CRITICAL ACCLAIM FOR LAIRD BARRON'S THE CRONING

"*The Croning*, then, is an unspeakably intimate novel of cosmic horror. From the darkly fantastic fairytale with which it opens and closes through to a deeply disturbing yet massively satisfying climax, via an assortment of effulgent intermezzos—gratifying in their own right, but also critical to the success of the central thread—it demonstrates Laird Barron is as adept a genre novelist as he is undoubtedly a purveyor of shorter horror. Episodic though it is, *The Croning* comes together in the end, again and again, making for a tremendous—if altogether disparate—debut."
—*Strange Horizons*

"It's a rare year in which a superabundance of fine horror novels—novels that reward rereading—appears. That said, most years bring at least a handful of novels whose titles can stand to be mentioned alongside Matheson's *I Am Legend*, Jackson's *The Haunting of Hill House*, and King's *The Shining*. To this year's list, add Laird Barron's *The Croning*."
—John Langan for *Los Angeles Review of Books*

"*The Croning* is the kind of book that burrows into your brain and has you jumping at shadows. Laird Barron has managed to create a universe as black and uncaring as any since H.P. Lovecraft. Not for the faint of heart, but if you can bear to step out of the light, *The Croning* will teach you why all men fear the darkness."
—Brett J. Talley, author of *That Which Should Not Be*

"Teeming with the cosmic horrors that distinguish the fiction of Lovecraft, Machen, and other weird fiction masters, this eerie first novel offers up a picture of human civilization as a plaything in the claws of malignant alien entities… The narrative toggles back and forth from past to present, establishing a rhythm between disturbing events and their foreshadowing that reaches a terrifying climax. Barron (*Occultation*) has studied the work of his predecessors well; already acknowledged a master of the horror short story, he shows himself equally skilled at novel-length work."
—*Publishers Weekly*, Starred Review

"*The Croning* is beautifully paced and wonderfully innovative."
—*City Book Review*

"*The Croning* is stark, literary cosmic horror… *The Croning* deserves a place in the bookcase next to T. E. D. Klein's *The Ceremonies* [illegible] Leiber's *Our Lady Of Darkness* and that is the high[illegible]
—*CrowsNBones.*[illegible]

CRITICAL ACCLAIM FOR LAIRD BARRON'S THE CRONING

(continued)

"This novel not only met but exceeded my high expectations. It is nothing short of a masterwork, comparable in so many ways to Lovecraft's 1931 classic *At the Mountains of Madness.* Powered by a luminously dark writing style, a phantasmagoria of nightmarish imagery, and a bladder-loosening mythos, this is exactly the kind of novel Lovecraft would've written had he been alive in the 21st century. Like *At the Mountains of Madness, The Croning* is a novel that will stay with readers long after reading. And if you don't think that you're truly scared after finishing this novel, just wait a while until you go to sleep…Bottom line: *The Croning* is one of the very best horror novels that I've read in decades—and Laird Barron is the next coming of H. P. Lovecraft. Mark my words."

—Paul Goat Allen, *B&N.com*

"If you're a fan of weird fiction or...simply love good horror novels, you must read *The Croning.*"

—Risingshadow.net

"Barron's storytelling has that rare power of grip, weaving a particular strain of beautiful, sinewy prose that somehow possesses enough tiny microfibers to pick up the grit and sharp things swept into the corners of forgotten history. Both beautiful and monstrous, his evocative imagery lures you into the forest with the cadence of lost eons, leaves you in expectant silence, and then rips back the shading canopy, exposing you to the terrible realities that lie waiting under the thin veneers of bullshit "civilization"…It's a gift of cosmic naturalist horror that will force you to re-examine everything and everyone around you, if only slightly. *The X-Files* in print, only infinitely scarier and hitting far closer to home. It will make you fear the trees. It will make you check for zippers."

—T. E. Grau, *The Cosmicomicon*

THE CRONING

OTHER BOOKS BY LAIRD BARRON

Collections
Occultation
The Imago Sequence
The Beautiful Thing That Awaits Us All

THE CRONING

LAIRD BARRON

NIGHT SHADE BOOKS
NEW YORK

Night Shade books may be purchased in bulk at special discounts for sales promotion, corporate gifts, fund-raising, or educational purposes. Special editions can also be created to specifications. For details, contact the Special Sales Department, Night Shade Books, 307 West 36th Street, 11th Floor, New York, NY 10018 or info@skyhorsepublishing.com.

Night Shade Books® is a registered trademark of Skyhorse Publishing, Inc. ®, a Delaware corporation.

Visit our website at www.nightshadebooks.com.

10 9 8 7 6 5

Library of Congress Cataloging-in-Publication Data is available on file.

Print ISBN: 978-1-59780-231-4

Edited by Ross E. Lockhart

Cover illustration and design by Cody Tilson
Interior layout and design by Amy Popovich

Printed in the United States of America

ACKNOWLEDGEMENTS

My thanks to the following for making this book possible: Amy, Marty, Jason, Jeremy, Ross, and the entire staff of Night Shade Books; my agents Brendan Deneen, Colleen Lindsay, Heather Evans, and Peter Rubie; Matt Jaffe; Jody Rose; JD and Lara Busch; Mark Ibsen; Larry Roberts; and Ellen Datlow.

Special thanks to my loyal companions Athena, Horatio, Ulysses, and Persephone; and my friends—you know who you are.

Extra special thanks to Jason and Harmony Barron; and the Langan family—John, Fiona, and David. I love you guys.

For Oksana, Julian, and Quinn.

CHAPTER ONE

Looking for Mr. R

(Antiquity)

1.

That venerable fairytale of the Miller's daughter and the Dwarf who helped her spin straw into gold has a happy ending in the popular version. The events that inspired the legend, not so much.

The Spy who was the son of the Miller embarked upon a perilous mission into the Western Mountains. The cart tracks and game trails he followed were tortuous, wending through darksome forests full of robbers and all manner of wild beasts. Such were the dangers of travel in most regions of the world in those days. He chose to walk and was accompanied by a grizzled mastiff who'd served him faithfully through many a bleak hour. He carried a dagger, a water skin, a few coins in a dried-up purse, and a tiny crucifix around his neck. Just those meager possessions and his heart, which burned for the Queen. That devotion guided him through thorn thickets and quicksand, over rockslides and across rivers. It comforted him all those dark, dark nights as he and the dog camped along the trail, wrapped in his cloak, fire dwindling to embers, wolves howling among the trees. The stars glowed cold as stones, cold as the snowy caps of the peaks he climbed closer to each passing day.

He thought of his sister, the Queen, also daughter of the Miller, albeit of a different mother. She'd elevated herself unto royalty by convincing the old King she possessed the secrets of alchemy, that she could spin flax into gold, or some similar horseshit. The Spy couldn't be certain what particular deception his lovely sister had practiced for this high-stakes roll of the bones. He loved her all the more for her foibles, her casual cruelty.

The Spy knew damned well, however, that while Sister possessed a golden tongue for sucking cock and other manipulations, she was no fucking alchemist. Thus, when the old King called her bluff and imprisoned her in a dungeon with a pile of straw and a dawn deadline, literally a dead-*line*, the Spy, who was at that time a humble groom, figured her head would roll into a basket before noon the next day. He sent his nicest black peasant ensemble to be cleaned, and picked a bouquet of white roses for the pauper's grave.

Imagine everyone's amazement when she emerged from the cell twelve hours later with several baskets of gold wire and a formula scrawled on a parchment for repeating the process under spectacularly rare astrological conditions. Her smug little smile and coy eyelash batting aside, the Spy sensed her fear.

In the three years that followed, all through her lavish marriage ceremony to the Crown Prince, which half the population of the neighboring kingdoms attended; the opulent honeymoon; the abdication of the old King, and her subsequent elevation to queen and consort; the gala balls and garden parties of epic extravagance; the rosy pregnancy; only the Spy detected a black cloud of gloom piling around her in a gathering storm. Only he paid heed to crows in the branches of the willow tree in her favorite garden.

Despite a ruthless nature and innate talents for subterfuge and skullduggery, he was the Spy entirely due to his sister's generosity. She'd rewarded their father with retirement to a country estate and her brother with a post at court in the clandestine services. The Ministry of Red Hot Pokers, as certain wits dubbed the office.

The Groom was happy to be shut of his prior job. No more getting kicked by nags during shoeing, no more pitching shit or fetching water for the irritable stable master. No more shagging brawny farrier's daughters and warty hags in back alleys (or so he thought)! It was going to be frock coats, feathered hats, and high-tone pussy until he keeled over.

Things went in that general direction for a while. Until the Queen showed pregnant and the creepy Dwarf started hanging around the palace…

During a polo match the Spy noticed the Queen staring at a dwarf in a cassock who was lurking near the bleachers. Horrible creature—and the Spy knew from horrible after his many misspent years on the mean streets among lepers and beggars, and maimed veterans of foreign adventures. He'd seen his share of pox-ridden, congenitally defective, gods-cursed twisted caricatures of the human form in alleys and brothels alike. The Dwarf, hunched and scabrous, peeping at the world through gimlet eyes and grinning with the malice of a butcher or coroner who enjoyed his job for all the wrong reasons, was something special indeed. The Spy figured the fellow for a mendicant or an entertainer, an itinerate jester. Then the Dwarf tipped the Queen a sly wink, eyeing her by then prodigious belly, and the Spy smelled trouble brewing.

That night he separated her from the entourage of ladies-in-waiting and snot-nosed footmen and brought her into the garden under the weeping willow. He came right out and asked if she was being blackmailed regarding the fact the baby did not belong to the virile young King who'd, ironically, made a virtue of siring hundreds of bastards during his boring wait for the throne.

"Have you told anyone it's mine?" the Spy said, holding her small, chilly hand too tightly.

"I'm not stupid," she said in a tone that indicated she thought *he* sure as hell was. "I prefer my head where it's positioned rather than mounted on the wall in my loving husband's study."

"Then who's the pygmy working for and what do they want?"

"The Dwarf never told me his name. He's an imp of Hell."

"This doesn't sound very good," the Spy said. "The pigfucker smuggled in the gold and now he wants a royal favor, is that it? God's blood, honey. You're in a real bind if it's political."

"He doesn't desire a political favor."

"Really. No maps, no troop movements, no appointments to the cabinet?"

"Nothing of the sort."

"Your sweet ass?"

"He wasn't interested in the royal preserves."

"Well, shitfire. Fuck. Piss. What's his game, then?"

"The Dwarf spun the gold, not I. He's come for his prize."

"What, dear sister, have you gone and done?"

Sister grinned exactly as a fox in a trap baring her teeth, and told him what pact she'd made to produce those fabled baskets of gold wire and thus get her family out of the poorhouse. It hadn't involved the Spy's biggest fear at the time—her blowing the misshapen Dwarf. No, it was far worse.

2.

A few nights after the Prince was born, the Dwarf arrived on a cold draft, then went away empty-handed. However, the reprieve would be short-lived. He vowed to return in three months to the minute and collect payment—the tender babe who presently nuzzled the Queen's fair breast. Although, if dear Queenie could learn the Dwarf's name during the interim, why then he'd declare the whole sordid pact null and void and they'd take crumpets and tea instead.

Fat chance.

The Spy learned of this the next morning when he was summoned to the Queen's parlor alongside several of her majesty's other best men. She kept the briefing short and sweet and the Spy figured he was the only member of the cadre to know the whole ugly truth of the mission. He also doubted that *even he* was privy to everything. Sister being a sneaky bitch and whatnot.

The Queen dispatched them to the four corners of the land. They had seventy days to learn the Dwarf's name, else there'd be hell to pay. Should someone happen to find the sawed-off bastard and stick a knife into his ribs, all the better.

Predictably, the other men, whipped into a patriotic lather, leapt upon their trusty steeds and bolted hither and yon to begin the search. As the best of the best, the Spy employed unorthodox methods to secure the lead that later sent him across the kingdom to the mountains and the darksome territories beyond.

He spent even more time than usual in taverns and nunneries. He poured drinks for off-duty bailiffs, finger-banged lonely scullery maids, beat merchants and pimps. He held a groom's left foot over an open flame. The Spy despised grooms with a passion. He bribed, blackmailed, and cajoled. To hilarious effect, if not much utility.

Everyone knew of the Dwarf, but not his name or whence he came. He was a shadow flickering in and out of reality. Rumors abounded—some claimed he was an assassin in the pay of a rival nation; he was the last scion of a ruined noble house, reduced to begging and prostitution; he was an evil magician descended from the Salamanca Seven who trafficked with demonic forces and had lived far in excess of any mortal span; he was a devil, an incubus, the decrepit human form of the Old One, the Serpent. One syphilis-addled courtesan claimed the Dwarf consorted with worms and the Lord of the Worms. She refused to elaborate.

Those who spoke of meeting the Dwarf made the sign against the evil eye and spat, or clutched their crucifixes. A strapping barmaid who moonlighted as a doxie for the well-heeled gentlemen in the High Market swore the Dwarf was in tight with mercantile princes, that he taught them secrets of the black arts in return for abominable favors. She'd seen him unhinge his jaw to devour a screaming baby which he'd received from a harlot as recompense for his services to a certain burgher. The barmaid had been sleeping it off after an orgy. None of the principals realized she was lying beneath a mound of cushions on the other side of an ornamental screen when the dark deal was consummated. She was a young lass, a former redhead, except her hair had gone white as the mountain snow, allegedly upon witnessing the horrible murder.

The Spy nodded politely, believing none of it. Nonetheless, he did due diligence and investigated the merchant in question—a burgher formerly of Constantinople named Theopolis who specialized in antiquities and dwelt in a posh manor on the upwind side of the city. Quiet inquiries revealed Theopolis to be no more devious or unscrupulous than any other of a hundred merchants; no more or less perverted or corrupt, no more or less exotic in his leisure proclivities.

Desperate for any lead whatsoever, the Spy broke into the house while its master and most of the servants were on the town drinking and whoring. Nothing seemed untoward. The house was sumptuously appointed in a variety of styles as befitting a man of Theopolis's means; a few tasteful volumes of erotic lore, a handful of risqué statuary, a titillating nude portrait of some long-dead diva. Perhaps several of the pieces of armor in the hall or a baggie or two of the spices in the bedside drawer might be of questionable legality, but certainly nothing sinister or helpful in tracking down the damnable Dwarf.

On his way out the window, he hesitated, then doubled back to check the bookcase in the master study, and Lo! did find a cunningly concealed lever. The cramped brick chamber hidden behind the case was fitted with shackles and chains and arcane torture devices. An onyx floor plate gleamed by the light of his candle. A skeletal serpent bent into a C configuration was deeply etched into the plate. *Serpent* wasn't accurate; perhaps a worm. Whichever, it was altogether unwholesome. In a bamboo hamper, its lid also engraved with the occult symbol, were the bones of children. The Spy counted enough discrete segments to constitute nine or ten infants and toddlers.

It appeared he had a lucky winner.

Later that night he abducted the drunken merchant from his bed and interrogated him in the wine cellar. All Theopolis would admit to was that the Dwarf belonged to a powerful family who dwelt somewhere in the Western Mountains. The man also predicted the Spy was going to wind up suffering a fate worse than death. The Spy thanked beaten and bloodied Theopolis for his information and dumped him in a burlap bag full of stones off the Swangate Bridge. While the bubbles were still popping in the water he set forth on the Western Road.

This was the end of the first month.

3.

He and the dog traveled on highways, then roads, then trails, and finally tracks that vanished for leagues at a stretch. The cities shrank to towns, villages, hamlets and thorps, each farther and farther apart, then there was only the occasional woodcutter's hut in the depths of the wilderness. Fellow pilgrims were seldom seen. It was a lonely journey.

After much hardship he came to a remote valley populated by dour, sunburned folk who tended sheep and goats and raised beets and radishes in the turf. A province of peat-cutters and burners of cow chips. The kind of place overlooked at court and likely awarded to some down at the heels shirttail noble as a booby prize.

The countryside was largely untamed beyond primitive farm plots and unfenced grazing lands. Copses of pine were broken by stony pastures and hillocks. A river thundered down from a glacier caked in black dust. The far end of the valley rose into a high, desolate moor stalked by wolves and dotted with the ruins of ancient fortresses and the weathered cairns of defeated barbarian tribes. A rugged and gloomy scene that disturbed the Spy's anxieties while also exciting him with its potential as the spawning ground of the miscreant he hunted.

The Spy struck gold right away.

A graybeard farmer had occasionally seen the Dwarf in the nearby village. Name? Who could say? Folks called him the Dwarf. He lived in a cave and came down to the lowlands for supplies once or twice a year during the festivals where he'd get drunk and dance with the pretty maids who weren't nimble enough to escape his lecherous advances, and horrify the children (mostly he'd horrify the mothers) with gruesome tales of sexually deviant fairies and monsters. Made his way in the world as a crafter of jewelry and a wolf trapper. Privately, the farmer suspected the Dwarf was a professional tomb robber who filched most of his trinkets from the ruins on the moor.

In any event, a right homely bugger, that little man, and long-lived.

"Long-lived?" the Spy said.

"Aye. First I clapped eyes on 'im, I was a sprat. Saw 'im again, caperin' along the Moor Road, just last spring. 'e 'ad a sack slung o'er 'is hump. Must've 'ad a goat in there...That bag was jumpin' somethin' fierce."

The farmer offered his barn as refuge since the village was full of wicked folk and no place for any God-fearing Christian. When pressed for examples of this wickedness he simply spat and made the sign against the evil eye and grumbled into his beard. On parting, he warned the Spy to beware the Dwarf. "Ye wanna steer clear o' 'im and 'is little friends. Ye shall come to a nasty end nosin' 'bout that gent."

The Spy knew the refrain. He wondered aloud as to the nature of these *little friends.*

"Ain't ever seen 'em, just 'eard of 'em. Cripples and deformed ones. Some ain't got no arms or legs is what I 'ear. They crawl along behind 'im, see? Wrigglin' in the dirt all ruddy worm-like."

"He's got an entourage of folk without arms," the Spy said, raising his brows toward the brim of his cocked hat. "Or legs. Following him wherever he goes."

"Some got arms, some don't. Some got legs, some don't. Some got neither. That's what I 'ear." The farmer shrugged, made the sign of warding again, and would say no more on the matter.

The Spy slogged his way to the village and took a room at the dingy inn. His disguise was that of an ex-soldier trekking across the kingdom to his homestead near the borderlands. He claimed to be a prospector and that he might linger a week or two surveying the hills for likely sources of gold or silver. None of the sheepherders or goatswains who staggered in for a pint of grog after a day in the heather seemed to give a damn.

He bedded a couple of the serving wenches who were pleased with his appearance and moreso by the fact he at least didn't smell of cowshit and actually had two silvers to rub together. Both had seen the Dwarf as recently as the previous month. Both were frightened and repulsed by the creature's demeanor, though he'd not done much to offend either of them directly. Yes, they'd heard of his deformed kin who were said to remain hidden in a mountain cave except rare occasions when they accompanied him on excursions into the moor. The rumors the wenches shared were not enlightening. Except for one—according to certain old goodwives, the Dwarf and his kin made mincemeat of babies and their cave was carpeted with the bones of several generations of wee victims. There'd be a proper torch and pitchfork army marching on those cannibals one fine day, avowed the wenches.

The Spy did not learn the name of the village. The buildings were from olden times, fashioned of mud and brick and thatch with small doors and smaller windows sealed with sheepskin. Doors got barred shortly after sunset. Pagan tokens hung above entry mantles and the bones of animals were common decorations in yards. Conversations dried up when he entered a room or passed by on the street and the people smiled at him and looked at their feet or the sky.

The local denizens were a queer lot—the folk dressed archaically and spoke with an accent troublesome to his ear, such that he missed every third word when they conversed slowly in normal tones, and lost the gist entirely when they muttered amongst themselves, which was often. On the whole, the population was homogenous as a pod of toads. Not counting the wanton barmaids, who'd been born outside the valley in a more populous area, the women wouldn't speak to him. The women weren't shy by any means; they smiled and winked and brushed him in passing, but simply wouldn't exchange words. Many of them were pregnant, but the Spy was surprised to see no other children in evidence. The youngest person he noticed was old enough to shave.

A half mile north of town lay a bluff upon which loomed a temple built in ancient times. On the Spy's first evening ensconced at the inn, he witnessed a commotion in the taproom. Proprietor, staff, and guests set aside mugs of ale and haunches of roasted goat and gravitated outdoors into the square. A procession of villagers marched from the square and up the lane to the temple, lighting the path with torches and lanterns. They marched in absolute silence, led by a trio of figures garbed in rust-colored cassocks and frightful pagan masks that resembled no beast of fact or legend familiar to the Spy.

Once the stream of petitioners had disappeared into the distant edifice, its exterior remained cold and dark for the better part of two hours, whereupon the procession returned to the village square and dispersed. The innkeeper was one of the bizarrely robed leaders of the ceremony. He removed his unpleasant mask that appeared to be a waxen hybrid of an eel and a predatory insect, and stamped about the taproom, stoking the hearth and clearing flatware as if nothing unusual had transpired. Later, the serving wenches kept their eyes downcast and deflected the Spy's queries regarding the incident with inelegant, but exuberant ministrations of love.

The next morning, he ate a hearty breakfast and decided to visit the site. The dog followed him with a decided lack of enthusiasm. The dog had communicated through growls and groans and baleful glares at every villager who passed that he didn't like this place one bit. The mountain air agreed with his canine sensibilities not in the slightest.

The temple on the hill was by far the grandest monument the Spy had seen since departing the capital; extravagant beyond the wildest imaginings for such a remote province of the kingdom while also existing in a fabulously decrepit state; certainly a relic from an ancient era. A forbidding structure of granite blocks and carven pillars, the whole shot through with cracks from age and earthquake (a massive shaker had hit the region about ten years ago, according to the innkeeper— *The Worm turned*, he quipped with a sour grin) and covered in unwholesome northern black mold and thorny vines.

Instead of the traditional crucifix, a massive ring of hammered brass hung above double doors the likes of which belonged to a fortress. The ring was broken in the upper corner, much as the monstrous symbol he'd encountered in the burgher's cell, and it canted at an extreme forward angle, presumably as a result of the earthquake. The effect was that of a giant torque poised to descend, literal hammer of the gods style, on petitioners shuffling through the gates.

The interior was dim and cavernous, reminiscent of Roman and Greek temples of the Hellenic; naves and altars to a dozen gods were arrayed in alcoves. The Spy recognized Jupiter and Saturn, Diana and Hecate, and busts of the Norse pantheon, in particular a feral depiction of Loki undergoing torture for his crimes against Baldur, and another of Odin weeping gore from his plucked eye socket. The Spy's father was a learned man despite toiling as a simple miller, and his sister a supremely ambitious woman, and between the pair it was books and lessons in classical history throughout the long, bleak winters.

There were other gods represented that he did not recognize, however. Situated deeper inside the temple hall these statues were much older and the writing upon their placards was foreign to him. Upon reflection, he concluded this place had been constructed or renovated piecemeal over the centuries, with the modern additions, gods and architecture alike, tacked on near the entrance. Thus, proceeding into the torchlit gloom was to travel backward into antiquity.

His hunter's senses were sharp and he knew a hostile gaze had fallen upon him. On several occasions he caught movement in the corner of his eye; small shadows moving inside the larger ones of the pillars and arches. Low and thin and fast; at first he thought it must be children, whatever the pagan equivalent of altar boys were. He soon decided this was incorrect, although he couldn't quite name how or why. He recalled what the farmer said of the alleged "limbless kin" of the Dwarf, and shuddered.

At the opposite end from the main doors were two huge pillars of basalt and a thick curtain of crimson. On the other side was a nave, larger than its neighbors, and a crude altar of primordial black stone, hewn from the spine of the Earth herself, and roughly fashioned into a pyramidal shape, flattened at the apex in the manner of certain jungle civilizations. The ziggurat was nine feet tall, and approximately twelve feet broad on a side. A shallow depression was carved in each face at eye level.

Above the altar and inset at the heart of a soot-streaked tile mosaic was another broken ring symbol the diameter of several men standing on one another's shoulders; this version was constructed of countless pieces of interlocking bone aged to a decayed black. Dragon's-blood incense wafted from wrought-iron braziers and mingled with the torch smoke in a haze that caused the ziggurat and the effigy to distort and bend like reflections in stained metal.

The Spy took a torch from a sconce and raised it high to better examine the broken ring and the mosaic of murky imagery that enmeshed it—a hunt or revel in a forest; maidens with babes in arms fled dark figures whose eyes blazed red and who grasped with elongated arms and spindly, clawed hands. He saw, as his light glanced from surface to surface, that the bones of the broken ring symbol were real human skeletons of all sizes, mortared and fused to create a piece of unholy art.

Upon determining the sheer numbers of corpses involved, and inevitably recalling the burgher's collection of children's bones and the tavern wenches' pillow talk of a cave carpeted with baby bones, his knees shook and he nearly lost his resolve. The Spy was by no means a pious man, nor afflicted by undue superstition. Even so, this sight quickened in his breast a chill dread and reminded him that he was a man without friends, far from home.

"Welcome to the House of Old Leech," a woman said. She stood in an alcove, watching him. Clad in a diaphanous gown, a crimson diadem at her throat, she was dark of hair and eye and lushly proportioned. Older than the Spy by a rather wide margin, her flesh was taut and she radiated carnality as voracious as fire.

A priestess, he assumed. Instantly smitten, only a sliver of his fevered brain was capable of rational thought. "Hullo, priestess," the Spy said. He affected an archness of tone. *Beautiful seminude women jump out of the shadows at me every day, cheerio!* He tried not to stare at her breasts, focusing instead on her eyes, and that seemed equally dangerous for she appraised him with a measure of intellect and cruelty that even his sister the Queen could not match. It was the kind of gaze to flay a man's soul, and it reminded him that not so long ago he'd mucked horseshit in a stable, far from the good silver and polite company. He cleared his throat and said gamely, "This is an unusual church, if I may say so. I confess surprise that such blasphemies are openly conducted. And the coin required to maintain the roof. Ye gods..."

"And you missed the orgy, too." The woman approached with a slowly widening smile. Thankfully, she possessed legs, and nice ones. Up close she smelled of perfume and pitch. Her eyes were painted in a soft glitter and her lips were the deep red of the diadem. "These lands are administered by Count Mock who is fond of the old ways. He's filthy rich and the crown seldom pays heed to the doings along the frontier. Left to their own devices are Count M and his people. You may find the Valley exists under a different set of traditions and customs than you are familiar with."

"Yes, if by different you mean uncivilized. The Count must've paid off the diocese as well. Yours is the only place of worship I've witnessed in the entire valley. That is passing strange, my lady. Surely there are Christians dwelling among you pagans."

"Christians are welcome. *All* are welcome. All flesh is food of the god."

"Who is Old Leech? The name isn't one I recognize."

"You're surprised? There are in excess of twenty thousand gods acknowledged to exist. Unless you are a scholar or a master theologian, you'd be hard-pressed to name a hundredth of them. You don't carry yourself like a philosopher. A mercenary, perhaps." Her accent was more foreign than that of the villagers. While the peasants spoke with a rustic twang, hers hinted of a cosmopolitan education in a distant land. There was a nearly imperceptible lag between her words and the movement of her lips; the sound of her voice echoed in his head an instant before it issued from her mouth. He wondered exactly what was in that incense...

"I'm an ignorant clodhopper, which means I should feel right at home here. Are you a caste of healers? A gaggle of old leeches?"

She laughed into her cupped hand and watched him sidelong. "Curiosity killed the cat." She boldly hooked the chain of his crucifix with her nail and its silver chasing reflected in her eyes. "Good Christians should not seek knowledge outside the Holy Book."

"Really, there's very little good in me," he said, trembling at the heat of her skin close to his own, the swirl of exotic perfume that clouded his mind.

"I bet." The priestess glanced down and seemed to notice the dog for the first time. "Oh, cute dog," she said and patted him on the lumpy head.

The Spy opened his mouth too late to warn her—the dog was a savage and had chomped off the fingers of more than one person who'd come too near, but now the brute whimpered, cowed, and shivered in ecstasy or terror at the woman's touch. The Spy understood the emotion. He said, "Priestess, are we alone? On my way in I could've sworn there were children moving in the shadows."

"Kids are in short supply around here," she said. "Unless we're talking the kind with floppy ears and an ivy fetish. What spooked you was probably a few of the limbless ones creeping up. Don't worry, they won't brave the light just for a taste of city dweller flesh." A gong sounded through the alcove and the air rippled and his teeth chattered. She stepped away from him. "By the way, I'm not a priestess. I'm a traveler."

"Your manner of speech...Where are you from?" He chose to completely ignore her reference to the limbless ones.

"Wouldn't mean a thing to you, handsome."

"Ah, a woman and her secrets. What are you doing here?"

"I am undergoing an initiation. A croning, of sorts."

"The rite of passage. Maidenhood and fertility giving way to wisdom."

"I'm impressed."

"Mum was a druid."

"Really?"

"No. I've shagged a pagan or two, though. When is the rite? Will it happen here?"

"It's already begun, and no. All of this," she gestured to indicate their surroundings, "is for the hicks. The real action is at the castle. Your turn. Why have you come to this charming nook at the ass end of the kingdom?"

"I seek the wealth of the mountains."

"All you'll find here is shit."

The gong sounded again; a bone-rattling vibration that caused dust to sift from the upper reaches of the chamber. She flinched and fear and exultation flickered in her expression. He grabbed her arm and stepped in and kissed her. It seemed the thing to do, under the circumstances. Her lips tasted bloody and hot.

She caught his forearm in a grip far more powerful than her stature indicated and pushed him back with the ease of a mother fending off a child. "That's quite enough out of you for today, Miller's son." She turned and moved quickly into the darkness. She called, or perhaps he imagined that she did so, as the echo was as from a canyon bed: "Go back, go back. There are frightful things. The stables never prepared you for this."

The Spy remained before the altar, dazed and rubbing his arm where the woman left her black and blue fingerprints. He'd traveled incognito, yet she'd known him and, by her own words, so did the Dwarf. This frightened him until he mastered himself and banished that futile line of conjecture. Every dram of his blood was property of the Queen. Danger was immaterial—he was in no position to abandon the quest regardless of what awaited him. As for the cryptic warning of the lovely petitioner, that wasn't anything to dwell upon or invest with greater merit than it warranted. Word in such small communities traveled like fire in dry grass. There was no mystery here. He truly hoped that thinking it made it so.

There are frightful things.

He glanced from the dog who yet cowered and skulked to the great effigy of Old Leech. Feeling as an actor highlighted upon a stage, an instant of dark epiphany assailed him, permitted him a glimpse of a vast, squamous truth of the universe as it uncoiled. Nay, despite its myriad constituent skeletons this abomination wasn't a dragon, or a serpent, or the Ouroboros with its jaws come unstuck—this was a colossal worm that had swallowed whole villages, cities… A leech of nightmare proportions, a constellation rendered against granite, and it had shat the populations of entire worlds in its slithering wake through the night skies.

He left the temple and kept his hand on the dagger hilt all the way back to the inn.

4.

The Spy banished the disappointed serving wenches from his quarters and slept with the door locked and barred and his boots on in case he was compelled to flee through the window in the middle of the night. This took him back to his days of sneaking around the boudoirs of many a married lass in the city.

A week passed and he dreamed of the woman in the temple. In these dreams a chasm divided the temple floor and she stood on the opposite side, shining with a crimson radiance. She laughed at him. Her eyes and mouth dripped black and she glided across the smoking fissure. When she was almost upon him she grasped her own face and pulled. There was an eggshell-cracking sound and her face came free, and he'd awaken in a sweaty panic.

By day he tromped through the fields and pastures, interviewing farmers and herders with a scant pretense. Most of the people refused to answer his questions and those few who were more forthcoming provided nothing of substance regarding the Dwarf.

His perambulations carried him to the moor and its leagues of foggy, marshy vistas. He poked around the foundations of ruined towers and barrow mounds and toiled like an ant in the shadow of the moss- and lichen-covered megaliths. He investigated a large cave on the rocky slopes of Black Bear Mountain, and there was indeed sign a bear dwelt in its depths—bones and scat. The bear itself was absent, however. The Spy was glad of that; he hadn't brought a spear or bow.

By night, he took his mead near the taproom hearth and dried his clothes which were invariably sodden and muddy from his excursions, and listened to the yeomen mutter and gossip at the big table. The peasants contended with boars and brigands, crap weather, mean wives, and occasional plague.

Of course, he knew an answer or two might lie within the walls of Count Mock's castle. Unfortunately, the Count refused to entertain strangers and without a pretext, the Spy would be clapped in irons or worse. Sneaking in was risky; the Count's abode was an old fortress after all, and designed to thwart such enterprises. So the Spy fretted and schemed and wandered the valley hoping the gods of light or darkness would take pity and throw him a bone.

A peddler stumbled in from the wet and cold one evening; a ruddy, lanky man from the capital, and he sat with the Spy and related news of the civilized realms and confessed, in a hushed tone and with many furtive glances around the inn, that the valley and its denizens were not pleasing to him by any means. The Peddler traveled many routes to ply his trade and had visited the region thrice in the past. He always concluded his business in the village and up at the Mock estate as hurriedly as possible. The Count extended an open invitation to the trader, desirous as the noble was for certain tobaccos the Peddler was sure to keep on hand.

Thus, the Spy asked the Peddler if he'd care for company upon the next morning's journey to Mock's castle; a strong arm to indemnify against the depredations of brigands and wolves. The Peddler was only too delighted and the pair departed the inn at dawn; the Peddler leading two surly pack mules, and the Spy with his faithful hound.

The weather was valley-fair, which is to say, drizzly and dreary. Rain led to sleet and threatened to become a blizzard. The men walked until sunset, following a path parallel to fog-shrouded peaks and a small forest of twisted, leafless trees, and arrived in the waning light at the gates of a crumbling castle. The building jutted from a mountainside, its gate accessible only after crossing a gorge via a rickety drawbridge. The drawbridge existed in a state of disrepair and was missing a chain and so remained permanently lowered. The rusty portcullis in the gatehouse also appeared inoperable. These details heartened the Spy who ever prized avenues of speedy retreat when encountering the unknown.

Standing in the dilapidated courtyard in several inches of mud, he surveyed the mossy roofs, potholes and smashed statues, weedy gardens and algae-choked fountains, and couldn't discern much difference between Mock's abode and some of the better-preserved ruins on the moor.

"Well, crap," he said. The dog growled in agreement.

"Aye, this place always gives me the shivers," the Peddler said as an aside.

A platoon of evil-looking servants in dark garb emerged to tend the mules and lead the travelers inside the main keep. One of the men made to leash the dog, but the Spy dissuaded the fellow with a cold, sharp glance. Inside they doffed soggy cloaks and were seated at a banquet table in the main hall. Oh, it was a gloomy and ancient chamber, its stones cracked and moldy, suits of armor gathering rust, pennants moth-eaten and rotting. The scents of smoke and mildew were strong.

Soon, the Count descended the grand staircase flanked by his sober, iron-haired daughters Yvonne and Irina, both of whom resembled in a familial way the woman hanging around the temple. Count Mock was a doddering shell of a man, quite elderly and bald; his chin receded and his eyes were filmed like a snake, and he drooled.

All three dressed in black.

The dour servants bustled in with platters of stringy roast beef and potatoes and a cheap thin wine. Irina fed her father by hand and dabbed his slack mouth with a napkin. Yvonne conversed on behalf of the Count and asked the Peddler many questions regarding his stock, most especially whether he'd brought the flatland tobacco her father loved. Neither woman expressed the slightest whit of interest about events in the kingdom or the wider world.

Neither directly addressed the Spy, as befitting his lowly status as a servant to the Peddler, however they studied him on the sly throughout dinner. For his part, the Spy kept quiet except to mumble superlatives regarding the overdone meat and stony potatoes. Through the course of casual discussion, he learned the Mocks commanded the vanguard that pacified the local barbarians a hundred and fifty years back and were awarded title to the region when the dust cleared. Apparently nothing of interest had occurred since those glory days.

Nobody mentioned anything about dwarves and the Spy didn't judge a good opportunity to work the subject into dinner conversation. Particularly since on occasion the Count's dullard countenance animated and he stared directly at the Spy and yelled, "Run for your lives! Run!" This followed by a bout of gasping and coughing, then a relapse into vacuous silence.

During a dessert of blood pudding and dates, Yvonne said to the Peddler, "It is meet that you arrive on this eve of eves, good Peddler. We've watched the calendar and the fogs of the season in anticipation of this moment, your fourth visit to our humble estate."

The Spy, wary as a fox near a kennel of wolfhounds, ate and drank modest quantities, and later, when deposited in his chamber for the evening (instead of the stables, as a courtesy to the Peddler), immediately searched the premises for dangers undreamt of by ordinary guests. In the span of minutes he uncovered a loose block beneath the bed that doubtless concealed a spring or spikes, and peepholes drilled in the ugly tapestry near the wardrobe. He estimated himself well and truly in a perilous circumstance and was comforted solely by the fact he hadn't spotted evidence of castle guards and the servants didn't handle themselves as trained fighting men.

The hour grew late and the halls quieted. He crept forth with the dog at his heel. Man and beast prowled those dim passages and winding, drafty stairwells, peeking into rooms and antechambers, in quest of *what* the Spy wasn't sure. The words of the sisters to the Peddler regarding their anticipation of their arrival haunted the Spy, as did the terrified demeanor of the Count during his interludes of lucidity. Clearly the noble sanctioned the pagan temple, else it would've been put to the torch and razed; and clearly the temple was connected to the Dwarf. For all the talk of caves and mountains, all roads to that sawed-off blackmailer led through this castle.

He and the dog descended from shadow to shadow down, down into the cellars. He encountered no guards along the way although the normal coombs for storage of wine and other goods roughened and became damp and showed evidence of having served as a dungeon He sneaked past a series of empty cells and a dusty room equipped with rack and iron maiden and dissecting table, then through a low arch scarcely wider than his shoulders and more downward curving stairs. The subbasement was correspondingly wetter and dimmer than the rest of the gloomy fortress, lighted by infrequent torches and dingy lanterns in recessed niches. Water dripped and small streams ran from cracks in the foundation and made the eroded stone steps treacherous. Bats squeaked and flapped, agitated.

Somewhere ahead came the low sonorous cadence of chanting.

The Spy had the queer and unwelcome sensation of sleepwalking, or trudging through a vivid dream that was rapidly becoming a festering nightmare.

Did they say it was beef at supper? You fool! The voice hissed from the deep black near his left-hand side and he almost went for a tumble down the steps such was his surprise. He squinted and found no evidence of a lurker, nor were any more whispers forthcoming and he soon wondered if his nerves were betraying him. Meanwhile he reached a landing and traversed a narrow tunnel. His path drew ever nearer the chanting and the hairs on his neck prickled. The words were similar to Latin, yet another language entirely. Though the chant was incomprehensible it conjured images in his mind of noisome maggot nests and a river composed of wriggling worms and gore, of himself and the woman from the temple coupling in a hellish cavern as a toothless maw of a colossus descended and engulfed them.

He cursed and bit his tongue until it bled, and kept moving.

The tunnel let into a small box canyon on the opposite side of the mountain. The area was illuminated by a bonfire near a dolmen of great, great antiquity. The dolmen, four vertical henges of prodigious girth surmounted by another flat rock, was graven with runes similar to the many barbarian megaliths and cairns upon the moor. A boulder lay to one side of the dolmen entrance and this stone was fitted with manacles and chains.

The beautiful woman from the temple languished naked, manacled at wrist and ankle. She serenely gazed toward the bonfire and its attendant figures in black cowls. There were thirteen hooded and robed figures and the Spy suspected that these were the servants of the estate gathered to participate in a blood sacrifice.

He and his hound observed this spectacle from a ledge perhaps fifty yards distant. He pinched himself, glumly hoping to wake from this awful dream, and surely it must be a dream for no confluence of malign events could logically occur in a sane universe.

Any shred of naïve assumption that the universe was in anywise sane dissolved, along with much of his *own* sanity, when Yvonne and Irina threw back their hoods and produced jagged daggers. Irina sliced the bound woman open from hairline to hip in a prolonged sawing motion. Blood spurted from the wound. The attendants chanted and the woman screamed and her screams escalated into a lunatic laughter that gathered strength and echoed like thunder from the canyon walls.

Summoned by the laughter, the chanting, the copious flow of blood gleaming dark as honey in the bonfire blaze, the Dwarf, garbed in a cassock, hopped and skipped forth from the dolmen. He tore away the cassock and his liver-gray flesh hung loosely upon his squat frame as if it were a hastily donned and ill-fitting costume. He leaped forward with violent alacrity and seized the woman in chains and wrenched at her. The Spy felt nauseated, convinced that the little man was actually peeling her alive.

Then the Limbless Ones squirmed from the darkness to join the fun. At the sight of them the Spy's perceptions bent and buckled inward and smote him senseless. He shrieked and ran back through the tunnel.

5.

He made it to the Peddler's quarters, his body bruised from many falls on the slippery stairs. The Peddler had been sleeping soundly and reacted in a groggy manner that suggested he'd consumed drugs. He'd eaten and drunk far more than the Spy himself had dared.

The Spy slapped and chivvied and threatened the confused man and drove him from the castle sans mules, supplies, or payment for the tobacco he'd handed the Count and daughters. They fled across the forsaken landscape. Eventually the Peddler shook free of his stupor and joined in casting fearful backward glances for signs of pursuit.

Upon reaching the outskirts of the village they composed themselves and repaired to the Spy's quarters at the inn. Safely ensconced, they shared a flask of wine the Spy had previously stashed in a cupboard and were soon three sheets to the wind.

Darkness engulfed the village. The men, shaking with cold and nerves, huddled around a candle. The Spy, numb from the horrors he'd witnessed and the knowledge he'd failed his sweet sister, grasped the Peddler's shoulder and confessed why he'd journeyed to the valley.

The Peddler finally said in a besotted slur, "Wait, wait. Not a traveling soldier or sell sword? The Queen's own spy… Are you by chance the son of a miller?"

Having difficulty lifting his head or speaking in complete sentences, the Spy grunted that this was indeed the case.

"By the gods," the Peddler said, his eyes as large and round as tea saucers. He told a story then of how once, as a young, green trader upon his first visit to the valley he'd gotten lost in the mountains during a thunderstorm and taken shelter in a cave. The Dwarf was drawn to the cheery blaze of the Peddler's fire and the two spent a long evening smoking from the Dwarf's hookah and swapping tales as the wind howled and lightning cracked the sky. The Dwarf claimed to be a hermit who subsisted by trapping and gathering herbs and that he dwelt in several caves and huts scattered throughout the area.

An exceedingly odd thing disquieted the Peddler. Perhaps his senses were distorted by whatever powerful herb was percolating in the hookah barrel; nonetheless, he'd received a fright when at one point it appeared the Dwarf's face was melting. Right before the Peddler collapsed unconscious, the Dwarf lifted the man's chin with a razor-sharp fingernail and told him to relay a message to the son of the miller when they met one day. The message was, *There are frightful things, Groom. Time is a ring. My name won't save you or your sister. We who crawl in the dark love you.*

The Peddler paused, lost in memory. His eyes cleared and he said, "I was alone come dawn. The storm yet raged, so I hunkered in that cave for three days and three nights. There was another chamber farther in back. I realized the Dwarf had dwelt there long ago by the rotted bedding and clothes, a few mugs and tarnished bits of silverware. The rest was dust, cobwebs, and bat shit. Or so I thought until I found a bundle of clay tablets beneath a loose stone. These comprised essays and a journal by a self-styled naturalist who'd been driven from his community. The charges against him included child murder and witchcraft and trafficking in black magic, all of which he adamantly denied in his notes. The people feared him because of his small stature, his misshapen bones, and claimed he was son to a warlock. I couldn't follow his words completely, for the language is difficult and the account had been carved before our grandfathers were even born. The gist of his latter entries was that he made friends with visitors from another kingdom or tribe who visited him from their own caves that lay deeper in the mountain. These men knew wickedness as a potter knows a wheel and over time they corrupted the Dwarf, swayed him to their cause. You say the Queen struck a bargain with this fiend and seeks his identity? That makes sense as a True Name is a token of power. Well, I beheld it all those years ago. His signature was engraved in the old tongue in the clay. I will not say it, for it must be one of the many names of the Prince of Darkness." He brought forth quill and parchment and scrawled with a shaking hand the name he'd seen written on the tablets.

"What a strange, ugly name," the Spy said, so drunk that two of everything shimmered in his blurry vision. He stared at what the Peddler had written and thought with grim amusement that in some ways the name made perfect sense, a cunning play on the Dwarf's stunted growth and the fact his flesh was rumpled as a bad coat. A demon jester. How droll.

"He is a strange, ugly little man," the Peddler said. "Although, I trow the Dwarf perished and what now walks the earth in his skin is something altogether different."

"If the worst should befall me, promise that you'll bear the Dwarf's name to the Queen. In the morning I shall depart via the West Road for the capital. You must take the low roads. One of us may survive to bear witness."

"Of course," said the Peddler. "God save the Queen."

"God save the Queen. But which god?"

The candle guttered and died.

The Spy lay helplessly against the warm bulk of the dog. The dog snored. The Peddler snored. A door creaked, then floorboards. There was a steady, thick dripping, the sound of bare feet squelching. The blackness reeked of copper and the Spy's heart beat too fast.

She said into the Spy's ear, "We meet again. Yes, time is a squirming, hungry ring that wriggles and worms across reality. It eats everything, lover."

He tried to speak, to cry out a warning. Too late.

In the chill gray light of dawn, the Peddler roused and discovered that he and the dog were alone in the room. There were a few bloody footprints. No other trace of the Spy, however. So, the Peddler hurriedly departed that cursed village and took the mournful dog with him. He traveled day and night, pushing himself past exhaustion in order to beat the appointed date. By miracles of perseverance and providence he barged into the Queen's court and delivered the message mere hours before the deadline. Afterward, he vanished from his guests' quarters despite the presence of a contingent of armed guards, and was never seen again.

Subsequent legends of the Queen's fateful showdown with the Dwarf notwithstanding, the creature's prophecy was quite accurate: knowing his name didn't save the Queen or anyone else.

CHAPTER TWO

One Time in Old Mexico...

(1958)

1.

The first time Donald Miller almost died was during a visit to Mexico, but later he didn't remember anything of the event, except in dreams that dissolved moments after waking. His body remembered, though. His blood remembered, and the black sap of his subconscious.

He and his wife Michelle took a spring vacation to Mexico City. Her umpteenth visit and his first. A well-connected colleague of Michelle's, one Louis Plimpton who had conducted a significant measure of research in the country, pulled strings and managed to get them into a suite at an international hotel. A gorgeous elevated view of the garden district, silk sheets, plush towels, fresh fruit, expensive coffee, complimentary brandies and margaritas. Walking through the mahogany double doors, Don took in the slate tiles, marble statuary, and gold-chased accents and raised a brow at his wife who merely smiled and advised him against looking the gift horse in the mouth.

Every morning began with a multi-course continental breakfast followed by guided tours of historic neighborhoods, lunches at sidewalk restaurants, then dinner and a show at the hotel nightclub, which imported Vegas talent to croon the tourists into buying a few more rounds. The days were breathless, the nights languid. They made frequent love with resurgent abandon—tied one another up with silk scarves, wore blindfolds and joked about paying a maid to join the merriment. They drank too much and for once didn't talk of their careers or how after seven years of marriage that it might be time to start a family, or anything to do with responsibility or sobriety. That part of the trip went off like a second honeymoon and lasted for a week. Among the best weeks of young Don's life.

One morning as the couple lay entwined and still drunk from the previous evening's excesses, Michelle received a call from, as Don barely managed to discern, Bjorn Trent, a professor at the University of Mexico, about a dig occurring at nearby ruins, south of the city proper. Something to do with work? Or was it more claptrap regarding the missing tribe she'd become increasingly devoted to the past couple of years? Although he wasn't entirely sure if she meant *missing* like the Mayans, or *misplaced* by anthropologists who hadn't quite nailed down seasonal migratory patterns.

While he shared her love of the cryptic and arcane, the intensity of Michelle's research worried him. Junk science was a keen way to get relegated to the lunatic fringe of the community. Tough enough she was a woman in a man's world…

Answers were not forthcoming. She slammed the phone, kissed Don goodbye, throwing on her clothes as she dashed from the suite. He did not see or hear from her again for two days and two nights. This incident was to change many things between them, most especially the power dynamic all couples share, although the full effects wouldn't be experienced until many, many years later. Good things were worth waiting for, weren't they?

Late into the first afternoon, real worry for her safety began to gnaw him. Don played the customary role of the concerned spouse—he rang the university and received short shrift from one ill-tempered secretary or intern after another, none of them the slightest bit interested in Don's plight, none of them knowledgeable of any professor by the name of Bjorn Trent. Thus he languished in loosened tie and shirtsleeves on the edge of the bed, phone cradled against his ear, an endless chain of cigarettes smoldering between his fingers as the sun fell and the suite darkened and grew black but for the occasional flare of his cigarette cherry and the reflected glow of the cityscape that softly swirled on the bedroom wall.

The weather turned nasty and dawn came through the gray underbellies of rainclouds and fired them crimson. The air tasted of creosote and burnt tar. Don slouched to a corner bistro in his slept-in-clothes and drank bitter coffee and sucked on a bitterer wedge of grapefruit and contemplated alerting the consulate, hesitating only because this wasn't entirely out of Michelle's character. She'd pulled similar, albeit less dramatic, stunts in the past, charging off to have beers with an old chum, or visit a remote site without notice or a how-do-you-do for poor worrywart Don. When the moment seized her, she could be impetuous as the wind, and just as indifferent to his feelings.

And so he lingered at the café, sucking his grapefruit and watching the rain, caught somewhere between sullen resentment of being tossed aside for this Bjorn fellow and dread that something terrible had happened—an accident, a run-in with the soldiers or the police, that she might be lying semi-conscious in a squalid hospital bed or trapped in a country prison and desperately awaiting rescue. He fumed and fretted by turns. A pigeon strutted up and shit upon Don's shoe.

Eventually he paid his tab and hailed a taxi to the university, determined to conduct the investigation in person. Perhaps the unhelpful secretaries and grumbling interns would be of sweeter disposition when confronted with the red-eyed and bewhiskered countenance of a frantic husband.

Not so, as it turned out. He spent a frustrating eight hours routed around the labyrinthine complex of tunnels and offices above and below the main university structures, finally landing in the subbasement cubbyhole of a junior assistant to an assistant of some middle manager of a scarcely spoken-of tentacle of the bureaucracy.

The alcove was dimly lit and hot as a furnace room, which considering the location, meant the boiler might've been perking along nearby. A pallid functionary showed him a seat at a desk mostly obscured by piles of folders and loose-leaf parchments. There Don waited, slumped and battered and beginning to lose his mind with aggravation and no small measure of fear for Michelle's imagined plights. He chewed the end of his tie in frustration, embarrassedly dropping it when an ascetic, elderly gentleman in a dark suit emerged from the stacks, silent and graceful and pale as a deep-sea fish and took a seat on the other side of the desk.

The elderly man wore a pair of tiny glasses that rendered his eyes quite strange. He leafed through papers atop the general stack, adjusting his glasses periodically. Presently, he fixed Don with the cold beady gaze of a bird examining a worm and said in cultured English, "I am señor Esteban Montoya. I am in command of campus security. You require my assistance."

Don noted the choice of 'command' and the customarily interrogative phrased as a declaration, and the tomb-like confines squeezed in a bit tighter. "Yes, I'm Don Miller and my—"

Señor Montoya wagged his finger. "No, no. Do not bore me. I know about you, señor. I know of this wife of yours as well. You've annoyed my staff for many hours today. Asking questions. Now I ask the questions. Start again, por favor." He didn't raise his voice, merely allowed ice to inform it.

"Uhh, right. My wife is missing."

"Your wife is not missing, señor."

"She's been gone for..." Don counted the hours on his fingers because he was too tired to trust his calculations. "Over thirty hours."

"I see." The way señor Montoya stared beadily and coldly indicated he did *not* see.

"No phone call. That's really why I'm worried."

"Because she went shopping or sightseeing in our lovely city and has not contacted you. Perhaps you missed her call while away from your hotel."

"Calls are being forwarded to the front desk while I'm out. I checked an hour or two ago. Still nothing."

"I see."

"Do you?"

"Frankly, señor, I think perhaps you are excited for no reason."

"Well, I don't know how it's done here, but where I come from—"

"San Francisco, USA."

"Right. In the USA, if a man's wife goes off in the morning and doesn't return for thirty hours, we alert the proper authorities. It means something might be amiss." Don was flushed and his dander was up. The official's cool, condescending demeanor almost made him hope Michelle was in trouble (God forbid!). He didn't wish to imagine the insufferable arrogance Montoya would exhibit when she came prancing along, blithe as a you please.

"Oh. That is what you do in the USA. Has this happened before?"

Don hesitated. "Er, not like this."

"So it has happened."

"But thirty hours! And no call! And nobody here has even heard of Professor Trent! How is that possible?"

"Your wife is an anthropologist. Well regarded. And you, señor?"

"Didn't you say you knew?" Don and the official stared at one another. Don sighed. "Geologist. I work for AstraCorp."

"That is not very exciting."

"No, it's not. Well, sometimes. There's the caving. That can be hairy."

"I'm sure." Señor Montoya scribbled something with a pencil stub. He removed his glasses. The sharpness of his gaze suggested that the glasses functioned as costume jewelry. "Professor Trent, you say?"

"Yes! Thank god! I thought either I or everybody in this place had gone mad. Yes, Professor Trent. You've heard of him."

"Of course. He works in Natural Sciences."

"That's swell. We find him, we find Michelle. They're investigating some ruins. I don't think she said which ones..."

The old man clucked disapprovingly. "You let your wife run away with Professor Trent? Muy mallow. He is muy handsome. He's Swedish."

"Swedish?"

"Si, señor. Swedish. Professor Trent is popular with the señoritas. The faculty know to keep their wives far away."

It didn't seem possible Don was hearing these words come from the official's lips; it was too dreamlike, as if he'd fallen asleep at the hotel and was simply in the throes of a nightmare, any moment Michelle would flip on the lights, or leap into bed and shake him awake for the tale of her adventures.

Señor Montoya waited, unblinking.

Don squared his jaw. "Fine. You don't want to help, I'll go to the cops. I didn't want to involve them, didn't want to make a fuss, but okay." He stood and straightened his jacket.

"Wait," said Montoya. "Perhaps we are hasty." He slipped his glasses over his nose and smiled, not particularly happily, but a degree or two warmer. "You don't understand. The policia are… Let us say, unreliable. They will want money or they will do nothing. As you say in America, sit on their hands."

"Yeah, that's what we say."

"I shall help you. It must not be held against me that the University was discourteous to a guest." Montoya clapped his hands briskly and dialed the phone and began speaking swiftly in Spanish to whomever answered. The conversation concluded quickly. He said to Don, "I have friends in the policia. These men are retired, so have plenty of time to assist you. Here, I shall give you their address. Go to them and they will escort you, help with the locals, smooth any difficulties. The city is beautiful. She is also perilous for foreigners, especially after dark. These men, my associates will keep you from coming to harm."

"That's gracious of you, señor Montoya. Perhaps I should speak with the faculty…Trent's supervisor. As I said, I'm not even certain which ruins they're visiting."

Montoya picked up the phone. He spoke rapidly, and impatiently, or so it sounded, and scribbled more notes all the while not breaking his gaze with Don, not blinking his cold eyes. "I apologize, señor Miller. Most of the administration has departed for the day. Professor Trent's secretary provided an itinerary. Unfortunately, no site was listed and I am unaware of these mysterious ruins you mention. There are many unusual attractions here." He tore a square of notebook paper and handed it over. "Some of those establishments are notorious. You will need Ramirez and Kinder, I think."

There wasn't much for Don to do thusly confounded by the certainty and finality of Montoya's statement. Deflated, he thanked the elderly gentleman and spent half an hour negotiating the subterranean maze before pushing through an unmarked service door into soft, purple twilight. He rented a taxi and hove off to track the policemen as Montoya had directed. The taxi driver frowned upon receiving the address and muttered sourly, but he threw the car into gear and careened through the labyrinth that comprised the surface streets of the city. Meanwhile, Don blotted the rivulets of sweat cascading down his cheeks and held onto the door strap for dear life.

He was dropped in a strange and largely unlighted neighborhood in a district he wouldn't have recognized in broad daylight. The street was unpaved and white dust covered everything, turning gray in the quickening gloom. A cat slunk through weeds in the cracked sidewalk, and a Mexican flag rustled limply where it hung from a deserted balcony rail. Faintly came the strains of a man and woman shouting and bits of music and canned laughter from a radio show, drifting through a window seven or eight stories up, the only one with any light shining out. This was disquieting—Don was wearily accustomed to the hustle and bustle of the mighty city, the pell-mell crush of millions of citizens packed like ants into a colony. Such silence, such emptiness, was unnatural, was claustrophobic and deafening.

He spied the twinkle of the cityscape between canted and decrepit brick apartments. The lights of the center of town appeared as remote as the constellations glacially coalescing overhead. This celestial glow permitted him to shuffle across the rutted avenue and barely make heads or tails of the building numbers. None of them bore titles, just numerals bolted or painted onto stucco or wood, if at all. The alleys were black cave mouths and odors of urine and decay wafted from them and his eyes and nose watered and he covered his mouth with a handkerchief. Someone whispered to him from the shadows. A trashcan lid clattered across his path, rolling on edge, rolling fast.

"Oh, Michelle," he said and picked up the pace, dangerous as that might be, and soon decided he was at the right door because it was made of rotten wood, its white paint peeling like dead skin, and because it was the only door in the wall that was otherwise crisscrossed with fractures and blurry graffiti and a few windows with iron grilles. No handle, though; the door fit square into the frame, rusty keyhole awaiting a key he didn't possess. Don was ashamed at the panic rising with helium lightness through his body, but the person in the alley called again, slightly louder, and there was an intercom with the letters worn off the placard, no taxi in sight, no nothing except acres and acres, and row upon row of menacing architecture. So he started pressing buttons. After a while, and a series of hang-ups, garbled responses, or plain static silence, a buzzer buzzed in the guts of the building and the horrid white door clicked open and he ducked through.

The door didn't have a handle on the inside either. "What?" he said, his voice rebounding unpleasantly from the walls. He stood in a caved-in foyer that smelled almost as putrid as the alley had and was illuminated by a greenish-red light in a distant aperture. The floor was a partially skinned aggregate of tile, slate and gravel littered with broken glass and shreds of packaging and tatters of fliers. The walls were soft and pocked, corroded rebar exposed. A rickety metal staircase spiraled up and up into the green-red gloom. The radio program he'd heard outside echoed from the invisible upper levels, muffled.

Away from the icy stare of señor Montoya, this entire endeavor seemed less of a wise idea with each passing second. Here was the kind of place a dumb, bumbling American might easily find himself set upon by vagabonds and held for ransom, or simply murdered and dumped in a ditch. He seriously wondered if it would be better to brave the unlighted streets and find a police station, or a payphone to contact the consulate and get the highest authorities involved. However, there was the small matter of no door handle or evident method of egress from the squalid foyer.

In his moment of doubt, the clang of a heavy door thrown wide rebounded down the stairwell and the music and recorded laughter tripled in volume. Footsteps and creaking approached at length. Minutes passed. From the shadows above, a man said, "Hey, gringo. Get your ass up here, pronto!"

"Who goes there?" Don said, not quite sufficiently gullible to traipse farther into the dark without verifying the identity of the speaker first. Ransoms and ditches, ransoms and ditches. Might already be too late.

"Listen, amigo—this is a bad neighborhood. There's some muchachos in the alley wanna slit your throat or make sweet love to your lily white ass and they gonna be tryin' the door. I ain't plannin' on hangin' out here all night. Come on!"

The man didn't sound Hispanic and that threw Don until he recalled that Montoya had referred to the contacts as Ramirez and Kinder. Etymologically speaking, Kinder was awfully Caucasian, and that was close enough for Don, especially as he was anxious about the potential appearance of thugs who wanted to make love to his ass or cut his throat, or first one then the other. Someone knocked on the door and dragged what sounded like a nail or knife across the wood. Don ascended the stairs to the second floor landing in three or four bounds. He stopped short of a man in a turban, v-neck silk shirt, cotton harem pants, and grimy sandals.

The fellow was extraordinarily pale, as if he'd given a bonus quart at the blood drive, and his eyes glinted blue as chips of ice. He was lean and his nose hooked at precisely the right length to be character-enhancing rather than repulsive. His voice was husky and raw; a drinker's voice. "Yeah, you're him. I'm Ramirez. Follow me." Don didn't have an opportunity to reflect on this turn of events as Ramirez turned and began to climb with the speed and agility of a mountain goat, remarking over his shoulder around the fifth floor, "Hug the wall, whitebread. Some of the supports are comin' unscrewed. Long way down."

Don, soaked in sweat and hallucinating from exhaustion, lacked breath to respond. He hugged the wall, though, and gladly. Sixteen months since his last caving expedition and he had seen his stamina decline to the degree his belly ever so slightly pooched over his belt. Michelle hadn't commented, although he suspected she wasn't impressed.

On the seventh floor, Ramirez led him through a swatch of near-perfect darkness and into a shabby studio. Wallpaper hung in loose flaps and bare bulbs dangled by wires from a water-stained ceiling. A radiator thumped and rattled under the single prison cell window. In the corner a stove and antique fridge sat covered in mold. A vinyl couch, gradually coming unstuffed, and two wooden chairs were the only furniture. Boxes of newspapers were stacked waist-high, their surfaces layered with the white dust. The floor was bare wood, notched and scarred and stained. A naked woman sprawled on pile of blankets near the fridge. Her hair was so blonde it was nearly white. She snored. A cockroach balanced upon her thigh, preening its antenna. On the wall above her, a nude Aztec princess and a jaguar in velvet. Doom sliding over a purple horizon, its wormy shadow a bruise upon the princess's bare shoulder.

A thick man in a serape sat on one of the chairs. His hair was blue-black, and thick and shaggy and fell to his waist. He hunched over a long, primitive stone knife, sharpening it with a whetstone. He glanced at Don and returned to his business.

"Kinder, it's our wayward gringo. Gringo, this is Kinder. Wanna drink, amigo?" Ramirez didn't wait for a reply. He threw the bolt on the door and peeked through the spy hole, as if it were possible to see a damned thing on the pitch-black landing. "Yeah, all clear. Sometimes the pendejos follow us. That's when I reach for this." The pale man slid a nine iron from a bag stuck between two piles of boxes, brandished and slid it back into place. "Okay. Time for a drink." He stepped over the snoring woman and retrieved a bottle of tequila from the shelf. He squinted, then poured some booze into a dirty glass and brought it to Don. Don had a sip against his better judgment. When in Rome, and so forth. Ramirez swilled directly from the bottle and wiped his mouth on his sleeve, and belched. "Yo, Benny, wanna slug?"

"Uh-uh." Kinder spat on the stone and kept grinding. He might as well have been hunkered near a prairie campfire. The muscles in his shoulders flexed and rippled through the fabric of the serape.

Don couldn't tell if that was a petrified worm at the bottom of the tequila bottle or a trick of the light. "Señor Montoya says you gentlemen can help me with a problem. He says you are policemen."

"Retired," Ramirez said. He didn't appear old enough to rate retirement. "Montoya sent you over here. That was dumb. We woulda come to you. But whatever, hombre, whatever. What's your problem, uh?"

"He didn't tell you?"

"No, amigo. Montoya only said a gringo pendejo was making waves at his office and we needed to take care of it. We gonna take care of it. You got money, right? American dollars. No pesos."

"Huh? Wait, he sent me to you because the cops would shake me down for cash."

"Damned right those pigs would. Never ever trust the pigs, my friend."

"But… *You* want money. And *you're* a cop."

"Of course we want money. That's how it works. Grease the wheels so they roll, amigo. I'm no pig, I gave that up moons ago. Trust me, I know how the pigs think. You're way better off with us. You're with the angels now. Right, Benny boy?"

Kinder spat and slid the blade across the stone.

"Okay, man. How much you got?" When Don hesitated, Ramirez rolled his eyes and snapped his fingers. "Let's go. How much?"

"Uhhh… Thirty-five, American. A couple hundred pesos."

"You…say what? Thirty-five American?"

"Thirty-five American."

"Throw him out." Kinder didn't bother to glance up this time.

"What the hell you doin' here?" Ramirez said. He took away Don's glass.

"Montoya sent me—"

"Oh, for fuck sake. Yeah, yeah. Why?"

"My wife. She's missing." Don found it difficult to form words. He swallowed and set his jaw. "I can write you a check for more. Or get it from the hotel, or whatever. Or, you know what? Forget it. I'm sorry to have bothered you."

"Slow down, don't be mad. I'm yankin' your chain. Montoya said to take care of you, that's what we do. Benny's into reruns of Bob Hope. After he listens to his show, we talk. Come to an agreement."

"This was a bad idea. The worst. Thanks for the drink. I'll show myself out." The very idea of navigating the stairway of certain death terrified Don, but he wasn't going to accept any more grief from these seedy characters. Likely true that the police would be unsympathetic, yet such was his predicament that calling in the cavalry, an cavalry, appeared the only tenable option.

"Hang on, hang on. Thirty-five is something. Not much, but something. I dunno. Maybe I could make a call. Besides, you'll trip and break your neck if I don't go with you. Montoya might not want it like that. Gotta picture of your woman?"

"Here." Don sighed. The mention of the stairs clinched it, though. He thumbed through his billfold and handed Ramirez a snapshot of Michelle standing on the lawn in her blue sundress, croquet mallet in hand, a floppy hat shading her face.

"Mother Mary, that's a fine-looking woman," Ramirez said in a reverential tone. He scooted over to Kinder and showed him the photo.

Kinder expertly flipped the knife and slid it under his serape. He stood and rolled his brawny shoulders and looked at Don with dispassionate hatred. "What the hell are we waiting for?"

2.

The trio descended into the lobby, Kinder at the fore, gasoline lantern lighting the way, Don in the middle, and Ramirez at the rear, tapping the nine iron against his palm. They went outside into the humid night, crossed the street, bee-lined through a deserted lot and wound up inside a locked garage that Kinder possessed the key to. Inside the garage were islands of tarps and machinery and broken cars. He whisked the canvas from a cherry Cadillac convertible. Don rode in back. Ramirez took shotgun and Kinder drove. Ramirez and Kinder chatted in Spanish, referring by the dashboard glow to the jotted itinerary Professor Trent's secretary had provided.

Ramirez whistled. "Amigo, some of these places are not so good. Are you sure your wife would go there?"

"No. It's Trent's list. She went with him to see ruins."

"I don't understand. Your wife got a boyfriend?"

"Jesus, no. Look, they're just friends. Not even friends; colleagues, like cops, you see?"

"But, man. These places… Okay, okay. You're the boss. Benny will take us right there, no problem. Right, Benny?"

Kinder stepped on the gas and the Cadillac's engine rumbled and wind whipped through Don's hair and stung his eyes. The lights of the metropolitan heart of the City didn't draw nearer, but slid sideways and receded as the car growled its way beneath a series of bridges and then climbed a steep switchback grade. Tenements and cinderblock and corrugated tin row houses crowned the rise. A large portion of the block appeared to be a ramshackle cantina. Cars parked at random angles in the dirt lot, the ditch and the road. People stood around drinking, or flopped in the dirt, loving or fighting, it was impossible to tell; dozens of them, and more lined the roof of the cantina like birds on a wire, bare legs hanging in front of the dead neon sign that spelled *Casa del Diablo*. Light fell from the stars and the batwing doors and a pole with a torch breathing medieval fire over the scene.

Don thought there must be a serious mistake. "This can't be right," he said.

Kinder parked in the middle of the road. There was nowhere else. "It'll be fine," Ramirez said as he hopped over the side, one hand on his turban. He waved impatiently at Don. "Don't lag behind the big dogs, amigo. This is no place for puppies."

"I'm sure it's not where my wife would've come."

"Don't be scared, puppy. Nobody gonna lop off your head with me and Benny in your corner. Stick close, hug the wall—it's a longer fall than them damned old stairs." Ramirez snickered and grabbed Don's shoulder and pushed him forward across the muddy lot and through the batwing doors into a smoggy, smolten den of crimson light and fire pit smoke coiling and roiling in a bloody miasma that rendered the occupants, of which there were scores packed into the oven, shadowy figures who stopped their boozing, dicing, and whoring to stare at Don. A yellow dog missing an eye snapped at him, all rotten teeth and lolling tongue, and tore off a chunk of his leg, putting action to the crowd's voiceless intent. People laughed and guitars and horns kicked back to life. He'd paid the cover charge of flesh.

"Haha, Benny, he's bleedin' like a stuck pig. Better sop it up, amigo. These mutts got the rabies. So do the dogs, harhar! Hey, give me some dough." Ramirez grabbed the notes Don blindly thrust at him.

They shoved him into a chair in the corner and he hissed through his teeth with agony as blood soaked his pants leg and he patted it with his handkerchief. Too much blood though.

"Ay caramba! Poochie took a whole piece," Ramirez said and pressed a bottle of warm beer into Don's hand. "Drink. It helps!"

Don swallowed and while he did, Ramirez cackled and dumped a stream of whiskey from a bottle he'd uncapped directly onto the seeping wound. White fire did a tarantella in Don's brain and he nearly fell backward off the chair. Ramirez caught him.

"Shh, amigo. Don't show no weakness. Gotta be strong, gotta have cojones. Dog eat dog in this town, harhar!"

No question remained in Don's mind that he'd royally screwed up with this particular operation. Instead of getting out of a hole, he'd continued to dig for China. He lay his sweaty forehead against the table and prayed for the searing pain in his thigh to relent, for the hyenas to vanish in a puff of smoke, for the whole quagmire to dissolve and reveal itself the effluvium of a nightmare. None of that happened. Instead, Ramirez massaged his shoulders while raising the bottle with his free hand and swilling inhuman amounts of tequila and muttering what had to be a slaughtered rendition of a Mexican lullaby.

Kinder returned, a couple of men in tow. "Good news, gringo. These guys know where the chica and her boyfriend went."

"Not her boyfriend, damn it!"

"What's that? Hey, this is excellent luck." Ramirez shook Don none too gently. "Open your eyes, sleepyhead. Clubbo and Günter here have brought the good word. Gimme your wallet." He snatched the remainder of the cash and stuffed the deflated wallet into Don's shirt pocket. He glanced down and shook his head sadly at all of the blood on the floor. "Man, he really bit the shit outta you. You need to see a vet."

Clubbo was a silver-haired Cuban in a white shirt and a shell necklace—Ramirez explained his friend was on the lam from revolutionary forces on his island. Günter was European. His hair was nearly as long as Kinder's, but dirty blond, and his beard was full and curly. He wore a leather jacket and leather pants and resembled an Ostrogoth who'd stepped out of a time machine, as painted by Frank Frazetta lacking only a sword in his hand and a nubile maiden wrapped around his leg. He'd tattooed skulls on his knuckles and a thick spiky bracelet adorned his left forearm. Kinder said something about a stint in a Russian gulag.

Neither of the newcomers spoke. Their gazes slid over Don and fastened to the cash in Ramirez's fist. Ramirez gave each a share. The men frowned and pocketed the loot. A topless bargirl with tits floppier than the hat Michelle wore in her snapshot sashayed over with a platter of beer and another bottle of rotgut tequila and everybody had a snort, including Don, who demurred and tried to squirm away, but Kinder pulled back his head by the hair and Ramirez cannon-balled the medicine down his throat and laughed as the American coughed and choked and thrashed around.

"So your lady, she's a scientist or some shit," Ramirez said, and knocked back another shot of hooch. He looked like an albino devil and the stone at the center of his turban glistened like a third eye, flickered with the inner fire of the Fabled Ruby Ray powering on. "Yeah, this is the question of the hour. Why she fuckin' around the ruins, huh? People around here don't appreciate gringas sneaking into our ruins. Uh-uh."

"Maybe she just fucking around," Kinder said, gazing at the door, one hand hidden under the table like he was waiting for John Wayne to strut in and open fire.

Don laughed crazily, and red hate shot through his vision. He reached across the spilled drinks, smashed tortilla chips and half-full beer bottles, and socked Kinder in the mouth. Don had boxed a smidge in his youth and this was a decent blow, delivered from the lower back and hip, thrown loose as an uncoiling chain until it snapped tight on impact. The kind of blow that when delivered with twelve-ounce gloves could lay a man on his backside. Bare knuckle, it was a wicked shot. It felt like hitting a sandbag.

Ramirez and Clubbo yanked him back. Each man drove his thumb under Don's clavicles and he lost most of the feeling in his arms and chest.

Kinder blinked and casually flicked a drop of blood from his dented lip. "Don't want me talking about your puta that way, eh? Okay, I'm sorry, gringo."

Again Don lunged and again the men restrained him, although this time Ramirez punched him in the heart and Don's vision went for a few seconds, along with his wind.

Kinder smiled slightly when the American ceased gagging and retching. "Forgive me. Sometimes I forget that not everyone is an animal. Lupe," he nodded at Ramirez, "give our amigo another drink. He needs it. You smoke, amigo?" He drew a cigarette from a plain white pack and lighted it with a match he struck on the sole of his boot. "Nah, you don't smoke. Climbing in and outta them caves, you gotta be strong." He flexed his biceps mockingly. "Too much smoke robs your strength. But listen, so does a woman. Don't hit me, hombre. I'm giving you some wisdom. Women like your wife, women who wear pants and run around with handsome strangers, you gotta watch out for those bitches. They don't care for nothing but themselves. I'm sorry to tell you this. It's the way of the world."

"Piss up a rope," Don said, hoping for Gary Cooper but probably channeling Andy Griffith. Cursing wasn't his forte, however the occasion seemed to merit it. The others had released his arms, but he'd calmed and his urge to kick the Mexican's ass or die trying had subsided. His rage smoldered, tempered by the change in Kinder's timbre, how the man's rough features had smoothed and taken on the aspect of an entomologist preparing to dissect an insect. Genie-like, Louis Plimpton's blandly superior face came to mind. "I sure as hell smoke." He clumsily snatched a cigarette from stoic Clubbo and lighted it from the candle in the bowl because his fingers weren't working very well. "How'd you know I cave?"

"Señor Miller, how do you think? Montoya told me over the phone."

"Yeah? Damned short conversation."

"Montoya is concise."

Don's pain receded to a dull throb in the background wash of light and noise. "You guys aren't cops."

"Real bright one here," Ramirez said.

Kinder sighed. "Shut up, Lupe. Look, amigo. Everything is going to be all right. The señora is fine. She'll come home tomorrow as if nothing ever happened. What say we enjoy a few more drinks then get you to your hotel and you forget about rushing into the hills looking for her and this Trent pendejo?"

"Do you know where my wife is?"

"Si, señor. Can't you relax and have a nice evening? Let your troubles resolve themselves. As I say to you before, these wayward women will only bring you sorrow. No use chasing after them like a dog chasing chickens."

"I say we round up some putas and go to the donkey show!"

"If you aren't cops," Miller said, "then what are you?"

"He's not gonna listen to reason and get whores with us," Ramirez said. "Montoya said so."

"Shut up, Lupe," Kinder said.

"Easy, easy. Just sayin'."

"Dirección Federal de Seguridad."

"Mexican Intelligence? Where's your suit, your badge?"

"I hope you can keep a secret, señor Miller." Kinder stared coldly at Don, and it was similar to the creepy look Montoya had used, except Kinder was built like a truck and carried a knife large enough to slice off a man's arm. "Sure, yes. You're all right, Miller. We can be friends."

"Mexican Intelligence… Good lord. You go after the real bad guys."

"Si, señor. We go after the bad men."

"You're surveilling Michelle? What on earth for? Is that legal?"

"Everything is legal in México, especially for us, stupido," Ramirez said and snickered in that ugly manner of his. "We make the rules."

"We're not watching señora Miller. She's not important. We're watching Professor Trent."

"Oh, that rat bastard. How I'm growing to hate that sonofabitch."

"Hey, there's the spirit," Ramirez said and slapped Don's shoulder.

"What's he mixed my poor sweetie up in? Oh, god, it's nothing to do with the Reds, is it? Jesus, she'll be blacklisted…"

The men exchanged glances. Kinder said, "Nothing to concern you, or your wife. This is an internal matter, a matter of state security. Come, finish your beer and we'll take you home. Tomorrow all will be well."

" 'An' all manner of things will be well'," Ramirez said.

"Lupe, for the love of fuck, please shut up."

"Okay, I am."

"No way, Jose," Don said, a tiny bit drunk on top of everything else. "She isn't spending another night doing god knows what with Mr. Sweden. No, sir. I insist, secret agent Kinder, sidekick Ramirez, your two goons, that you escort me at once to these precious ruins of yours." He slapped the table for emphasis.

"But, señor… What will you do if we find them?"

"I'm going to challenge him to a duel. Anybody got a gun?" Don swayed in his seat, steadied by Ramirez and one of the aforementioned goons, Günter.

"Ay yi yi," Kinder said and again glanced at his friends. "So be it. Montoya promised you'd prove intractable. Lupe, my apologies. To the car, then. Ondalay."

3.

The brutes Günter and Clubbo assisted Don to the car as his legs had all but given out from exhaustion after the adrenaline rush, loss of blood, and the free-flowing booze. The trio sat in back, Don wedged in the middle, his head resting on Clubbo's shoulder. Clubbo smelled pretty good; a combination of liquor, smoke, and aftershave. Don drifted in and out of reality as Kinder dropped the hammer and they hurtled along a winding road that led ever farther from the city into the night.

"My people were Celts," Ramirez said.

"Celts, really?" Don was slurring. "I thought there was something different about you."

"My clan is special. Real black sheep. We were into the groovy shit, hombre. We danced to the music of the old black gods."

"Celestial music," Kinder said, his voice heavy with melancholy. "Those must've been the days."

"Don't be sad, compadre. The wheel rolls round and round all hail Old leech!" And this shout was echoed by Kinder and the heretofore silent Clubbo and Günter.

"My wife would love to talk with you," Don said.

"Oh, yeah!"

"Shut, up, Lupe! The fucker will climb over there and kick your ass." Kinder feathered the brakes and slewed the big car wildly, throwing everyone around.

After they'd straightened out and things were calm for a few moments, Ramirez said as if muttering to himself, "Yeah, yeah, yeah. At the fall of the Western Roman Empire in Britannia, we were there, man, sticking the shiv to those wop fucks. We limed our hair and fought butt naked, painted in blue and red. We set ourselves on fire, hacked off the heads of our enemies and made fruit bowls outta their skulls. Got one in my pad, too. Fought with copper and bronze and flint. Men fucked men when putas were scarce, and the dogs ran scared. Everybody ran scared. So don't screw with me." His eyes were wild in the rearview and Don waved at him, limply.

"Nobody's screwing with you," Kinder said. The pair passed a marijuana cigarette back and forth and the Cadillac swooped in broad, stately arcs across the faded centerline. Too dark to be certain, but it felt mountainous.

"I'm okay," Ramirez said after taking a manly drag on the cigarette. He popped his eyes at Don in the mirror. "Be good, puppy. You're under surveillance."

Something huge and dark blotted the stars, and snuggling into Günter's armpit, Don realized his instincts were absolutely correct—they were in the mountains. Even then, the powerful Cadillac toiled beneath the shadow of a tower of rock. The warm wind grew dense with the tang of pollen and sap, a cloying sauna humidity that instantly stuck Don's shirt to the small of his back and caused him to imagine Aztec ziggurats wreathed in vines and a terrible shadow of winged lizard gliding across the rainbow landscape, an Aztec Princess, nude as fire and over her shoulder a storm cloud, a cloud of something at any rate, a ball of raveling yarn crackling with lightning and closing fast. He groaned and Ramirez barked laughter, and then the car stopped.

Don tried to make a break as soon as the doors opened; jackknifed his head into Günter's jaw and then flung himself across Clubbo, elbowing and clawing the big man as he went. Günter wasn't any more fazed by the headbutt than Kinder had been by getting socked back at the cantina. The brute caught Don's belt and he and Clubbo threw him from the Cadillac. Don landed face down in the dirt and the goons casually kicked him in the ribs and thighs until he couldn't suck enough air to scream.

Kinder called a halt to the beating.

Günter and Clubbo helped Don to his feet and led him by the headlights' shaft to a mossy boulder and propped him against it. Things happened as if in a dream—someone stripped his jacket and shirt; a quick yank and there went his belt and pants, everything dumped into a canvas bag Kinder held open. Don didn't resist; his limbs were heavy as lead and focusing was impossible.

In his delirium he was far past resistance or holding grudges. He said, "Am I being Shanghaied?" and everyone chuckled and Ramirez patted his arm, careful to stay clear of the blood pumping from his nose and the gore yet trickling down Don's leg from the savage dog bite. To Don, his thigh and lower leg were a mass of grue, no better than a deer haunch smashed by a car, but he felt only the dullest sensation of pain at this point. Insects churred in the thick brush that surrounded them. Rocks and gravel everywhere, the dim outline of a cliff just at the edge of the headlights' glow; a cave mouth. Someone had painted an inverted crucifix and a crude devil face against the pale rock of the mountainside and other, obscure symbols and glyphs whose significance escaped him. "Are these the ruins?"

"There are many, many ruins in Mexico." Kinder straightened and handed the bag to Clubbo. Clubbo walked to the car and tossed the bag inside. "There are many wonders. I regret to say, compadre, that these ruins your wife spoke of do not exist. I could not take you somewhere that does not exist, so I bring you here. This is the Cave of the Ancients.

A dangerous, dangerous place, unless you know where to step. There is a hole inside the entrance. Not far, not far. It may interest a man such as yourself. The hole is bottomless. I ask myself if such a thing as a bottomless hole is possible. We shall go see it now, eh?"

Don briefly contemplated the panic that should've coursed through him. He felt most excellent, adrift on a pink cloud. These men were his facilitators, solicitous to his every need, and his need was to continue floating, to feel the balmy breeze rushing over his damp skin. Michelle's face bobbed to the surface of his muddled consciousness and gazed at him with loving disapproval, then burst into vapor and troubled him no more as the men hoisted him upon their shoulders and carried him like a football hero. Ramirez walked ahead with a torch he'd fashioned from a stick and some rags and by that queer and reddish light, devils, or the shadows of devils hooked to the shoes of the men and capered across the stony earth.

The walk lasted an eon and the stars hardened and fossilized in the heavens and Don's blood slowed to stagnancy in his veins. Ramirez began to sing as the path rose and the group came to the mouth of the cave, and though completely incapacitated physically and mentally, Don was amazed by the size of it. The thing yawned like the spiked maw of the Ouroboros and what Ramirez sang was a song of death, of sacrifice.

They proceeded into the cave and along a tunnel. The floor was sandy and occasionally the men's shoes crunched upon bits of shattered bottles of revelries past. And they continued through a snaky side passage, emerging at length into a great cavern. Stalactites spiked the ceiling and the torchlight reflected from deposits of quartz and mica. Even to Don's reduced sensibilities, the chamber felt ancient and malign, a cyst in the granite sinew of the mountain, and fear kindled in his belly. A feeble thing, his fear, pacified and quieted by whatever drug his companions had slipped him at the cantina.

"Aw, shit," Don said to no one in particular as he was laid across a slab of worked stone with a smooth concavity marking its axis and a series of deep grooves carved into its foot. The surface of the slab had been fashioned and planed so that it canted toward the edge of a pit. The pit spanned perhaps six feet. An odor of decay wafted from its depths.

The men lighted more torches that were fixed to sconces of blackened iron in the walls. Each man stripped to the waist then donned the headdress and mask of a demon or beast, or demonic beast, and joined his fellows in the wicked chant, this accompanied by the blowing of reeds and clashing of cymbals and piercing ululations that echoed most alarmingly from rock that had seen slaughter and sadism aplenty in its epochs as sentinel and receiver of blood.

Clubbo and Günter were monkey demons, Kinder a bird of prey with a yellow beak, while Ramirez had donned the trappings of a monstrous bat. Kinder took the ugly stone dagger from his belt and held it loosely, like an ice pick. Ramirez brought forth a similarly brutal stone tomahawk and danced recklessly near the pit, waving a blazing torch in his other hand.

Their dreadful song reached a crescendo. Don considered struggling, tried to flex his hand, tried to swing upright, and found that his extremities were beyond leaden and now short-circuited, nerveless lumps. He closed his eyes and waited. There came then a strange and hypnogogic interlude which might've lasted seconds or minutes and the song resumed altered; shriller and discordant. When he managed to summon the strength to look, he beheld the wondrous sight of Ramirez levitating as if a puppet jerked off his feet by a string, then flying in reverse into the greater darkness of the cavern. He shrieked piteously and flailed with the torch and vanished.

Don couldn't see any of the other men as their screams and wails diminished in opposite directions. However, the acoustics were treacherous. He fell unconscious for a much longer duration. When he awoke, the torches had died, leaving him in blackness. His body and mind were free of the drugged lassitude. He shook violently with chill and pent animal terror and those were bad moments.

Someone whispered, "Let the dark blind you on the inside, Don. There are frightful things."

A family bound for market found him on the road near a small southern village two days later; cut, bruised, suffering from exposure and a gash on his temple likely received in a fall. He'd lost twenty pounds and skated very near death. Michelle came with the police and officials from the U.S. Consulate. Even Dr. Plimpton frantically hopped a flight and ensconced himself in the hallway, berating himself for some mysterious reason Don was too addled to comprehend.

She sobbed and lay with him on his hospital bed and kissed him a thousand times, explaining that he'd completely misunderstood her last words the morning they'd parted—she and Professor Trent hadn't visited any ruins. There were no ruins. Instead, they'd attended an informal lecture at the home of a German scientist at his villa in the hills. No phones, as the fellow was a notorious recluse. The bus had blown a gasket, so the guests were detained for nearly a day waiting for fresh transportation. An awful misunderstanding.

Naturally, the local authorities questioned him regarding who he'd spoken with and where these people had taken him. Already, the details of names, faces, and events slipped through his memory as eels through a skein.

Don remembered nothing of his escape from the cave. Within a few years, his only solid recollection of that Mexico vacation was the superheated romance with Michelle in their hotel and vague impressions of snooty bureaucrats, menacing street thugs, and a parade or party where everyone had worn horrible masks. The rest was simply smoke. For her part, Michelle never spoke of it again.

CHAPTER TWO POINT FIVE

Wenatchee, 1980

The entomologist died with his bloody lips pressed to Agent Crane's ear; a slimy crimson seal that burst when the scientist's head lolled, fell to the pillow. Agent Crane stepped away from the bed and its glassy-eyed passenger. The dead black bulk of a revolver lay near the corpse's left temple. The revolver was still warm, still reeked of oil and scorched metal. So much for their Person of Interest. He pulled a handkerchief from his pocket and dabbed his gory earlobe.

The wind came against the farmhouse. A draft licked Agent Crane's ankles. Limp drapes breathed like balaclavas to the small-mouthed windows. The windows were dark and cold. Everything rattled, sighed, subsided.

"Melodrama, day-o." Agent Barton leaned against the door jam. A tall man, he appeared huge because the doors and halls were tacked up in the '20s when economy of design was king. "What did he say?"

Agent Crane wiped his hands.

An antique clock ticked and clicked on an antique dresser; a bulb sizzled in a brass lamp. There were many framed pictures; generations of them, arranged by columns. The pictures existed under foggy glass, subjects made spectral by shadows, their abrupt irrelevance to any living being. Below Agent Crane's shiny wingtips, the tattered throw rug and warped floorboards, came dim, aquatic creaks and bumps of other agents on the ground level. Men in crisp suits knocking about with flashlights and cameras.

"Hey, Tommy," Agent Barton said.

"Yeah."

"Did he *say* something?"

"Yeah." Mr. Crane finished wiping his hands. He didn't know what to do with the cloth, so he held it between thumb and forefinger. Something crashed downstairs; nervous laughter followed. A dog barked in the yard. "Goddamn it. Fifteen minutes sooner…"

"Fifteen minutes sooner he might've plugged you or me instead if himself. Want coffee?" Agent Barton didn't wait for an answer; he went to the dresser and used the phone to brief Section. Section had alerted the local authorities, would coordinate the necessary details. After disconnecting with Section, he took a deep breath, visibly composed himself for the call to their field supervisor. It was a short conversation—*Yes, ma'am. No, ma'am. We'll be back tomorrow in the PM, ma'am.* He shuddered, smiled in a perfunctory manner. "We're done here. Want coffee? Let's get some coffee."

Agent Crane nodded. The techs would scour the room, ants on jelly. Maybe there was a note, a recording. Probably nothing. He followed his partner into the narrow hall, down the narrow stairs. They acknowledged the other men, the ones with the gloves and the specimen bags.

Once they were in the car and crunching slowly along the gravel lane, Agent Crane began to relax. He lighted a cigarette. Bony poplars clawed at the stars. Clouds blacked a steadily widening swath of the lower heavens. Three cruisers from the Chelan County sheriff's office met them head on, ghosted by, trailing rooster tails of dust. Red and blue flashes wobbled through the empty fields and imprinted behind Agent Crane's eyelids.

"What's with you?" Agent Barton said.

"I couldn't make it out."

"Couldn't make out what? What Plimpton said?"

"Yeah."

"Looked like he had something on his mind."

"Did it."

"Yep. Hey, there's that truck stop on 97. Burger and coffee."

"OK." Agent Crane cracked the window. Agent Barton hated it when he smoked in the car. Agent Crane lighted another. His head felt thick, felt like a lead ball. The adrenaline was seeping from his system, leaving him shaky and depressed.

They made the highway. Every mile reduced Agent Crane's sensation of dread, until what remained curled in the pit of his stomach. It hit him this way sometimes, but not often, not in years. This wasn't the suicide, either. Plimpton was a photo, a paragraph in a dossier. A pathology report now. Meat.

No, it was something else, some *indefinable* thing. The other team members had felt it too, judging by their flared nostrils and unhappy smiles. Agent Barton felt it as well; he drove too fast. Barton always drove fast when he was in a mood. Maybe the team *would* uncover something. Maybe there was a secret stash of chemicals, guns, incriminating documents. Bomb-making supplies. Agent Crane didn't want to go back and hang around. He preferred to wait for the report.

He said, "You think *she* knew?"

"She called it. She must've known something."

"Could be a coincidence..."

"And what do you say about coincidence?"

"Fuck coincidence."

"Right. So she knew, she was right about that much. But, if they don't find anything hot, it's going to look like another circle jerk."

Barton said, "You think they're going to post us in Alaska, huh? Don't worry—Alaska's pretty nice in the fall, long as you pack some electric underwear."

They drove in silence for a while. Then, Crane said, "I wish I could've made out what Plimpton was trying to say."

"Uh-huh." Barton's eyes were slits in the dashboard glow.

"He...slurred. Mumbled. You know."

"Probably didn't see you, Tommy."

"Yeah?"

"Yeah. Brains all over the wall. He didn't see you."

"He was pretty gone."

"That's what I told Section."

"Good."

"Good. Not our problem."

"We got enough of our own."

"Yep."

The men chuckled, and now it shrank to a sliver, the wedge of ice in Agent Crane's gut. Later, after a greasy dinner at the Rattlesnake Prairie truck stop, they checked into a no-tell motel, left a 5am wakeup call with the night clerk.

Crane donned his bifocals and burned the midnight oil, scanning a briefcase load of papers, including geological surveys on the substrata of the Wenatchee Valley region and a corresponding environmental report documenting its effects on the local ecosystems. Then there was the twenty-page compilation of homicide, assault and missing persons statistics. This latter read like a segment from the *Detroit Free Press* crime insert rather than the description of an agrarian county populated by vineyards, orchards and farms. Eventually he switched off the bedside lamp, sat against the wall, sipping bottled water. Barton snored across the room. Agent Crane couldn't banish Plimpton's red mouth from his mind. Freezing rain pelted the roof. The wind returned, hungry. The tall lamp in the parking lot emitted a cheerless glow and at some point it wavered and snuffed like a blown candle.

Black.

Right before Agent Crane went down for the count, the night terrors of childhood rushed over his skin and paralyzed him on the cheap bed in the unlit room. A door squeaked softly as it swung to and fro, to and fro, and stopped. The blinds shivered as if beneath the faintest stir of breath. He was a child in dread of the yawning closet door, a grown man pinioned to a bed, a federal agent leaning over a dying man in a rundown farmhouse, and his personal gloaming approached from all points at once.

Plimpton whispered, *They Who Wait love you, Tommy.*

Agent Crane inhaled to scream, but the blood was already pouring in.

CHAPTER THREE

The Rabbits Running in the Ditch

(Now)

1.

Autumn was around the corner after a scorching summer. Of late, the days remained dry and hot, while evenings saw starry skies and crisp temperatures. Don wandered to the yard some evenings and watched the star fields blink and burn, his heart filled with a profound sense of disquiet he couldn't identify. The cold impassive stars didn't bother him so much as the gaps between them did. He was old, though. Old and unsteady in mind and body. A real flakey dude, according to his loving wife.

The feeling was always gone by morning.

During the last official week of summer, he dusted off his beloved 1968 Firebird and squired Michelle into town for dinner and drinks as an early sixtieth anniversary present. Don had booked reservations at the *Inn of Old Wales*, a traditional Welsh pub and restaurant incongruously transplanted inside a refurbished Spanish mission, half an hour from their farmhouse in the Waddell Valley. Due to a combination of circumstances and her reticence to appear anywhere within a thousand yards of a tavern, this was but the second occasion he'd managed to drag her to the inn.

It was a now or never sort of proposition. The twins would arrive for an impromptu vacation in the morning: Kurt and his new wife, the princess from Hong Kong; and Holly with a girlfriend who accompanied her every summer on various adventures. Next week, Don was scheduled to moderate lectures regarding the Cryptozoic Geomorphology exhibit at the Redfield Memorial Museum of Natural History, and Michelle would leave for an anthropology summit in Turkey, the latest destination of her annual Eastern pilgrimage. Don wished like hell he could hop a ride with his wife; he dreaded moderating the panel of stuffed-shirt academic rivals, all of them with axes to grind and scores to settle, before an audience of, well, dozens, if one included the light and sound technicians, the caterers and custodians.

Don and Michelle took the impending hubbub in stride. Theirs were lives characterized by steady, placid routine, punctuated with moments of absolute anarchy. Hers was a formidable presence in the field of comparative anthropology, due in part to no mean skill at writing brilliantly flamboyant papers and securing lucrative grants through savvy and guile. Her detractors grumbled that she wasn't likely to depart the game unless it was feet first, and probably in the belly of an anaconda, or after succumbing to some dreadful foreign scourge such as malaria. Meanwhile, Don served the Evergreen State University as a geophysics professor emeritus.

The drive went pleasantly enough, even if the Firebird's brakes were tight and Don tended to overcorrect on the bends—he'd packed the beast away a decade past and only fired it up for a yearly shakedown cruise. His wife preferred he stuck to the Volvo or their minivan, especially now that he wore thick glasses and his reflexes were nearly shot to pieces and he tended to forget things, although that part had gone on for several decades, at least. She claimed it was against her policy to ride around in a muscle car with a octogenarian at the wheel.

We must hurry, my sweet, or the Grand Prix shall start without us, he'd said when he zoomed up to the front door. She frowned in dismay at his prescription sunglasses, driving gloves, and the checkered scarf wrapped around his neck—which he'd worn just to get her goat. Don eventually coaxed Michelle into the car by champing a rose in his teeth and patting the passenger seat. *Oh, you old fool*, she said, tittering into her hand.

They crossed into Olympia under orange skies, and followed potholed avenues through historic neighborhoods, winding serpentine along the ridges; then, racing between the majestic shadows of one-hundred-twenty-year-old maples. The road continued until the coastline curved and separated from the city proper.

Michelle gasped happily when the inn hove into view atop a bald crest several switchbacks above their rapidly moving car. "Oh, my—I'd forgotten how lovely it is." Her sunglasses reflected the fires of sunset. She wore a kerchief and bonnet like Vivian Leigh.

He cast sneaking glances at her, admiring the exquisite beauty she'd matured into, feeling a pang of lust that he hadn't shaken since their first date, the first time she'd lifted her dress and wrapped her powerful legs around his waist—and he belayed that line of thought immediately lest they fly off the road into a ditch due to his amorous distraction.

At eighty-two and a half, Michelle conceded to a solitary vanity: her long, dark hair had bleached dead white and she preferred to disguise that fact in public. The scars, on the other hand, didn't affect her self-confidence. Her face and torso bore marks from injuries suffered during a jeep wreck. Years and years ago, while on an expedition into the heart of Siberia, her driver flipped their vehicle on a muddy road in the foothills two hundred miles from the nearest town. She'd nearly died on the forty-hour trip to the hospital and no amount of surgery ever disguised the disfigurement—a jagged, white valley that slashed from her left temple, across her breast and arced to its terminus at her hip bone. Don was consulting a mining firm in the wilds of the Olympic Peninsula and didn't receive news of the accident and Michelle's brush with death for nearly a week. Yet another hazy interlude of his past that he'd resigned himself to never fully recollecting. Perhaps it was better to forget.

Don smiled at Michelle to disperse his sentimental melancholy and talked about their destination. He'd been meeting Argyle Arden, Robby Gold and Turk Standish and the rest of the boys here for fifteen years to drink and play at darts. In 1911, the mission had been transported, brick by brick, from San Francisco and reassembled at its current perch above the Olympia Harbor. It was soon converted to a Roman Catholic priory at the behest of local founding father and resident eccentric, Murray Blanchard III.

The building changed hands numerous times during the Depression, and again after the turmoil of the '40s and then sat vacant until 1975 when Earlagh Teague bought it from the city for a song. The Welshman, with the assistance of a dynamo wife and five doughty sons, transformed the relic into something of a monument; a cross between fine contemporary dining and old world hostelry. Inside, it was vaulted and airy. Balconies formed a wide crescent above the oak bar and the scatter of small dining tables and booths. The darts room lay beyond an arch just off the main gallery, sporting the requisite cork targets and a set of shopworn pool tables. There, a handful of bawdy old salts and genteel ruffians congregated daily, slugging beer and laying wagers on their shooting hands or whatever sporting event might be televised on the ancient black and white.

Miller, party of two, Don told the hostess, a mildly impatient girl with preternaturally rosy cheeks. She was new; staff came and went with regular frequency. They were escorted to a table on the northeast balcony with a lovely bay window view of the distant swath of darkening water and countryside. Tiny lights of sloops and barges bobbed on the harbor, glittered on the wooded hillsides where deep green gave way to streaks of red and gold, and approaching night.

They ordered a bottle of wine. The waiter lighted candles in elegant wrought iron sconces. A few couples drifted in, trailing murmurs of conversation and laughter. Finely dressed seniors; the men wore oversized watches and crisp silk ties; the women were decked in stately dresses, feathered hats and pearl necklaces; and everybody's dentures snowy white and aglow with petroleum jelly. Below, on a small dais, a white-bearded fiddler in a plaid jacket and a bowler tuned his instrument and began a Celtic jig. Michelle sipped her wine. She studied the pennants and heraldic shields, and the stained glass mosaic of Mary that reflected its colors across nearby tables.

Don adored his wife; her radiant joy warmed him more thoroughly than the half bottle of Merlot had. At moments like these, the wrinkles and seams smoothed away, she very much resembled the baby-faced bride he'd whisked off to that quaint resort in Maui for their honeymoon. It boggled him Truman manned the Oval Office while they spent the last of their meager savings on two hedonistic weeks of sun, surf and sex.

Dinner came and went, and most of the wine too. For dessert, the staff lugged in a six-layer chocolate cake, and, on a silver platter, the imperiously decorous headwaiter presented Michelle with a platinum chain in a mother of pearl box. Don secretly ordered the gift at Malloy Jewelers some months prior to this joyous event. Michelle dangled the chain in the candlelight, cheeks flushed, lips quivering, and burst into tears. She buried her neatly coiffed head between her forearms.

"I'm just glad I've still got what it takes to make you happy after all these years," Don said drolly. He quaffed the remainder of his glass. Michelle's shoulders shook harder. Her answer was muffled by her arms and when Don said, "What's that, dear?" she raised her mascara-streaked face and sobbed, "I *am* happy, damn it!" He considered this development and poured another glass for both of them. *Silence is indeed golden, my boy*, his grandfather had often muttered as a piece of advice gleaned from a long, rocky marriage to a woman vastly more temperamental than Michelle. Dear old Grandma. She'd been a case to the end, God love her.

Michelle snatched a hanky from her purse and bolted for the ladies room. Don noted she'd taken the chain with her, which was a good sign. He hoped. Michelle didn't cry often—she'd never been an overly emotional girl. She claimed high passion dangerous to people in her profession, especially afield. Peruvian Bushmen and New Guinea headhunters weren't impressed by weepy foreign broads.

Don gazed out the window, down into the parking lot, and noticed a couple of people lurking near his car. For a moment he stared, bemused, leaning sideways in his seat, the glass halfway to his lips. The parking lot was rather cramped, and populated by perhaps a dozen vehicles. The sodium lamp had fizzed to life, thus he easily discerned the dark figures on the passenger side. He hesitated, wondering if they might belong to the Studebaker parked two slots over; but no, the shadowy fellows were quite plainly crouched to get a better look at the interior, and gads! had the Firebird slightly rocked, an unmistakable precursor to the door or window being jimmied?

"Well, good luck, mate," said an elderly gentleman in a leisure suit and bowtie. He patted Don on the shoulder in passing. The man's companion, a handsome woman with tall, burnished hair, smiled at Don. *You pathetic lout*, her cold, pitying expression seemed to say.

"Eh?" He groped for understanding of this exchange, and then realized they thought Michelle had fled their romantic dinner due to some churlishness on his part. "Er, yes, thank you." He quickly checked the lot again and caught not one, but *four* mysterious figures skulking away into the deeper shadows—and they hadn't been crouching; they were kids. A gaggle of miscreant children, he realized. Brazen hooligans having a last bash before summer vacation came to a crashing halt and they went swept into the loving arms of the public education system. Their handiwork was everywhere these days; the downtown bus terminal vandalized with graffiti and broken windows, shattered street lamps and mangled mailboxes. Luckily, the blinking red dash light of the alarm system was sufficient to deter would-be scoundrels.

"Honey, look who I found," Michelle said. Her face scrubbed and cheerful in a runner-up at the beauty pageant kind of way; the chain gleamed between her breasts. She stood arm-in-arm with a matronly woman Don vaguely recognized. What was her name? He racked his brain while Michelle smiled expectantly and her friend waited with the blandly uncomfortable expression of a confirmed stoic. "You remember Celeste, don't you, dear? We worked in Alaska on the Tlingit cultural study in '86. Her husband's Rudy Hannah. Rudy Hannah? Lead occupational therapist for North Thurston Public Schools."

"Why, of course," Don said, not remembering anything of the sort, although it sounded right. Another example of the white gaps in his mind. Now that he was old enough to be entombed in a pyramid, everyone wrote his lapses off as incipient dementia—during middle-age his distaff students thought his stammering and stuttering to retrieve an elementary fact or quote, or his constant neglect of personal grooming, or his tendency to misplace his glasses and notes, were endearing qualities. In his prime as a spelunking, devil-may-care geologist, that stuff had made his friends and colleagues very nervous. It used to make Don nervous as well, but he'd learned to adjust. No other choice besides madness.

As for this vaguely familiar Celeste person, he gave himself a pass. His wife was a popular lady; from Washington to Beijing, her associates were legion. "Hullo, um, Celeste. A pleasure." He rose and pecked the woman's hand, surreptitiously checking the window in the process. Mr. Bowtie and his big-haired wife were slamming the doors of the Studebaker. When he looked up, Michelle pretended not to be annoyed, and Celeste gave her a patently fake smile, a perfunctory gesture of civility. *We both know your husband's an ass.* She might as well have rolled her eyes. Don had that effect on women. Invariably, and despite his best efforts at urbanity and charm, they sniffed out his essential oafishness, or so he'd come to believe. There were worse curses. Michelle put up with his occasional bouts of idiocy and that paid for all.

"I asked Celeste to join us. Look, Celeste, there's an extra chair at that table." Before Don could open his mouth to express an opinion one way or another, they were all cozy and ordering another bottle of wine. Don listened to them chatter and considered asking where Rudy might be, and decided against it. One never knew when one might be setting foot in a bear trap. He smiled aimlessly when the cone of conversation turned his direction; otherwise his mind wandered.

He eventually stood and walked to the landing, ostensibly to stretch his aching back. He flagged the next waiter, a tall kid named Roy Lee, according to his tag. Don requested he compliment the chef, and also, management might wish to know some local kids were scoping the parking lot.

The waiter nodded. "Yes, thank you, sir; I'll relay your concerns to my supervisor." He lowered his voice in a gesture of sincerest confidentiality and said, "One of the girls chased them out of the ladies room earlier. I guess they were vandalizing the stalls. We don't get this sort of thing too often. Middle school pranksters, I'd wager."

"Heavens! You alerted the authorities, I presume..."

"We don't like to disturb our guests. Besides, Marie never really got a close enough look to identify them." Roy seemed embarrassed. "I think they scared her. She won't talk about it."

"Really?" Don said. "That's despicable. Poor girl."

"Yeah, she's rattled. I hope you don't mind me saying I'd like to thrash those little punks if they threatened her." He cracked his knuckles.

"I understand," Don said. "Thank you again."

Roy shook it off and his mask of obsequiousness snapped in place. "By all means, sir."

2.

On the way home, he said to Michelle, "What did Celeste say about Istanbul?" They'd exited the well-lit city streets and were zipping along stretches of pasture broken by hills and copses of old-growth trees. He kept his eyes glued to the road, alert for deer. Clouds crept in during supper and it was black as a mine shaft. The radio was down so low it might as well have been off. She didn't care for music anymore unless it was tribal or certain strains of Bronze Age Korean court music.

"Oh? She asked if I'd packed for the trip yet. She procrastinates—like you."

"I don't procrastinate. She's going too, eh?"

"Every year, dear." Her face was slack from too much wine, and slightly green in the eerie dashboard glow. She slurred ever so faintly when she said, "Me an' Barbara, an' Lynne—"

"Lynne Victory? Oh, man alive. She's a looker."

"Shaddup. Barbara an' Lynne, and Justine French. An' Celeste. Girls Club."

"I'm sure it's a hoot." Don took a sharp corner. Something rolled over in the trunk. A solid, *ka-thump*. "Probably just an excuse to get soused and watch dirty movies—if your friends are anything like mine." He had scant idea what format these summits followed. They occurred each year a different city in a different country—last year Glasgow; the year before that Manitoba; and before that Peking; although it was frequently held in relatively unknown regions of satellite states that came and went, formed and dissipated in the shadows of their mother lands—the Soviet Union, Africa, and Yugoslavia. *Anywhere there's a party*, Michelle had quipped.

"It's an occasion to discuss important scientific theory an' bond socially an' professionally. An' for your information, we drink wine coolers an' watch art films." She chuckled and tilted her head back, allowing gravity to slide her around in the bucket seat like she was on a kiddy version of a tilt-a-whirl.

"Hey, one of the waiters told me the ladies restroom was vandalized. Was it pretty bad?"

"Huh-uh."

"Oh," Don said. "Roy mentioned some kids fooling around in there."

"Who's Roy?" She slurred more as her head lolled.

"The waiter I talked to. He said they vandalized the stalls."

"Wha—oh, that. It wasn't much. Just some graffiti. Celeste was kinda scandalized, but you gotta laugh at these things. *Tagging* is what it's called. We got gangs here too, y'know."

"As long as the buggers don't tag my car."

She turned to regard him. "Oh, they were messing with the car?" Her eyes were owlish.

"Eh. Everything's in order." He laughed and patted her hand and she nodded and closed her eyes.

The Firebird hugged another corner on a steep grade. As Don downshifted, something in the trunk *ka-thumped* again. "Okay," he muttered and pulled over where the shoulder widened in a saddle of foothills. Off the passenger side, a steep slope climbed rapidly. Farther up, near the snowline, lay a radio beacon, a ranger station and an observatory owned by a co-op of three universities and a board of wealthy private citizens. He and Michelle had driven there once; the view from the observatory encompassed the valley. He cranked the emergency brake, hit the flashers and leaned over Michelle to retrieve a flashlight from the glove compartment.

"Huh, whazzat?" she said, plucking at his sleeve.

"Don't worry, sweetie. I have to check something. Just be a minute."

"Huh-um. Don't get hit," she said drowsily.

"Righto." He took a breath, steeling his nerves, and climbed out. There weren't any other cars on the road. The air pressed chilly and damp and the darkness seemed vast around the feeble bubble of the Firebird's headlights, the flashlight in Don's hand. Treetops soughed in the grip of a high, rushing breeze that funneled through hidden creek beds and hollows. Branches crashed at some distance as the wind shook them.

Storm coming. Don opened the trunk and shined the weak flashlight beam over the tire, the tire iron, a box of flares and a bandolier of wrenches and sockets. The culprit was the jack; it had come free of its mooring and jounced around. He sighed and secured it, casting brief glances over his shoulder to ensure another vehicle wasn't slaloming around the corner—Saturday night and drunks cruised the highways and byways.

His giant shadow spread on the white gravel and the asphalt. He gasped then at the face in the brush that overhung the ditch at the perimeter of his light. The face was flat and misshapen as something from a dream, with a cruel black mouth and black eyes, a shark's eyes, but horribly askew. Don shined his beam directly at the spot and an eddy of cool, damp breeze caught dead leaves and swirled them to pieces. It swept bare the crosscut of a large chunk of slate. Alkaline drainage dribbled across its face and congealed in inkblots.

My lord, getting jumpy in our old age, aren't we? I shouldn't have let those hooligans spook me so easily. He preferred to blame this latest startle on the rational after-effects of worry for his beloved car, the knowledge his best years were long gone and he and Michelle were vulnerable even to rowdy kids acting with malice aforethought.

However, the snapping branches, the moaning wind, the absolute impenetrability of the darkness oppressed and intimidated him. Incipient nyctophobia; he'd self-diagnosed by plugging the symptoms into Web MD. Unlike his darling wife, he wasn't cut out for wilderness expeditions anymore; not after dark. Even the prospect of pitching an overnight tent at one of the nearby parks unnerved him. In the latter stages of his career he performed his vocation from the safety of an office, a lab, or the infrequent daytrip. His youthful postings to remote research camps gradually became a source of major anxiety; occasions to be endured as a necessary evil. He enjoyed the country as far as that went, just so long as when night fell he could flip the switch and have lights go on.

Don raised his eyes to the seam between the hinges of the trunk and the rear window. This revealed a sliver of the interior of the car, faintly illuminated by the radio dial. Michelle had twisted in her seat and swung her head toward his activities. She was silhouetted and thus utterly inscrutable. The wind pushed the trees around again; handfuls of twigs pinged the canvas; a dust devil skated circles in the road. Glad to shut the trunk, he hurriedly retreated into the shelter of the car. "All fixed," he said as he buckled in. Michelle didn't reply. She slumped, fast asleep; a trace of drool glistened at the corner of her mouth. Don dabbed it with his sleeve, mildly perplexed at how he'd so clearly, yet mistakenly, saw her gazing at him moments before. His brain was apparently deliquescing.

He rolled onto the road. From the trunk: *ka-thump*! "Hang it." Don stamped the accelerator.

3.

Come the dawn, the sky threatened and fumed, but no storm descended upon them. The radio girl said be ready, folks, it's only a matter of time.

The Millers' home was located in the bucolic and slightly depressed Waddell Valley, a shallow, crooked notch in the heavily forested Black Hills a few miles from the state capital. A potholed country blacktop wound past quiet farms where cattle and horses lazily grazed in the few fields and pastures not lost to creeping wilderness. Michelle inherited the Olympia residence in 1963 from her aunts Yvonne and Gretchen, who'd lost their husbands in the First World War and later moved to New Hampshire to spend their declining years with the eastern branch of the Mock family. The ladies bequeathed Michelle most of their possessions—nearly a century's worth—and to this day, the Millers had yet to replace the original antique furniture, paintings and knick-knacks, much less sort through the troves in the attic, the huge, labyrinthine cellar, or the barn loft.

The building was a yellow and white three-story farmhouse with two large additions (one being a half-tower of ivy-twined brick that rose a solid story above the roof peak) and a stone chimney running up the side. It sat on a hill at the end of a dirt lane and at night theirs were the only lighted windows in the area. Twin magnolias loomed in the backyard near the barn he'd repainted and converted into a garage and workshop. The trees were monsters, studded by thick, mossy knurls and scaled in tough bark that reminded him of ossified crocodile hide.

As a boy, Kurt drove Don batty by climbing into the uppermost branches and swinging like his idol Tarzan. He'd recently discovered Edgar Rice Burroughs and Robert E. Howard and for the next few months there was hell to pay. Kurt only quit his brachiating hijinks after Don vowed to cut the trees down and make a complete set of dining room furniture. Kurt had been, and still was, a monumental pain in the ass compared to his sweet sister. Michelle snorted and shook her head when she heard Don talk about Holly as if she were God's own angel. *Dream on, bucko; she's her mother's child*, Michelle would say with a cryptic arch to her brow before resuming her absorption of raw data in the form of moth-eaten journals, blood-stained logbooks and typewritten reports stacked knee-high to a giraffe in the study. The "keep out, if you know what's good for you" room.

This ancient farmhouse had been the Millers' summer home until nine months previous when Don finally agreed to sell the Spanish colonial in San Francisco, which they had lived in and done business from two-thirds of each year during the 1970s, ideally situated as it was at the plexus of Michelle's international travels. Don certainly preferred the hacienda in the city, a smaller, brighter, inarguably cheerier domicile, but ages ago his wife insisted they remove themselves to Washington State during the summers—the children required fresh air and an at least minimal exposure to nature.

Of course, around 1980 with the kids going to college and both Don and Michelle receiving excellent offers from Washington-based institutions to work and teach, they'd divided their years nearly in half between the Bay Area and humble Olympia, with friends and associates by the gross pulling them in twain. Thus, the Millers never did quite become settled in either locale—an experience akin to migrating constantly between two familiar hotels on never-ending business trips.

Now that quasi-retirement had segued into the real thing, it seemed prudent and sensible to relocate permanently. Living expenses were substantially lower and the country setting far more tranquil than in San Francisco. Finally, Michelle had expressed the ambition to conduct a genealogical survey of her ancestry, and the old farmhouse was literally stuffed with books and notes from generations as far back as the Huguenots' expeditious retreat from Europe, although Mock family origins predated that era by an inestimable margin.

Many a lazy afternoon found Don lounging in the porch swing, a glass of lemonade in hand, fanning himself with a good solid naturalism book while squirrels chattered in the trees and an occasional vehicle trundled past on the main road. The property, like most land in the Waddell Valley, originally belonged to a gentleman farmer, a Dutchman, who sold Yvonne Mock the parcel in 1902. God alone knew for certain when the house itself was built (however it was renovated twice), but rumor had it the foundation was laid in 1853, which placed it as one of the oldest surviving residences in Olympia. One could only imagine what its walls had witnessed. The surrounding field spread in an irregular rectangle for several hundred yards, hemmed by a rusty wire fence. Grass and wildflowers and sapling birches overran the environs. Forested hills reared at the boundaries. Don's black Labrador Thule went crazy chasing rabbits from one end of the property to the other.

The closest neighbors were the Hertzes just up the road—a blond, ruddy family. Blonde wife; three or four blond, chubby boys; two blonde girls, the elder of the pair in junior high; all of them a matched set like a nest of goslings. Only papa Hertz with his rugged, sunburned face and unflinching Icelandic eyes seemed more than a Disney caricature made flesh. Dietrich was a dirt-poor dairyman, who'd sold off the majority of the acreage his dad, a second-generation farmer, had bequeathed as his legacy. Dietrich was down to a half dozen cows and the plot his house and barn occupied. A laconic fellow, he curtly tipped his hat to Don in passing and slid his gaze around Michelle, content to pretend she didn't exist. She laughed and explained that was typical of salt of the earth, God-fearing men, certainly nothing for Don to bristle at. Besides, Dietrich appeared capable of ripping off her husband's arms—*My goodness, the size of his hands.* Only auto mechanics, stonemasons and dairymen had hands like those.

Misty Villa lay a quarter mile in the opposite direction. The greenbelt subdivision had gone in around 1969 and was populated by middle-class folks who lived in newish houses with vinyl siding and faux brick and rock exteriors. Don and Michelle were once acquainted with an architect who designed a modernized cabin at the end of one of the subdivision's ubiquitous circle drives. They attended a few barbeques and cocktail parties, exchanged Christmas cards. The architect moved to Brazil in the early 1990s after being drafted by some corporation that built skyscraper offices and luxury hotels in the poorer regions of the world so the executives and business partners would have a clean, air-conditioned habitat while they organized and consolidated industry in developing countries. Dan something. The Millers hadn't occasion to meet anyone else in the neighborhood; their friends lived chiefly inside the city limits of Olympia, Tacoma and Seattle, and to the four corners of the continent. They'd chosen the Waddell Valley precisely for that reason—close enough to whisk into town at a moment's notice, but remote enough casual visits were unusual.

This morning, Thule lay snorting and whimpering on the kitchen tiles near the back door that let out to a covered walkway and Michelle's greenhouse. Last night's storm had arrived in furious glory. Rain poured down the windows. Wind slammed the roof and rapped the doors, whistled in the gutters and the chimney. The buzzing transistor on the counter reported heavy weather was here to stay—three or four days minimum. High wind and flood warnings had already been issued for Pierce and Thurston counties.

Don sat at the kitchen table in the predawn gloom. He wore his bathrobe and a pair of fluffy slippers and sipped a mug of instant coffee. The porch light shuddered with each savage buffet and momentarily dimmed as if plunged underwater. He listened for the sound of Michelle stirring from bed to make breakfast in advance of the kids' arrival, but she was still sleeping it off, for which he was thankful. She absolutely never slept in, unless she'd been drinking or taking heavy duty cold medication, and even then she usually dragged herself out of bed to carry on. *Carry on, carry on*, was Michelle's motto and Don could only surmise this comprised a Mock family tradition.

Don knew precious little about the Mocks beyond hints and rumors. As with Don, Michelle's parents died young: Theresa Mock (none of the women took married names) from tuberculosis contracted during an adventure in China at the age of forty-eight, and Landon Caine by a stroke eleven years and one remarriage later. Don shook hands with the parents during his own wedding, the sole occasion he'd ever seen or spoken to them. Michelle had made it clear early on that her familial relations were strained. She wasn't kidding.

On Holly's sixth birthday, Michelle flew her (but not little Kurt) to a family conclave in New England, but as for Don, besides his brief encounter with the parents, he'd only met a younger sister, and before that, an aunt Babette; a mummified lady who dressed in basic black. Her eyebrows were permanently inked in lieu of the real thing. Babette Mock grudgingly consented to meet Don after she discovered he moonlighted as an antiquarian and a journeyman bibliophile with expertise in geomorphic history. In her declining years (that dragged on for two and a half decades) Babette had frequently toured the West Coast for rare manuscripts, which sounded far more interesting than the reality.

Unfortunately, Don had been unable to procure certain texts pertaining to geophysical anomalies and that was the last they'd spoken.

There were several other aunts, a bushel of female cousins and Michelle's stepmother Cornelia, but no uncles. Michelle's twin brother Michael had served as an Army sniper. The military loved his hands; stone steady were those hands, those steely fingers that once tapped the ivories of classical piano. No Millers possessed musical talent to speak of, although most suffered an acute appreciation of the sublime art, and thus Michael fascinated Don.

The subject of Michael inevitably provoked a melancholy sigh from Michelle. *Mom wanted to ship him to Julliard. Damn it, Mikey, you decided to be a lifer in the military instead. Selfish bastard.* He and eight other soldiers were lost in a helicopter crash during a mission near the South Korean border in the fall of 1952. An eerie analogue to how Don had lost his own father a few years earlier. *Mock men die young*, his wife said with grim cheer whenever he'd pressed the issue. Don had last spoken to her brother over the phone when he called for Christmas. They'd vowed to buy one another drinks when Michael's tour in Korea ended.

Sometimes Don pondered on the sort of man Michael would've become if the rocket had spun eight feet to the port side. He imagined the clean-cut boy from the pictures in Michelle's wallet coming home, eyes a bit wiser, face worn from the jungles and the worry, dressed now in the formal wear of a Beethoven or a Bach in some dim concert hall, bent over the keyboard of a grand piano while the gentry in the gallery leaned forward in their massed and breathless silence, hanging upon the movements of those fingers poised to work their prestidigitation upon the sacred keys, those same fingers that cradled a walnut stock and squeezed the trigger on God knew how many targets, had instead curled tight and black in the heart of a conflagration and were reduced to dust.

Don was uncertain if this was the reason Michelle had had a strained relationship with her relatives, most of whom, obviously, were passed on to the Great Beyond. In any event, they'd almost never visited, seldom called, just sent the occasional handwritten letter done in script so cramped and esoteric, it proved unfathomable to Don's weak eyes.

Michelle, as per her custom from the first date onward, kept mum, except to say her relatives were *odd ducks*, and better off in Maine and New Hampshire. According to Michelle's admittedly vague accounts of her genealogical origins, the sprawling family tree sank its roots in the Balkans, and to a minor degree, Eastern Germany and obscure territories along the Pyrenees. Researching that tree had become yet another of her all-consuming passions and appeared as if it might keep her occupied until the Reaper came to collect his due.

Numerous photographs of the Mock clan decorated the parlor; more were scattered about the house on the landing and in various alcoves—the formal kind where the men stood rigid as wooden posts in top hats and coattails, and the women sat primly in dresses with bustles that made their rumps resemble cabooses; everybody posed and shot against featureless backdrops. An austere and decidedly unfriendly lot, judging by their sallow, joyless faces.

Don's own family were Midwesterners, lapsed Catholics, mainly. His younger brothers were long-retired attorneys. His elder brothers, now dead and gone for several years, or so the rumors had it, were odd ducks who'd gone the route of iconoclasts and professional dilettantes; however most of the family worked in law offices, museums and private schools. Lots and lots of curators and English professors in the Miller line. He joked that family reunions resembled conventions of J.R.R. Tolkien fanatics; everybody wore tweed, smoked a pipe and smelled of chalk dust.

The most interesting of the lot were benevolently eccentric and this disappointed him. All of the truly remarkable persons, persons of zest and vibrancy had died, like his parents and war-hero grandfather, or vanished, like his elder siblings, consumed by time and life unceasing. Maybe that was one's reward for coloring outside the lines. His attraction to eccentricity, while being somewhat of a fuddy-duddy in his own affairs, was likely the secret to sixty years of marriage with Michelle. She was precisely loony enough to keep his heart racing.

Cold hands fell upon his shoulders and he spilled coffee onto his robe. Michelle kissed the top of his head where the remnants of his hair held the line. "Whoops. Better trim that hair in your ears, yeah?" She tweaked his lobe to accentuate her point. "I'm going to get dressed. Put more coffee on, will you? And peel some potatoes. There's a dear."

"Ack!" Don wiped at the widening stain. "For the love of Pete, don't sneak around like that! This isn't the jungle, y'know!" He called after her shadow as it floated up the staircase.

4.

Saturday was also Don's day to walk the dog around the tree farm on the other side of Misty Villa. He dressed in sweats and a windbreaker and pocketed a can of pepper spray as a precautionary measure. The packs of roaming neighborhood dogs were unpredictable and vicious, thus a circuit of Schneider's Tree Farm was as potentially fraught with peril as stuffing ham sandwiches into his backpack for a hike across the Serengeti. Don knew this because he had seen them cruising the byways and the unfenced yards—a border collie, a poodle, a beagle (although Don suspected the beagle was just along for the ride) and two or three mixed breeds—and, more succinctly, because the pack had once chased him from the mailbox to his front porch.

The quarter-mile walk went slowly, Thule hell-bent on sniffing every bush in the ditch and then hiking his leg for a squirt.

The subdivision was arrayed around the streets of Red Lane & Darkmans like a body on a crucifix. The biggest and boldest house in the neighborhood belonged to the Rourkes, half a block in. Barry Rourke was an executive for AstraCorp (and thus one of Don's current bosses), his wife a semi-retired cellist and fulltime gadfly who played with the Seattle Symphony Orchestra, and their home was very old and ponderously stylish; a Victorian number raised months after the First World War. Then Red Lane and Darkmans were the *only* lanes, and made of good, honest dirt. The woods had lain even deeper and darker in those days when wolves roamed the forest, and black bears and cougars from the hills, and according to the coots at the Mud Shack, the occasional escapee from Wharton House, the old asylum that got shut down in the '90s. The wolves were long gone, the feral inmates shipped off to Western or wherever, but coyotes still laired in the woods; deer, and of course the packs of dogs that swelled with the inevitable wave of abandoned pooches each frantic tourist season and encouraged people of wisdom and prudence to arm themselves for the daily stroll.

The Rourke manse and environs had history, all right, were fairly steeped in it like an old blackened tea bag left to wither at the edge of a saucer. Don had several occasions to venture inside the house during the late '70s and early '80s—Kirsten Rourke threw frequent and lavish parties and because Don was a minion of AstraCorp at the time, Michelle was invited into the Friday afternoon pinochle club for awhile, and of course, Rourke invited Don over periodically to indulge his impulse for slumming with the help. The place was imposing and decorated in a museum-quality fashion that discouraged touching a blessed thing on pain of arousing the housekeeper's ire.

One could scarcely move in a straight line without tripping across metastasized lumps and growths in every cavernous room, the benighted accretion of ineffable superiority through breeding and fortune: Circassia walnut Victrolas dredged from the wreckage of East India Company outposts; Flemish oak paneled armoires brought West in the face of marauding red devils; wicker baskets threaded by the cracked fingers of villagers long subsumed unto the dull gray chalk that collects as a mantle over everything everywhere; oil paintings from estate sales and private auctions; Ming vases and Tiffany lamps; Kirsten's million-dollar shoe collection, an affectation she'd contrived after following the exploits of Imelda Marcos. Rourke collected Western European medieval art—swords, shields, ragged banners and a library of withered books behind glass. Rourke knew a bit of Latin and recited Olde English poetry when he got drunk, or, as Don suspected, when he pretended to be drunk.

Rourke had been an affiliate member of the John Birch Society; an amiable elitist, a masterful badminton player with a savage left-hand serve. He subscribed to *Foreign Policy* and a clutch of peer-reviewed journals pertaining to historical research societies of which Don had scant knowledge.

Back in the day when everyone was young and busy, sometimes Don had seen one of the Rourkes in passing when he walked down his own long bumpkin drive to fetch the mail or the paper from the roadside mailbox, the old star route, as the postal workers dubbed them—Kirsten cruising in her Jaguar, squiring the two-point-five children (twins Page & Brett, and Bronson Ford the adopted boy from a village in Angola) to or from recital (soccer, ballet, gymnastics, chess club, etc); or Rourke, in his mega-sized diesel pickup, which sounded like a piece of industrial equipment idling in the yard on blustery mornings—and he would wave or nod in greeting. If the elder Rourkes weren't too preoccupied they'd usually return the favor. The platinum blonde girl had regally ignored him (her brother, also a blond, died tragically; Don never heard the particulars), although Bronson Ford sometimes turned in his seat to stare through the rear window, impassive as a totem mask.

The dry breeze quickened as Don trudged by the Rourkes' iron gate. When had he last spoken to them? Ages—Kirsten was shriveled as a prune. Don chuckled wryly. *Ah, but haven't we all?* Too late to speak with Rourke now, anyway. The smug bastard had vanished in the Olympic Mountains years ago. Very mysterious circumstances. There were rumors of banking scandals, embezzlement, a Cayman Islands account. A number of folks agreed Rourke probably parachuted out of his loveless marriage and collapsing business empire and ran out the clock on a tropical beach.

Don scrutinized the lengthy gravel drive, the looming outlines of the house and the dazzles of glass and metal through the hissing trees. Shadows rose and fell like inhalations and a man, probably a gardener, in a shiny red shirt flickered briefly across a swath of razor-precise green lawn and vanished when the shifting branches clasped leaf to leaf.

Don and Thule continued down to the cul-de-sac and its trio of pedestrian homes. A footpath curved into the shallow copse of alders and termite-bored stumps of fallen pines and a man had to watch his step for the all the mounds of dog- and horseshit. About two hundred yards farther on, the trail intersected a dirt road, a combination of rutted gravel and mucky sand, that divided and divided again like the spokes of a wheel and cut numerous paths through the many acres of tightly packed dwarf evergreens; none crowned more than eight feet tall; a veritable forest of Christmas trees.

The farm had been around since forever; it was a formidable enterprise bordering a stretch of the distant Yelm Highway and sprawled inward from there in the shape of an irregular fan some four miles wide at the junction of its service road and the path from the Misty Villa Home Owners Association. The road was popular with joggers, dog owners and rowdy teens on dirt bikes. Dirt bikes, four-wheelers and the like were expressly forbidden, not that such edicts ever discouraged kids hopped up on testosterone, and drunken rednecks who'd achieved the adult instar stage, from roaring around the track after dark, tearing up the place and leaving beer cans everywhere.

A wooden sawhorse with a peeling gray placard was jammed upside down into the teeth of a row of trees near the entrance. The placard shouted in huge, black letters,

KEEP OUT! THIS AREA
HAS BEEN SPRAYED WITH PESTICIDE!
DANGEROUS TO PEOPLE & PETS NEXT 14 DAYS!
YOU ARE ON PRIVATE PROPERTY!

The sign migrated about the perimeter of the farm and had done so perpetually for several years.

A yellow lab trotted past and lifted its leg to hose a baby Douglas fir before moving on, snout to the earth. Thule strained at his leash and whimpered excitedly. The lab's owners, a couple of yuppie kids in matching polo wear, ambled along a few dozen yards behind Don, placidly oblivious to the cryptic sign or their wayward pet. Far off, somewhere beyond pickets of greenery, a saw whined. Everything smelled humid and bittersweet and gnats danced in his hair.

The workers who tended the farm were around this morning. A crew of seven or eight arrived every few weeks to clean the undergrowth, trim the branches and remove any diseased specimens. The laborers were uniformly male, organized by a patriarchal countryman with a barrel chest and a frightful scowl. They wore coveralls and wide-brimmed hats and swung machetes with the casual efficacy of butchers.

Don assumed them to be Hispanic because he'd heard them conversing in Spanish, albeit overlaid with another language he couldn't identify. He'd never spoken to the workers, just nodded in passing; a friendly smile or wave, which was always reciprocated. His Spanish was bad to nonexistent. That last detail aggravated and mystified him in equal measure since the day last winter he'd rummaged through some long-lost files and discovered journal notes he'd written entirely in *Español* during his youth. These were field notes he'd taken while surveying a cave system in the Aleutians during the Nixon administration. Long time gone, but god... How did a man forget a language? How did a man forget he'd even once *known* that language? Wracking his porous brains, he couldn't dredge much detail regarding the expedition either. Darkness, a cavern, him suspended by a line above an abyss, his headlamp beam not touching anything solid, the drip and gurgle of water everywhere...He blinked and shook himself as Thule did after coming in from the rain, and kept moving. Moving forward from a past that became more the realm of a shadow life every day.

Today, he spotted a couple of the younger men near the road, and instantly knew something was different, wrong somehow. Thick and broad, their coveralls caked in dust and sap. Flat, sallow faces already alight with sweat, they muttered and hacked at dead limbs, dropped them into wheelbarrows like tangled stacks of deformed arms and legs. Yes, there was a difference in their movements, a queer, vaguely inimical aura radiating from them and their half smiles that resembled sneers. He glanced down and noted that Thule's fur was ridged and ruffled as when he was pointing toward a threat such as a hostile dog or an unknown critter in the bushes.

The pair gradually became aware of Don's presence and ceased their labors to study him and converse furtively. One called out in a shrill, fluting voice to his brethren hidden among the deep rows and the eerie cry was immediately returned from several, widely scattered locations.

His mouth, my God! Don gasped and averted his gaze from the man uttering the strange bird cry; the fellow's mouth shuttered like an iris, a toothless hole as big as a fist. The other man licked his lips and slid his machete against his pants leg in the manner of a barber stropping a razor.

Don nodded with a sickly smile, pretending obliviousness of this most palpable unwelcome and ambled onward as fast as dignity permitted. Their deadly obsidian eyes swiveled to track him until a curve of the road intervened. He spasmodically gripped the pepper spray in his pocket. His teeth chattered.

Too many joints in their necks. He hadn't noticed that during his previous encounters with the crew. Both of these men had possessed the same deformity, and a crazy, paranoid thought occurred to him—the pair were actors, doubles in a film who stand in for the name actor, always filmed from behind, or in soft focus. Put a uniform on someone and that person could pass as your best friend from a distance. Crazy and paranoid in spades. Who the hell would bother to impersonate migrant laborers on a country tree farm? Why did he have a sneaking suspicion he'd seen them before under different circumstances?

They watch. They watch you, Donald. They love you.

The impingement of this unbidden whisper from his subconscious galvanized him even as he crammed it back down into the cellar with his childhood fears of spiders and the boogeyman. He trotted all the way back to the house, racing the storm, the devil.

5.

A pot of coffee later, Thule growled and headlights turned into the driveway. Don squinted at his watch, *Here they are.*

Kurt and Kaiwin arrived in a rental car. Kurt owned four cars, including a Lexus and a classic, fully loaded Mini Cooper that formerly belonged to a B List action star; but as he once remarked, it'd be a cold day in hell before he'd risk one of his babies on the back roads around Olympia. The sky had brightened by inches, outlining the soft shapes of the barn, the trembling magnolias. They emerged from the car and splashed through a mud puddle and burst into the kitchen.

Kaiwin was dark-eyed and slender, delicate, yet wiry, like a dancer. She dressed simply in a peach summer dress and sensible shoes and appeared much younger than her likely age. Her purse was transparent plastic, the current affectation of trendy metropolitan girls and girlish women everywhere. She stood nervously, wiping raindrops from her eyes. Her eyelids were painted a delicate butterfly-wing blue.

Thule sniffed her warily, and then wriggled and frantically kissed her hands. Don, who beyond a short conversation at the wedding reception, hadn't chatted with the lady, accepted her then and there sans reservation. Kurt's judgment was suspect. On the other paw, anyone good enough for Thule was A-okay in Don's book.

"Pop. We made it. A real shit storm out there." Well into middle-age, Kurt was nonetheless tall and bronze and built like a power lifter; he'd played ball in high school and college, a first team linebacker at the University of Washington. He might've been on his way to a business meeting, such was the elegance of his hand-tailored suit, the slick blue-black sheen of his three-hundred-dollar haircut; the kind of haircut the governor himself might've favored. "Well, Winnie, this is the old homestead." He put his massive arm around her fragile shoulders. She nodded and smiled a bright, superficial smile.

Don had to wonder exactly how fluent her English might be. He gave her a kindly smile and told them to hurry up and grab a seat. He took their coats and poured more coffee, although it developed Winnie wasn't much for coffee, tea being her preference, and in that case, Kurt no longer drank coffee either. *More for me*, Don said, and scrounged in the cupboards until he unearthed a rusty tin of herbal tea that likely gathered cobwebs before the kids ever left for college.

Once Kurt and Winnie were sipping their tea, Don washed potatoes and started peeling them, a task he'd become rather adept at over the years, if only as a matter of self-preservation. Michelle was many things, but a cook wasn't one. He made small talk, noting Kurt's expression of mild boredom; the lad drummed his fingers when his attention began to wander. Don had always harbored the suspicion his son suffered from attention deficit disorder. Michelle disagreed, noting that Don wasn't a sparkling conversationalist and an appreciation of rural life certainly hadn't trickled down through the paternal genes. Nonetheless, he'd always wanted to try Ritalin on the boy in the interest of science. He inquired about his son's job as the vice president of operations at an aerospace contractor in Seattle.

Kurt's was a position that required extensive travel—the company outsourced its manufacturing of electronic components to Taiwan and China, which was incidentally how he met Winnie. The youngest daughter of a minor Hong Kong executive, they'd sat adjacent at a dinner party. The marriage date was arranged a mere six months later.

Kurt's job also necessitated absolute secrecy and draconian security procedures. He showed Don the back of his left hand. "The company implanted a chip under the skin, right there—microscopic, like a grain of rice. It has my security clearance, medical information. They track it via satellite so I can move freely throughout our office and from building to building. There are a dozen checkpoints, sealed doors, security elevators, you name it. It'd be a flaming nightmare without this puppy."

"Are they tracking you now?" Don said. He looked at the ceiling.

"Uh, no, Dad. That'd be an infringement of my privacy. I'm on vacation for Pete's sake." It was always difficult to tell whether Kurt's exasperation was a reaction to Don's dry needling or impatience with his father's presumed ignorance. Kurt was far from stupid, but even farther from imaginative.

"Yeah, but how do they know where you are, who're you're talking to? Jeez, this could be a nest of commie spies."

"I signed a nondisclosure form. Standard procedure. The penalty for violating that is about twenty-five years and forfeiture of my left nut, minimum. Besides, we provide ops a detailed itinerary of where we're going and what the purpose of the visit might be. Bloody hell, this tea tastes like rotten leaves. Winnie, you don't have to drink that." He gently extricated the teacup from Winnie's hand and slid it across the table. Her eyes glinted dangerously, a glint that subsided almost in the exact same instant. Kurt remained oblivious. "We got any of that coffee left?"

6.

Holly and her girlfriend Linda arrived around nine o'clock during a respite in the weather. Holly, independent and rugged as ever, piloted the ancient Land Rover her mother once shipped to South Africa for a six-month odyssey across the Dark Continent; she'd bequeathed it to Holly as a college graduation gift. Don guessed the engine had clocked enough miles to reach the moon and slingshot back to Earth.

Holly leaped from the truck and seized her father in a bone-crushing embrace. Short and stout, her hair a shaggy blonde shot with gray; her tanned face bore the pits and pocks of an adventuresome existence. Like her mother, she possessed a quality of essential agelessness, a quirky, youthful passion toward life that did not engender frailty, be it physical or otherwise. Her eyes flashed with bleak humor, no doubt born of twenty-odd years as an elementary school teacher.

"Hullo, brother," she said when Kurt ambled onto the porch, smoothing his fantastical hair. She socked him in the arm, hard, and Don winced in sympathy; he'd roughhoused with her when she was a teenager and even then her scarred fists were clubs.

Kurt grunted and rapped his knuckles on her forehead and Don stepped between them to defuse the semi-playful aggression before matters escalated and his children were rolling in the mud pulling each other's hair and biting; his role of referee had become reflexive over the years of broken noses and bruised egos. Nothing changed; they would hit the big five-oh come December, and yet they reverted to adolescence at the drop of a hat. The friend, Linda, joined them on the porch. An attractive, albeit hard-bitten, woman with a buzz cut. She wore a heavy flannel shirt, khakis and logger boots. She shyly said hello to everyone and her voice was quite soft; she meticulously enunciated in a fashion that suggested European nativity.

Rain closed in again mere moments after the luggage was unpacked and piled inside the front entryway. The house had many smallish windows, but the structure was built to 19th century standards. The rooms, staircases and connecting halls were low-ceilinged, narrow and dark, especially in dismal weather. A house of nooks and crannies, funny doors and storage cabinets in unusual and unexpected locations. Throughout childhood, Holly expressed an abiding fear of certain rooms. She complained of scratching and whispering emanating from her closet and the staircase that led to the attic. Some nights she refused to sleep in her own bed.

The cellar was right out because she swore that once when she ventured down to fetch a jar of preserves, the venerable tomcat Boris (whom they'd inherited along with the house) had chuckled from his perch high up on a wine rack, and crooned, *I'm a good kitty*. Boris wandered off one day not long after that alleged incident and they didn't get around to bringing home another cat, despite the perennial mice problem.

Kurt had mocked Holly by saying maybe what she heard was one of Mom's little people. Don immediately shushed such talk with uncustomary bluntness. Mention of The Little People, so called, was strictly verboten around the Miller household. He knew from bitter experience precisely how sensitive his wife was regarding even the most innocent slight of her decades-long investigation into the existence of uncontacted tribes and hidden cultures. As a man well-acquainted with similar foibles, such as cryptozoology, he tended toward sympathy.

Yet Michelle had pursued the topic with evangelical zeal, albeit in quasi secrecy, as only cryptobiologists such as her once great friend and mentor Louis Plimpton and the more radical members of the scientific community like renowned kooks Toshi Ryoko and Howard Campbell could be trusted to keep a straight face while discussing such esoteric theories.

Thank the heavens she'd later given up before it wrecked their marriage and drove herself or Don, or both of them, to lunacy.

These days, Don didn't often think of Michelle's quest, that apocalyptic obsession she'd cultivated during her early years at university of proving the existence of a particular extant family of men, likely tribal, who dwelt on the hinterlands of civilization—the Antarctic, deep in the jungles of New Guinea, or the amid the wastes of the Gobi, or, if her painstakingly collated sources were to be trusted, in *all* of these places. The theory was absurd, of course, and would've gotten her laughed out of mainstream academia had she not also demonstrated reliable brilliance in traditional research, or if she hadn't written two nonfiction books that sold sensationally and garnered overwhelming critical praise. The powers that be chuckled at her Hollow Earth theories and wrote them off as regrettable, but perhaps essential kookiness in an otherwise genius scientist.

To the twins, the mountains of data, dry as chalk and coupled with thousands upon thousands of hours logged on planes, boats, and in hard library seats, had always boiled down to "Mom's looking for little people!" Cute when the kids were kids and Michelle's optimism and humor were peaking, less so with each passing year, until finally at a family dinner she'd grimly announced sans preamble that her research (thank the gods a sideline to her real work) had all been a wild goose chase and was officially terminated. Henceforth, her spare time would be devoted to a genealogical survey of her extensive family tree. Afterward she drank half a bottle of white wine and fell asleep on the living room floor. The subject was seldom mentioned in the wake of that extraordinary evening and within weeks everyone stopped talking about it altogether.

As for Holly's contention she'd heard the cat talking, Michelle scoffed; as with many old houses, the pipes knocked and moaned, shrews nested in eaves, and above all, kids were endowed with hyperactive imaginations.

Don seldom reproached his daughter, however. He too dreaded the attic and the cellar. There were other little incidents, a string of them, in fact, that he wrote off as a product of his phobias, or, when expedient, promptly forgot. He'd become very good at putting these unpleasant details from his mind until the next time Michelle went away and it was late and the power flickered and something bumped in the night—a tipped chair, a cracked vase, the tinkle of glasses moving in the kitchen cabinets, things of that order. Items went missing; food, forks and knives. The knives bothered him; it was always the big ones, the butcher knives and the cleavers. Sometimes Thule whined like a puppy and glared at the walls and the ceilings. *Then* Don's fears came home to roost.

He bustled room to room clicking on lamps. The cheery glow comforted him, although the light could only do so much as the cubbies and corners lay in deepest shadow. His foremost lament regarding life at the old Mock residence was the fact he couldn't utterly banish the darkness.

Soon chaos descended. Luggage lay strewn from the front door to the landing below the attic which doubled as a guestroom. Kurt and Winnie agreed to accept residence therein, although he grumbled at the tight quarters, predicting he'd whack his skull on the beams. Holly told him to *shut it* and be a trooper. He responded with a colorful epithet. They preferred to converse while each was in a separate room, if not on a separate floor, which necessitated shouting, and set the dog to barking and bounding up and down the stairs. Michelle loudly admonished them to lower the racket because she was hung over. The phone rang off the hook. As it was never for Don anyway and Michelle refused to answer the bloody thing, he appointed Holly receptionist pro tem, and she in turn passed the buck to poor, shell-shocked Linda who walked around in a daze with a pencil stub in hand.

"Argyle is coming for dinner," Linda said. "He's bringing champagne."

"In this weather?" Don said as thunder rumbled. Argyle Arden was a phylogeographer who'd retired from Caltech, then again from Saint Martin's, and currently served the Redfield Museum as a consultant. The kids still referred to him as Uncle Argyle.

"He won't drown," Michelle said. "Besides, we can't leave him alone in that huge house of his; we're bound to lose power. Can you get that suitcase for Win, dear?" She'd drawn Winnie, Holly, and Linda away from Kurt on some pretext or other. They sat on the leather couch in the parlor with a box-worth of photo albums spread open on the chairs and the floor. The quartet seemed perfectly content to camp there indefinitely.

"Which one?" Don morosely eyed a full set of matching designer luggage.

"The heavy one." Michelle waved absently.

They all looked heavy to him. He decided this was his cue to slip away and take his arthritis medicine with a belt of Glenlivet he'd cunningly cached in the pantry behind a row of mason jars and cans of stewed vegetables. He didn't indulge much these days; just when stressed. He poured a triple, estimating this would suffice as an anesthetic until Argyle arrived to rescue him from the clutches of his wife and children.

Kurt stumped into the kitchen and caught him red-handed. "For the love of Christ and the Apostles, hand that over quick!" He barged into the pantry, snatched the bottle and reduced its contents by a quarter. "I hope you haven't become a closet lush, Dad," he said after wiping his mouth with his knuckles, then registered they were currently holed up in a pantry the length and width of a janitor's closet. "Literally."

"Well, gee, son. I don't guzzle whiskey like soda pop."

"Yeah, yeah. I need to mellow. My blood pressure's through the roof the last few weeks. We might lose a contract to Airbus and the machinists are threatening a walk-off. Another strike! Can you believe that garbage? They get a sweet new contract three years ago and look how they repay us. Extortionist bastards." Given Kurt's lofty position and the attendant responsibilities, hypertension seemed an obvious occupational hazard.

"Ah, well, *I* live with your mother." Don retrieved the bottle and had another dose. Before he knew it, the bottle had run dry and he was beginning to take the entire hullabaloo quite philosophically. He and Kurt eventually emerged, snickering at their own witticisms like a pair of prep school cadets, and tackled the daunting task of dragging a half dozen bags up the stairs, a chore that proved surprisingly hilarious, all the more so when Kurt admitted five of them were his.

After the second trip to the attic, Don slumped on the double bed, which Michelle had taken pains to beautify with new sheets and a counterchange quilt, and tried to catch his breath. He considered himself in decent shape for a flabby-assed geezer. He ran every other day and lifted a set of dumbbells Kurt had left in the garage. This, however, was a bit much. He put his head between his knees. Thunder crashed much closer than before. From this height, the crow's nest as it were, the storm was impressive. The roof seemed as if it might be torn apart at any moment. Gray, bloodless light came through a single window smudged with grime and fly droppings.

The room was crowded by racks of mothballed clothes, bookshelves crammed with moldy picture books and magazines such as *Life* and

Time—and an array of antique dolls. Aunt Yvonne had been a collector; some of the dolls went back to the Civil War; she'd even acquired a wooden Indian, the kind shopkeepers once set on the sidewalk. It waited in the shadows, dust-caked, its termite-riddled aspect rather ghoulish, hatchet-edged and emaciated; the portrait of a Cherokee chief cut down by starvation and smallpox, an angry soul condemned to haunt the attic.

Tucked in an alcove was an ancient Westinghouse projector alongside dozens of film canisters whose labels were mostly illegible due to yellowing and that awful Mock handwriting. Those few that proved comprehensible were pure argot: *Hierophant Exp. 10/38; Mt. Fuji Exp. 10/46; Crng (Beatrice J.) 10/54*; *Astrobio Smt. 5/76(keynote T. Ryoko & H. Campbell), Ur-trilobite organizational patterns (L. Plimpton) 8/78, Ekaltadeta spinal column, Duin Barrow 11/86, CoOL 9/89*, and so on. Stacked in the corners were dusty wooden crates and steamer trunks papered with stamps from exotic ports of call. A handful of these objects were newer, holdovers from Michelle's expeditions to Africa, Malaysia, Polynesia, and a dozen other regions.

Several oil paintings lay under canvas, propped against an easel, and largely unfinished; the labors of an unknown artist. The pieces were disquieting. Impressionist work; the subjects were deformed humanoids dwarfed by unwholesome man-beast figures and indistinct objects of unremittingly baroque dimensions. These latter struck him as tribal renderings of anthropomorphic gods and the cyclopean ziggurats wherein such beings would naturally dwell, the whole as filtered through the lens of someone possessed of a Western European sensibility. Possibly someone with a psychological disorder or a deviant fetish for the grotesque. He'd avoided mentioning the paintings to Michelle for fear she'd form a morbid attachment to them and insist on hanging the "masterpieces" in prominent locations.

Even worse was a poster-sized black and white photograph of a tall, gangling figure in half profile looming over a misshapen dwarf against a featureless background of white and gray. Both wore stiff suits and Homburgs; the freakishly proportioned thin man, whose hands and neck possessed all too many joints, wore rimless black glasses while the dwarf grinned at the camera through a devilish beard. The photo was likely shot during the Prohibition or Depression era going by the striations and patina of composition, although identification was difficult due to yellowing and a layer of dust. *R & friend* was scribbled in the corner. Don didn't care for either of the men and wondered who they were and what became of them.

He smiled wryly—if this was what Mock men looked like in their declining years, no wonder they maintained a low profile. Behind the photograph were several others, but these were scorched and ruined, edges curled and charred from flame, giving the impression someone had tossed them in a fire and then relented too late, and neither heads nor tails could be discerned regarding the subjects.

"I see you never got around to clearing out this junk." Kurt lighted a cigarette. "It's stuffy as hell in here. And those bloody dolls. They scared the crap out of me when I was a kid."

"Ahem, you can't smoke in the house." Don widened his eyes melodramatically and drew his thumb across his throat. He pointed at the floor where muffled laughter occasionally echoed through the grillwork vents. "It's the law." He'd quit tobacco periodically since Sputnik.

Kurt puffed vigorously with the rapturous expression of a satiated addict. "Screw going outside in this shit. If I don't have a drag my head will explode. Want one?"

"Lord yes." Don practically snatched the proffered cigarette. They smoked in contented silence for a bit and Don's whiskey buzz began to evaporate, usurped by the rush of nicotine. He said, "So, what's the occasion?"

"What do you mean?"

"I mean, we get Holly once a year, if we're lucky. And you, you're always busier than a one-armed paper hanger. But here both of you are; out of the blue I might add. So, what gives?"

Kurt puffed smoke from his nostrils. "Mom threatened us. You telling me you aren't in on it?"

"Postcards suit me, son. I cherish my peace and quiet. Threatened you how?"

"With being disinherited, what else?"

"She's too late."

"Ha-ha. I'm kidding—she asked Holly to visit, not me. I came because I want to talk." Kurt dragged on his cigarette, face screwed up in concentration, as it always had when he confronted a problem too big for his eminently prosaic brain. "It's…Well it's weird."

"Uh-oh," Don said. "Quick!" He crushed his cigarette and hid the evidence in the front pocket of his shirt and frantically swiped at the smoke circling his head.

"Oh, boys," Michelle called from the landing. Backlit by a lamp, her shadow flickered on the ceiling where the stairs slanted downward. "How's it coming?"

"Er, ahem—fine, dear! Almost done," Don said, fighting the itch in his throat, the maddening urge to cough.

"Fabulous. Come right down, if you please. Holly has another trunk on the porch and we can't have her spraining something trying to lift it, can we?"

"Right, right, she's a delicate flower," Don said. He shrugged at Kurt. "Hold the thought, eh?"

"Yeah," Kurt cracked the window enough to create a whistling suction and smoke streamed forth into the maelstrom. "We'll talk about it later."

7.

There came a golden and crimson break in the weather. Black and purple for miles all around, Jupiter's gory eye fixed directly overhead. The girls sent Don and Kurt into town for emergency supplies—more wine coolers and candles.

Don decided to make the best of a raw deal and took Kurt to visit Grandpa Luther, a chore he'd neglected for six months, much to Michelle's growing irritation—she coming from the blood is thicker than water set. Don shrugged off her disapproval, turtled stubbornly. Luther had been a force of nature and Don didn't like visiting the old man's patch of dirt. It reminded him of his own crow's feet, how the flesh of his triceps had begun to loosen, dimpled and pallid as a plucked turkey.

Kurt drove him to the cemetery and said, "Hey, do your thing. I'm no good with this sentimental crap. I'll get the booze and swing around to grab you in a bit."

Don lingered a moment in the entrance lot, breathing in the salt tang mixed with decomposing soil and wet grass. He walked slowly then, a bouquet of parti-colored supermarket flowers drooping from his fist. On the left was the mausoleum, a low, brick rectangle, crosses graven at intervals where windows might've served. To the right, a dirty white marble Christ knelt upon a knoll, hands clasped, face upturned. The stone split along Christ's jaw and temple; a scar. Perhaps this was his portrait after Golgotha, the wounds yet sharp. Behind the statue, a storm fence leaned crookedly, a spine of plastic slats and mesh separating the cemetery from a warren of duplexes and tract houses.

Numerous bedroom windows overlooked this field of crumbling markers; he considered the irony of how at night the living and the dead slept crown to crown. Did the flimsy barrier represent something more than its makers intended? Possibly a subconscious demarcation between the Here And Now and the Hereafter.

Passing a naked flagpole near the granite Civil War Monument, he came toward the oldest sections, the plots where the founders of Portland were buried. The rough-cropped turf was largely innocent of paths. Those that existed were uneven, asphalt-rutted from the crush of years, and slimy with needles and pollen. Trees reared in disorderly copses. Evergreens dominated, limbs heavy and low, creaking as the wind nudged them. Birches hunkered as poor relations at a banquet, their mottled skins cold and white, black branches haggard even in summer. Periodic attempts to dress up the grounds were evidenced by the symmetrical shearing of hedge trees.

Markers radiated unevenly to the cardinal points—rain-slick headstones of marble and granite, and a few of dull metal. Most were simple affairs, comprised of names and dates etched in rock. Gray plates lay half-sunken in the turf; hungry green moss filled the grooves and hollows of the most venerable carvings. Under these markers, in the wet, dark soil, nested the bones of pioneers and politicians, fishermen and fishwives, cowboys and bankers, immigrants and vagrants, ancient dowagers and newborn daughters, boys lost at war, girls lost in the cannery, atheists and parishioners alike.

Beyond the brief fields of colonial interment, he approached the cemetery's opposite flank, the newest portion. His grandfather's plaque was simple—a plate bolted to a flat wedge of stone. It said:

LUTHER ANGSTROM MILLER
CAPTAIN UNITED STATES ARMY
BORN AUGUST 3RD 1882
DIED JANUARY 14TH 1977

They'd buried his wife in Bellingham in the family plot, so it was only Grandfather here.

"Brought you some flowers, Grandpa." Don arranged the flowers in what he hoped was a decent presentation. The ground was too wet to sit.

1945 was the year the world raveled for Don, the year he'd gone to live with Luther in the old homestead cabin among the hills outside of town. Mom wrecked her car and Dad went off the deep end, volunteered for some kind of suicide mission on a remote and long since forgotten piece of island real estate in the Philippines—the true circumstances of his death buried in a government vault for forever plus a day. Don's older brothers, Colin and Robert, were out of the picture by then: Colin moved to Wallachia and became curator of the venerable museum of natural history ensconced in Castle Mishko; Robert ran away and did a tour with the Marines, then joined a commune in San Francisco in the latter '60s and disappeared completely except for a half-dozen bizarre letters he sent to 'Whom it may concern' across the next three decades. Younger brothers Stephen and Ralph spent the summer across the pond with Aunt Muriel, a London socialite. Don's long-lost sister Louise had also disappeared into the world, touring Eastern Europe in the company of rich, urbane men, although she too wrote occasionally; last anyone heard she'd emigrated to Central America in the 1980s and performed relief work on behalf of various charities.

Luther had taught Don to smoke in the summer of '45 when the boy was fourteen. Luther was suffering through his third year of retirement from the military and picking at a book of poetry he'd been writing since WWI. The brass had sent him to pasture after a long run—the time was nigh for a fresh vision, younger, more ruthless men were needed; bastards even sneakier and more bloody-minded who could face the intricacies of a rapidly changing intelligence-gathering model. His wife, Vera, died the winter previous and the big house on the hill seemed cavernous with just the old man and grandson for inhabitants.

Grandfather's bitterness was tempered by a keen black humor, a refined, yet earthy, knack for self-deprecation that, in the final analysis, bolstered more than condemned. *We're ants. Not even ants. We're gnats, kiddo. Don't neglect your prayers.* He'd chuckle his horrible, phlegmy chuckle and clap Don's shoulder as if they were junior officers sharing a wry joke.

They didn't discuss family. Instead, they debated where Don should go to college, what he'd do for a profession. At the time, Don had his eye on Rogers and Williams with a mind toward oceanography. The reality became four years at Western Washington State and two more in Stanford and getting hitched to sweet Michelle in between. Luther footed what his three scholarships didn't cover. Those summers with Granddad when school was out were from another life, but he recalled them with a clarity that frightened him.

The weather was apocalyptic. Sluggish days framed by metallic skies and brown grass. Dog days of heat and flies. Flies crawled everywhere, buzzed inside light fixtures, made mountains of their corpses in the porcelain coverlets, clung as blue-green tapestries upon the ancient screens; humming a death drone.

Luther sat on the porch during the worst, empty and half-empty glasses gleaming around his feet, the flowerbox above his head, scattered like tiers of candles in a medieval church. He slumped in the sweltering blue shade, chain-smoking and draining bottles of scotch without seeming effect, always dressed in a conservative suit, of which there were perhaps a dozen in his closet. He flipped his tie over his shoulder, eyes muddy behind thick-rimmed glasses. The Philco crackled from the living room, carrying fragments of baseball heroics through the screen door. He glowed in the dead light, a shade of himself, the dimming bell of a supernova. The steady fossilization had crept into his face, marbled the veins of his once delicate hands. Those hands had hardened into the knotty, blunt-fingered hands of the elderly, the spent.

Don knew things about Grandfather, there were many things to know. Luther Miller was, in some murky era of prehistory, a minor legend. The massive house his own grandfather, Augustus, had built in the spring of 1878 was a repository and a testament of the rich mythology steeping the Miller lineage. Don had many occasions to examine the artifacts cluttering the study. Diplomas from Columbia and Princeton; yellowed certificates and dusty ribbons awarded by the U.S. Army. Besides the requisite family snapshots and wedding pictures, there were galleries of black and white photos of Luther as a whip-thin young man in an officer's uniform set against exotic backdrops—ruined cathedrals and monasteries, crumbling plazas and pyramids, Old World markets, desert encampments and jungle fortifications, destroyers and camel trains. In these pictures everyone was burned by the sun, everyone smoked cigarettes, everyone was armed and smiling like movie stars between takes in a historical production. And a hundred more, until the photos merged into a camouflage pattern that gave him a headache and a profound sense of inferiority. Grandfather had *done* things, and in the doing the man himself was shaped and scarred, his blood thinned, his emotions rarefied.

Luther didn't say much about that part of his life either. He didn't talk about his year in China as a liaison to the Shanghai Municipal Police, his affiliation with the likes of Fairbairn and Applegate who became close friends. Nor his missions in France during the First Great War, never spoke of the papers he had authored, the congressional reports he had participated in. If asked, he shrugged and told the curiosity seeker that his life was archived in the Army record—look it up. And that particular statement was a fitting summation, in Don's mind. Luther Miller was a ponderous, open book with some of the pages carefully removed, others encoded.

That filthy, humid summer of '45 was the summer of the bloody war in the Pacific that would end in the bloom of two new suns, the annihilation of innocence, even in savagery. Luther taught him to smoke by example. And once, when the old man was so drunk his speech became deadly precise, his movements the functions of an automaton, he instructed Don to dress sharp and they drove the Studebaker into Olympia. Luther gave him a tour of the State Capitol, introduced him to a smattering of men in Brooks Brothers suits and Rolexes and smelling of expensive after-shave. Important men who smiled and shook hands with Luther, addressed him almost reverently, turned beaming eyes and shark teeth bared in shark grins upon Don.

Through it all, Luther smiled a windup smile Don found alien as the ice in dark canyons of the Antarctic, and called everyone by his or her first name. This ordeal lasted minutes, it lasted hours. When it was over and they were driving back into the hills, Luther, both hands locked on the wheel, asked what Don thought of the esteemed representatives of the people. After his grandson muttered whatever answer, Luther nodded without removing his eyes from the road and said, *There is not enough rope on this wobbling ball of shit to hang those bastards*. The conversation ended there.

Don trudged back to the entrance. Night fastened upon the cemetery; lamps fizzed alight, mapping the perimeter. Again the breeze freshened, damp in his mouth. Branches groaned as if to promise, *Go to your warm house and leave us here in the dark. Do not worry, friend, you will be back for a much longer visit one day.*

CHAPTER FOUR

The Séance

(Now)

1.

It grew late.

Holly nipped out to chauffeur "Uncle" Argyle as his license had been revoked going on ten years. He lived at the Arden House located in an historic neighborhood on Olympia's eastside. The morning deluge resumed, driven by more powerful gusts of wind and the lane melted into a quagmire and her Rover was the most reliable all-weather vehicle. Argyle's arrival set the household on its ear again. He lumbered through the front door cursing the gods and the weather in a baritone that was the trademark of Arden men.

Argyle was large, bluff, and commanding in his classic gray suit, a Brooks Brothers inherited from his great-grandfather, which rendered the ensemble unspeakably ancient, practically an historical artifact that might've interested a museum or two. He'd pursued an extravagant and fruitful life—soldier, dilettante, author, historian, scientist, and professional ne'er do well just a hair this side of royalty. He'd certainly inherited a fortune sufficient to make a run at the Prince of Monte Carlo, much of it, as the whispers went, from his grandfather's criminal empire during the Roaring Twenties.

His presence among the proletariat Millers was often remarked upon as slumming; this whispered by his presumed equals. The Arden clan extant comprised the inner circle of local old money families, the crème de la crème, the very royalty of three counties, and included such luminaries as the Redfields, Rourkes, Wilsons and Smiths and in roughly descending order. The middle sibling of eight Arden brothers, and the lone scientist from a brood of lawyers and playboys, he was the last standing and the least likely to consider peerage when making associations. His brothers had fallen by the wayside due to wars, duels, disappearances, and in one notable instance, natural causes. Not that he'd escaped unscathed; a confirmed bachelor who'd stepped out of character once and married a lovely girl from Nice, a nurse who died young and made an embittered widower of him. Sometime during his seriously squandered youth, he'd gotten his nose lopped in an accident—no one knew precisely the circumstances of the mishap—and wore a gold-plated prosthetic to conceal the damage.

Michelle's inexhaustible fascination with the arcane was responsible for their friend's inimitable fashion statement. A popular form of punishment in the Byzantine court involved severing an offending noble's nose, followed by the wretch's permanent exile; a fate periodically visited upon even the high and mighty emperors and their luckless consorts. One such emperor fled to a neighboring kingdom and had a golden nosepiece made to salvage some meager shred of his dignity. The emperor returned to court at the fore of an army of disaffected citizenry and slaughtered the would-be usurpers—after hacking off their noses, naturally. The notion appealed to Argyle and he commissioned Llewellyn Malloy himself to craft a number of the ostentatious prosthetics in gold, silver and platinum. When the kids were in elementary school, he gave each of them a fake nose; ivory for Holly, and bronze for Kurt. They wore them with embarrassing regularity and tried to emulate Argyle's distinctive accent.

Dinner was roast pork, Don's specialty. He put the end leaves on the dining table and the seven of them enjoyed a lengthy banquet characterized by great quantities of champagne and rowdy banter that spared none. There were revelations: Winnie was nine weeks pregnant; she and Kurt delayed their announcement to ascertain the tests were correct, complications could've arisen since she had entered her forties, but the prenatal signs were reassuring. The latter breaking news concerned Holly's last-minute decision to accompany Michelle and associates to Turkey. Holly was free to partake of such an excursion because she had secured a one-year leave of absence to pursue a masters in education, the prerequisite for a transition to an administrative career. It developed that Michelle campaigned long and hard to convince her daughter that a vacation prior to the fall semester was just the ticket.

Between a dessert of orange sorbet and sponge cake, the lights brightened, then died. For several moments all conversation suspended as they sat in the darkness, surrounded by the roaring gale, the rattle of rain against the shutters. Don had prepared for this eventuality. Via penlight, he fumbled out a box of wooden matches and lighted kerosene lamps placed strategically around the house. Originally the property of Aunt Yvonne, the Millers had cause to use them frequently over the years—blackouts were part and parcel of living in the country.

Everyone eventually relocated as a herd to the parlor, amid much stumbling and nervous repartee, and sat near the crackling orange blaze of the fireplace, which Kurt had stocked with seasoned birch. Wind shrilled in the flue, and sparks showered the screen. Don brought out a battered camp stove and boiled water for hot toddies.

Waiting in the darkened kitchen for the kettle to heat, he felt isolated. Hushed conversation echoed down the hall and seemed to issue from a far more remote locale than the parlor. Thule slunk from under the table, a large, black shadow, and growled his fear-growl. He crouched, nose pointed at the cellar door. Not only was the door narrow, but also seemingly designed for midgets. Michelle at five-foot-three ducked whenever she passed through. The creaky wooden stairs descended some fifteen steps and made a ninety-degree left-hand turn. Fractured, sunken flagstone gave way to hardpack dirt about two-thirds of the way in and the enclosure smelled of wet earth and rotting wood. Don minimized his excursions down there, had pared it to once or twice during each summer visit.

Thule whined. Don shooed him into the hallway. He fixed the drinks, standing in an awkward way at the counter so he didn't put his back to the cellar. Which was worse than silly; it bordered paranoia. He ferried the refreshments from the kitchen and passed them among the assembly. He experienced a short-lived fright upon realizing Michelle had disappeared. He nearly panicked, nearly went tearing through the house searching for her. Such an overreaction could've proved disastrous as he was blind as a bat in low light, glasses or not. Fortunately, his wife materialized from the gloom, a trifle confused why her excursion to the bathroom to powder her nose was suddenly a federal issue. Don mumbled an apology about being jumpy and gave her a conciliatory peck on the cheek.

That matter settled, they waited there in the parlor, sipping their toddies and reminiscing, voices subdued as if the loss of electricity had sunk them into the Dark Ages when peasants scurried into their cottages before dusk and barred their doors and made signs to ward evil.

It was Argyle who suggested a round of ghost stories. How could they in good conscience waste such a perfect alignment of inclement weather, candlelight and agreeable company? No one leaped to second the prospect, but it hardly mattered. Once Argyle seized upon an idea, he proceeded inexorably and heedlessly along his charted course. He launched into a travelogue account of his infamous journey to the interior of China to document migratory patterns of a particular tribe that hunted near the Gobi Desert; incidentally his work netted some obscure, albeit immensely satisfying award. His oratory was punctuated by knowing asides to Michelle who smiled indulgently and certified the veracity of his observations through her very silence.

Don conceded that Argyle spun an excellent yarn. It possessed the proper elements—star-crossed lovers, cruel fate, revenge from beyond the grave, a rare flower that bloomed precisely where the lovers were stoned to death, the haunting legend that echoed down through the generations as a cautionary fable. Everyone clapped at the dénouement, whereupon Argyle, who had likely recited this exact tale in a hundred seedy cantinas across the globe and twice as many lecture halls full of drooling grad students, half rose to execute a gallant bow.

"Well done, Argyle, well done," Don toasted his old friend. "Too bad you're full of bull chips. Who's next?"

After an uproar of laughter that served to cut the tension, Kurt said, "Well, how about it, Holly? Spin us a haunted house yarn, will you? The thing with poor, hapless Boris—"

"Nobody wants to hear about Boris. They've heard all my stories." Holly had long resented Kurt's opportunistic mockery, the insult doubly painful by her mother's collusion. She'd first confided this to Don when they were moderately toasted at Kurt's wedding reception and the conversation turned to the subject of the afterlife and whether Grandma and Grandpa might be floating about as ethereal presences.

"Ah, right, it's true." Kurt grinned. "But you tell them so well. As for Boris, I think you came up with that humdinger because you're allergic to cats. You had it in for puss from day one—admit it." He ducked the mug she chucked in the general direction of his head. "Or maybe you just wanted to help Mom prove her Hollow Earth theory..."

Don cast a sharp glance at his wife to gauge her reaction, but she continued to smile and he suspected she'd had more than enough to drink at that juncture. Or, miracle of miracles. maybe the wounds had actually healed.

Then, quick as a serpent her eyes changed and she stared at Kurt with great intensity. "My hollow whatsis?" she said with the sugary inflection that emerged only when her mood was wrathful, the tone she'd adopted before flexing her claws to shred a hundred hapless colleagues in a hundred debates.

"Uh, the, well, you know what I mean." Kurt coughed and looked around for rescue.

"Oh, sweetie, everybody knows there's no such thing as little people," Michelle said. Her grin was feral. She showed too many teeth, still perfect after all these years. "But there are better stories. I ever tell you about the time Dr. Plimpton took me to a whorehouse in Spain to meet his sister? She was highly placed. Ran all the other whores ragged. Just a happy coincidence as Louis was pursuing rumors of a community dwelling in an uncharted cave system. Don, too bad you were done with caving by then. The stalactites! The stalagmites!" She tossed her drink back with that same awful grin plastered on.

"Linda?" Don said quickly to Holly's girlfriend. "Do you have an anecdote you'd care to share with our humble gathering?"

Linda declined, citing the fact she couldn't watch a horror movie unless she covered her eyes during the scary parts. Don waved off an opportunity to join the fun. The conversation lost momentum and he thought perhaps everyone would call it quits, which suited him. It had been a hell of a long day.

Winnie looked at Kurt. "Tell them about the witch."

"Uh, that's not interesting, Win. Trust me, Holly's are whoppers." He wasn't laughing now. His mouth tightened. Don noted him clenching and unclenching his fist.

"Your story is very frightening. I shivered when you told it to me." She smiled innocently, her tiny hand pale against his arm, her face tilted upward so their eyes met. Don stifled a chuckle because he knew feminine revenge when he saw it in action—damned if she wasn't inflicting reprisals for her husband's overbearing behavior. He made a note to avoid crossing the demure woman from Hong Kong.

Kurt's flush was apparent even in the shadowy light. "Bah. Mine's hardly a ghost story. Mom, surely you've got one." He sounded vaguely desperate.

Michelle said, "I don't know any ghost stories; just true ones." From her smug tone Don knew she was high as a kite on the champagne. He'd surreptitiously stolen her glass three times during supper, to no avail.

"Tell us one of those, then." Kurt came as close to pleading as he ever got. "Surely the primitives and their ancestor worship are good for a tale. Something with sex magic and human sacrifice."

"We don't call them primitives these days—they're indigenous peoples. Anyway, I can't think of anything that isn't excruciatingly boring. Yours sound more interesting. I can't recall you ever mentioning it before."

"Good grief, lad. Are you whining? Stop that nonsense," Argyle said, grinning.

"Yeah, bro. Let's hear it." Holly raised her brow in a way that rendered her expression slightly diabolic. At least she didn't combine the arched brow with rolling up the whites of her eyes like she'd often done in school to impress her classmates, or terrify them, as the case might've been.

The others rumbled approval and imprecations and finally, Kurt shrugged in defeat. "Jesus. You people are relentless. Fine, if I'm going to do this, I need another toddy."

2.

Kurt stared at his drink. He shuddered when a blast of wind broadsided the house, muscles jumping in his clamped jaw. At last, without raising his gaze toward the expectant audience, he began to speak. His voice was thick and he enunciated with the care of a man deep into his cups.

"Okay, Uncle Argyle and Linda, bear with me on the details. Senior year in high school, I saw a witch. That's what we called her, anyhow. 'Witch' isn't the right word, not by a long shot, but you'll see what I mean. That summer, I stayed in San Francisco while Mom and Dad came out here as usual.

"I remember what a big deal it seemed to be—left in charge of the house, paying off the meter guy and making sure the lawn got mowed and whatnot. Not that it should've been, considering how often the neighbors watched us all the time. Mom, you and Dad weren't around much in those days, always traveling to one jungle or cave complex, or another. Still, seventeen was the tipping point—this marked the first occasion I was left alone, the man of the house. Everything was copacetic. *For awhile.*

"I'd made varsity linebacker for the Rams my junior year. Led the team in sacks. Third most tackles by a Pac Nine player ever. Everybody knew I had a shot at All State. That got me in like Flynn with Nelly Coolidge, one of the best-looking cheerleaders at school. Everybody sucked up to her—the jocks on account of her being a 'hot chick' as they used to say, and all the girls fawned over her because she had plenty of folding green and didn't mind spreading it around to her clique. The girls were afraid of her, too. She was popular and powerful, a dangerous combo. Her dad gave me a summer job at the department store, stocking shelves and closing shop. The gig put enough spare change in my pocket to take Nelly dancing and drinking—cover your ears, Winnie dear—in hopes of scoring more than a touchdown. Never happened, alas. Quite a bummer, considering the crap I was soon to endure on her behalf.

"This was 1979. Thanks to my stellar performance knocking poor sophomores around the gridiron, I managed to land that scholarship to UW and that settled matters. Tell you the truth, Dad, if the scholarship hadn't gone through, I'd made up my mind to enlist on my birthday and go into the military with Frankie Rogers and Billy Summerset. Frankie died in the Beirut barracks explosion, and Billy was one of the unlucky bastards shot during the Grenada invasion. They were Marines, though. Marines see the worst of it. I still exchange Christmas cards with Billy's younger brother, Eli. Eli joined up for the Gulf War and managed to make it home with all his parts.

"Anyway, senior year. Graduation nine months away and coming fast, coach counting on me to lead the defense to a state championship. I knew damn well he held the keys to my scholarship, and Coach wasn't exactly peaches and cream, not with the booster club and the principal on his ass to bring home the hardware every year…I had a lot going on; my mind was racing a thousand miles an hour. Seemed as if half the time I was a little woozy, almost in a dream state, and that could've contributed to what came later. Certain people are susceptible to hallucinations. Perhaps that's me—Mr. Cotton Head. Dunno. I'd love to believe it.

"Me and the boys—Frankie, Billy, Toby Nethercutt, and Mike Shavenko, and a couple other guys from Oakland—raised a bit of hell at night. We'd gather at the old Celadon Park—definitely not wise with the druggies cutting each other to ribbons with broken bottles—or that deserted carnival by the boardwalk. Sometimes, when there was a party, a bunch of us loaded into Mike Shavenko's Caddy and cruised down the coast and stood around a bonfire with kids from half a dozen other schools, and drank beer and played football on the beach. The whole *Sometimes a Great Notion* deal sans anybody as gray or cantankerous as Henry Fonda. There were a few brawls and the usual fooling around, but things were remarkably innocent. Nothing like the kids get up to today. I think the worst thing I did was get drunk a few times and fall into the habit of smoking. Frankie and Billy got me hooked. Especially Frankie, who was a pack of Lucky Strikes a day fellow. Hell everybody smoked; it was the height of cool. I remember sneaking into the bathroom to get a couple drags in between classes. What did we know?

"Frankie's parents were divorced, had been since he was eleven. I knew him since second grade. Happy kid. Class cutup, though the teachers loved him because he was so damned quick with a wise-ass remark. You know the kind. He'd make you want to punch him except you were laughing so hard you were in danger of pissing your pants.

"His mom lighting out for parts unknown changed everything. She met an advertising exec and left with the guy—packed a single case and was gone forever. His dad went over the edge. Jack Somerset worked on the docks as a longshoreman. Shoulda seen his arms and shoulders—a bison stuffed into a plaid shirt. Scary. He took to drinking—would stop at Clausen's Liquor and pound a sixer on the way home from work—occasionally, when I came over to visit Frankie, I saw his old man slouched in that Chevy of his, knocking back a half case of Lone Star. He sluiced those cans into his mouth; one after another, like a machine. Then he'd carry another half rack in and polish it off while he watched basketball. Never said squat, either. Just sat there like a boulder, face white as a sheet from the T.V. glow. You could practically hear him ticking.

"Worse part was, he started slapping Frankie around; and for nothing. Well, maybe not for 'nothing'—Frankie was an inveterate smart mouth, after all. This was different, though. No warning—Jack would just walk over and pop him one. He couldn't fight his dad, of course. Tried it once and the old man chucked him through the screen door like a sack of meat. He smashed into the sidewalk and skinned his hands. The doc had to tape them like a boxer's. So, yeah, here was my boon comrade living in hell for seven years. He couldn't get into the Marines fast enough. Not fast enough to keep from going bad. When Frankie's personality turned dark, I wasn't exactly surprised. Yet, even knowing his damage, the transformation chilled me, drove an icy spike right through my guts. I watched him rot from the inside…an apple being eaten from the core by a worm. Broke my heart.

"It got worse that spring of '79 and went to complete shit by summer. Jack went from the once a week whippings to kicking his kid's ass every day. Sickest part? The guy got real careful not to leave marks. He'd rabbit-punch him, squeeze his neck until his eyes bulged, that sort of thing. I wasn't there to see it, thank God. Frankie told me what happened, made a black comedy of the account. He'd laugh and shrug and say something along the lines of, 'It's just T.V., Kurt.' His laugh had changed, too. It sounded like the bark of a crow.

"He got mean at the end of our junior year, became savage as a junkyard dog. He stole money from his dad and paid the goons who loitered outside the brick and bar liquor stores on 10th and Browning to buy booze for him. Not beer, either. Nah, he graduated directly to Jim Beam; stashed the bottles under the seat of Mike Shavenko's car—Shavenko was kind of Frankie's squire. He drove Frankie to all the backyard beer parties, especially the cross-town mixers where trouble could be found if one was sufficiently determined. They'd get good and scotched, then Frankie would pick a fight—one, two, three guys, didn't matter to him. He'd take all comers and beat them down. The kid was scrawny, which goes to show viciousness is more important than natural athletic ability during a brawl. He became something of a legend, honestly. Frankie took plenty of licks, but I guess it wasn't anything compared to what his old man laid on him.

"Now, it can be told—I gave Frankie a key and let him crash on the couch whenever the scene got too heavy at home. He was there, dead to the world on a few mornings, both eyes blacked like a raccoon's, and snoring loud enough I thought he'd choke in his sleep. And once, Jesus, Joseph, Mary I found him sprawled on the couch literally covered in blood, so much blood I scarcely recognized him. He looked like he'd been in a car wreck; his face was pancaked with gore, his tee shirt was black and hard as a plaster shell. For a few seconds I figured he was dead—then he started snoring that honking, godawful snore of his. I drove him to the clinic. Turned out he'd been in a hell of fistfight against two college juniors at a bonfire party. Frankie had one of them on the ground and was tattooing his face with a sealed can of Black Label when the second dude tried to kick a field goal with his head—the asshole was wearing hiking boots with studs, too. Frankie finished off the first one, then jumped up and chased the other guy along the beach for half a mile and beat him to a pulp. He was frothing at the mouth; tried to drown the guy until cooler heads prevailed and a bunch of kids dragged them apart. Frankie lost three teeth and needed forty-odd stitches in his scalp. Nasty deal.

"The whole arrangement was a kind of betrayal of your trust, letting somebody the entire school considered a bad element flop at the house while you were out of town. Believe me, I wasn't happy about the situation, skewered on the horns of a dilemma. I had to choose between helping my friend and keeping the faith with my parents. It was a tough call. I asked myself what you would do in my shoes, Dad.

"As it developed, Frankie was a perfect gentleman. He didn't touch a blessed thing. He even helped me with the yard work a couple of weekends.

Looking back, it's lucky for us his dad didn't put two and two together and come hunting for Frankie to use as a punching bag. Maybe Jack didn't give a damn. He was so screwed in the brain by then he'd managed to get fired by the union—which gives you an idea what a colossal mess he'd become to provoke that drastic a move. Last I heard of him was during college—he finally lost his house, and relocated to an Airstream trailer in New Mexico and was living with a prostitute who made her bones, so to speak, under a freeway overpass.

"While all this drama with Frankie was coming to a boil, I reported to Coolidge's store every other evening at eight o'clock sharp and worked until midnight. Unless we had deliveries; then Coolidge's assistant manager, Herb Nolton kept me around until one or two A.M. It wasn't exactly backbreaking labor. Herb usually stayed in the office and watched the tube, or fell asleep in the comfy leather swivel chair Coolidge referred to as 'the Captain's Seat.'

"I worked with another guy named Ben Wolf. He'd graduated two or three years before and got married to his high school sweetheart. They had a baby, so Ben worked three jobs trying to keep the roof nailed down over their heads. We took long breaks smoking in the alley and talking football. Ben had played running back for the team. Didn't get bupkus for playing time, although he sure looked fast enough. Nice fellow—he even brought his wife and baby to watch me at the home games later that fall.

"Then there was the other member of our nightshift fraternity—Doug Reeves. Reeves was way older than us; did piece work for a few local businesses. A jack of all trades type; not an electrician or a plumber, yet he could rewire faulty outlets in a pinch and knew how to sling a monkey wrench. He usually kept to himself and that's probably because he toted a hip flask. He wore heavy aftershave to disguise the whiskey reek. At least once a night I spotted him ducking behind boxes in the storeroom to take a swig. Poor Reeves couldn't go fifteen minutes without lighting up, either. Mr. Coolidge forbade us from smoking in the building. Smoke got into the clothes and sleeping bags. He woulda been pissed if he knew Reeves walked around with a cigarette hanging from the corner of his mouth. I imagine he woulda fired Herb for letting it go on. Fortunately, Coolidge didn't drop in for any surprise inspections. Nelly told me once that her parents fought like cats and dogs. Eventually they just came home, had a few scotches and stumbled off to separate bedrooms. That's how divorce was done back then, right? Still, their misery was our salvation.

"Things took a turn for the weird. Reeves started hanging with me and Ben during our smoke breaks in the alley. It seemed odd—he didn't say anything, didn't want to join the conversation. He smiled at our jokes in the half-ass way people do when they're trying to get along and not draw too much attention to themselves. At first it happened once every couple of shifts. By the last three weeks I worked there, Reeves was connected to my or Ben's hip wherever we went in the store. He slunk around back there, puffing his cigs and slugging booze. Got to the point me and Ben couldn't even sneak off and leave him. Soon as the coast was clear and we'd tiptoe for the door, I'd hear a paint can or a crescent wrench clatter on the floor and here'd come Reeves like a bat outta hell. In hindsight, that might've been the case.

"Ben's the one who finally decided to pull him aside and have a man-to-man chat. He planned to set Reeves straight, break it to him as gently as possible that he might want to crawl out of the bottle and get his act together a bit. The stalking routine was getting on our nerves and it better stop, pronto. I remember Ben's expression about ten minutes later when he came back with Reeves in tow to where I was stocking tennis rackets and baseball bats. Ben asks Reeves to repeat what he said and Reeves shrugs and stares at his feet. Eventually we got him to spill that he's scared shitless of somebody lurking in the storeroom. 'The Witch,' he called this person. Claimed she was tall, spindly, and white as chalk. She wore a dirty dress that dragged the floor. That's how he noticed her—he saw the hem of her dress disappearing into the shadows from the corner of his eye. He thought it was a hallucination, his wacked version of a pink elephant. Until he saw her in the flesh a few minutes later when he walked by the office and she's in there leaning over Herb, who's sleeping, as usual. Reeves shook while relating this yarn. Guy's teeth were clicking like he was freezing. Allegedly this had gone on for two weeks before we got tired of him grasping after our apron strings, as it were. That's why he didn't want to be left alone in the store—once, he turned around and there she was on the other side of a rack, grinning at him with pure evil. He wanted to quit, except he was too in hock at the bar and a month behind in rent. If he left, he'd starve. Or have a heart attack from DTs.

"We didn't know what to make of it. Ben took the lead again. He patted the guy on the back and made me cough up twenty bucks so the old-timer could go get hammered Friday night—said it was the least we could do. There went my dinner and movie plans with Nelly. Irritating thing about dear, sweet Nelly—free as she was with treating her friends, she fully expected me to pay the freight during our liaisons. That girl was a cock tease and all around power-tripper. I'm shocked she didn't go into politics, what with her gift for manipulation.

"As it happened, Herb called me Friday morning to say an unexpected shipment of exercise equipment was sitting on the loading dock. Neither Ben nor Reeves were scheduled to work, so he begged me to come in and do the heavy lifting because he'd slipped a disk in his back. Since I was flat broke and dateless, I jumped at the offer, although lugging barbells and cast iron plates wasn't my first choice for an evening's recreation. I ran into Nelly at the soda shop. One thing leads to another and pretty soon we're necking in the back of my—uh, your car, Dad—and I'm not really getting into it because my mind is on the freaky revelations of Doug Reeves. Nelly asked me what's wrong, so against my better judgment I gave her the whole story. She took it seriously.

"The store was built in 1916 and the Coolidges took it over in 1950. Nelly leaned close and whispered conspiratorially that she'd heard from a friend of a friend that an employee died in the store during the Roaring Twenties; hanged themselves from one of the railings. Only a ghost could come and go like this figure did. I asked if she'd ever seen anything. Not exactly; nonetheless, she remained convinced something spooky was afoot. She'd been sweet on one of the stock boys a couple of summers back and he'd mentioned the ghost too. Same description of a tall, spindly woman with a wicked grin. That sealed it for her.

"Right there, in the middle of our preempted make-out session, Nelly's eyes brightened and she pinched me and said what we needed to do was provoke the spirit into appearing, then perform a ritual to banish it from the property. My jaw dropped. I didn't quite believe what I'd heard. She worked herself into a lather and nattered on about these two friends of hers, outcast girls who dressed in black and moped around and how they were into all kinds of occult bullshit. One of them had promised to show her how to use a Ouija board and take her to a séance they planned for Halloween. Precursors to Goth chicks, those two. Samantha and Cassie. Nobody liked them, not even the chess nerds, or the stoners, or even the fat kids in band. Nelly was slumming, sampling their 'quaint' lifestyle; no doubt so she could mock them to her circle when she grew bored. Once she'd decided to bring her pals to the store, I couldn't get a word in edgewise.

"Still bemused by this turn of events, I showed up at Coolidge's that evening. Herb handed me the keys on his way to his twice a month wild Friday night at the Elks Club; he wore his orange blazer and a bowtie—I can't adequately express the dizzying effect of that ensemble. From what I understand, Monday mornings he'd skip into the store chipper as a squirrel; the one day he wasn't sober as an accountant. To this day I'm a little curious what he got up to at those soirees. Maybe he hit the jackpot with one those old flames he'd reminisced about on occasion.

"After Herb made his getaway, I got busy with the mountain of heavy boxes waiting for me in the receiving area, which was sort of a warehouse attached to the rear of the building. Metal racks went to the roof, jammed with stuff and crowded in tight. It's by the grace of God nobody ever got clobbered by a loose unit of tile, or an unsecured fridge toppling from the top shelf. We stacked that junk to the rafters, literally.

"Coolidge inherited an antique forklift when he bought the store, the type with a clutch. Ben usually drove the pallets in and dropped them close to the main display room. No way I was getting on that thing in those tight aisles, so that meant hand-trucking the deliveries inside one or two pieces at a time. No fun, particularly because the place was dark and lifeless the way buildings are when they empty for the day and everything falls quiet—and Coolidge's Department Store was huge. Remember? You guys used to get camping supplies there. Two floors and half of a third with a crappy escalator and narrow stairs with awful carpeting—lime green!—steering the mobs from women's clothing to sporting goods and housewares. God, that place was so packed with merchandise only three or four people could stand on queue without doing the bump and grind.

"I realized this was the first time I'd been alone in the place. It was gloomy in there, but I was leery of lighting the building like a Christmas tree. I contented myself with switching on everything in the storage room, which sorta helped, although the effect left much to be desired—everything turned sickly green and there were plenty of shadows in the deeper stacks. It didn't do a thing for the main floor which was illuminated by light strips inside the display cases and two or three puny brown bulbs upstairs. Honestly, I glanced over my shoulder every five seconds, sort of expecting to see a Halloween mask of a face leering at me. Every shadow was a menace waiting to pounce.

"About nine o'clock Nelly banged on the glass of the front door for me to let her and the Gloomy Gus twins inside. The sisters were so pale and sickly they could've doubled for ghosts themselves, or walking corpses. They sure as hell stumbled around like mini Boris Karloff clones and communicated in monosyllables. Real charming.

"Those girls were all business, though. While Nelly stood over them, twitching and frittering, Samantha and Cassie broke out the tools of the occult trade—black and red candles, white chalk and a thick black book bound in faux leather—and meticulously scribed a pentagram, or pentacle, or whatever, and a slew of arcane symbols on the concrete floor near the tool department. Coolidge was a first class cheapskate. When the contractors hired to renovate the store for its grand reopening had gone over budget, leaving unsightly loose ends such as bare sheetrock in the loft and carpet that ended ten feet short of the end of some aisles, he booted them from the premises and called it 'close enough for government work. Who looks at the floor, anyway?'

"The circle—as Nelly informed me, tittering in her sudden anxiety at committing black magic rituals in the sanctity of the family business—served as a conduit and symbol of protection. Basically, it was supposed to suck in and trap any evil spirits floating around. I thought they were all effing loons and abandoned them to their fun. Oh, not so fast! I was in the middle of unpacking another pallet of boxes when Nelly rushed over and informed me everybody's waiting. Waiting for what? I received an answer soon enough after she herded me back to where Sam and Cass had lighted the black candles and were hissing incantations. The tool aisle smelled of bubbling fat and burning hair. One of them had chopped off a hank of their hair, tossed it into a tin bowl and doused it with lighter fluid. Whoosh! Too bad the sprinklers didn't trigger. That woulda been classic.

"Meanwhile, the black candles were melting in gloopy puddles. Nelly clung to my arm as the red glow of the makeshift brazier lit the scene. It must've looked like something from the cover of a pulp comic. Normally, I'd have enjoyed Nelly Coolidge pressing her heaving bosom against me, but I was transfixed by the sisters rocking on their heels, babbling in tongues, fragments of which definitely referred to *Beelzebub* and *The Prince of Darkness*.

"Cassie looked at me and Nelly; Goth girl's pupils were dilated to the max. She ordered us to sit Indian style. Of course I said, not no, but *hell no*. Nelly gave me a look like you wouldn't believe. Her queen of the realm glare that spoke volumes—it was a *I'd never work in this town again* warning via telepathy. She brushed her lips against my ear and whispered, *Cluck, cluck, cluck!* I sat and we all joined clammy hands while Sam called for the 'restless spirit' to show itself. Deep down, despite being cold to the scene, in my heart of hearts I wanted to see what happened next. Nelly's fascination was contagious.

"This went on until my butt started to ache from the concrete; then Cassie pulled a dagger out of her purse and pricked her finger. It wasn't actually a dagger, just a cheap replica she'd picked up at a Chinese gift shop. She dribbled blood into the bowl. Sam went next and then Nelly. I said nope, no way, and passed it back to Cassie. She smirked and poked me in the forearm. Dull as a letter opener, but she'd jabbed me hard and I was on my feet, cursing like a sailor. She flicked blood droplets from the point of the blade and into the brazier. I'd thought the thing was cold because the hair and powder and God knows what else had burned to ashes. Damned if flames didn't shoot forth again, two, three feet high. The flames died and I stood there swearing. Nobody else uttered a peep; they stared into the bowl, swaying as if they'd been smoking the reefer.

"The power died. For a few seconds it was pitch black. The girls screamed. I couldn't see my hand in front of my face. That freaked me a tad. To top that, the air felt electrified, thick as if a humid fog bank had settled over me. Maybe ten feet up the aisle, someone laughed—just once; high pitched and drawn out, it cut through the caterwauling. Mocking us.

"The light in the office suddenly kicked in. It flicked on and off, repeatedly, faster and faster in a strobe effect. Between flashes I saw…someone standing in there, watching. Coolidge kept some mannequins in the front window to model the flannel jackets and ladies' underwear, that whole bit. I convinced myself later that Herb left one of the dummies in there, propped in front of the desk. Another cycle of flashes and it was gone. Now *I'm* considering joining the scream fest. The phones started ringing. We had seven or eight—one at each till, the office, at a kiosk on each upper level, another in storage—and they all went simultaneously. I covered my ears and decided it was high time to bail. Great minds think alike: the girls almost knocked me over as they scrambled for the exit.

"We piled onto the sidewalk, stood, gaping into the black pit. The darkness was shot through with the wildly flickering light way in back. It was chilly and lonely. Damp wind swirled up from the bay. There weren't any cars moving, nobody walking. Just the four of us clinging together and whimpering. A pay phone across the street rang, and a tick later, the one by the old drugstore. I made the ballsiest move of my entire life—I walked over to the door and locked it, and went through the alley and made sure the receiving door was locked too. I wouldn't have gone inside for a million bucks, but I didn't want Coolidge to skin me alive if somebody looted the place after we ran away. Which we did.

"And...that's it. I handed in my resignation the next day. Didn't give two weeks, which royally pissed off Coolidge. Nelly dropped me like a hot rock and went steady with one of the defensive linemen, not that I cared at that point. I had nightmares until Thanksgiving and would come to in the middle of the night with the cold sweats. *Don't think I got more than four hours sleep an evening during that stretch.*"

3.

Lying awake later that night, Don stared into the dark. Michelle snorted and mumbled; Thule curled on the bed at their feet, a ninety-pound lump. The dog twitched and moaned with each flash of lightning, each crack of thunder rolling down the valley. Blue-white pops and sizzles illuminated the room, sent bony shadows of tree branches raking across the ceiling, across the bedcovers and Michelle's humped form; spectral claws intent upon peeling back the sheets to have at sweaty, naked flesh. Don counted between the stroke and the clash—one, two, three, BOOM! The jar of water on the dresser vibrated, and his dentures bobbed, distorted in the momentary glare. At least the rain had slackened and the wind died down to intermittent gusts.

His joints throbbed and he contemplated taking another pill to quiet the pain. Instead, he flopped over to spoon with Michelle. She smelled strongly of night sweat and something deeper; a dank, earthy taint that caused him to recoil and breathe through his mouth. Her hand clamped his forearm, an unconscious gesture. Her flesh was cold, like a fish left to smother on a wet clay bank, a pike hoisted from the depths of a northern lake.

He lay there and held his breath, listening hard to the night sounds, the creaking timbers, the faint, mournful jangle of wind chimes smacking against clapboard. Someone giggled in another room; the laughter drifted through the vent and reminded him of the twins as toddlers whispering their plots and schemes. A frog croaked just outside the window, perhaps trapped in the lee of a dormer, its complaints joined by a dim chorus from the yard among the weeds and the shelter of the magnolias; a gloomy litany, magnified somehow by the acoustics of the storm. The frogs seemed disturbed of late, didn't they? Perhaps, like dogs, they sensed impending disasters. Mice skittered in the secret hollows of the walls and Don wondered if they should get a cat, then he was asleep.

4.

The storm front passed through before dawn and sunrise lighted the bedroom in pinks and blues. Don could not remember his dreams, but knew they'd been rough from the bags under his eyes when he shaved. His hands quivered with exhaustion and he nicked himself three times and had to stick bits of toilet paper to his face to stem the blood. Making up the bed, he discovered a muddy handprint on his pillow and clods of dirt in the sheets. He frowned and stripped the sheets and dropped them in the linen basket.

A chorus of exclamations brought him downstairs in a hurry. It seemed Kurt had gone sleepwalking during the night—probably in response to the filthy weather and his reliving that decidedly unnerving tale. This happened to him as an adolescent; he occasionally woke up in the closet or the pantry, or the attic. This time he wound up in the greenhouse, sprawled between the tomatoes and the squash. Michelle had stumbled into the kitchen to get an early start on breakfast preparations and discovered the back door ajar.

Kurt didn't have an explanation and decided he must've tripped and knocked himself in the head; a lump swelled over his right ear and he'd received a number of scrapes. Worst of all, a damned rat had bitten him in the hand and arm—nasty punctures, too. That meant X-rays, tetanus shots and the unhappy revelation rodents had invaded the green house. Don scratched his head over that one. He hadn't seen any rats around. They were obviously lurking in the cellar or the barn prior to this incursion. Oh, well, while Kurt was getting the needle, Don would nip over to the hardware store and purchase rat traps and poison.

As the others mobilized to pack Kurt into the Rover for a hospital visit—except for Argyle, who sat at the kitchen table drinking coffee with liberal dollops of whiskey—Don grabbed his plaid coat off the hook and noticed that the cellar door hung open by a couple of inches, revealing a wedge of musty darkness. He resented the chill that ran through him, reduced him to a cub scout shivering before the campfire, and slammed the door with his hip on the way out.

Everything turned out okay—Kurt claimed to have heeded the call of nature in the predawn hours, although he must've been inebriated because he couldn't put together what had happened to him after he ascended the stairs. Don, who'd spent ten minutes running around frantically searching for the car keys, until he stuck his hand in his pocket and found them, sympathized completely.

Don saw Michelle to the SeaTac airport on the Wednesday before Labor Day weekend. By his calculations he would be home alone with Thule and the mice for the better part of seven weeks. Luckily, his mornings and early afternoons were full with the panels and the seminars at the Museum, and though he inherently despised the insufferably dull nature of these activities, they provided a respite from his recent bouts of nerves, his spikes of nyctophobia and short-term memory loss.

Don's memory was faulty during normal operating hours, but his dreams were an entirely different matter. Though these dreams evaporated within a few minutes of waking, while in progress they unspooled in Technicolor with a grainy, yet vibrant and coherent inexorability that forced his mind's eye to rewind and play events from the ancient past.

On the night Michelle left for Turkey, Don drank some white wine that had languished in the cabinet for the gods only knew how long—the bottle label had peeled away. It was Kurt's tale of teenage terror, the gangly apparition at the department store that triggered Don's own dream, perhaps. Whatever the cause, he dropped like a stone into a deep slumber and his consciousness was whisked back to 1980.

CHAPTER FIVE

The Exhibit in the Mountain House

(1980)

1.

Don surfaced from a nightmare of drowning in the dark, and realized somebody had called his name from the far bank as he drifted the Yukon in his leaky old Zodiac raft.

He glanced around somewhat wildly—had he even heard another human voice? This was deep, dark wilderness, miles from the nearest native village, much less the summer cabins or suburbs of white men. He was also drunk off his ass. Seemed as if he'd been floating forever and anyway it was during the Luminous Period so all bets were off. Time was nebulous. Time glowed, trailed sparks.

He would not feel better on the return flight to Olympia. Looking down at the busted skulls of nameless ranges, his thoughts were lizard-thoughts. The DC-10 bucked and flexed while he peered through foggy glass at the interminable sweep of prehistoric America and pondered how it resembled the folds and cockles of a calcified brain. Black Hills Dakota was the legendary heart of the world. This, then, the utter north, could be the brain of the world. Forward arc of the Ring of Fire, Land of Ten Thousand Smokes.

For now, he flickered between the plane and the raft, future and present; between nursing a brandy over the black and white wasteland, and sprawling shit-faced at the bottom of a raft, gawking across the flat muddy expanse of river to a sheer bank and its fence of cottonwood trees.

The park service boys had warned him about restless natives back at Kyntak Landing. A Gold Rush mining outpost crumbled into a historical asterisk, Kyntak Landing was comprised of a Quonset hut, a handful of outbuildings and a radio tower in the foothills of the Brooks Range. Alaska had its share of these relics; graveyards of the Frontier spirit.

The rangers suggested in not too gentle terms Don was looking to get his head blown off. The veteran of the pair, the one who did the talking, said some of the locals held a grudge that went all the way back to the days of Seward. The man doubtless knew what he was talking about, he appeared at least a quarter native himself. He couldn't grasp what possessed anyone to raft from the Yukon headwaters 1200 miles to the Canadian border if not for hunting or shooting nature photographs.

Don didn't carry a rifle or a camera. Didn't have much more than traveling clothes and a Navy sea bag jammed with C rations, a case of Wild Turkey and a genuine leather flask of rye straight from his pal Argyle Arden's bathtub back in Olympia. He declined to mention the plastic baggie of peyote buttons tucked in his shirt pocket under the pack of Winston 100s. Another of Argyle's essential survival kit items. *Don, my lad, if you wanna vision quest, here's your ticket. As the kids said in our day, Happy trails, muthafuckah!* Neither did he inform them that he'd spent some months among the Yukon tribes, back when he was doing grad work, and knew a thing or two about the unpleasant side of Alaskan race relations firsthand.

Was he an experienced outdoorsman? He'd hiked canyons in New Mexico with a burro looking for copper veins; he'd gone camping in the Cascades a few weekends as a kid. He'd inherited several boxes of *Field and Stream* from his granddad. He knew how to use a John Wayne, so he figured his bases were covered.

Is it a dare, Mr. Miller? You out to prove something?

Don chuckled and promised them it wasn't a dare, wasn't a suicide ploy, nothing like that. Maybe a midlife crisis come five or six years early. He needed space, needed room to breathe, needed to sort some things out. A fellow couldn't ask for much more space than the interior of the Land of the Midnight Sun.

The rangers grimly dusted their tall hats and left him to his own devices, promised to send word to the family if and when he disappeared.

Actually, it was a dare, at least in part. He was here because he made a list once—the Twelve Labors. Granddad had commanded him to write down a dozen things he wanted to accomplish before he died. The *Do or Die List.* Granddad had been keen on that sort of thing, did the very same himself, only instead of screwing Debbie Harry and navigating the Yukon it was making love to Louise Brooks and climbing Mount Everest. Granddad had gone after thirty-plus years of twilight decline; then he got the twenty-one gun salute, Old Glory folded into a sandwich wedge and presented to his dry-eyed daughter, the obligatory sendoff in the Daily O.

So here Don floated, on a sabbatical from his job as a managing consultant at Pacific Geo, as it were, assuming one could take a break from doing basically nothing and go on vacation, getting piss-drunk and living out number twelve on a list of childish feats of derring-do that only grew exponentially fanciful should he happen to survive the current enterprise. Trying to impress a dead man when he didn't even believe in ghosts, trying to exorcise demons when God was the least of his manifold fears.

The first night out he beached on a gravel bar, made a bonfire from deadwood, and uncapped the Wild Turkey. He saved the good stuff, the genuine moonshine, for later. This was autumn in Alaska and the nights got bitter when the light finally gave up the ghost. He sat wrapped in an army blanket, slugging his booze and watching the stars burn coldly in the gulf.

His dreams were torments, full of fire and demons and reed music.

Next, there was a fuzzy period where he couldn't sleep, couldn't keep his eyelids fastened for more than a few seconds. Newtonian law was intermittently enforced, it faded in and out like a degrading radio signal. Euclidian geometry became elastic to say the least. He hallucinated natives in war bonnets stalking him from the bank. He hallucinated cottonwood logs were Nile crocs waiting for him to dip his grimy hand in the cold water. He hallucinated a spider dangled beneath the blurry white sun on a strand of razor wire. The wind whispered in an old baby's voice even when the air was still as lead. The wind's voice tickled and crooned in his bones, subsonic, subatomic. *The deepest cavern in the world is the human heart.*

The Luminous Period.

Luminous was *the* entertainment industry argot of the month, the watchword for that which was all style and no substance. Prose was luminous. Film was luminous. The river, grey as a quivering lung, was *luminous* grey. Don suspected his brain was grey too. He didn't know if it was luminous; sure as hell felt like it quivered with every throb of the pulse in his temple.

Alongside stark weather and mosquitoes, a man can expect bad dreams, nightmares perhaps. He knew there was a season for everything. He admitted himself as being foolhardy, but Mother hadn't whelped a fool, had she?

Certainly a man could expect bad dreams and even nightmares when he'd been swilling homemade rotgut hooch from a leather flask like the old boys in coonskin caps did it in the 1840s. A white man was letting himself in for danger floating down the Yukon River in a rubber raft, a leaky Zodiac; drinking dirty whiskey and sucking peyote buttons and it was no wonder he had dreams that weren't exactly bedtime stories. When they fractured at the point of consciousness he would be hurled from the saddle, rouse to the slosh of bilge water, the omnipresent nothingness that permeated the atmosphere like white static.

Problem was, as the trip progressed he couldn't always be certain when reality ended and dreams began, couldn't be certain at any given moment whether or not he'd crossed that thin black line. Couldn't stop drinking the firewater or eating the devil plants.

The motor dead as three o'clock and he wasn't particularly concerned. He was sliding toward the sea; King Arthur sans horns, hounds, or the epic pyre. He wasn't sure how to classify his condition. A midlife crisis? Too bad, so sad it hadn't manifested as a yen for a Jaguar and a fling with a nubile secretary half his age.

He didn't give a damn about fancy cars, or manly adventures, not even this one, really. As for nubile young women, well, as he'd muttered a time or two during his long marriage—*I didn't go blind when I put on the ring, baby!* That said, Michelle was the only woman for him. God knew, he could barely handle her. The idea of an affair was laughable, exhausting, depressing, and knowing Michelle as he did, scary.

She'd inhabited his dreams the past two nights. A younger version of herself from college days that truly wasn't much different on the surface from the woman of fifty. Michelle was possessed of an ageless charm reminiscent of great classical beauties such as Sophia Loren, Jacqueline Bisset, or Elizabeth Taylor. Her skin remained flawless and taut, her hair sleek and dark as the proverbial raven's wing. For her, age burned from the inside. Gazing into her eyes, there was no mistaking her for a naïve girl. He wasn't entirely sure that such a girl ever existed.

He'd met Michelle Mock in the spring of 1950. This was during their junior year at university. Don's classmate and best friend Custer Bane was pursuing a coed majoring in sculpture and she'd invited him to a show in the Ballard neighborhood; a house near the water, currently rented by a professor named Louis Plimpton, a man Don would come to know quite well. At that juncture, he was just another faceless instructor Don had heard speak once and estimated as dry as the chalk he scratched on the board. Custer explained that Professor Plimpton was a scientist, but had eclectic sensibilities when it came to art and culture. Scuttlebutt was the prof dipped his toe into all kinds of exotic sensations.

In any event, Custer needed a wingman, and so Don rode across town in the fellow's jalopy along with four other guys from school. Somebody passed around a bottle of vodka and the lot of them were toasted and singing bawdy roadhouse ditties when they piled from the car and descended on the wine and cheese event.

Don remembered the clapboard house being dark as a pit, illuminated by candles and a couple of paper lamps tinted red like a boardwalk brothel. Many of the windows were blocked with plywood; stars glinted through a hole in the roof. There was a cold hearth, some rickety furniture, and a natty couple entwined on the couch. A man in a dinner jacket slouched in a doorway. A glass of absinthe dangled from his left hand. He grinned and patted Don's cheek, pointed him toward the bead curtain and a claustrophobia-inducing stairwell that led to the *real* party.

The basement was a labyrinth of subdivided cubbyholes and closets, exposed pipes and chipped cement; cobwebs and dust and lots of shadows, and an overwhelming smell of mildew. The guests, a mix of college kids and their off-campus pals and some creepy-types that gravitated to such spectacles, had gathered in a long, skinny L-shaped section to admire a handful of wax sculptures and oil and charcoal paintings that resembled lousy Picasso imitations. A flautist sat cross-legged on a mat and played. The air was heavy with smoke from the candles and cigarettes.

Professor Plimpton stood at the heart of the gathering next to a display of rusted bedsprings, wax drippings, and copper tubing with his arms clasped behind his back. A short, wiry man in a blue suit. He kept his gray hair tied in a pony tail. He ignored the trio of undergraduate supplicants arrayed before him and nodded at Don. His smile was quick and sharp; much sharper than the softness of his features or voice would indicate. "Young master Miller. Glad you could tear yourself away from the quarry."

Don was exactly buzzed enough to second-guess his own recollection—they hadn't met, had they? He grinned noncommittally at the professor and waved the way a man does from a speeding car, or from the deck of a boat to acquaintances on the shore.

"We meet again," a beautiful girl in a mohair sweater said to Don, her breasts flattened against his shoulder as she leaned in to fix him with her dark, dark eyes. Those eyes belonged to a much older, more worldly soul than fresh-faced Michelle Mock, however precocious she might've been in stodgy 1950.

A magical moment, in a black way. It was as if they'd known each other forever. Don was neck deep in trouble before he even opened his mouth to stammer his name. She smiled and held his hand and said she already knew, they'd taken a philosophy class together. He didn't believe it—surely he'd remember sitting in a room with this gorgeous woman, and she grinned in a sexy, feral manner and said maybe she'd worn glasses and a sweater.

"I blend in when I want to," she said. "I'm the hidden figure in the grotesque of a tapestry. Look closely and I'm the one sitting in the background under a tree, naked, drinking from a horn."

He still didn't believe it. A sweater and schoolmarm glasses wouldn't do much to obscure her erotic lushness. He nodded and went along with it, determined to get the real story at a more opportune time; say after she'd had a few drinks. This never occurred.

Three dates later they were in her apartment experimenting with Tantric sex, and a month after that they got engaged and eventually eloped for a civil ceremony in Eastern Washington. Professor Plimpton got wind of the news and wired Michelle, his favorite student, some cash, and directions to his farmhouse in Wenatchee so the couple had a honeymoon retreat. There were hills and trails for romantic hikes, a clear, cold lake, vineyards…

Amidst the confusion and excitement, it completely slipped Don's mind that he meant to ask his bride to confess where and when she'd actually seen him before.

2.

Don had achieved quasi-sobriety when he bumped into the rotting docks of Ruby, an Athabascan village that had sunk deep into a curve of the mighty river. Fish wheels languidly churned the water, although the kings had long-since spawned; now the machines dredged for pinks and whitefish; dented Smokercraft skiffs bobbed at the end of slimy tethers and the air was ripe with cottonwood smoke and the stringent musk of curing chum salmon. The only modern buildings were the school and the armory—all else dated to the 1930s or further back in the dim prehistory of territorial conquest. Satellite dishes perched atop shingle roofs, incongruous and alien as deep sea flora.

People parted like smoke when he limped up the sodden dirt path of the cutback. The villagers observed him with flat-eyed stoicism he recalled too well from previous visits. They would, according to his experience of their traditions, suspect he was a demon, or demon-inhabited. Considering the volume of alcohol saturating his liver, that ancient gateway of spirits, of course they were at least somewhat correct. His skull whispered, whispered in the tongues of burning leaves, the corrosive drone of carcinogens metastasizing to membrane. The world enveloped him in shades of jaundice and bruises.

He paid ten dollars to borrow the radio phone in the post office and check his messages. He imagined he cut a melodramatic figure, leaning into the low, rude wall with its scaly-yellow flyers and disjointed wanted-posters from faraway lands, receiver tucked in the crook of his neck and ear, a mostly-drained bottle of brown liquor clutched in his free hand.

Michelle crackled on the line, or, her day-old echo, melancholy and wan. She said, *—Lou's dead—come home.*

3.

Michelle awaited him at the Olympia house, freshly returned from her latest expedition to the Congo, burnt to a crisp and with new lines around her eyes and mouth. If anything, she appeared tougher and more hard-bitten than Don did after his odyssey of self-destruction on the Yukon. They made love with passion sufficient to leave marks. Then, they fought for two days, and it was time for the funeral of a man Don scarcely knew despite the scientist's presence in Michelle's life for more than thirty years.

Louis Plimpton had passed away at a rented farmhouse near Wenatchee, Washington, but the Plimpton family plot was in nearby Levitte Cemetery where Tumwater and Olympia overlapped.

Don finally dragged Michelle out the door twenty minutes before the service began and he had to drive like hell to make the opening ceremonies, which included a blustery oration delivered by the Dean of Columbia who'd been flown in thanks to the largesse of Barry Rourke; the eulogy, delivered by Lou's surviving brother, Terrance—a hoary octogenarian stricken with Parkinson's; and the requisite bagpipe dirge courtesy of a quartet of ruddy Scots from the VFW hall. Lou had never set foot within a hundred yards of a recruiting office, much less gotten shipped overseas to pump old-fashioned American lead into the enemies of the Republic, but nobody seemed to notice the discrepancy.

The pavilion was reserved for family and close friends, colleagues and associates, and there weren't many folding seats. Don and Michelle stood in the rear, fanning themselves with programs in the sweltering heat. Don had hastily shaved and doused himself with cologne, dusted off his funeral suit, a Windsor tie, the nice shoes and everything.

He was fanning himself with his hat when he noticed two men in off-the-rack suits staring at him and Michelle. Both wore dark glasses and serious expressions; one had an impressive mustache. The men loitered on the periphery, making no secret of their presence as outsiders, interlopers.

Michelle was oblivious to them, busy as she was wiping her eyes and blowing her nose into a hanky. Don decided not to point them out and after a few minutes they climbed into a black car and drove away.

When it was a wrap, he and Michelle shook hands with a few people who noticed them lurking, and afterward, beelined for the parking lot and had nearly made their escape when Paul Wolverton intercepted them behind the street-side hedge and attempted to extract a promise to appear at a special reception in one week's time for a round of *do you remember when's*, and *for he's a jolly good fellow*, and to pay obeisance to the Widow Plimpton, a self-made royal. Paul Wolverton, middle son of the famed playboy Marcus Wolverton, was taller than Don, and only a few years junior, although he was what Mama Miller would've called "well-preserved", and unlike the oft-accepted characterization of bankers as porcine, Wolverton was gaunt and urbanely boisterous, if stereotypically fashionable in his double-breasted suits. Don promised to consider attending the reception.

4.

Once they were alone in the car, Michelle responded to Wolverton's invitation with a rather pronounced lack of equanimity, exclaiming, "Oh, sweet baby Jesus, Paul's cousin Connor Wolverton was Lou's benefactor. There's a museum in that house. It's incredible. We're going!" She explained that Connor Wolverton was sort of a northwest Howard Hughes who made like a hermit in rural eastern Washington on a huge estate. The man was rabidly passionate regarding the sciences, collecting everything from pottery to the bones of obscure war leaders and unusual animals. While not formally trained or inclined, Connor Wolverton did what rich, obsessed patrons were best at—contributed enormous sums to various foundations and projects. Michelle, via her longstanding association with Doc Plimpton, had benefited magnificently from that largesse.

"But, um, my sweet, that's in Spokane," Don tried.

"Ho, ho, nowhere so civilized. It's at least sixty miles south of the city. Nowhere near an airport, either. Completely in the sticks."

"By car? Egad, sweetheart."

"Six-hour drive, tops."

"More like ten on those roads and with someone behind the wheel who doesn't have a death wish."

It went like that all the way back to the farm. Upon arriving at the house, Michelle tabled the discussion and made a few phone inquiries before engaging Don for round two.

She said, "Naomi and Paul are hosting. She's doing all the legwork. They're tight with the Wolvertons."

"Our vacation…relaxing, screwdrivers on the veranda, screwing…"

"Don't be unseemly. Show proper respect to our dead colleague."

"Whom we've spoken to half a dozen times since the Moon Landing."

"Wrongo. I corresponded with Lou plenty. Our interests coincided. Who do you think put me in touch with Toshi and Campbell? Why do you suppose they agreed to help me secure funding, charts, maps? Hells bells, Howard lent me his data for the Pyrenees expedition."

"Oh, right—the tour of exotic whorehouses and Plimpton family reunions. Honestly, hon, I just figured you flashed your lovely gams and those lecherous swine fell all over themselves securing the dough." He was no fan of Ryoko or Campbell, a pair of crackpot scientists who'd kept tinfoil manufacturers busy for the better part of a decade. He suspected it was their ilk who'd infected Michelle with the whole Hollow Earth delusion, and later that duo fostered and fed it with praise and monetary support. He'd met them way back when during a visit to Bangkok. Vainglorious frauds who'd made a fortune by peddling quack science to the gullible public. The evening was a disaster. Don lost his temper and engaged in fisticuffs with someone, though as usual the details slipped away.

In any event, somehow the fools hadn't managed to torpedo Michelle's career as he'd seen befall other, less fortunate researchers caught in their draft.

Michelle closed the book on the debate. "We are going."

She was correct, as ever. So correct, in fact, that she'd prevailed upon Argyle Arden to emerge from his badger burrow, otherwise known as the Arden House, and to join them for the excursion. Argyle declined the offer to hitch a ride, preferring to be driven by his own dashing chauffeur in a Rolls Royce.

"Argyle's coming?" Don had said, annoyed as if his friend had betrayed him, albeit unwittingly. On second thought, Argyle was hardly unwitting and he unerringly took Michelle's side in political matters.

"He's certainly breathing hard," she'd said and pecked his cheek.

The following week, husband and wife cruised through Seattle and out into rugged country toward the Cascades in a sedan Don had borrowed from an intern at Evergreen who was a little sweet on him and would be for maybe another semester before she too whiffed the scent of unshakable loyalty to his often absent wife of thirty years.

The thermometer at the rustic gas station where they serviced the car read 99 in the stifling shade of the awning. This was late August and rain hadn't fallen for the better part of two weeks. Don bought fuel and a six-pack of Coke and an ice cream bar, and rambled on, rambled on. Michelle licked the ice cream bar, hoarding it with mischievously selfish pleasure.

She went down on Don after he took the East Valley exit off I-5 and rolled through terrain that alternated between fields and hills verging on low mountains. He nearly crashed the sedan in surprise at his pants buttons being expertly undone and her red lips closing on his manhood. Her tongue was hot beneath a veneer of ice cream chill as it circled and pressed. He glanced at the speedometer and noticed the needle had jumped to the 70 mark.

"Well, all right," he said. "I concede: this *is* a wonderful plan. You are right as always, my dove. Let's pray I can keep us pointed between the ditches…"

She chuckled and nipped him. Then she sat up and smoothed her hair and casually reapplied her lipstick in the side mirror. Her hair whipping about her tanned cheeks lent her an aspect of unearthliness, a beautiful, ambivalent creature, half woman, half goddess of the brambles, with the requisite affection and cruelty of both halves.

"Hey, uh…I was joking," he said, gloomily trying to figure out how a man went about buttoning his pants with one hand while sporting a considerable erection.

"Better safe than wrapped around a tree," she said, and smiled.

"Really. I think it's proper to finish what you start."

"Don't be such a tough guy."

"You love it."

"I love you. I also know a few tough guys. *Real* hard cases. Don't tread in those waters—you'll catch cold, dear."

He sighed and she smiled a secret smile and tuned the radio to a blues station. The country road wound before them, often narrow and unpaved, margined by wild forest and marsh and creeks, and occasionally a house or a farm. Golden fantail dust rose in their wake and drifted toward an enamel-blue sky. Late afternoon came down upon the land and occasionally, he slowed to avoid a cow or a string of goats wandering the road. The beasts sought the deep blue shade of overhanging willow limbs. She rolled the window down and trailed her bronzed arm against the rushing wind.

Even though the nest was empty going on five years, Don felt a pang whenever he glanced in the rearview at a blank seat and no children pulling one another's hair, or causing him to pull the last of his own in exasperation at incessant yammering questions, or the interminable monotone naming of things kids were wont to undertake.

He swerved around a black Labrador and hoped all concerned were having a swell time traveling on his dime. Kurt in Cape Cod with a gaggle of affluent chums he'd met in college, Holly abroad in Europe with a girl named Carrie. Backpacks and a stack of travelers checks and mommy's bank number were all the ladies needed—Holly had promised to drop a postcard in the mail when they hit Rome.

He smiled with fondness and melancholy. None of this felt right. The family shouldn't be scattered to the wind, yet there it was.

Dinner was a leisurely affair at the quaintly named Satan's Bung tavern in Ransom Hollow, a venerable chain of valley settlements and home to several of Michelle's ancestors on the Mock side. Allegedly cousins of the Mocks (she couldn't recall the family name) had settled hereabouts before the Gold Rush and founded a lodge; the family had owned half the valley during their heyday.

The couple knocked back a few rounds and devoured exquisite venison steaks and held hands while the Blackwood Boys, a highly polished local jug band, play several sets. Matters came to a head when, as the entire taproom crowd was clogging in unison to a drawn-out fiddle solo, Michelle drained her glass of whiskey (it was whiskey, beer or water at Satan's Bung) and leaped atop the table and danced a jig she'd learned in a similar backwater village in Ireland. The men hooted and cheered and Don laughed and covered his eyes as she swished her leopard stole under his nose. Michelle had bagged the cat herself with one clean shot from a borrowed Winchester. She was no Jane Goodall, that was for sure. Were a seal hunter to toss her a club, Don suspected she'd cheerfully march for the beach.

A logger with a furry beard punched a beardless logger who wore a plaid coat and in short order bottles were flying and teeth as well. The jug band upped the tempo and the lead man yowled a tune about a bad person named Black Bill coming into the hollow to rape the goats and carry off the women-folk. A fire started near the bar and Michelle and Don took the opportunity to split.

All in all, Don thought as he revved the motor and burned rubber out of the parking lot, a typical evening abroad with his dear wife. He didn't allow himself to contemplate the trouble she got into when wasn't around to whisk her away.

5.

He took a wrong turn and they lost two hours before stopping at a mill and getting directions from the fellow who was locking the place down. Don shouldered the blame with as much self-deprecatory grace as he could muster. Michelle kissed his cheek and said nothing. At times during their journey she was entirely present and focused on him with the heated intensity he recalled from their courtship in school; at other moments she drifted miles away and was hardly with him in the car.

Bumpy blacktop road unwound before their headlights. A lonely night in the mountains; moonless, starless. The heat had dissipated with sunset. Mist rolled across the fields and through the trees and boiled in the ditches and conjured images of cloaked highwaymen and wolves howling on Scottish moors.

Don switched off the radio and pushed in the knob of the dashboard lighter. He stuck a Gauloises cigarette into the corner of his mouth while he waited. He'd tried to quit since Sputnik with intermittent success. Recently, Michelle had brought home a knapsack of brunes direct from Paris. "It's dark-dark," he said. "Anything could be out there on a night like this."

"What? Why do you say that?" Michelle pulled the collar of her jacket tighter. "Good lord, it was roasting an hour ago. Now it's practically winter."

"We're getting pretty high."

"How I wish. I wasn't going to tell you. But..." She rummaged in the glove box and came forth with a baggie. She expertly rolled a joint and had herself a toke. "Don't you touch that window and whisk away my lovely fumes, Donald Miller, or I'll break your fucking arm."

He sighed and released the handle as blue exhaust clouds swam before his eyes.

She said in a deep, rasping tone, "Good kitty."

"Excuse me?"

"What do you mean 'anything can happen'?"

"Just look. Might as well be in the Dark Ages, baby—"

"Don't call me baby, baby."

"Okay. Here we are in the countryside at night in the middle of even Daniel-Boone-wouldn't-know-the-hell-where. Peasants locked in their cottages, windows shuttered. That's how we lived for centuries. Huddled around fires, listening to the howls from the wilderness."

"Take a ride with me into the non Anglo-world one of these days. Business as usual for a lot of folks."

"Kinda my point. Baby. The night hasn't changed. It's the same as it was a hundred years ago. A thousand." He didn't enjoy how the headlights seemed dim and yellow against the dark and the fog. The dashboard panel flickered ominously. It was a quarter past eleven. The lighter popped and he pressed its glowing coil to the tip of his cigarette. Despite, or because of, the pleasant fuzzy aftertaste of whiskey in his mouth, he wanted a drink; a single malt scotch, cooking sherry, shoe polish, anything. Nerves did that to him—excited his desire for booze and smokes. "How'd the Wolvertons get so rich? How come Paul and Naomi don't brag about this relative?"

"They aren't braggarts, dear. It's the kind of clan where having a job as a banker is hopelessly plebian. Wolvertons aren't supposed to work, they're supposed to lounge around and admire their statuary. The original fortune was made by the family industrialists. Big wheels during the late nineteenth century. This was their bolt hole from civilization."

"Railroads? Bombs? A zeppelin manufacturing company?"

"Rivets and doorknobs. The family died out, mostly. There's only a couple of them left. The guy who owns the property is one. He doesn't do anything. Lives in South America, or something. Rents the mansion out for tours and special events. They shot a movie on the estate last year. *Beyond the Valley of the Dolls* rip-off." Michelle coughed and waved her hand to clear the air. "Aww, damn. That's enough of that. Go ahead, and get some air in here."

"You promise not to hurt me?"

"Never mind. You bruise easily. Just drive." She lighted a cigarette and cracked her window. The wind whistled eerily. "Ha! Funny you should mention it, but yeah, they made parts for zeppelins too. On the side."

"No kidding?"

"I think it was a short-lived venture. I didn't do much research on that angle."

Don tapped the wheel and frowned. "I read something about that house. Damn it…a bunch of murders."

"The place has a bloody history. One of the Wolvertons got pissed outta his gourd and shotgunned the gardener back in the 1920s. There was a jealous mistress and a hatchet murder around World War Two—"

"This was more recent. The past couple of decades for sure. And a high body count."

"You're thinking of that bloodbath in Amityville. Guy slaughtered his family in that big old house."

"I'm not feeble, woman. Recent, but not last year."

"Huh. It's possible, I suppose. After what I've seen I wouldn't be surprised if there was a Lizzie Borden style massacre on the Wolverton property at some point."

"Oh. It sounds lovely. That black book got anything about a kitten torturing festival? We could hit that next. "

Her eyes were large and dark. She placed her hand on his thigh.

They emerged into a stretch of field in a massive, glacier-dug valley. With the fog and darkness pressing against the windows, it felt little different than the previous tunnels of forest. A moment later the road curved and they were in the firs again. Don resisted the urge to press harder on the pedal. Already the car floated as if unmoored from the pavement. If a deer jumped into his path, he'd never have time to brake.

He said, "My dad hit a deer with our truck once. I was a tyke. I hate driving in this weather."

"Want me to take over for a while?"

Don remembered how erratically his wife drove, and shuddered. "No, no. That wasn't a hint. Just thinking aloud."

Their weekend tour of the Wolverton estate might be the very thing to kick-start his ambition, galvanize a final push to completing the cursed book.

Don glanced sidelong at his wife, taking in her "civilization camouflage" as she called it: bouffant hair and hoop earrings, lots of eye shadow, a slinky dress, heels, all a far cry from the pith helmet, mosquito netting, pants and hiking boots that often comprised her field attire. A strong, lean woman, Michelle appeared much as she had during college. She wore the same yellow-tinted starlet glasses day or night, the same indistinct perfume from the same unlabeled bottle.

She said, "There should be an intersection in a mile or so. Go right. It's about fifteen miles after that—the place is above the snow line. Too bad we got such a late start. Damned thing is mostly over by now. There was a fancy dinner and a slide show."

"A slide show!" He chose not to remind her that the reception was to be spread over the entire weekend. Very likely the mind-numbing biopic of Plimpton and his life poking and prodding surly country folk to get access to their burial grounds was yet to come. At least there'd be a boatload of free booze to dull the pain.

"Hmm, yes… So I'm mistaken that your eyes glaze when I show mine to my friends from the institute?"

"I'm a victim of bad lighting. Not to mention a bit glassy-eyed by nature."

The intersection was a T illuminated by a blinking amber caution light that seemed a forlorn reminder of civilization here among miles of peaks and evergreen forests. Don turned right and continued along a steadily ascending grade. Except for his impulsive adventure on the Yukon he hadn't strayed far from the suburbs for what had it been? Five, maybe six years? So, not only had he lapsed into the role of prune-dry fuddy-duddy with the sense of adventure God gave a stick, he'd slipped into a sedentary routine like a foot into a comfortable old boot. Gods, the crow's feet around his eyes and the softness of his belly weren't just cosmetic; atrophy was spreading throughout the entire mechanism. Dashing Don the Caver out to pasture with nary a whinny of protest. This gloomy realization heightened the sense of mystery and danger plaguing him since Michelle plucked that skinny black book off the tourist shop rack.

Despite that warning in the back of his skull, he did as he'd become accustomed and followed Michelle's marching orders, cliffs be damned.

6.

And he laughed ruefully a few minutes later to see that the Wolverton Mansion indeed perched upon a cliff. The cliff overlooked a swath of forest and the rocky sandbars of a shallow river. The house was a truly palatial cabin hewn from massive timber, huge as the wood and rock castle of a Viking lord. Don recognized it instantly from his recollection of at least a half dozen exterior shots in low budget films, although its majesty deserved the cinematographic genius of an artist such as Bergman.

He was surprised to see a handful of smartly dressed guests standing around the colonnaded porch, drinks in hand, sweaters drawn up to their chins. The double doors were open and warm light from a chandelier illuminated their faces, rendered their figures soft around the edges in a bloom effect.

A valet trotted over and took the keys. The young man pulled the car down a side drive and disappeared into well-groomed ranks of hedges. Don breathed in the bitter pre-dawn air. Michelle winked at him and moved toward the congregation. Their footsteps crunched on the gravel and Don had a vision of a carpet of dried yellow finger bones snapping beneath his shoes.

Michelle introduced him to a man in a turtleneck—Connor Wolverton himself. He was a few years younger than Paul with a full head of black hair, the crow's feet just beginning to set in around his eyes. He smelled of good whiskey and fir needles and his entire demeanor was that of Christopher Lee welcoming victims to his castle. Don hated guys in turtlenecks. Guys in turtlenecks reminded him of the ivy tower princelings who'd lorded it over their domains during college years. Middle-age had tenderized him in many ways, but it hadn't dampened his fire-hot antipathy for preppie assholes.

Connor said, "Ah, you made it! Paul was getting worried. These roads are hell at night. One of my boys will come around to escort you to your rooms. Meanwhile, permit me to show you a much more important feature of Wolverton Mansion." He led the way through a foyer with a ceiling that vaulted to imposing heights and into a drawing room. He left them at the bar with a bartender in a white tuxedo. Michelle handed Don a Canadian Club and clinked glasses hard and the liquor splashed onto his fingers.

Standing there near the bar, slightly apart from his wife, Don watched guests trickle in to refresh their drinks. He inclined his head toward Michelle and said, "How many guests are there anyway?"

She sidled closer and hooked her arm with his. "I don't know the roster. Not many. Twenty, twenty-five. It's an exclusive club."

"Damn, what am I doing here?"

"Hanging onto my coattails. And Argyle's. Speaking of the devil, he doth appear. Argyle, my dear!" She extricated herself with the efficiency of a serpent and intercepted Argyle Arden as he entered the parlor, shining like a subdued star in his cream-colored suit and golden nose cone. They kissed and Argyle introduced his chauffeur, a brawny lad with short black hair and eyes perhaps a scooch too close together. Don thought all of Argyle's young, strapping companions were "sorts" as opposed to real people, and they blurred into a composite of beautiful and sullenly aggressive American masculinity. Winter would bring a new class and a new companion for the white-haired aristocrat.

This new fellow, Mickey Monroe, as Don soon learned, was working his way through graduate school at Saint Martin's. "Mick's going to be a librarian when he grows up," Argyle said in his thunderous voice as the second round of introductions were made. "Almost as boring as licking stamps or sorting rocks, hey, Donald?"

"Stamp-lickers and frog dissectors and sorters of index cards have me beat by a country mile," Don said with a broad smile. "Luckily, I've lost the craving for traipsing about bogs and falling down mineshafts."

"He isn't kidding," Michelle said. "Except, it's worse. Can't get him to budge from the sofa without a red hot poker to the ass."

"Oho! Is that how you chivvied him along this arduous wagon trail?"

Michelle grinned at Don. "Honey, bend over and show Uncle Argyle the handle."

"To the moon," Don said, making a loose fist, but the others had already turned from him, Michelle quickly changing the subject to her most harrowing and infamous hike through a stretch of jungle ruled by headhunters and jaguars. The expedition had been organized by several foundations and included photographers, journalists, guides, and a small army of porters. The expedition leader, a Russian anthropologist named Boris Kalamov, had made his bones unearthing Aztec temples and other ruins and he'd claimed to possess documents legitimizing legends of a city in the heart of the Congo. The team never located Ophir, but three porters were dragged away by leopards or jaguars, two knifed each other in a dispute, and everybody down to the pack mules contracted dysentery and almost died.

No great success story for Kalamov or his backers. On the other hand, Michelle landed on her feet as usual and documented a connection between the local headhunters (some of whom actually came down from the hills for a friendly campfire chat) and two other large and modernized tribes dwelling thousands of miles away. The connection was tenuous and compilation and collation of data remained for the drones who performed such labor, and given the glacial pace of such work it would be years before she received any real recognition; nonetheless, here in the latter half of her highly decorated tenure, she continued to produce the goods, so to speak.

A third book was doubtless in the works, if only she'd relent on her most recent passion—the Mock genealogical survey—long enough to get the manuscript typed. Or her clothes changed and hair washed. Her elegant and admittedly sexy coiffure for the Wolverton shindig notwithstanding, Michelle was the picture of a crazed Macbethian crone when she emerged from lengthy stays in the den in the Olympia farmhouse, her hair in disarray, her dark eyes wild with chaos and malignant rapture, fingers cracked and ink-stained from pen and quill. Sometimes she wrapped herself in a filthy, tattered robe, sometimes not, and skulked through the kitchen and pantry in the small hours of morning, foraging like any wild animal.

Don missed his children. He also thanked the gods that they weren't often around to test their mother's patience these past several years. Kurt especially might've suffered a grievous injury.

Leaving his wife, Argyle and friend to their devices, he went into the parlor where many of the guests had gathered chatting quietly, then ducked out again, following strains of chamber music. Don floated in a decaying orbit of that murmuring magnetic cloud, content to exile himself to an antechamber populated by a handful of disaffected partisans and bastard princes. Don was no stranger to many of them. His presence provoked a visible ripple of unease. Many had known him off and on since his youth and noted a dramatic change in his demeanor over the last few years. He'd become tougher and more reckless, his humor sardonic.

None of the dandies, playboys or pampered dilettantes that comprised this particular subset of the elite strata could be completely certain where he roosted in the pecking order. It was quietly acknowledged that while being a lowly middle-class lout, he possessed entirely too many connections to be dismissed outright. They settled for exchanging brittle smiles and hollow pleasantries and watching from the corners of their eyes for signs of weakness. Then, because Plimpton's influence had extended to the academic spheres, a motley collection of professors, administrators and civil engineers mixed freely among the nobility, albeit with gawky discomfort. This latter consortium were guzzling champagne and wolfing down the smoked salmon and cheese with fanatical zeal and surreptitiously (or not) ogling the décolletages of simpering trophy wives.

Don had ignored the ritual for years, grown a thick skin, cultivated a wary obliviousness. He frequently swiped drinks from the trays of circulating waiters, which made the proceedings a touch more palatable, and shortly the crowd resembled clockwork automatons bunched in awkward groves, smacking glasses of Glenlivet and blurting cynical apothegms by rote as their glittery, lifeless eyes rolled about like ball bearings.

"Mr. Miller—" Don caught that snippet as a sort of cocktail party effect. He glimpsed a swarthy fellow with a bushy mustache, a Latin Tom Selleck, raise his hand in a drowning gesture. He struck Don as familiar somehow...

The dark man was body-blocked by a cataclysmically stoned surveyor from the Army Corps of Engineers, then Paul's wife, Naomi Wolverton, sailed into the room, regal as Queen Victoria in her austere mourning dress and elegantly somber mien, lacking only tiara and scepter to complete the image. She waved to Don as he endured the verbal crossfire of a man in a bad tweed jacket, a history professor by the look of him, and from across the state line, Melvin Redfield the prodigal poet and heir apparent of the Pierce County Redfields, who owned enough of said county to convert it to a duchy were they so inclined. Melvin was a one-time high school baseball captain, fulltime wastrel, and prematurely gray. He'd always been shrill and his voice was in fine form after a snootful of Hennessy.

"My lord, Don, are you okay?" Naomi wrinkled her nose in mock horror at the sight of him shambling her direction.

Don casually shouldered aside a journalist from the *Spokane Star* and the journalist's date, a leggy blonde who dressed as if she'd come fully accessorized from one of the local escort services, and kissed Naomi Wolverton's gloved hand—it smelled of lilacs. His lips were rubber-numb and it was like nuzzling a piece of wood. He winked. "I've been abroad. Does it show?"

Naomi drew him aside, put a towering rubber plant between them and the bickering duo and assorted gawkers. "Paul was hoping you meant it when you said you'd come by. My bet was Michelle hopping a ride with a motorcycle gang and leaving you at the ranch with the cat and the tumbleweeds."

"It's a farm. Lots of weeds, true." He glanced around for Lou's ex-wife. "Cory—is she—"

"Oh yes, over there." Naomi frowned in the direction of the parlor where Corinthia Plimpton held court, flashes of sequins and crimson through the sea of black suits. "The bitch brought a date to her husband's funeral. Some sleazy producer. Can't go without a man for ten seconds, can she?" When she was angry her lips made a ruby slash, her cheeks paled.

There was no safe answer to that one, so he changed the subject with cumbersome gallantry. "I wouldn't have figured Lou to draw this big a crowd at his going-away party." Don tossed down the dregs of his bourbon, craned his neck to catch a glimpse of Corinthia's companion, the sleazy producer; a short, pasty guy in a charcoal suit, wraparound shades and a fistful of rings that twinkled in the dull chandelier blaze. All kinds of teeth. He was apparently in his element.

"He didn't. The crowd is for *her*, obviously." Which precisely mirrored Michelle's sentiments regarding the funeral gala, except his lovely wife had deployed exceedingly colorful language to enhance her opinion.

There was no love lost between Naomi, Michelle and Corinthia and that simmering resentment went way back to some prep school feud, an aborted teen romance—the women had suffered crushes on Melvin Redfield's elder brother, Kyle, who, according to all reports, was cut of a different cloth than his dilettante sibling, had made lieutenant in the Navy, gone into the family law business. Too bad Kyle clipped a power line while cruising around the Hanford Nuclear Reservation in Luke Whitman's ultra-lite. The Whitmans were still smarting from that public relations disaster.

Naomi kissed his cheek and departed, swept up by a passing throng of Fortune Five Hundred types. Don grabbed another drink and pressed through the bodies and possibly someone called his name again, that celebrated phenomenon of biological acoustics. He kept pushing until he'd gone past the French doors onto the veranda where all was cool and subdued. The chairs glimmered rain-slick, so he leaned against the railing, bourbon in hand, and toyed with the notion of lighting his second cigarette of the season and dooming himself to yet another failure of character. Instead, he regarded the gathering darkness while his blood pressure descended and his nerves steadied.

Finally, he noticed a boy sitting in the opposite corner on a fancy iron bench. Bronson Ford, a preadolescent Ethiopian boy the Rourkes (who'd lost their first child under mysterious circumstances) had adopted the previous summer. Somebody, probably Kirsten Rourke, had dressed the kid to the nines in a Little Lord Fauntleroy getup complete with spats and a soft cap.

"Jesus," Don said and gulped his triple Jim Beam in commiseration.

Bronson Ford stoically rolled a cigarette, lighted it and smoked. His eyes floated oily and diabolic in the cherry glow. His skin shone like petrified mangrove. Don realized the boy was one of those who seemed ageless, a glider in the twilight between youth and maturity and the only clues were the lines on his brow, his cold eyes and the pockmarks of an impoverished ancestry.

Don wrinkled his nose at the pungent odor of marijuana, was touched by dizziness. He sneaked a few more glances at the boy before he mustered the courage to commit the egregious inanity, "Some party, huh?"

Bronson Ford exhaled and smirked knowingly. Amber light from the windows splashed his face as if it were the black oval of a projector screen. Don shivered and his glass was empty. He considered assaying the maelstrom inside.

"Mr. Miller!" The swarthy man with the heroic mustache emerged from the house. A second man, much taller and leaner, followed. Both men wore serviceable suits; nothing shabby, although hardly on par with the heavyweights, yet a cut above the professors and assorted engineering types.

Don had dealt with enough governmental agencies to recognize the handmaidens of the bureaucracy when they appeared; devils sans the requisite puff of smoke. "Well, well," he said. "You two were at the funeral. The lurkers."

The swarthy one made the introductions. "Vaughn Claxton. You remember my colleague Maurice Dart. Nice to see you again. We'd hoped to chat." Not, *So sorry, old chap, about your mate what offed himself*, or, *Condolences, my friend, sorry for your loss*. Instead, *We hoped to chat.*

See him again? Chat? Don automatically disliked the sound of it, whatever it meant. The duo smelled of airport aftershave and Mr. Claxton smiled fiercely as they shook hands. Mr. Dart didn't smile at all. His face hung oblong as a waterlogged piñata and was utterly melancholy. Mr. Claxton nodded at Bronson Ford. "Hiya, kiddo. California Gold? Nope, too dark—no offense. Colombian, then. Make with the bud, eh?" There was no warmth in the greeting, only a queer, pseudo familiarity, the implication of accustomed authority lent by official credentials and jackboots.

Bronson Ford expressionlessly took another long hit. He slowly held forth the joint in his left hand and Mr. Claxton strode over and took it and squinted as he dragged. He coughed and his cheeks darkened. He handed the joint to Mr. Dart and Mr. Dart drew in the smoke, held it expertly in the manner of a blooded veteran, before exhaling. His expression was a pallid, moony reflection of Bronson Ford's. The tall man offered the rapidly dwindling joint to Don.

"Um, thanks anyway," Don said, edging from their tribal campfire circle toward the doorway, from which spilled light and the tidal roar of tipsy conversation. Civilization and its protections seemed suddenly remote. Three pairs of eyes focused upon him and Mr. Claxton frowned ominously.

"It's easier than slicing our palms, trust me," Mr. Dart said.

Don said, "Okay, sure. One can't hurt." He accepted the joint and inhaled clumsily; it had been ages since his days of rebellious toking behind the bleachers at school and later in the dorms at college. The rush almost knocked him over. He tried to speak and ended up hacking and retching. Claxton smiled benignly, as if to acknowledge that all was well, that they had forged a brotherly compact and now secrets could be safely exchanged, and retrieved the joint.

No one spoke for a minute or two, or fifteen, Don wasn't certain because time had become rather elastic and he was dizzy. He gripped the rail for dear life and peered at the black masses of tree tops on the hillside below the house and wondered about the songbirds in their secret nests, the scrabbling mice, the silently gliding owls. The stars jumped. He could not remember the best grass ever having such a visceral effect upon his senses. Kent Pepper had confided that the native strains were getting stronger with each new crop.

Bronson Ford rose quickly and scuttled back inside and the men watched him depart.

"I'm Sicilian with a Welsh influence," Mr. Claxton said, his voice booming like a god speaking from the clouds. "Tom Jones meets the *Cosa Nostra*. You were staring."

"The Sicilian for cruelty and ruthlessness, the Welsh for his charm," Mr. Dart said. "You should hear him in the shower. Lawrence Welk more than Tom Jones, I'd say. Vunnerful, vunnerful."

Mr. Claxton said, "You work for AstraCorp."

"I'm a consultant," Don said.

"A long-term consultant."

"Eh, the projects last as what they last...Say, what is it you fellows do?"

"We've got government jobs. Great dental." Mr. Claxton showed his teeth. "Yeah, AstraCorp. Man, the Rourkes sorta own that baby. Don—

may I call you Don?—you're working on a job on the Peninsula. Lot number, oops, lost it. Slango Camp it's called. Timber company logged the shit out of those mountains during the 1920s. Now it's being prepped for some new development, yeah?"

Don nodded warily. "Sure, that's public knowledge, I guess." He didn't volunteer the fact AstraCorp was conducting its portion of an environmental impact study for some energy development company in California. Don hadn't gotten physically involved—his task was to line out the surveyors and other specialists and ride herd on the paperwork. He eyed Dart and Claxton (instantly dubbing them Frick and Frack) and tried to guess their angle. Possibly they weren't feds after all, and instead represented rival interests to AstraCorp; espionage was common in the industry, but seldom this overt.

"Right on. Slango's got a history. How many loggers disappeared from that camp in 1923? Two hundred wasn't it?"

Mr. Dart said, "You have a big-time physicist on the clock up there. Vern Noonan. Hot shit dude, huh? Kinda like swatting a fly with a sledgehammer bringing in a gun that size. Come on, level with me—what's really on the agenda at Slango?"

"Gosh, I wouldn't be able to venture a guess," Don said. A small lie; he'd seen Noonan's name on the manifests and felt a twinge of curiosity regarding the man's presence on an involved, if pedestrian, feasibility study.

"Have you met Dr. Herman Strauss? Old evil German scientist, did big things at R&D for the company back during the height of the Red Scare—became Herr Director, in fact. There's the secret to how we won World War Two—our Nazi scientists were better than their Nazi scientists."

"Er, no. Should I know him?"

"Hah, well, maybe. Mrs. Miller interviewed him for her first book. The interview got edited for content or length, or whatever. Very interesting fellow, Herman Strauss. Specialized in mind control and unorthodox applications of medicine and technology. Heh, if he hadn't gotten press-ganged by the Allies, he'd probably be sipping mint juleps on one of those plantations in South America."

Mr. Claxton tried next. "Hey, ever hear of a physicist named Nelson Cooye? Great big Lakota Indian. Chummy with Plimpton. He did research for Caltech, Stanford, MIT. A real stallion for an egghead."

"Never met him," Don said, trying to picture Cooye. He had the unhappy premonition that the guy was famous and something bad had happened to him and that somehow this terrible thing presaged something equally dreadful for Don himself. He recalled a newspaper photo, two and a half inches of print, rumors of uncontrollable violence, of public tirades. He didn't normally keep track of physicists.

"Ah." Mr. Claxton nodded. "But you hearda Cooye. Rather a renowned figure among the radical elements, the lunatic fringe. He was buddies with that one dude, Toshi Ryoko, guy that made a movie about his expeditions in the Far East. Another classic, lemme say. I heard a rumor he's in the planning stages for a trip to some deathtrap of a wildlife preserve in Bangladesh. Bet he gets a Nobel if he can find backers."

"Oh, Toshi," Don said. Everybody in the civilized world knew of Toshi Ryoko the same way everybody knew of Jacques Cousteau or Dian Fossey. "Did something blow up in his documentary?"

"No. It's about an expedition, is all. Nothing to do with the price of tea in China. Anyhoo, Cooye was a smidge wacko; a saucer watcher. Got himself and a few radical kids from Stanford arrested for trespassing on a government research facility in Nevada. Nothing important there, by the way—it's the thought that counts."

"Yeah, I don't recall. Who do you gentlemen work for? FBI? CIA?"

"CIA doesn't operate on American soil," Mr. Claxton said. "That's the line, anyhow. National Security Agency."

"Uh-huh. Y'know, my grandfather always warned me to never talk to spooks."

"Yep, he was a smart guy, your gramps. We'll get to him. Back to Cooye. He rolled in a teeny Volkswagen. Can you imagine this six-eight dude jamming himself into one a those contraptions? Went off the road near Eureka. Burned up on the rocks."

"When?"

"About six weeks ago. Sad, sad, y'know. Wonder what he was thinking about on the way down."

"The highway patrol couldn't locate the body," Mr. Dart said. "Cops say he was thrown from the wreck and taken out to sea."

"Yep, like a commode flushing." Mr. Claxton mimed pulling a chain.

"There's a bore tide along that stretch of coast. No way they'll ever find him unless he washes up somewhere, which I doubt. But on to the good parts: Plimpton," and here the agent gestured to encompass the party being thrown in the dead man's honor, "and Cooye moonlighted for the CIA during the '60s. Cooye was a few years younger than you. CIA likes'em young and dumb. Your granddad knew Cooye pretty well, like a grandson, in fact; we're confident Luther handled him during his tour in Bali. Course this is speculation—the company boys don't play nice. But we're betting Luther was the control. Small, small world, ain't it."

Don hadn't given the matter much thought since he was a kid—it was simply a dab of color in the magnificent canvas of his grandfather's larger-than-life persona, a childhood fascination stowed in the trunk where such dusty recollections languish. "I never met Cooye, despite the fact you say he was close to my grandfather. Granddad didn't work for the CIA. The brass forced him out years before the company or the NSA even formed."

"He worked for Army Intelligence. Same diff."

"He was old, decrepit. Died not long ago… 1977.

"1977, there's an excellent year."

"For some, I guess."

"Well, three years, you should be done with the grieving and on with the spending of that inheritance loot. Old bird had a few bills stuffed under the mattress, I'd bet my left nut on that." Mr. Dart grinned when he said it, like he was relating a dirty joke. "This leads to the next piece of the puzzle and how your wife was Plimpton's star pupil and all those mysterious vacations they took together."

"I'll thank you to consider very carefully what you say about my wife." Don loosened his tie and turned slightly sideways. His hands flexed, loosened, flexed.

The agents exchanged a glance. "Don't get crazy, Miller," Mr. Claxton said.

"Let's see some ID," Don said, and that also hit him with a powerful sensation of déjà vu. He glimpsed, a shadow in his mind's eye, some rough men laughing, then wearing devilish masks while the fires of hell burned away the darkness. He swayed as the room dilated and contracted.

"Hell, man. We're undercover. We don't carry badges undercover."

"Hey," Mr. Dart said, "I'm curious—you ever ask yourself what the connection is between the Wolvertons, Rourkes, and Mocks? Other than big fortunes?"

"You gotta include the Redfields too," Mr. Claxton said. "Although, I don't know how deep *that* goes."

"Let me think...They all live in Olympia?" Don said. "The Mocks aren't moneyed."

"Oh, come on," Mr. Dart said. "Those old bitches are sitting on millions. Besides, I said it isn't just the money. And Plimpton mixed with them. His line was almost as mind-numbingly boring as yours. How did he fit in? Look at these clowns—they drove hundreds of miles to this joint in Timbuktu to pay homage to a lab jockey. Not like the guy did anything sexy—no Nobel, no famous dino discovery, no Einsteinian breakthroughs on the true nature of reality...he always just plugged along researching the mundane stuff that only excites other lab jockeys and review boards. Odd, huh?"

"Wake up, Miller," Mr. Claxton said. "We're watching out for you. Something's rotten in Olympia and these rich assholes are in cahoots."

"Cahoots?" Don blinked and tried to wrap his mind around the notion. "You mean like spies and Deep Throat? Cloak and dagger? Commie moles?"

Mr. Dart smiled. "Everybody knows who the commie moles are. You see them in small-town obituaries all the time."

"Think worse," Mr. Claxton said. "Think bigger."

"I don't know what my grandfather was into," Don said. A half lie—that Granddad and Dad had done dirty business of the U.S. of A. was implicit in their very nature, the artifacts they'd left behind. He'd heard of the secret government black lists, and not only the kind McCarthy reserved for the un-American Activities Committee. Oh, no; the FBI kept tabs on all kinds of people from environmental activists to Pinko college professors to subversive authors and reformed hippies. Thus, in a way, given his relatives' exotic background, and the company Michelle had kept over the years, he wasn't entirely surprised to occasionally encounter federal law enforcement types sniffing around like jackals on the scent of blood. His family had surely collected enemies.

"Here's the inside scoop. Plimpton committed suicide," Mr. Dart said. "The coroner's report is a dummy."

"Baloney. Lou had a heart attack."

"Wrong, my friend," Mr. Claxton said. "Any idea why the good doctor would want to off himself?"

"I wasn't close to the man. I don't believe you, though."

"That's okay, Miller. Your wife might have an answer."

"Sure. She'd be the one to ask."

"We're not allowed to speak with her," Mr. Claxton said. "She's an untouchable."

"You can't talk to my wife?"

"Nope, indeed we cannot. It's a real pain in the ass."

"She's in the parlor, last I noticed. Not a hard lady to find..." Don trailed off, belatedly noting how serious Frick and Frack were.

"Don't you get it, Miller?"

"He doesn't."

"This is what we're trying to make you understand. Michelle Mock isn't...How shall I put it delicately?" Mr. Dart paused and stroked his chin. "She's got powerful friends. I don't often run across people blessed with the kind of friends as these. You?" He nodded to Mr. Claxton.

Mr. Claxton said, "I've shot at potentates who aren't as secure as your woman. Truth be told, this whole visit is unauthorized. Our superiors would have our guts for garters if they knew we were here gathering intelligence. Spying on Mrs. Miller. Warning you."

"That's why we decided to pay our respects and get to know you, Mr. Miller. Of all these splendid folks you're the only one who isn't protected by the forces of darkness. The only one who's in a vulnerable position."

"Protected from what?"

The agents stared without answering.

Don had had enough. "This is the goddamned *Osterman Weekend* or you two are having me on. And I don't see Bob Ludlum anywhere, so... Please excuse me, I'm going to take a piss now."

"More like *Rosemary's Baby* writ large. Illuminati level shit. The Mayans vanishing en masse and leaving us a calendar that rolls over to zero in about thirty years."

"Easy does it. Man's got to piss, man's got to piss." Mr. Dart's lachrymose expression became pleading. "This I have to know—what went on in Mexico?"

"The records say you were playing chicken with the reaper," Mr. Claxton said. "Somebody used you for a piñata. Almost bit the dust is what I get from the file."

"Nothing happened." Don slumped with exhaustion. Mexico, 1958. He'd gotten lost in a bad neighborhood and some thugs hassled him. Alcohol was surely involved. Michelle played deaf whenever he started reminiscing about their trip to Mexico City. The truth was, most of the details were fuzzy. "I had a nice time with my wife. Drank a wagon load of Coronas. Came home with a sombrero. It's hanging on a hook in my den."

"See, we heard that in between the Coronas and hanky-panky you lovebirds were spotted lurking in interesting places with the wrong kind of people." Mr. Claxton wasn't smiling anymore. "Are you aware that your wife went to an enclave of a certain Nazi scientist who'd managed to escape the Mossad? Or that Plimpton, Josef Wolverton, the former owner of this magnificent estate, and several luminaries in the fields of eugenics and tinfoil hat science theory were invited to that party? There were also several of those scary people who play with Tesla coils and test tubes in their basements, trying to design homemade atom smashers. Best of all, no fewer than nine all-pro practitioners of the occult made the trip. I'd give a testicle to find a video of that little hoedown."

"Yep, she's sipping champagne and schmoozing with Anton LaVey and the Goering fan club. Meanwhile, you're playing fuck-fuck with some dirty agents in Mexican intelligence." Mr. Dart shook his head. "You drop off the radar and resurface a couple of days later, covered in blood, raving mad, though nothing that a week in the loony ward and a few high-powered injections couldn't fix. Two of them Mexicans were heavy hitters, by the way. Double-breasted sonofabitches I surely wouldn't want to meet in a dark alley. Contract killers, the lot of 'em. Kinder, during his troubled youth, was chief torturer for el Presidente. Ramirez specialized in political executions. He loved bumping foreign nationals. The authorities spared no expense searching for the bodies. Neither hide nor hair was ever found."

"Hell of a mystery," Mr. Claxton said.

Don said, "Excuse my language, but I don't have the first damned clue what you're on about. This is a fantasy."

"*I'm* on Black Beauties and copious amounts of blow," Mr. Dart said. "We're here to save the free world. We're all that stands between your overeducated ass and the Not With a Bang, But A Whimper ending of the world. We're also high on vengeance. A couple of our brother agents recently disappeared while investigating Plimpton's death. Kind of how them loggers went poof in 1923 and them Mexicans disappeared after they tried to snuff you, Don."

Claxton sneered. "Man, your wife was at an overnight cocktail social with a member of the Third Reich and a cabal of Satanists while you're getting kidnapped and tortured and you don't bat an eyelash. You need a fucking clue all right."

"It's a conspiracy," Mr. Dart said. "I'm guessing you're exactly the rube she needs to maintain her cover as a cute little lady scientist. Who'd suspect her of anything with Gomer Pyle hanging around? She didn't fool your grandpa. Remind me to let you listen to the piece of audiotape I found in the archives. Ol' Luther was chatting with his handlers in Washington. This was '76. Not even five years ago. He wanted clearance to terminate a certain unnamed female in-law with extreme prejudice. Pretty sure he was talking about Mrs. Miller. Washington denied the request, apparently."

"Yeah, and here's the kicker. You don't know Cooye, but you wanna take a wild stab in the dark at who was really chummy with the dude? I'll give you three guesses and the first two don't count."

Don gaped at the men. His faculties were fried. He didn't trust his mouth to form words without spluttering or foaming. Everything the agents said was penetrating, digging furrows into his gray matter. He just hadn't registered the impacts yet. "I don't think so. No way." He shook his head in the stubborn and ungainly fashion of a man who'd drunk or smoked to the point of believing himself sober.

"Goodbye, Don." Mr. Claxton dusted his sleeve and flashed his lion smile. "We'll see you later."

"By later, he means real, real soon," Mr. Dart said.

"God, I hope not," Don muttered.

7.

Don returned to the bar and hunted for Michelle who was nowhere to be seen. He managed to catch the host, Connor Wolverton's attention and that worthy informed him the house was enormous, the lady could be anywhere. Had he checked their guest room—third floor, eighth door on the left near a stuffed bear head. Their luggage awaited them and a bed was laid out. If not there, Connor couldn't hazard a guess. But never fret! She was likely kibitzing in one of the antechambers with some of the girls and would doubtless turn up as bad pennies always did.

Don rubbed his numb cheek and tried to shake the uncomfortable feeling this was the latest occurrence in an ongoing pattern between him and his wife. He did stumble upstairs and poke his head into what was actually a decadent suite, and sure enough, their bags were piled near the poster bed and the sheets were laid down. No sign of Michelle, however. So, back down to the reception and more trudging from room to room, interrupting conversations with his assuredly haggard countenance and protuberant red-rimmed eyes—his drinking face.

The smoothly neutral expression of each guest he approached to inquire if that person had seen her got under his skin, but vaguely, mitigated by the booze and the dope. The only useful intelligence he gathered in fifteen minutes of wandering was from one of the servants who informed him Mr. Arden and his chauffeur had retired to their room for the evening.

He climbed a spiral staircase with a fluted marble balustrade and crossed a landing of marble veined with gold. The pungent aroma of marijuana tickled Don's nose and ahead and to the left someone moved in the shadows and pushed open a door and disappeared.

Poster-sized photographs of Wolverton luminaries hung upon the walls like pieces at a museum and indeed, though the hall was empty but for the photos and small potted trees, he too pushed through an ornate blood-red door and entered a large, twilit gallery.

Tall glass cases were arrayed long one wall where the vaulted roof angled downward to create a seam. The glass appeared thick and tiny dim track lights, similar to the kind on airliners, glimmered dimly at the base of the daises and did more to suggest than actually illuminate. In the first two cases were models of leafless trees. A badger, stuffed and lifelike, crouched at the base of one tree while several large hook-billed birds perched among the branches of the next. He wasn't familiar with either species, but recognized them to be extinct. They reeked of the Stone Age, if not an epoch of deeper, darker antiquity.

The contents of the next cage stopped him cold. Suspended from a delicate and nigh-invisible frame of wires draped the skin of a humanoid figure, emptied and stretched on a rack as if it had been ripped whole from the muscle and bone of its previous owner. Eye sockets, nostrils, mouth, sagged agape; coarse, wiry hair spread thick across the loose curve of chest and belly. Stacked to one side, an array of spears with rudely chipped flint broad-heads, arranged and labeled.

A placard indicated the fellow was unearthed from a cave in upstate New York in 1949. Impossible, and thus this was a hoax, a PT Barnum special calculated to impress the rubes. That fit—celebrity mediums, séances, paying guests jaded out of their minds; similar shenanigans went back to the Edwardian Era, maybe farther. Connor Wolverton possibly wasn't as wealthy as his digs might represent. He wouldn't be the first aristocrat to find himself with a castle and no gold to pay the utilities. Such men would go to extravagant lengths and perpetrate intricate charades to pull in the dough while maintaining the illusion of royalty at leisure.

Nonetheless he lingered, enraptured by the exhibit. The skin, desiccated, yet oddly thick and weighty in appearance, gave him the creeps despite his confidence it was a fraud. Michelle mentioned the mansion's museum earlier. Had she seen this before? He very much desired to know what she thought, if so.

The whiff of grass grew stronger and Don spied Bronson Ford seated cross-legged upon the floor in the shadows of a heavy oak table. A cloud of smoke swirled around his head and rendered him more inscrutable than ever.

"Hi, Bronson. Fancy bumping into you here."

Bronson Ford laughed. He tossed the stub of his joint into a ceramic pot that allegedly originated in Tibet and hopped to his feet and approached Don with a queer, hitching stride that was nonetheless rapid. He tapped the glass of the exhibit. "It is real." His voice was strange; pitched like an old man's and rusty from disuse. "Those men, those government men... You shouldn't talk to people like them." He grinned at Don and his teeth were crumbling and black. "My kin will get them soon. Never fear."

Don said, "You got any more grass?" After Bronson Ford produced another joint and lighted it and they'd each toked heavily, Don wiped his eyes, fascinated at the odd blurriness of the lighting and the background textures while the boy, or whatever he was, became sharper and more in-focus.

An ineffable *something* about the boy disturbed him on a more immediate and much deeper level. Don couldn't recall ever attributing the word evil to a casual acquaintance, but that appellation fit. It was evil that animated Bronson Ford's smirk, the light glittering in his eyes, the hateful merriment of his tone. As this sank in, Don noted how lonely and isolated the gallery was; the two of them might as well have hunkered on tree stumps around a fire in the wilderness.

Bronson Ford regarded the caveman exhibit and his expression shone with the light of unholy joy. "*They* took his skin and wore it for a while. It's not real skin. More of a hide. Yes. They made a suit from his hide the way my own people skinned lions once upon a time. The way my people wore lion hides as capes, took the claws and fangs for jewelry. Yes, yes."

"They."

"Them, they. The Children of Old Leech."

"The children of what? What tribe were they?" At that moment, trying to regain mental equilibrium and regain some control of the conversation, he felt akin to a swimmer who finally glances back toward a distant shore and realizes the tide has carried him into cold, bottomless water. *It's the dope, screwing with your mind. You're going to wake up in the morning and discover this whole evening was a trip on the magic bus.*

"Don't you know? Isn't it why you came? This is for the special people."

"No, kid, I really don't know. Who are these children?"

"Friends of Mum and Dad." Bronson Ford crow-hopped to the next case and pressed a button. The curtain parted and a dim track light flickered on. "A sea cave in the Shetlands, spring of 1969."

"Bronson, you're freaking me out, man," Don said, and meant it. The object in the case might've been a behemoth of a quadruped in its life; a bear, a small elephant, a giraffe. He couldn't get an intellectual fix because his perception of the object shifted with quicksilver fluidity—ten or eleven feet on the vertical axis, three feet wide, multi-limbed, elongated neck, the powerful torso of a large land animal, a cranium of prodigious girth. Another skin, or in this case a pelt, also stretched on wires. Its fur was black against bone-white flesh. A bear, miraculously skinned as the Cro-Magnon had been skinned, nothing particularly special about taxidermy or the furrier trades…He sweated and the animal skin gathered height, loomed over him. "Why does the skull…" He couldn't, wouldn't take it a syllable farther.

"It doesn't come from the Shetlands. I'm not from Ethiopa." Bronson Ford wore a dreamy, maniacal expression; the smile of an elderly sadist trapped in a child's body. "The suit just got left there in that wet old cave when *They* returned to the dark."

"Another bloody fake," Don said. His stomach heaved and he covered his mouth. His boozing on the Yukon, all the partying he'd done during the drive and here at the mansion was coming home to roost. His gorge settled and he repeated, "Bloody fake," in case it might make him feel better. "Where are you from, really?"

"Russia. The mountain on the plain. Coldest fucking place you've ever seen."

"No shit?"

Bronson Ford rolled up his sleeve, revealing a classy stainless steel wristwatch. Also, a livid white scar that arrowed from his wrist along the ulna toward his elbow; a raised zipper seam. "Oops, it's past my bedtime." The boy saluted with three fingers and sidled away, slipping through the blood-red door and leaving Don alone with the horrors of the gallery.

Not horrors, damn it. Sideshow fakes. He only lasted a few seconds before the nausea threatened, and he fled. Frick and Frack were waiting on the other side of the door. He caught them with their backs turned, one peering north, the other south. A sack dangled from Mr. Dart's fist. Mr. Claxton brandished a syringe.

Don pin-wheeled his arms for balance in silent terror and at the last moment managed to stop short, recover and pull the door shut again, and as he did, he glimpsed Connor Wolverton ascending the stairs, smoking a pipe and waving at the agents. Don locked the door and his stomach finally won the battle and he vomited onto the carpet. Heart convulsing, he sucked air and listened for the thud of fists on paneling that would indicate his hunters were alert to his presence; but nothing of the sort occurred. The gallery was a velvety tomb.

He tried to regain his composure with some sensible and rational self pep talk. The very notion that the two men were plotting to kidnap him was preposterous; surely his perceptions were askew. It beggared belief that such an event could even conceivably involve a nobody such as himself, and in the middle of a mansion crawling with guests. *Right, right—bag and a needle and two creepy strangers who seemed to get their jollies menacing you earlier. Better find a service door, my friend.*

His thoughts jumped to Michelle. Oh, no! What if they were after her too? There'd be another door in the back, surely. The light in the gallery changed subtly and he whirled and saw someone approaching him from between the exhibit cases. The individual moved with alarming speed, bent low to the floor, but straightening as he or she drew nearer. Unfolding…

"I guess you'd best come with me," Bronson Ford said. It sounded like Bronson Ford, at least. The voice quavered on the edge of diabolical laughter. The figure was too tall—it loomed over Don. He yelled, albeit a cry that was silenced in an instant. This figure reached for him with a splayed hand both spindly and large. All Don could smell as it snuffed his consciousness was the whiff of his own puke.

8.

He was shambling along a hallway and the realization he couldn't remember *getting* there was jarring as a broken reel in a film.

There'd been a surreal conversation with Bronson Ford about art, or anthropology, and prior to that, an even more fanciful exchange with the two feds who'd seemed intent on convincing him his granddad was a super-villain, Michelle was a double agent, and that the moon landings were faked and half the aristocracy of Olympia participated in Black Mass or worse. A wave of dizziness and disorientation swept over him, and for a few seconds he swooned, nearly overcome by the sensation he'd wandered these gloomy halls for an eternity. He also recalled fragments of voices, the rustle of fabric, of being smothered, and then these impressions were swallowed by the mists of amnesia.

The other guests had retired and the houselights were dim. He groped his way back to the guestroom, praying Michelle awaited him there. The interior was mostly dark except for a pocket of light in the living room. He found Michelle curled on the couch near the mammoth rattan floor lamp very similar to one back in San Francisco they'd bought at a bazaar in Hong Kong nearly a decade ago when their relationship was in the final legs of a second honeymoon phase. He'd attended a geophysics conference, and she, being on sabbatical to write a book about multiculturalism, traveled with him for research purposes. They skipped the conference and spent a week sightseeing, losing themselves amongst the mazes, and gambling and partying at the nightclubs where Mandarin-speaking locals whined American pop classics in passable English.

There were a few tense moments upon returning safely stateside when it seemed possible a brand-new baby might be on the way—but one wasn't; thank God for a weak sperm count for once and crisis averted! The twins, God bless 'em, were plenty. These many years later, neither of Don nor Michelle was sufficiently comfortable to examine his or her feelings in light of current events and the benefit of hindsight.

Michelle had been crying; her blotchy face shone pale as an egg. For a queasy moment seeing her camped beneath the tall lamp as if posed by a photographer, memories of the Hong Kong excursion and the resultant baby scare caused Don's pulse rate to accelerate again, precipitated the looming disorientation and sickness.

"Honey, sorry it's so late. Whatsa matter?" he said. "Sweetie..."

She had wrapped herself in a raggedy quilt her grandmother sewed at parochial school. She pulled the quilt tight under her chin and stared at him. "Tell me a secret. One only you and I know."

Don sat on the edge of the couch. He awkwardly took her hand; it was cold. "Honey, what are you doing out here?" It occurred to him that this might be a ploy to deflect his natural peevishness at being abandoned earlier during the reception. He squashed that line of conjecture and put on a brave smile.

She left her hand in his, limp as a dead fish. She stared at him with that queer, drugged expression and said nothing.

"Okay. What kind of secret?"

"Anything," she said. "As long as it's ours."

"Um. That was kind of bitchy abandoning me to the wolves, this evening. Er, I guess that's no secret since everybody saw the dust cloud, right?"

She stared at him and he guessed then that she too had been drinking and more heavily than he first presumed.

Don swallowed and forced a smile. "I can't match my socks and, uh, I wear 'em inside out. Oh, oh, and I forget to change 'em more often than two or three times a month. How's that?"

She squeezed his hand and seemed relieved. "It's you."

"Yeah, babe. Hope to God you weren't expecting Don Juan." He stroked her wrist.

She nodded. Her expression slackened, became heavy with exhaustion. Don coaxed her from the couch, and together they swayed and stumbled into the bedroom.

Don clicked off the light and was instantly weightless upon the king-sized bed, cocooned by the blankets and the swaddling darkness and had almost fallen into the well of sleep when Michelle mumbled at him across the swells and swales, the inland sea. "Huh, whazzat?" he said.

"I thought you came in earlier," she said, her voice muffled by a pillow. "A while ago. I was reading and...I went to sleep and something woke me."

"Yeh? What did."

"You."

"Oh." Don lay face down, engrossed by intestinal gurgles, the womb-noises of his guts rebelling at their contents. "I did? When?"

Michelle remained silent. Then, even as Don decided she'd fallen asleep, she said dreamily, "I dunno. Earlier. I opened my eyes and there you were, watching me sleep. You used to do that, 'member?"

"Sure do, mm-hm."

"Why would you be standing in the closet? Just standing there between my dresses. Couldn't figure that out."

"Honey?" Don rolled over. "This is crazy, I know. Do you happen to know a physicist named Nelson Cooye? These two weirdoes claimed you're an evil, evil woman. A mistress of skullduggery. Our taxes in action, eh?" He reached toward her, but she was too far away across the water and he fell back. He stared into the gloom and listened to her breathe and after a bit she began to snore.

He dreamed of walking naked across a savanna toward a stand of Eucalyptus trees. Agents Frick and Frack stood to his left in the tall grass. The men were naked but for loincloths and sunglasses. Both were shouting at him; their voices didn't carry and he walked onward.

A piece of the earth rose between the trees and pushed one over with a series of low cracks. The thing was a sloth, or an elephant. It watched him and as he approached, legs propelling him against his yammering instinct, he soon saw that it was neither of those animals. Then he was in its shadow.

In the morning he recalled a fragment of his vision with a small scream. Five seconds later it had evaporated from his mind and was lost.

CHAPTER SIX

Bluebeard's Husband

(Now)

1.

Though his days were busy after Michelle departed, Don initiated further measures to minimize the solitude of the empty house. He invited Argyle Arden and Turk Standish for a barbeque over the weekend, and inveigled Harris Camby, the former Pierce County Sheriff, to attend as well—promising ale and horseshoes. Harris was a formidable presence in the pits; even when the sheriff was dead-drunk none of his friends or colleagues could hope to match his prowess.

Saturday proved lovely; a bright, warm afternoon hinted at the possibility of a prolonged summer. Don grilled ribs and served steins of Irish stout to his friends. As midday slowly ceded to a soft, hazy twilight, he lounged on the porch with Argyle. Harris and his grandson Lewis were methodically drubbing Turk and Argyle's companion for the day, a preppy grad student named Hank. Hank, a beefy kid in a heavy Norwegian sweater and fancy slacks, sweated and scowled, apparently displeased at Harris's wry commentary regarding the boy's game, and possibly even more so with Turk's complacency about being thoroughly shelled. His face flushed red as a fired brick and he drank too many rum and Cokes for Don's comfort.

The conversation meandered, being of no consequence beyond a pleasant diversion, when Argyle took his pipe stem from between his teeth and said, "Has Michelle gotten anywhere with her survey?" He meant, of course, the genealogical research and translations she'd chipped away at for decades. It had once been a hobby, a method of easing her tensions and frustrations during the inevitable setbacks and disappointments in discovering the Lost Tribe.

"I gather yes. She's in there, going great guns."

Argyle chuckled. "She's a terrier with a bone. Always been that way when it comes to her passions."

"We don't discuss it, really. Over my head."

"Hrmm. You've got rocks for brains, is why. I hope she publishes her findings. The work is quite intricate. Her piece regarding the demographical data of her ancestors' principal migratory trajectories is remarkable. Admittedly, I did collaborate on particular bits of procedural documentation—"

"If you look closely, you'll note my eyes are glazing."

"Bah. How's Kurt doing?"

"Fine, fine. I called him yesterday. He's laid up at home. Says Winnie's rubbing his feet and feeding him grapes."

"Hah! I hope she doesn't hear him running at the mouth or I'd bet good money he's a dead man." Argyle sucked on his pipe. "If Kurt's okay, then what's the matter?"

"Nothing. I'm happy as a clam at high tide. The weather is marvelous, yeah? The house is all mine for a while—"

"About that."

Don waited and when it seemed as if his friend wouldn't continue his thought, he said, "What about it? Afraid I'll go stir crazy? No chance of that, not with tending Michelle's vegetables and puttering about."

"Yes, it sounds swell. But that's not what I meant. What I mean is, it's a shame you two inherited this place." Argyle swallowed some beer and gestured vaguely with his pipe. "Let's face it, with the exception of Michelle, the Mocks are seriously strange. You've never even met any of them, thus there's absolutely zero familial attachment. Must be like living in a cheap, bizarre museum. You're more curator than owner."

"Not true. I met Babette, once."

"For about thirty seconds, sure. Didn't that dame stay at the Samovar instead of here? There you go. Anyway, back to you and your lovely wife. I'm thinking you two are looking like a couple of silver foxes—"

"Thanks."

"Don't mention it. Really, though. If your back gets much worse, those stairs will be impossible. When you go senile and start drooling into a bib Michelle will have to set you up with a gurney in the parlor, because she won't want to jog back and forth. And that'll just be tacky. People will be too embarrassed to visit—"

"Ah, at least there's a silver lining."

"You think so now. Michelle will be forced to meet her friends at their houses, the Kiwanis club, or, sweet Lord, bingo—"

"Michelle doesn't like bingo."

"The hell she doesn't. See, that's the problem. She's got interests you don't have the foggiest notion about. It'll get worse. Pretty quick she'll be shacking with the pool boy from the Broadsword hotel and spending your retirement on the slots at the Happy Eagle."

"If I'm senile, I don't think any of this is a problem."

"Trust me, lad. What you two need is to sell off this place and get into a nice updated rambler in town, close to the bus lines so when you become incompetent and lose your license you can still go fill your little canvas bag at the supermarket. Hell, you're a stubborn goat—I know you aren't listening to a damned thing I say. Try this then: get that no-account son of yours and do it up right. Cart off a mountain of the junk, slap on a coat of paint and some trifles you've got in storage, and *voila!* It'll seem more like home. Think on it. I know a guy who'll take most of this crap off your hands."

Don laughed and poured Argyle another beer.

2.

That evening after his company had gone home, he repaired to the parlor and rested in his favorite chair, a compendium of subterranean geophysical studies resting heavily across his thighs, and conceded that Argyle had raised a valid point. The house *was* a museum. They'd never gotten around to boxing things up or shipping unwanted items away to the Salvation Army, or Goodwill, for the bald fact four months a year seemed too short and there were numerous, more pressing tasks, the inevitable backlogs of work-related business, and the torpid apathy that accompanied hot weather. Now he had no such excuse. Nine months they'd lived here full time; nine months of him picking about the edges, wary of tackling the Herculean Labor, his greatest obstacle being Michelle's diffidence. If and when they decided to overhaul the décor, she insisted upon itemizing and meticulously cataloging everything down to the last spoon, the last shred of paper.

Well, he could handle something as simple as that, couldn't he? *I'm a grown man—a PhD, for Pete's sake! And I'm not afraid of my wife*! Which wasn't quite true, but nice to believe, if half-heartedly. A faint doubt nagged him, however; this doubt forced him to question whether he harbored an ulterior motive. He'd long sublimated a growing desire to poke about the place in depth, and, horrors of impropriety! peruse the materials in Michelle's study, the books she pored over with indefatigable determination, yet never brought to bed or spoke of with any candor.

It was difficult for any degree of mystery to survive eons of marriage. Historically, he'd welcomed the enigma of his wife, cognizant they'd managed so swimmingly because of their frequent and lengthy separations due to work, and no less the professional compartmentalization they maintained even in these, their golden years. Lately, though, he felt dissatisfied and mildly resentful regarding this aloofness, perhaps goaded by the awareness that while his life and work were slowly succumbing to entropy, hers flourished magnificently as ever. She remained exotic and he had been relegated to pasture, effectively condemned to isolation in a house that unnerved and depressed him. And why? Why her fixation upon this plot of land, this building? He thrust aside the thought as unworthy and convinced himself his motives were altruistic, or at least pragmatic.

Girded by this new-found resolve to transform the house into a more agreeable habitat, he rang Kurt at home to request his support and physical assistance in the endeavor. Don prepared for his son's inevitable protestations of business deadlines, domestic crises and the like. Thus it was to his bemusement that Kurt hesitated briefly and then said he'd drive down in the morning and stay for a couple of days. He promised to bring a truckload of boxes and packing tape, but on one condition. Don had to agree to a campout at the fishing hole about a mile up the creek from their house. Don opened his mouth to protest this ridiculous notion and the line went dead. He hadn't gotten around to modernizing their communications system, so he repeatedly tapped the reset hook to no avail. Thule raised his head and growled. Raccoons came onto the porch for late-night snacks. Don listened for the garbage pail getting knocked about. Thule put his nose between his paws and dozed again.

A campout? What foolishness was this? He decided it was idle chatter, perhaps a way to invoke some semblance of the bond they shared during Kurt's boyhood. Don stared into the fire and turned the conversation over, searching for clues to explain Kurt's mysterious exhibition of philanthropy. Perhaps his son wanted first crack at some of the antique collectibles, although that seemed far-fetched and uncharitable of Don besides. Kurt hadn't the slightest clue as to evaluating such things and he didn't need money. His company paid exorbitant wages supplemented by lucrative retirement programs and medical benefits. Don scratched his head, then let it go, loath to look askance at good fortune. In the morning he'd zoom into town to stock plenty of Kurt's favorite beer, mildly worried that maybe the boy had abandoned beer for white wine, or mineral water, or whatever affectation struck the fancy of his generation's rich, Patagonia-clad suburbanites.

Before bed, he jogged around the house and made sure every single light was in working order and switched on. Heaven help him if Michelle ever checked the bill and put two and two together; he'd be blackened toast. He fell asleep with the massive geophysics tome weighing against his chest, soft light from the nightstand lamp warm across his cheek.

The thud of the book sliding from his lap and hitting the floor brought him to the surface. The room was dark as dark gets, although as his rheumy eyes adjusted, he discerned a blurry crack of light beneath the bedroom door. He groped for the lamp, upsetting the glass of water that soaked his dentures. Pulling the chain had no effect; it only produced the dry rattle that bespoke an open circuit. Sweat popped out on his face and he froze, trembling in his pajamas, inexplicably consumed by an image of the cellar door swung wide like a mouth skinned open to reveal a throat.

Water dripped from the overturned glass on the stand to the floor. Then new noises came: squeaking and rustling. He understood even in his blindness the closet door, a wooden panel that folded like an accordion, had slid on its track.

Oh, boy. Adrenaline squirted into his blood. There was a presence in the room. Unless, oh, of course—the dog. Thule was a hunting dog at heart. He often nosed about, sniffing for vermin. Thule must've moved the panel after smelling one of those blasted rodents that hid in the walls. Don raised himself in bed to admonish his pet and floorboards shifted in the closet, followed by a low utterance, a cross between a wheeze and a drawn-out croak, although he knew instinctively that wasn't quite it, but his mind couldn't fix upon the proper description; it lay beyond his experience. Don's heart skipped and he thought, *Here comes the big one*, as his chest tightened. Clothes hangers jostled and clacked. Something under the bed scraped, like nails gouging wood, and the groaning croak came again, slightly muffled and directly beneath him, a pneumonia victim's burbling, gasping inhalation.

Don shouted and threw back the bedcovers. He clambered from bed and lurched to the door. He flung it open and light from the hall illuminated parts of the room. The closet appeared empty except for shirts and pants and jackets hanging neatly from their hooks. Clothing swayed gently. He couldn't make out anything in the darkness under the bed. Poor Thule cowered on the opposite side of the room. He shook in brute terror; a pool of urine spread along the dips and warps of the floorboards. Don, not daring to reenter the bedroom, beckoned him with quavering reassurances and eventually the dog came, tail tucked between his legs, foam dripping from his muzzle as if he had gone mad. Together, they retreated to the kitchen and Don saw the cellar door was indeed open by several inches. He shut the door and wedged a chair under the knob, a trick he'd seen in the movies, along with using a credit card to pick a lock. He put on a coat and dialed the sheriff's office to report a possible burglary in progress. The dispatcher promised to send a car right away.

3.

"Right away" turned out to be forty minutes. Don developed a migraine from squinting; he'd left his glasses upstairs. He finally calmed enough to boil coffee. Two sheriff's deputies arrived in a Bronco and came in and took his report. The pair were amiable men who were duly impressed he was friends with old man Camby. They searched the house, clumping room to room in their heavy boots, shining flashlights while their radios squawked and crackled. They checked the cellar (refraining from comment about his wedging the door, although they exchanged looks) and performed a sweep of the barn. Meanwhile, Don waited on the porch, his arms crossed to ward the damp and chill. Frogs rasped in the black sea of grass. Don's knees knocked and he spooked himself with the thought the men might not emerge from the barn, that he would huddle, petrified, until some unimaginable doom slithered forth to drag him from the face of the earth.

The officers returned and stood around awkwardly, uniforms smudged with cobwebs and dust. During their sweep, they spotted a raccoon in the eaves toward the rear of the house and startled a possum near the barn. Possums and raccoons were bitter enemies and a noisy fight could've been what Don heard, explained the younger officer, a round-faced farm boy who doubtless knew his nocturnal critters. Don served them coffee and apologized for the false alarm. In the stark light of the kitchen, he inwardly questioned whether it had indeed been a false start, the byproduct of paranoia and isolation, or, saints preserve him, incipient dementia. Already, the incident threatened to fade into the morass of regular bad dreams.

The veteran of the two asked why he had removed the lights in the bedroom. Don didn't comprehend until the officer explained the bulbs were missing from the reading lamp and the overhead light. In fact the latter fixture had been unscrewed so that the globe dangled from the end of the threaded bolt and the wires were exposed. A definite fire hazard, the man warned, eyeing him sidelong as one might regard a potential kook.

Don was ashamed. He stammered another earnest apology, at a loss to reconcile this strange information with the lack of evidence of an intruder. The deputies assured him it wasn't a problem—a senior home alone in a semi-remote setting...better safe than sorry, right? Would he care for an escort to a friend's place for the night, a motel? He declined, professing foolishness at his overreaction.

It was three A.M. when their taillights dwindled into the black. His bladder had expanded to the size of a football and he fairly hopped into the bathroom to urinate, cursing his failing eyesight, his weak bowels and apparently diminishing numbers of brain cells.

He spent the rest of the evening in the parlor, sleeping in fits and starts, jolted by every tiny sound. In the gaps between dozing and waking he remembered the first night he'd ever heard strange noises in the house; 1962, the summer after they'd inherited the place. He'd awakened to creaking floorboards—the odd clink and scrape as of something small and metal dragging in the hallway. He'd sat up to investigate, when Michelle gripped his wrist. *Her hand was cold, wasn't it? Like it had been in a meat locker. How unreal the white oval of her face hanging there in the gloom. Her hair floated black and wild and her fingers tightened until his bones gritted. A purple ring puffed his wrist the next day.*

Honey, don't, she'd said in a soft, matter-of-fact tone, and pulled him against her breast. Don't leave me. The bed is cold.

No, she was cold; her hands, her body, frigid as a corpse through her thin gown. Yet he'd streamed with sweat, his chest sticky, his pajamas drenched and he'd been breathing like a man who'd run up a steep hill.

Had he protested? He didn't think so. Something else happened then—he became leaden and sleepy and Michelle soothed him and stroked his hair and he drifted away. In the morning it faded into a dream, could truly have been a dream for all he knew. Another of those unsettling occurrences he almost forgot, almost buried for good, until nights like this poked him in the tender spot that never quite healed.

4.

"I'm surprised Winnie let you come," Don said when Kurt arrived later that morning to begin their Great Reconstruction of the house. They'd decided to start with the attic. He documented their progress in a blank journal while Kurt wrapped objects in newspaper and then stuffed them into boxes. It was slow, dirty work.

"Oh, she didn't *let* me—she basically threw me out of the house." Kurt clapped his work gloves and dust smoked in the bluish light. He patted his stomach. "Morning sickness, bloating, I dunno. She's bitchy. Frankly, I'm happy as hell to get away."

"Um," Don said, trying to remember what Michelle's mood had been like during her early pregnancy, chagrined to realize he couldn't. "I know how it is." He tapped the list with his pen: *a rusty bicycle; moth-eaten corduroy children's clothes; eight boxes of crumbling Christmas tree ornaments; five boxes of water-stained children's books; four boxes of marbles, jacks, playing cards, chess boards, wooden blocks, jigsaw puzzles, etc; two boxes of homemade candles and soap, mostly melted; five boxes of penny dreadfuls and counting; two boxes of phonograph platters; a Philco radio from the early '30s*; and they weren't even warmed up. He still ached all over from dozing in the chair.

Moth-eaten canvases lay stacked like animal skins upon a crumbling easel deeper in the blue shadows; more of the bizarre grotesqueries he'd encountered in the past. This particular stack was of a highly stylized technique, a combination of oil and charcoal, unsigned and incredibly weathered to the point of ruin. That made him glad for each of nine or ten paintings he skimmed through dealt from individualized perspectives with a train of child-figures moving in a column across a plain toward a cavern in a mountainside. The plain was marked by a scatter of henges and megaliths. A muddy inscription near the bottom of one canvas read, *Fathers and mothers come as slaves and depart as kin. The children slake Old Leech. They entertain him with their screams.*

The name *Old Leech* struck a chord in his subconscious. He covered the pile with a drop-cloth, determined to burn the whole mess later. "Oh, hey, don't touch those," he said as Kurt rummaged in the cabinet of the dolls.

Kurt turned a rag doll over in his hands; a horrid thing of matted yarn, floppy, segmented limbs and coveralls wrinkled with age and mildew. Its eyes had fallen out. "Eh? This thing is heavier than it looks. Swear to Christ it's full of wet sand."

"Would you—? Your mother's got her mind set. She'll cook my goose for sure if we mess with them. We'll come back to it later."

"I doubt it," Kurt said. He laughed and tossed the doll aside. He looked around. "We've been at this for three hours. No end in sight. This must be what Purgatory is like."

"Sisyphus and son."

Kurt moved to the Westinghouse projector and the film canisters. "Ever watch any of these?" He picked up a couple of the canisters and gestured. "I mean, wow. Some of these babies are old as the hills." He began stacking them inside a box, pausing to name the titles of those that bore one. Most of the labels had faded to white. There were several dozen canisters, approximately a quarter of which contained Michelle's personal collection from various travels abroad.

"There's not much to them," Don said after a period of cataloging the boxes, labeling with a magic marker, and stacking them. In truth, he'd only glanced at a few of the films, and those at metaphorical gunpoint, usually in the company of Michelle's anthropologist friends following one of her trips; a gaggle of bluff academics in Hawaiian flower print shirts and Bermuda shorts, or in the case of the more staid variety (like Don himself), cheap suits they wore to every occasion, including the grocery store for cigarettes; everybody sipping gin and tonic and laughing uproariously at the in-jokes while Michelle put on her dry-as-bones deadpan narration and Don melted into the background, content to weather the tedium by passing among them with the drink tray.

"What?"

"Bird watching, picnics, travelogue rubbish. Nothing interesting." Don winced at the paucity of creativity in his fabrication. He couldn't fathom his embarrassment. Michelle wasn't particularly enamored of his rock collection or his treatises on glaciations, was she?

"Bird watching?" Kurt frowned. "This must be from one of Mom's trips. Yeah, right here—*Papua, New Guinea. Crng (Lynn. V) 10/83*. What's on it?"

"You've seen your mother's slides. This is probably the same, but longer."

"Ugh. The bloody slideshows; how soon we forget." Kurt chucked the canister in with its mates. A couple minutes later, he whistled to Don. "Hey, Pop. Check this out." He waved an envelope of photographs he'd discovered in one of Michelle's waterproof belt pouches; the kind she carried when afoot in jungles and deserts. The pouch had been mixed up with the film canisters. "I was doing a wee bit of snooping when we were over last week. Win is so taken by Mom's adventurous ways and I showed her some of the stuff she'd left here. Anyway, I came across these. See, these were taken in the '30s or '40s judging by the car there, and the house..."

Don accepted the photos; less than a dozen low quality black and white shots of the house with a Model T parked in the yard, and the barn a gray rectangle in the background. Other photographs featured pastorals: the field; the hill and stream; one from atop an elevated vantage in the valley. The last four were murky, overexposed—the dim interior of a forest revealed as an indistinct gallery of ghostly trunks; a pile of misshapen stones backlit by sunset; and two more of a person standing near the stones, facing the photographer, arms spread in a vee, a dark, indistinct object dangling from his or her left hand—a satchel, a sack, something lumpy. These last were shot in darkness at the edge of a bonfire. The figure was terribly out of focus; a blurry white cloud mottled in splotches of black.

"Aren't these odd," Don said, eyes widening as he realized the person was in the buff. Only flesh gave forth such a diffuse, moist glimmer. He checked the reverse; someone had written in faded ink: *Crng Patricia W. 10/30/1937*. He intensely disliked these pictures, and could tell Kurt felt the same. He slipped them into the envelope and put the envelope into his pocket for future perusal.

"Those rocks are familiar," Kurt said, oddly excited. "When I was a kid. Holly and I got turned around in the woods. That's where I saw them. In the woods."

As Don recalled, those two had done more than gotten turned around: they'd been lost for nearly eight hours, wandering circles in the densely wooded hills where one hollow and briar patch soon resembled another. Luckily, they'd happened upon the creek and followed it home at roughly the time Don had gotten dressed to come hunting for them. They were ragged and dirty and traumatized, but essentially unscathed. The incident had become something of a family legend, although none of them spoke of it in recent years; a childhood experience Holly had grown resentful of and preferred to ignore—and pointedly suggested that others do the same.

"Pop, what about this? I found it last time I was here, took it home.

Like I said—I was snooping. Occupational hazard."

"Eh, what do you have?" Don adjust his glasses as Kurt reached into his jacket and produced a book and handed it over.

"It's...actually, I'm not sure. Got me thinking, though."

The book proved to be an almanac of some manner, quite slender, its black cover embossed with a cryptic broken ring in crimson bronze. Don loathed and dreaded it on sight, was instantly repulsed such that he took an involuntary backward step and nearly fell. He'd seen this symbol. Lord knew where, for the details remained obscured in the muck and mire of his porous recollection, yet branded with a white hot current into his gray matter and muscle memory.

You've most definitely seen it, chum. Here? No, not here. Not here— elsewhere, in a book, at a gallery, a film... He doubted the memory spawned from any of the schlock cinema he'd so loved; this was too raw, too visceral.

It wasn't pleasant to contemplate the mysterious circumstances of his prior encounter with the broken ring, the skeleton of a demon Ouroboros. Grappling with the fact his brain increasingly resembled Swiss cheese each passing day hurt like hell; grasping the notion that this rune had meant something once, probably during his adventurous youth, and that it had frightened him, *cowed* him, was worse. Don Miller didn't consider himself as a particularly brave man in his dotage; nonetheless, he'd possessed more than his share of grit in the old days. If this mounting sensation of terror had taken root back then, dear lord, what could it mean?

He clenched his teeth and opened the book. The title page said *Morderor de Calginis* with a notation this was the fifth printing, 1959, and authored by Divers Hands. The pages were thin and pulpy and contained endless tiny monospaced font paragraphs detailing queer and unusual locations across Washington State, Oregon, Idaho, and Montana. In the appendices were numerous occult diagrams and hand-scrawled maps. *The Black Guide*, was the rough translation from Latin. He rolled it on his tongue and it tasted bitterly familiar as an epithet. *The Black Guide*.

Abruptly, and with the galvanizing force of an electrical current zapping him, a piece of memory returned. Michelle bought the almanac at a shop in Enumclaw, tickled by its novelty. The family was on vacation for the summer. He couldn't remember if they'd actually tried to track down any of the listed sites. It seemed probable, but the specific details evaporated as he strained to dredge them. There was more to dig up, more to unearth. He snapped the almanac shut and tossed it aside. He wiped his hands on his pants, rubbing at an invisible taint that had already seeped into his blood, already spread a chill through him.

"Pop, what's the matter?"

"Hmm? Nothing, Son. Too much blood to the ol' brainpan. Stuffy, isn't it?"

"There's some really nutty entries in there. I read part of one on the Valley; typeset about split my skull, though. Gonna need glasses as thick as yours. Some of it is explicit and kinda hokey. Other parts, not so much. Raised the hair on my neck. The Waddell Valley chapter mentioned a house and a rock, but only in passing. The Sanguine Stone. Have to look up the name of the house; something to do with children. Damndest thing, too. It's supposed to be within a few miles of here."

"The other shoe droppeth. Your motives become clear. Helping me clean, the camping trip..."

"C'mon, Pop. Don't be like that."

"Children, huh?"

"Yeah," Kurt said and rubbed his chin. "House of the children of old leaves...Nah, that's not it, but close. Damndest thing, though. I swear to shit it's impossible to locate entries in there after you close the thing. Like they move around."

"Uh, well, some of the worst typesetting I've ever seen. Should use a magnifying glass when you read it."

Kurt said, "Right. I'm hungry as a bear. When do we eat?"

Don fixed ham sandwiches while Kurt lugged the boxes downstairs and out to the barn. They rested on the porch and smoked cigarettes. Late afternoon had already come sweeping down from the Black Hills and the breeze was chilly. He cast sidelong glances at his son. Conversation was always difficult, points of commonality sparse and shallow. He considered relating his previous night's adventures and couldn't summon the energy to bear the incredulous response, the lecture about living so far removed from civilization that loneliness had surely begun to play tricks on his mind.

"Mom call you yet?"

"No," Don said too quickly, eager for any bridge. "She gets involved in sightseeing, or what have you, and forgets, I think. I might not hear from her until she flies back."

"Jesus, Dad. Next thing you know it'll be separate beds."

"Well, she does snore..."

Kurt took a deep pull from his bottle of beer. His eyes were slits, focused on the field, the flattening grass, dry as baked straw. Don realized Kurt had drunk the six-pack with mechanical efficiency.

Don also stared into the field. He remembered Kurt in kindergarten, their first summer here; he'd raced into the field, charged headlong into a hole hidden by that tall grass. Minutely serrated edges of grass blades dug a trench across the last three fingers of his left hand as he tried to brace against pitching on his face. Kurt had staggered back to Don and Michelle, blood leaking from his fist. They drove to the clinic, the one that used to be on Prine Road but had been bulldozed and replaced by a mini-mart liquor store. Kurt got stitched by Doc Green, two or three dozen and he didn't shed a tear. He observed the operation with the innocent fascination peculiar to most children of that age. Don noticed Kurt make a fist now as he stared bleakly at the undulating grass. "Okay, then. Ready for round two?"

They cleaned up in silence and went back to work.

That evening, they ate hamburgers for supper and watched John Wayne in *The Fighting Seabees* until nearly one in the morning. The television was a beast; a home entertainment center in a long box, an oversized coffin, complete with a Philco radio and record player. He and Michelle picked it out from the Sears catalogue in 1971 and they'd recently gotten an adapter when the FCC decreed all old sets had to be digitally compliant. A couple of burly Italian gentlemen had originally brought the set in a van and spent the better part of two hours maneuvering it through the house and into the parlor on a dolly. Afterward, Michelle made a pitcher of ice tea and little cocktail sandwiches and they all sat around and watched *Leave It To Beaver*. Don had spent many a sleepless night sacked out at the foot of that behemoth. He drank a cup of tea and soaked his aching feet in a pan of water with mineral salts and fell instantly asleep.

He dreamt of becoming lost in the dark woods, of being chased by children with knives, of stumbling through the trees and falling among rocks piled high in a clearing, of lying helpless as a turtle on its back as the sun boiled red and dripped away into blackness.

In the morning, he heated coffee while the floors were yet cold and starlight leaked through the window. He warmed milk in a saucepan for Thule, who waited patiently beneath the table, his long pink tongue nearly dragging. Don hunched at the table and studied the photographs. He didn't like them any better than before, and even less when he considered their at least tangential relation to *The Black Guide*. Eventually, he stuffed them into the envelope and dropped it into a drawer and set to fixing breakfast.

5.

Monday, Labor Day, was more of the same. They began at daylight and quit only when darkness stole over the land.

Kurt collapsed on the couch during the ten P.M. news and fell asleep with his mouth hanging open. Don left the television on for white noise, not tuning in to whatever atrocity the media had fastened on today. He idly rued the fact he'd lost track of current events—on the domestic front, he was aware of the current president, but had not a clue what the man's policies were; when it came to foreign events, he was marooned on a lee shore. If pressed, he seriously doubted his ability to quote the latest big ticket crises; he couldn't even name the current Canadian prime minister. The whole political mess, the universal squalor, the essential pettiness of mankind oppressed him and he'd submerged himself in work and writing and books.

When the late show started, Don rose and went to Michelle's study. He hadn't exactly planned to bust in. The day's events had effected a sea change in him that eluded definition. He thought of Bluebeard's young bride, of locked doors and dire warnings, and smiled feebly. The image of Michelle as Bluebeard was far less amusing than it might've seemed.

The door was locked; not to bar Don, who knew better than to disturb her things, but from ingrained habit of raising nosy, destructive children. Fortunately, he knew she kept the key in a decorative dish full of antique and foreign currency such as Buffalo nickels and rupees. It had been a while since he last entered the study. He'd probably ventured inside less than a dozen times since they began spending summers at the house. Michelle discouraged it, claiming it as a sanctuary. She professed fear her unorthodox filing system (scattered papers and open texts everywhere) would be disrupted by a careless intrusion.

The room was large and stuffy in the manner of chamber a 17th century historian might've called home. Ceremonial spears and knives, and pink sandstone figurines of Brahma, Shiva and the celestial court contributed to the East Asian and British-India motifs. Michelle tried to hang one giant wooden fertility mask specific to an Aboriginal tribe deep in the Australian Outback over their headboard until Don emphatically put his foot down; there it stood, canted in shadow, grinning terribly behind a wicker shield. She'd developed a love for Aboriginal art in recent years; she accumulated carvings and etchings, figurines of skinny, cadaverous Dreamtime spirits, an authentic didgeridoo (despite it being verboten among the tribes for a woman to play the instrument), and a boomerang cut from light, lacquered wood.

Leather and clothbound tomes weighted floor-to-ceiling shelves, overflowed her desk, a relic she'd imported from the British Consulate in Indonesia, which had in turn recovered it from a local museum that specialized in artifacts from the days of the East India Company, and it might very well have originally furnished the office of a company governor. Also upon the desk were a skull, an hourglass full of white sand, and a laptop; paper weights and inkwells, a calligraphy kit in a teak box, and cubes of sealing wax. Maps and parchment cascaded amid the piles of books.

The majority of the documents were scribed in Greek, German, and Latin. Michelle collected scholarly papers much as her aunt had collected dolls; a substantial portion of the material was purchased from European libraries and churches and private dealers; the remainder were transcriptions she endeavored during her spare moments. He was struck simultaneously with childish wonder and claustrophobia, the latter sensation serving to fend his natural curiosity more than Michelle's mild neuroses could've managed.

He ran his hand over the spines of Michelle's books, brushing fine dust from them, studying the titles, albeit randomly, uncertain why he'd chosen to snoop among her belongings, or what he expected to find. Most of it proved to be the usual fare: thoroughly pedestrian texts, a goodly deal of which he'd personally acquired for her, such as *The Golden Bough*. Then there were the books Michelle had secured during her travels; primarily accounts by obscure (to Don, at any rate) anthropologists and daring explorers regarding remote expeditions to jungle tribes, replete with illustrations and the occasional photograph. Nonetheless, the majority of the books came with the house; these latter comprised fragments of the celebrated Mock collection. According to Michelle, Aunt Babette's portion, for example, rivaled the archives of a city library.

He'd counted seventeen encyclopedias in five different languages, and two hundred textbooks of varied subjects that ranged from architecture to metallurgy. There was a lesser sampling of esoteric manuscripts detailing occult practices and theory by authors of formidable stature. Among them, Dee's *Liber Loagaeth* and *De Heptarchia Mystica*; and Trithemius's *Steganographia*; and a smattering of other masters, the likes of Agrippa, de Plancy, and Mathers. Don dabbled in comparative religion and European folklore as an undergraduate, had taken semi-permanent residence in off-campus bookstores and antiquarian shops—this morbid preoccupation with the macabre and the uncanny served as a useful counterbalance to his overwhelmingly rationalist bent, plus, it impressed the hell out of Michelle, who was quite scandalous when it came to reading habits. On the other hand, he suspected such hoary tomes might be a contributing factor to his nyctophobia.

Spread across one wall and a portion of a bookcase was Michelle's great genealogical map in progress; a colossal mosaic consisting of dozens of parchment scrolls taped together at the edges. The Mock family tree branched and forked and branched again like multitudinous veins radiating from a burst capillary, the whole of this diagram taller than Don and twice as wide. Quite obviously the ongoing project of successive generations, it began in quill and was illegible to Don's eye, what with bleeding ink and moisture and mold discolorations, and, not the least of which, the fact it vacillated between various foreign dialects. Also, despite the enormous amount of labor, it seemed raw and incomplete; many of the branches and tributaries dwindled to dead ends and question marks. Michelle had checkered its width and breadth with pushpins and sticky notes.

To supplement her drafting, she had stacked ten or eleven books of the Mock family history on a worktable and nearby stools. These dense, leathery tomes belonged to a nineteen-volume series normally tucked in a corner behind a low stand surmounted by a flock of stuffed Canadian geese. The books were products of exemplary craftsmanship. A number of her ancestors had earned livings as printers and lithographers, including several of moderate renown; a handful served at the courts of French and Spanish Kings, and, according to legend, the Vatican itself during the latter days of the Renaissance. These nineteen volumes purportedly documented the Mock lineage and historical accomplishments, warts and all, and would constitute the primary source of Michelle's genealogical inquiry.

He asked her once if she intended to write a book; this exasperated query came on the heels of a particularly unpleasant summer wherein she'd locked herself into the study and refused to come forth for days at a stretch, leaving to him the housework, the bills, the raging bundles of hormones the twins had metamorphosed into when Mom and Pop weren't paying attention. Haggard and ill-tempered, she snapped something to the effect he was a blockhead. *You are a Goddamned blockhead*, was how she put it, in fact. He agreed with the correctness of her assessment; however, this in no way explained the nature of her obsession, nor mitigated her dereliction of duty. She'd given him a long, wintry look, the coldest he'd ever received prior or since. Then she said, *Leave a girl her secrets, Don.* And he had; although neither of them were kids at the time of the exchange—Kurt and Holly were seniors and already had their letters of acceptance to college. Don pretended disinterest in his wife's endeavor; a disinterest that became more or less reality as the years rolled by and they settled into their respective roles with clearly delineated boundaries. Accommodation had ever been a cornerstone of wedded bliss.

Don hefted a book that lay open on the table amid a clutter of Michelle's crude charcoal sketches of female nudes. It bore a publishing date of 1688. Several pages were scorched; a circumstance shared by the majority of the books, indicating the collection had been rescued from a fire. The author's foreword, one Fedosia Mock, explained her work was undertaken solely for posterity. This declaration echoed down through the generations. The books were intended as heirlooms to be kept within the confidence of the family; and from what could be inferred, women had scribed all of them.

Curiosity piqued, coupled with the dread of sleeping in his bedroom, Don cleared a spot on the desk and switched on the wicker-shaded reading lamp. He unfolded his bifocals from his shirt pocket and casually flipped through thin, wrinkled pages of Old Church Slavic in block text. The whole was marred by copious handwritten notations and doodles in the margins. Quickly examining random volumes (the latter of said having reverted to standard nineteenth century English), hesitating over the last, which bore a printing date of 1834 by one R. Mock, he determined the scribbling was a recurring affectation of whomever perused the manuscripts, and judging from its angular, cramped style, most definitely signified the handiwork of a Mock scion. He rummaged through the many drawers of the desk until he found a notepad and began to jot down observations of his own.

Following two hours of lackadaisical study, he began to build patterns of association between the half-dozen texts Michelle seemed to have currently settled on; collectively, their scope spanned from 1618 to 1753 and represented the labor of four successive authors. Originally called Velicioc, or Belikcioc, confusion reigned over which was correct, the Mocks had indeed emigrated from southern and eastern Europe, chivvied by enemies or misfortune—the antecedents were vague on the matter; nor was the year recorded anywhere; authorial assumption placed their arrival in Britain between 1370 and 1400, although this struck Don as extremely fanciful conjecture. The histories, what he could decipher via the English notes, proved by turns excruciatingly dull and titillating. He was interested to discover the bulk of the sprawling family hadn't embraced Christianity as per the social norm of the age except as a matter of expedience, a behavior reminiscent of the Vikings' grudging capitulation when the Great Church first laid claim to the souls of northmen. Instead, the Mock ancestors stubbornly clung to agnosticism, and, in less frequent instances, outright pagan customs. These customs derived from sects of ancient Slavic cults; secret societies that hearkened back to the nomadic tribes.

The references were manifestly intriguing, but equally oblique, as if the historians preferred to obscure the nature of their spiritual doctrine from all save the initiated. This frustrated Don, although he sympathized with the authorial discretion—in those times, men were often persecuted, even burned at the stake for the merest intimation of blasphemy. Yet, laboring to untangle the circuitous language of an entry regarding the year 1645 that touched upon various, evidently unwholesome ceremonies certain elder family members brought to Essex, Suffolk and Cumberland from the Carpathians and environs, he cursed the dearth of concrete details, the maddening ambiguity that hinted of the carnal and the sinister.

The narrative appeared in a volume wherein Michelle had inserted scores of old, old bookmarks she'd plucked from various specialty booksellers; a peacock fan of faded reds, blues and purples, each marker labeled with enigmatic abbreviations and notational symbols and cross references. The passage in question was accompanied by an elaborate woodblock illustration inscribed, *The Croning* (*fig. i*); a depiction of thirteen naked, apparently middle-aged women encircling a massive boulder. A buxom figure lay supine, draped across the face of the stone, shackled or bound in some manner. Don instantly recognized this piece as the subject of Michelle's sketches.

The drawing was exceedingly baroque, freighted with peripheral figures: winged gargoyles; demonic beasts that resembled kangaroos with tusks (these latter feasted upon the carcasses of men in Conquistadors' distinctive armor); cherubs; flautists; and, peeking from the roots of a mighty oak tree, shadowy woodland sprites, imp faces twisted in dark merriment. Its overall effect was singularly disturbing, like a Bosch simplified and shrunk to minuscule dimensions. Michelle had scratched in a list of initials and alchemical symbols; she'd even gone so far as to make a charcoal sketch of the original on a piece of textured art paper. Aggravatingly, figures ii and iii (as promised by the index) were casualties of the fire, damaged beyond recognition by charring and smoke.

When the antiquated orange rotary rang, he nearly leaped straight up out of his chair. He picked up on the third ring.

Michelle said, "Hi, dear. Just checking to see how it's going there." The connection was poor; her voice buzzed, fading in and out.

"Um, everything's fine. How are you girls?"

"What?" The roar in the background sounded like a jet lifting off.

"How's everyone?"

"We're all lovely. What are you doing, dear? It must be beastly late there."

Don flushed. "Oh, nothing much. Couldn't sleep."

There came a long, humming pause. Michelle said, "What are you doing, then? Surely you must be doing something. I don't hear the telly."

"No, no television. I'm reading—"

"Reading! I'm shocked. Anything good?"

He sweated now. His pulse throbbed in his ears. Thousands of miles away and he felt no less guilty than a boy caught in the act of some dastardly mischief. "Oh, nothing good. Just the usual. Rocks." He laughed weakly. "Isn't it always about rocks?"

More static, then, "Yes, except when it's not." Her tone was unreadable over the connection. "Beastly hot here. We're on the cruise, by the way. We docked in Istanbul this morning. Holly's burned to a crisp—she's keeping below decks for a day or two. No air conditioning, can you believe it?"

"It's a crime."

"What?" Michelle shouted.

"I'm sorry to hear it," he shouted back.

"Are you sure you're quite all right, love?"

"Why wouldn't I be fine?"

"No reason. Everything's jolly, then? No problems?"

"Problems? Heavens, no dear. Don't worry about me. Enjoy your trip."

"I've got to go. Give Kurt my love. I'll call you from town, later." Michelle disconnected while Don was fumbling his goodbyes.

He stared at the mess of books and papers spread everywhere and shook his head. "Good lord, whatever Kurt's got is contagious. Don, old bean, you need your head examined." He put everything away and kept a couple of the latter editions for bedside reading. He locked the door behind him, chuckling in retrospect over his foolishness. A bit of domestic skullduggery had never killed anyone.

Much later, he paused to wonder why she'd called him at that hour, knowing full well he'd be fast asleep.

6.

Don saw to the record-keeping, Kurt performed the hefting and toting. As Don sardonically pointed out, occasionally the lad's brawn was good for something besides swelling his collar. By noon they'd amassed an impressive stack of boxes. Unfortunately, they'd but scratched the surface of the project.

"At this rate, it'll only take another five or six months and we'll have all your junk buttoned up and ready to go," Kurt said, wiping his brow on a beer bottle. He was into his second six-pack of Rolling Rock and getting mellow. He'd stripped to a pair of running shorts and a sleeveless tee shirt. His neck and shoulders flushed deep red from exertion and alcohol. That's when it happened, the lightning bolt of inspiration that ruined Don's day. "Say, Dad. I think tomorrow we should take the day and go camping like we talked about the other night. I haven't gone since—well, since me and Holly were kids." He nodded, animating as the notion took root. "I've a few more days of vacation. We can fish for trout up the creek, roast marshmallows; the whole bit."

Don swallowed bile. When he became capable of speech, he said, "I hoped you were joking. Where on earth did you dream up this cockamamie scheme?"

"Exactly," Kurt said. "I dreamed about camping."

"What the blazes—"

"I was in grade school again, nine or ten. It was late summer and you and Mom and me were on the hill behind the house. You'd caught some fish and Mom was frying them in a skillet. Then you took me hiking into the woods. We were hunting for rabbits or something—you had on your old Elmer Fudd hat with the dumb ear flaps, and carried that single shot .22 we used to keep lying around. Whatever happened to that rifle, anyway?"

"I don't recall. Rusting away in the barn, I suppose. Hunting's not for me, you know that." Guns made Don nervous. The idea of shooting an animal made him slightly sick to his stomach. His youngest brother, Tom, hunted squirrels as a boy when they were growing up in Connecticut and it always disgusted Don to no end.

"We got separated. In the dream. I wandered through the woods and started getting panicky, like someone or something was watching me, chasing me. That's how dreams are, right? There were kids playing in a meadow. I called to them for help, but they didn't hear me. They were dressed in dirty pajamas and playing near some big rocks. The pjs kinda make sense since the kids were bald like those poor tykes in cancer wards. They sang a nursery rhyme that I couldn't make out and when I got close, they ran behind the rocks and disappeared. Then you put your hand on my shoulder and I woke up. End of dream. Thing is, I've been dreaming about this area for a few months now, going back to the days me and Holly ran wild. Once or twice a week, I get these."

"And that makes you want to go camping?" Don suspected his son's sudden interest in exploring had everything to do with their recent discoveries in the attic. His hands shook.

"Nostalgia, Pop. It reminded me of when I went exploring around here. Holly tagged along and...who was that kid? One of the farmboys who lived around here I think. There's this enormous tree in the hills back there. I ever tell you about the tree? Petrified wood." Kurt rapped his fist on the wall. His manner seemed more manic than usual; his eyes darted and he paced. "Yep, and we found some other things. A shed, some fire pits, pieces of rusted metal like the doors on a box car. Hell, Lyle claimed he saw some skulls, but he couldn't find the place again. Crazy."

Nostalgia, my eye, Don thought with mounting unease. "There were some logging camps in the hills. Many, many years ago. They shut down before we moved into the area. Sheriff Camby said a few tramps lived way back there in tarpaper shacks and lean-tos like Snuffy Smith up until the '70s. Mainly Vietnam vets who couldn't adjust to the civilian life. Everything's gone by now."

"I know I've seen those rocks in the photos. I wonder if Aunt Yvonne knew about an Indian burial ground or something. Maybe I can find them again."

"Holy cripes. You're really convincing me to go camping with that malarkey."

"It'll be fun. We've got nice weather all week. Call Uncle Argyle; he's not doing anything."

"I don't know—"

"You owe me for all this backbreaking labor. Besides, if you're nice, I'll help you move more of this stuff next weekend. What do you say?"

There wasn't anything *to* say. Don felt like a rat in a trap. He rang Argyle and relayed the invitation, hoping the old boy would beg off. Argyle prided himself the consummate outdoorsman and had indeed spent a good deal of his life tromping in the wilderness. He said he'd be thrilled to "wallow about the brush and bivouac for a night in the wild" and promised to conscript Hank to serve as a porter. Ten in the morning sound about right? Don's fate was sealed just that quickly.

Good grief, don't be such a ninny! He slapped his hand on the table. *You're afraid of the dark; won't go into the cellar to save your life; avoid sleeping in your own bed if you can humanly avoid it. My word, Don. Are you the same fellow who once caved the Dahl Sultan with a miner's lamp and a knapsack? What's done you in?* The self-motivation didn't help much. Dread remained, a clammy vise on the back of his neck. He hoped he wouldn't disgrace himself by succumbing to hysterics or wetting his pants. To be on the safe side he packed three gas lamps and a bottle of Valium he'd saved as insurance against Michelle's threatened hike into the Appalachians. At least *that* trek never materialized, praise the gods.

CHAPTER SEVEN

The Backyard Expedition

(Now)

1.

The hike was predictably delayed—Argyle didn't bother to inform Hank of the camping trip the day before, thus they arrived two hours late. Worse, Kurt was notoriously disorganized, while Argyle was the polar opposite; the type who suffered near paralysis from dithering over the most trivial detail. Come noon, the Miller kitchen proved a disaster area of loose camping gear, sleeping rolls and various articles of mismatched clothing.

"Gads, people!" Don brandished a sock hat and a pair of insulated gloves. "We are not sailing to the Antarctic. The weather forecast is sixty with a low of forty-five. It isn't even going to rain. And if you think I'm walking more than a mile, you're off your rockers. Let's get moving before nightfall, eh?" The idea of spending a night in the dark still made his stomach roil and his palms sweat. Since the situation appeared to be inescapable, the sooner they got started, the sooner they'd come home.

No one bothered to answer him, but they began to pack more quickly nonetheless and by mid-afternoon the small company trundled up the hill behind the house and followed the trail along the creek bank. It had rained the previous evening and the grass soaked the cuffs of their pants.

"Does the county own all this?" Hank said, sweeping his arm in a vague arc. "Or is it private land?" His broad face shone with sweat.

"Some of this is ours," Don said. "Darned if I know where the lines are, though. Somebody else owns a big piece of this area—Goodwyn or one those other lumber companies. Goodwyn owns mineral rights to every parcel in this county from what I understand; it's in the fine print on the deed."

"Crooked bastards," Argyle said and spat.

"I think the state controls a lot of this," Kurt said. "You'll notice the logging is selective and there's some prime areas completely untouched. I bet the boys at the capitol are saving it for a rainy day."

"Ever walk all the way to the source?" Argyle said, indicating the creek. He wore heavy lace-up boots, a wool coat and a soft cap and carried a madrone staff that he constantly used to flip rocks and sticks. Don couldn't help but see the truant schoolboy masquerading as a white-haired old man.

"It peters out a couple of miles farther on," Kurt said over his shoulder. He and Hank wore big packs. Kurt seemed to be more comfortable than his huffing and puffing counterpart. "The brush gets thick and it basically disappears. We aren't going that far. I want to pitch the tent up ahead at this one spot—remember the fishing hole, Pop? Then we can explore a bit."

Explore a bit. Don wondered what that meant. Kurt's sudden interest in checking out his old stomping grounds seemed increasingly out of character. He'd long since professed to set aside childish things in favor of career ambitions and the manly hobbies of collecting cars and women. *He wants to find that pile of rocks. Lord knows why, but the boy's got his cap set.* Don studied his son's powerful, determined stride. Maybe Kurt's dreams were worse than he let on. He was the stubborn type, prone to exorcising demons via head-on confrontation.

The lazy, golden afternoon was further mellowed by a cool breeze and lengthening shadows. The creek gurgled through rocks and rushes and songbirds chirped in branches that yet kept most of their leaves. Clouds hung white and fat; they shifted and wobbled and remade themselves as animals and faces. A flock of geese honked as it skimmed low over a marsh across the way, then climbed rapidly and vanished beyond the ridgelines. Thule barked and raced ahead, peeing on every other bush and hunting for more birds to rubberneck.

After a bit, Hank called for a break; he and Kurt lighted cigarettes while Argyle scoped the valley with a pair of Zeiss field glasses he claimed to have looted from the corpse of a German Lieutenant during World War Two. That would've made him a stripling pup of seventeen or eighteen, a mere four years Don's elder, but he figured the tale was true. Beneath the genteel exterior, Argyle seemed rather fierce. He habitually concealed a bayonet in its honing scabbard at his belt—another wartime memento. Don begged him to leave it home when they gathered at the tavern, convinced the old goat would stick some loudmouthed lout and get hauled to prison. Argyle grinned and told him not to worry so much—he'd go gray before his time.

Don shaded his eyes and studied the valley behind them. The house was tucked like a matchbox in a fold of the terrain, partially obscured by the barn and the trees; reddish, westerly light illuminated its walls, pooled in its dead glass windows. Don thought its windows resembled a spider's eyes, its body a spider's body, its legs folded in the waving grass. He considered bumming a smoke from one of the guys and instead took a drink from his water bottle and watched Argyle who'd squatted near a rotten stump alive with termites. Don had an uncomfortable epiphany—he wondered who was watching him and his friends. A goose ran across his grave and the bucolic panorama attained a sinister grandeur.

Cigarettes finished and water swallowed, the party commenced moving again.

2.

Eventually, they arrived at the proposed campsite, a shady bower beneath a stand of maples ten yards from a pool that teemed with minnows and trout. The area had overgrown in the many years between visits, but the four of them soon trampled the bushes and cleared off the ring of stones that formed a fire pit. Despite himself, Don was taken aback by the rush of memories of bringing Michelle and the kids here to fish and tell stories around the fire, and after, look at the vast expanse of stars through the telescope he rescued from the attic and brought along on their excursions. Kurt and Don pitched the tent while Hank gathered deadwood. Argyle supervised, his professed area of expertise. Dinner was pork and beans and a half case of import beer.

Velvet darkness settled upon their tiny hollow of light. It grew chill and a damp breeze rustled in the branches and scattered leaves. Argyle announced he needed his beauty sleep and turned in. Hank followed suit a few minutes later, his face red from fatigue and too many beers.

Kurt said, "I think Winnie's going to leave me. At first I figured she was having an affair. It's been less than two years. That's not long, really. She's alone…her temp job at the college—she helps the Chinese kids who don't savvy English—it's only part time. I work fifty, sixty hours a week. I'm gone ten days out of the month. India, Asia, you know. Wherever. She's got a lot of time to kill. Bored and lonely can be a bad combination."

Don stirred coals with a stick and kept his mouth shut. The wind moaned and darkness shifted around them.

Kurt said, "Winnie started acting strange a few weeks ago. She'd be missing when I dropped in at the house unexpectedly. She'd be late from work. Then I caught her on the phone in the middle of the night. I'd been drinking, well, tying one on, I guess. So I woke up to take a piss and she's gone. I'm groggy as hell, but I decide to find her and she's in the den whispering on the phone. I can't make out much and she hangs up. I got back into bed and pretended to sleep just before she came sneaking into the room. She never said anything. I was upset, but I didn't confront her. Instead I intercepted the phone bill when it came in—she usually handles all that stuff. Know where she was calling?"

"Hong Kong?"

Kurt turned his head and actually laughed. "Nice one, Mr. Comedy. You're a regular George Burns. She called *here*. Three times in the middle of the night, each one maybe five days apart. You didn't talk with her, did you?"

"No. Are you sure you've got the right number?"

"I'm sure. She was calling Mom."

Don frowned. He couldn't recollect Michelle taking any calls at odd hours. On the other hand, he usually slept like the dead and she kept her cell phone set to vibrate—a matter of habit from enduring a million meetings and debriefings with officials who weren't the type to brook interruptions. "Why would she call your mother? Are they close? She hasn't indicated they've talked outside of your visits."

"I don't know. There's something funny between them."

"Perhaps it's a conspiracy," Don said, trying to lighten the mood.

Kurt didn't laugh at this sally. "I've considered that. You learn to spot certain behaviors in my line. I work with human resources and screen a lot of employees. Our data is extremely sensitive and it'll sound corny, but we have to guard against corporate espionage. Hell, we've been compromised by foreign governments. Lemme tell you, I've got a keen eye for suspicious persons. Winnie and Mom…they worry me."

"For the love of…This is why you agreed to help me clean the house, I take it. To get me alone. Good grief, Son."

"Yeah. I wanted to sound you out on this. Win's parents were eager to get rid of her."

"Really?"

"Yeah, Dad. I thought there'd be trouble, her folks being well-connected; that maybe they'd think I was too low for her station. Her father made no secret he despised Americans. At the dinner they threw for our delegation, he joined the toast only after one of his superiors gave him a look. Should've seen his face, wrinkled like he was drinking vinegar."

"Well, maybe you won them over with the old Miller charm. Or, maybe they wanted your money—Mr. Big Shot corporate fella." Don winked.

"Her parents are loaded. They pushed her out the door. Winnie clammed up about the whole deal. Put it on the tab, I guess. I tell ya, Dad, I'm getting scared to see the bill."

"Well, she could be a corporate spy. Marries you to steal secrets. Pretty clever."

"Oh, God. Don't even joke about that."

Don sighed. "It's also pretty melodramatic. Didn't your company screen her? Good lord, all the questions your mother and I had to answer before they gave you the job…"

"She's not a spy, okay? No, I have a domestic crisis brewing here."

"Why would your mother conspire with her…take sides? She isn't the sort."

Kurt nodded, as if convincing himself of a dubious theory. "Jeez, I dunno. Probably Win's asking for marital advice. Maybe she's scared about the baby. When we were here last…When I whacked my head. I wasn't sleepwalking." He gulped the remainder of his beer and rolled the empty bottle between his big hands. "I'm a pretty light sleeper these days. Win had gotten up to use the bathroom or something. I went downstairs for a glass of water; y'know, feeling my way in the dark. Candlelight was coming from under the door to Mom's study. They were in there talking; who knows about what. Me, I bet. Anyway, I figured to hell with Win if she wants to cry on Mom's shoulder. I went to the kitchen and got a drink."

"Then, what happened to your head?" Don felt uneasy now. He disliked the haunted light in Kurt's eyes.

"There's a mystery for you; I don't remember hitting it when I fell. Maybe I got short-term amnesia from the blow. The room sort of spun and I blacked out. Next thing I know, I'm in the greenhouse with Mom leaning over me, calling my name. It's weird, Dad. Really weird. Only thing is, I have this recurring dream of the incident, of being dragged. Like somebody had a hold on my pajamas and started pulling me away. There's giggling and whispering."

"I think maybe you *did* rattle something loose. You fainted, obviously. Then, delirious and disoriented, you crawled outside. Not much of a mystery if you ask me."

"Think so?"

"I do."

"You're probably right. I've just been doing the math and things don't add up, is all. Like, why Mom always insisted we spend the summer here. What is it about this house? None of us ever liked the damned thing. Except her."

Don wasn't feeling well; his skin clammy with thoughts of the lights in the bedroom, the long, strange history of inexplicable occurrences he'd learned to ignore. "You're drunk. Go get some sleep."

"I'm not drunk. And I'm serious about what I said."

"That seems to be the case. Let it lie for now, okay?"

"I'll let it lie, all right. Something else I gotta say, first. The story I told you guys about the séance at the Coolidge department store, how I saw a figure in the office…" Kurt let the moment drag on as he visibly steeled himself for whatever was to come. "To be honest, I actually got a better look at it than I let on that night we were sitting around with the storm going and such. Didn't feel right to say what really happened in that damned store. Not with Mom watching me like old Boris the cat used to right before he pounced and scratched the shit outta me."

"Why didn't you want to tell the whole story in front of your mom?"

"Because, that person I saw leering at us from the other side of the glass...the fucked up witch-thing that terrified Reeves. It was her."

"Who?"

"You know."

Don rose as quickly as his creaky knees permitted. "Yep, past my bedtime." He made a point of not looking at his son on the way to the tent.

Asleep moments after his head hit the bedroll, his dreams were sepia-tone twilightscapes of taiga frozen to iron. His astral self rocketed across the wintry panorama at frightening velocity. A light drew him; the mother of all bonfires, and it was bones, just like the old tribes did it, that crackled and emitted sulfurous black smoke and gouts of red fire.

Michelle, naked and lithe in a middle-aged incarnation, was chained to a boulder that had been shaped first by primitive hands, then eons of wind and rain. It was the lumpen altar of a nameless dark god. She smiled at him across time and space as figures in cowls danced around the base of the rock. There was a dolmen nearby; a pile of henges large enough to entomb a giant. The dolmen radiated the implacable cold of space; it hissed the frequency of gamma radiation, of stars.

"I love you," Michelle said, her voice carrying faint as a ghost radio signal. "We all love you." Her face began to change and crack apart. He screamed and the vision shattered.

He lay sweating and shaking in the tent in the darkness and did not sleep again. Those long hours he spent yearning for daylight and cursing Kurt for putting such fool notions into his mind. *Reinforcing notions in your mind*, a submerged and less pleasant aspect of himself muttered from the cellar where Don routinely banished all unpleasant facets of his personality.

3.

At dawn, heavy mist rose from the damp soil and drifted through the forest until it filled the valley. The men huddled near the fire, boiled coffee in a dented kettle and ate cereal for breakfast. Argyle dug a bottle of Irish whiskey from Hank's pack—he'd blithely loaded the poor sap like a donkey—and dumped a good pint into his thermos of coffee.

"Jesus, man! Did you haul a bar up here?" Kurt said. He lighted his cigarette.

Hank moaned and rubbed his thighs. "Ahh, my legs are sore as all hell."

Don supposed racquetball and badminton at the health club weren't quite the same as a real hike. He stifled his own complaints and picked at his breakfast in morose silence.

"Well, this is pointless," the younger man said. "I can't see ten yards in this fog. Why don't we head back to the ranch, huh?"

"It'll burn off," Kurt said. Don very much disagreed. Possibly the fog would lift in a few hours, although he doubted Kurt would be patient enough to cool his heels that long. Still he kept his peace and waited to see if Argyle would weigh in to second the kid's sensible idea to trek home.

Argyle peered into the trees and rubbed his chin. "It might lift if you're willing to wait it out."

"Let's see what happens." Kurt took the pans and the tin plates to the creek and scrubbed them briefly. The other men exchanged glances.

"It won't do any harm to hold off a bit," Argyle said. "The lad's determined to track down this alleged site of his. I must admit I'm intrigued. This part of the country has had its share of unorthodox religious customs."

"Er, what kind of religious customs?" Don said.

"Oh, the usual—Wicca, the druidic orders. Satan worship is another popular one."

Hank looked stricken. "No way."

"You must be kidding. I knew this was a dumb idea," Don said.

"Don't fret. *Most* of these people are amateurs. Kids acting out. You've seen the gothic silliness that's been the rage for years now. I credit rock bands for the whole mess. There's no real menace unless you happen to be a goat or a rabbit."

"Or a virgin."

"Haven't seen one in years."

Around noon things weren't much different except the mist was set afire and it hung in luminescent sheets. Kurt declared a brief foray into the forest. There were two compasses, thus the search would be most efficient if they split into parties. Don ended up with Hank. Thule abandoned him to trail after Kurt and Argyle. *See where you're sleeping tonight, traitor!*

After Argyle and Kurt and Thule disappeared into the mist, Hank said, "Y'know, we could just sneak back and call it a day..."

"Gosh, and miss all this wilderness adventuring? In for a penny, sadly enough."

"I hope you brought a flashlight. We're gonna get lost and spend the night out here. Yep, I can feel it."

Don sighed. He checked his canteen and took a compass reading. They set out toward the northwest as agreed upon earlier. The plan was to move generally north in a vee pattern for no more than three-eighths of a mile and then sweep back toward the camp. Even stubborn Kurt conceded that would be sufficient for this particular trip. Either they'd stumble across the site, or late afternoon would find them trudging home.

4.

Hank stepped behind a tree to "get rid of some coffee" and Don ambled on another twenty or so paces to give the fellow privacy. He stood quite still, and listened to faint woodland rustles, the drip of the branches. Trees and underbrush were black silhouettes floating in the shining white. The foliage blocked the sky, but for notches where sunrays slanted into the steaming earth. Birds called far off. He flicked his compass open to take a reading and found the glass was milky with internal condensation; no amount of rubbing with his sleeve helped. The silence began to creep into his ears and he abruptly called out for Hank. His cry echoed impotently, quickly snuffed by the smothering fog. He knew with the certainty of a lucid nightmare Hank wasn't going to answer.

"Over here," Hank said. A whisper that might've originated inside Don's head. Only the voice, though. Hank remained hidden by brush and mist.

My lord, I'm turned around. Hank had replied from a completely different direction than he'd expected. *Thank goodness Michelle isn't here to see this debacle. She'd fall down laughing at me…*

"Hey, Mr. Miller!" This time the younger man shouted, and from a good forty or fifty feet behind Don.

Don homed in on Hank, caught sight of him stepping from the shadowy bulk of a fir. They joined forces again, Hank patting him on the shoulder in passing, a gesture of sympathy. "Take it easy, old-timer. You look a little green around the gills. Bring your glycerin? Think I got hemorrhoids. Of all the luck. "

"Don't concern yourself with me, young master Hank. I'm…fit as a fiddle." Don faked a smile. As they continued onward, he sneaked a few glances over his shoulder without the faintest notion of who or what he expected to see lurking back there. Shadows, mist, a wall of sodden shrubbery; he was a young explorer again, brush knife in one hand, map in the other, with a cave to discover, groundwater to divine, a seismic survey to initiate, and anywhere from days to weeks before he'd stumble forth from temperate rainforest or highland desert to civilized, pacified lands once more.

Sure, sure, rejuvenated, reincarnated and on the doorstep of adventure… Yet had he been so skittish in the halcyon days of yore? Was it a consequence of age—the night terrors, paranoia toward Michelle, his fear of the dark, and now hallucinations of voices in the gloom? He had to ask himself just how much more of this getting-old stuff he could take.

A sharp slope greeted them. It was littered with rotted logs, a loose bed of slimy leaves. Underbrush thinned near the brow of the hill and the forest peeled away to reveal a clearing.

Don gasped. "What the dickens?" He *knew,* though. He'd seen it in the photograph. It had awaited him since forever.

"Funky ol' rock, ain't it?" Hank said, bored and weary.

The clearing was nearly level; a semi-crescent of dark, gritty soil patched with weeds. Wisps of mist rose like smoke. At the heart of the opening lay a massive boulder rooted deep in the black earth. The boulder rose to eight or so feet and was easily double that in circumference. Twined with creepers and evil green moss, it radiated an aura of malignance like a slumbering beast from a fairytale, one of the awful kinds in Michelle's books. This illusion was reinforced by the joyous dirge of nearby crows. More rocks lay scattered across the field, some as small as a man's skull, others on the order of a compact car. The trees that hemmed the clearing were quite large, old-growth forest to rival the twin monsters in Don's yard.

Don wasn't much of a tracker, but he figured no one had set foot on this ground for decades. His chest pained him and sweat and rocketing blood pressure clouded his vision, and he staggered. The big central boulder was without question the same as that in the photos, yet his sudden queasiness sprang from a darker, hidden source that he couldn't name. He imagined debauched reeds and clashing cymbals, demonic masks bathed in bloody firelight, an axe…

"Hang on, old-timer," Hank said and helped him kneel. "You having a heart attack? Oh, man alive—don't do that to me. Here, take a drink." He pressed his canteen to Don's lips.

Don swallowed and coughed and in a few moments the fugue lifted and he was himself again, but for trembling hands and a racing heart. "Thanks, lad. No, I'm A-okay. Getting too old for this nonsense, heh."

Hank had already turned away, rubbing the neck of the canteen on his sleeve before he screwed the cap back on. He stared at the mossy boulder, cocking his head. "Man, something odd about that damned rock, ain't there? Rest a minute, huh? I'm going to check it out." With that he slung his canteen and tiptoed across the clearing. His tracks, scuffing aside dead leaves and needles and indenting the soft, dark earth, were the only tracks. No animal sign. The drone of flies and mosquitoes, nothing larger.

Don stood, and quieting a chorus of ghostly misgivings that arose from the pit of his subconscious, he carefully made his way to Hank's side, snapping a few pictures to compare with the set at the house.

A portion of the boulder was concave along its vertical axis and a broad, shallow channel scored its length. Spaced at wide intervals were four brackets of tarnished and corroded bronze. He had no difficulty imagining a figure pinioned spread-eagle upon the stone, manacled hand and foot. Several feet off center, and obscured by a layer of needles and dirt, was the fire pit—one of several that lighted the scene of ritual and revelry. He said with a lightness that was superficial, "Argyle wasn't kidding. People getting up to hijinks and such." But not children, not amateurs.

This was too elaborate, too serious.

"I dunno," Hank said. "Kinda weird. Yeah." He scratched his head and frowned, conveying annoyance rather than curiosity. Obviously the implications of the groove, the brackets, the fire pit, were lost on him. Likely he was too young to appreciate the multitude of Hammer films that Don and Michelle had devoured in their prime (this despite the fact such fare always gave Don dreadful nightmares). Don knew how this went down in the creepy occult flicks of the gory-hoary '60s and '70s.

"I'm going to ring our fellows. Kurt will be ecstatic." Don hit Kurt's number on his cell. While listening to the rings, he adjusted his glasses and scanned the surroundings, momentarily visualizing a mob of hooded figures poised to swoop from the forest, scythes waving with murderous intent. The call went to voicemail. "Well, that's odd."

"Odd, what's odd? Don't say 'odd' in the woods. You got service? I got bars on mine. Lemme try." Hank did indeed attempt to raise Argyle, with no effect. "Not answering. What the hell are they doing that they can't answer huh?"

"Let's not fret. They'll be along soon." Don skirted the edge of the boulder, noting that its creepers and vines appeared simultaneously vibrant and voluptuously decayed; spoiled sap and pulp had burst through and made puddles in the weeds, and these reeked as befouled vegetation does. On the far side, the clearing narrowed to a saddle between the trees. On either side of the four-foot span was a sheer drop of fifty or sixty feet into a tangle of brush and more big rocks.

The narrow ridge had once served as a path; the depression made from countless tramping feet remained in evidence despite encroaching bushes and weeds. Ahead was another opening ringed by a stand of old firs, and within was what Don took as a queerly jumbled pile of huge white stone slabs. "Oh, my Jesus," he said after a moment, and stopped. The vertigo returned, as did the pain in his chest. He closed his eyes and concentrated on breathing slowly, calming his thoughts. He looked again, and the pile was still there. "Oh, my Jesus."

"Hey, I've seen this before." Hank stepped past him. "On National Geographic, or on one of those history shows. It's a megalith."

"No, it's called a dolmen," Don said, professional pique overriding his anxiety for the moment. "A tomb. *Maybe* a tomb. Nobody is certain."

"Cool as hell. Indians built these?"

"Neolithic tribes constructed them. But not here. Dolmens are in Europe, some other foreign locales. There aren't any in North America."

"Huh. Well, I'm looking at one, yeah?"

"So it seems." Don wiped his glasses and then simply gaped in amazement. The dolmen was built from a horizontal slab of granite weighing at least one hundred tons, supported by several crudely shaped vertical stones of similar size; these pillars were carved with mostly obliterated symbols that might've been an alphabet. The entrance was an off-kilter rectangle, and overhung by vines and morning glory. Its lintel was fashioned into a visage ruined by decay and mold. The faint light coming through the canopy combined with the mist, tinting the structure an eerie blue, as if he were observing it through smoke or a distorted camera lens.

"Lover mine, this is a bad idea," Michelle said. Don whirled, almost spraining his knee, and a few dead leaves fluttered past. His heart, his heart… He rubbed his chest and groaned.

Hank didn't notice. "Man, this has to be forgotten tribal grounds, or something. You think it's safe to go inside?" He shrugged off his pack and rummaged around until he retrieved a flashlight.

"Hank, that's not wise. It could be unstable. Could be a deadfall, or wild animals…" Don watched him click the light on and off. "Really. I don't recommend this course of action. I know some fellows at the university. We'll head back to the house, give them a ring. Probably be a team out here tomorrow. Best to wait. Safe before sorry, eh?"

"Animals? Nah, no tracks. Hang tight. Be a sec." Hank flashed the light at Don's face and then trundled away, pausing to examine the entrance; an ant inspecting a mausoleum. He scrunched his shoulders and ducked inside. His tiny beam of light vanished instantly.

"Oh, boy." Don should've protested more strongly, made further attempts to stop the boy. He didn't possess the energy or the will. He settled onto a rotten log and unrolled a paper sandwich bag and huffed into it until he felt more well, and after he'd recovered a bit, he sipped brandy from the stash of mini-bottles in the bottom of his pack. Michelle had stockpiled them from hundreds of international flights. He fidgeted.

The dolmen was an impossibility. Surveyors would've noted it ages ago, sitting as it did on county land. It had to be visible from the air and someone, somewhere would've laid in its coordinates, marked it on a topographical map. The Redfield Museum would have sent a team of photographers and archeologists. There would be a display, a documentary, a book. If the dolmen existed, if it were possible, then it would be on the record and Don would know everything about it.

"I should've stopped that fool," he said, fully aware of the absurdity of his wizened and decrepit self attempting to prevent a young thug such as Hank from doing whatever he wished. At twenty-five, hell, even forty-five, Don would've cheerfully rabbit-punched the bugger and laid him out for a nap. He glanced at his knotted and knurled hands and winced in sorrow and regret. Meanwhile, a fractional piece of his worn soul was slightly interested in what might happen. For some reason he began to mutter the old advertising line *Roaches check in, but they don't check out!* And promptly forced himself to desist.

Time passed and nothing happened, so he finished the brandy and tried Kurt's cell again, which came to naught, and then he cracked another little bottle and sipped that and waited, and as he waited, like the encroaching shadows of the forest, the shadows of dread in his subconscious lengthened and stretched across his entire mind. He was nervous that Hank didn't return, nervous that Kurt and Argyle didn't answer their phones, nervous that mid-afternoon was sliding past and the world remained a murky fairy ground that would soon enough become pitch dark and wholly dangerous. Certainly nervousness was in order. None of this explained his rising fear, an emotion more powerful by magnitudes than mere nervousness, however. Fear that crept from the middle of his belly and spread into his chest until he shook and sweated and imagined phantom music, phantom shrieks.

"Yes, love, it's going to get *so* dark," Michelle said. More leaves, floating in their death spirals to the ground. "The servitors will be waking up."

He clapped his hand over his mouth—Michelle hadn't said anything; *Don* was talking to himself, and heaven have mercy, that wasn't a positive sign. Against his palm he said, "Good grief, talking to myself? How long has this gone on?" No reply, not in his head, nor elsewhere.

In due course he heaved to his feet and shouted for bullheaded young Hank, received the echo of his own cry, muffled and impotent. Even the crows and mosquitoes had fallen silent. By the reddish slant of a falling sunbeam, or configuration of shadow, a tree opposite the dolmen caught his eye. A redwood of significant girth, and as old as the hills, its limbs the size of smaller trees and its scales of bark as tall as a man. Easily one of the largest and hoariest specimens he'd seen north of California.

The broad sheaves of bark drew his attention from the dolmen and whatever drama occurred within; drew him shuffling and stumbling closer until his nose was inches away, and still he required a few more seconds before he recognized the hidden puzzle.

A symbol was etched into the wood at eye level; a reverse C, albeit with a narrower gap. The symbol was blackened and glazed and partially refilled by the growth of the tree, and it measured on the order of a basketball, and upon closer scrutiny, he beheld delicate variations and lines that suggested the object represented the spinal column of a sinuous creature, a serpent, although the skull was enlarged and cruelly horned. Of course, this was none other than the embossment upon the cover of *The Black Guide.*

He retreated several steps and the larger picture coalesced, natural splinters and fractures aligning to form a door, or hatch, in the bole of the tree. He recognized knotted sinews as hinges, a knothole as a latch in a sheaf of thick bark scarcely wider than his shoulders and thrice his height—a neatly fitted panel that blended into its surroundings as to be nigh-invisible. Braced against the trunk was a long, slender rod that tapered to a hook, not unlike the poles he used at university to open classroom skylights. Obviously the crook was intended to snag the knothole and pop the panel ajar.

"Are you really thinking about it?" He imagined Michelle clearly and unambiguously at his side, dressed in blue, a blue wrap and fancy sunglasses disguising her expression. She was always her younger self in his daydreams, while he remained leathery and spent. He'd never been capable of matching her. "Stop and use your brain. What's in there? A hunter's cache? Moldering pelts, spoiled meat? A drug lord's bale of cocaine? Or worse—a body! What if it's murder? This deep in the woods, it just might be nefarious. You're too old for nefarious doings, Don. Your hands are shaking, you're making pee drops in your underwear. Baby, you've got every reason to be afraid. *The Black Guide* is bad medicine. The worst. Don't pull a Hank on me. Sweetie, are you really going to do this?"

Don was indeed considering the crook and the panel and what might lay inside the hollow tree, although not from simple curiosity as might've compelled him once upon a time; *dread* compelled him, the way it compels a man to look into an abyss, to entertain the notion of leaping in. He actually touched the rod before jolting to his senses and withdrawing his hand as if from a snake. He wiped his sweaty brow and cleaned his glasses and walked back to the path and stood twenty yards from the entrance of the dolmen, that keyhole slot in its dour face, and called for Hank. Again nothing, and this time when he tried to ring Kurt and Argyle the pane said NO SERVICE.

The forest closed in and the air dimmed. He shivered, hot and cold, and zipped his coat as Michelle would've chided him to do. He grimly studied the dolmen, hoping it might appear less gargantuan and passively inimical if he stared long enough. Twenty minutes since Hank vanished inside. Twenty minutes was an eon. He squared his jaw and fished out his own flashlight. "Oh, bloody blazes. I've got to go in after him, don't I?" Ghostly Michelle said, *Is that rhetorical? By the way, the servitors are coming.*

At the threshold of the prehistoric tomb, the powerful stink of mold and rotting vegetation obliged him to pinch his nostrils while brandishing the flashlight at arm's length. Only vines and spongy moss, and not a rank carcass in a pool of maggot-clabbered blood that his morbid imagination conjured on the spot. He called, "Hank! Hey, kid, where the blazes are you?"

The interior shouldn't have encompassed more than fifteen to twenty feet as the massive slabs were of such a dimension as to leave a mere pocket within their confines relative to the dolmen's overall size. Also, despite gaps being covered by brush and vines, sunlight should've seeped through and provided at least dim illumination. Yet his flashlight beam revealed a floor covered in dirt and creepers and the suggestion of a rude column decorated with more carvings, and penetrated no farther into the black. The relic's spatial incongruity summoned Don's dizziness and he fought to maintain composure.

His phone rang. Retreating to fumble the cell from his pocket, Don tripped and sprawled in the leaves. He managed to connect before it went to the recording.

Kurt said from a gulf, "Dad? Dad? You okay?"

"Yes, right as rain," Don said, trying to ignore the hundred firecrackers popping in his right knee and ankle, the scrape on his palm where he'd skinned it across the ground, the bruise to his dignity. "Where are you two?"

The line hissed and snapped and howling overlaid this interference. Kurt was shouting, though his words were faint. "Dad, get back to camp. Wait—fuck camp. Point toward the house and get moving. We'll meet you there. Dad, you hear me?"

"Son, I hear you. Problem is, young master Hank went exploring and I've lost him—"

"Dad, forget Hank! Get your ass moving! I repeat, forget Hank. Oh, shit!" The call dropped to static, then silence.

Don awkwardly regained his feet, and the firecrackers became dynamite and he yelped. He spent a few moments listening to the forest, listening for either Hank in the tomb or the other men somewhere in the omnipresent mist. Night was on the wing; already the pale sky had dimmed to red.

A moan or a cackle emanated from the dolmen and Don, with the molasses speed of a man in a nightmare, turned toward the black slot of an entrance. "Hank?"

He was running, crashing through brush and smashing into trees, rebounding from them and charging onward, heedless of injury, intent solely upon flight in a straight line. His breath exploded in sobs of exhaustion and he couldn't recall what spurred him, except that his fear had escalated to mindless terror, the terror of an animal fleeing before a cyclone of fire. He was away from the dolmen, and that was good, very good, and every stride took him farther into the trackless forest, which wasn't so good, but better than the alternative, better than being caught. He mustn't be caught. Mustn't be caught.

Run, baby; they're coming! Michelle said, floating over his shoulder.

A branch slashed his cheek and ripped his glasses free. He ran and then it was too dark for running and he collapsed, curled tight, knuckles in mouth, retching and gasping.

Later, Don dragged himself under the sheltering boughs of a granddaddy fir tree and rested with his cheek pressed to a bed of fir needles.

His pack was gone, his clothes in shreds, he'd lost the phone, and his knee was swollen as a cantaloupe. As he calmed and adrenaline trickled away, pain filled the gap; pain sufficient to cause him to rip strips from his pants and fashion an impromptu gag to bite upon. Despite the void whirling in his brain where a record of his last few minutes at the dolmen belonged, it seemed vitally important that he meld with the environment, that he become an unobtrusive creature of the wood. He jammed the fabric into his mouth and clamped tight, and gibbered involuntarily while leaves whispered and water dripped and an owl hooted softly overhead.

Don swatted at the hungry mosquitoes and tried to concentrate. The dark was so complete he couldn't see his hand in front of his face. Bit by bit fragments fit together like puzzle pieces and he remembered staring into the gloom of the dolmen as he now stared into the nothingness of the night forest. He remembered a low, throaty moan drifting from the tomb. He'd seen abrupt movement, a shadow within shadow, rapidly approaching and retreating simultaneously. A moist, pallid figure; tall, yet hunched, all angles and fluid in its motion. A faceless apparition, its head clouded in shadow.

The proportions were wrong for Hank. If not Hank, then who? It all distorted and zipped away from Don and the rest was a complete blank; the sequence only picked up again with his flight and fall.

All of this seemed familiar, somehow. The abject terror, the impossible dolmen, a missing companion, the experience of frailty and abandonment in the maw of the wild. He was reliving a nightmare that taunted him with its opacity.

You've been here before. Here, or somewhere very close. You've seen that... person. Oh, a person, was it? He didn't need his muse Michelle to laugh him off the stage. Shade Michelle put a finger to her lips and shook her head, then evaporated.

A fox screamed. The mist filled his bower and wormed into his nose and mouth, and he shook with violent chills. There was a terrifying moment when he jolted from a doze to the crackling of leaves and something heavy slammed into him—a beast with heaving wet fur and raw, heated breath, and Don cried out. Thule whimpered and buried his blocky muzzle under Don's arm.

"Oh, doggie," he said and hugged his trembling pet and together they cowered in the primeval darkness. A breeze came creaking and squeaking through the forest. Don imagined many doors opening in the trunks of cedars and firs.

Darker, and darker.

CHAPTER EIGHT

Mystery Mountain Stomp

(1980)

1.

Monday morning after he and Michelle straggled home from the funeral reception for Louis Plimpton, Don went into the Olympia office of AstraCorp where work deluged him. His supervisor and company comptroller Wayne Kykendahl fumed and boiled like old angry Vesuvius; his florid jowls quivered wrathfully. Something was amiss. Nobody dared ask and Don was too exhausted to care.

He passed through the day in a kind of stupor, doing his best to forget the hideously strange weekend at the Wolverton estate, the bizarre interrogation by the weirdoes claiming to be federal agents, the equally unsettling conversation with the Rourke boy, the monstrous museum display...

Then, a few moments before he managed to slink home, a flat package arrived via courier, no return address. He initially assumed the package contained a bundle of requested materials from one of his ongoing projects and didn't get around to cracking the seal until after dinner. Michelle was locked in her study, ranting and raving over the damnable family history she was assembling, so he camped in the parlor and went through the briefcase load of paperwork he'd lugged from the office.

What he discovered in the anonymous package proved incomprehensible at first, but after a second read through his neck prickled and he was reminded of the horror he'd felt gazing upon the Cro-Magnon skin hanging on display.

He poured himself a glass of bourbon. And another. Sleep was fitful, his dreams macabre and disjointed.

At the office the next morning Don slumped over his desk. He clutched his skull, vowing to never touch another drop of hard liquor if he lived a hundred years, all the while suffering sporadic catcalls of the boys as they poked their gleeful mugs into his broom closet of an office.

Around eleven o'clock, he asked Ronnie "Cub" Houghton from R&D to walk him the several tree-lined blocks to the Flintlock Hotel. The hotel basement constituted a substantial commercial annex, including a classy barbershop, shoeshine station, cigar emporium, an international newsstand called The Carrier, and The Happy Tiger Lounge, home of the ten-dollar martini—a hidden lair of legislators and the slick lobbyists who followed them in shoals. The Happy Tiger was Ronnie's preferred lunch hour haunt—he endeavored to snag a booth with an opportune view of the gaggles of secretaries and paralegals and interns perched on leather stools flanking the silky-bright granite bar. Don's head hurt too much for him to appreciate the cavalcade of high heels, short skirts and hosiery. Clouds of hairspray and perfume made his eyes water. He sneezed into his hanky. Michelle had stopped wearing scents out of a tender and rare inclination toward mercy.

No martinis for Don. The day-shift bartender, a hulking bruiser named Vern, took one look at his pale, sweaty face and mixed tomatoes, lime and ice in a shaker and had the waitress deliver it to his booth with a complimentary plate of gourmet crackers. Ronnie threw back his shaggy head and laughed good-naturedly at Don's misery; he ordered an import beer and a Caesar salad (God knew why he bothered, the boys nicknamed him Cub on account of his behemoth pear-shaped torso and copious patches of wiry black hair that grew wild and the fact he packed enough lard to hibernate) and plunged into an earnest monologue regarding the latest remote sensing device, a prototype model designed by some firm in Norway, and he was practically salivating about the possibilities. Don nodded and smiled noncommittally and thought about the government men, the spooks, who'd braced him at the reception.

What was it with all this recent weirdness? Montoya (and why was that name so familiar?), Cooye, Bronson Ford, and Louis? Poor Louis. So much for the story about a coronary conclusion, although one wit said long ago that the ultimate cause of all death was heart failure. He sipped his hangover antidote and tried not to worry where it was leading, or how Michelle might be involved. Grandpa, that secretive coot, had loved her dearly. Don paused now to speculate whether it was the out-to-pasture spymaster in him that responded to her so well.

What if Frick and Frack were right? *Everybody knows Sinatra worked for the CIA on his road shows. Michelle travels to a lot of dicey places on her little special visa. It's the perfect cover for an operative.* Goddamn those guys for putting such moronic suspicions in his head.

For dessert, he passed an envelope full of aerial photographic plates to Ronnie and watched with guarded interest as the bearded man unclipped his glasses from his shirt pocket. Nine plates were a sequence depicting Plimpton's farmhouse shot via satellite, or so Don assumed, but they lacked time signatures and that was odd, very odd indeed. The photos zoomed in by a magnitude of ten, and the final image reduced the peak roof to X-ray transparency and captured Plimpton on his bed, revolver to his temple, face contorted as if he were shrieking.

The tenth through twelfth pictures tracked a car on a winding coastal highway. The final shot was a dramatic overhead zoom, another muddy X-ray that dissolved the cab and caught a man staring up at the camera which could've only been mere inches from his gaping mouth. Ronnie shuffled them repeatedly and that was obviously no help. His jaw tightened and he squinted in confusion.

"So, what do you make of them?" Don said. Ronnie had served in the Navy as a communications specialist; it seemed worth a shot.

"You want my opinion? I mean—Jesus. Military satellite? Does NASA have anything like this?"

"Dunno what else they could be." Yes, Don was an expert in the field of high tech imaging, although that expertise hardly extended to more clandestine or esoteric applications.

"But this material. What the hell—swear to God it's synthetic parchment..." Ronnie flexed a plate between his hands. "You can roll it into a tube, cantcha? Whoa."

Don was equally mystified. He'd certainly never encountered any photographic print on the order of this stuff that flexed and deformed like a weird, Nuclear Age vellum. He said, "Sure, sure. We got eyes in the sky that can snap a picture of your driver's license from twenty miles up. Infrared; ultraviolet; electromagnetic; X-ray; and so on. These photos could've been taken from an orbital spy sat, I suppose."

"Unless they're fakes. I mean—they gotta be fakes."

"I wish." If the plates were forgeries Don hadn't been able to deconstruct their artifice via training or equipment. He concluded what they depicted was horribly authentic.

"Jesus, H. Do you know these guys?" Ronnie glared at the shots of Louis and Cooye in their final moments of extremis. "Where'd you get these anyway?"

"They said I couldn't tell anybody or they'd roll 'em in a carpet."

"Huh?"

"Nothing. Look, a couple of spooks cornered me this weekend. Cloak and dagger to the hilt. My guess is that these plates are a warning. I can't figure their angle—"

"Watch your butt. Sounds like shysters. You see ID? No ID, then who knows. Couple of conmen running a scam."

"Do me a favor. You still tight with that guy on Whidbey Island?"

"Ferrar? Yeah."

"Maybe you could get him to run an analysis for me."

"I'll give him a call—but I bet my ass he'll want a look at this radical shit." Ronnie meticulously slipped everything into the envelope, held it in his giant hands with something like reverence.

The men finished lunch and drifted back to the office, promising to keep in touch over the next few days before separating to follow their routines.

Don's punishment descended near quitting time when Wayne appeared at his door with a carefully smooth expression and informed him that he'd be flying to the Peninsula in the morning alongside an impromptu team consisting of a lawyer, a medical doctor and an architect. Some kind of difficulty with mapping the mountainous region for mineral deposits.

AstraCorp was commissioned to record seismic data, take water and mineral samples, the usual. The camp was rugged and the crew a notoriously surly bunch, but the wrap-up would only require two or three days—a week tops, ha-ha. Sorry about the last-minute notice, but you know how these things sneak up, right, right? By the way, didn't Don minor in psychology back in the days of the dinosaurs? Don explained that he'd taken a course in abnormal psychology related to the stresses inherent in remote wilderness and subterranean operations conducted over lengthy durations. And as his boss absorbed this, Don said, "This is all rather mysterious, isn't it, Wayne?"

Wayne rolled his eyes and blustered that consultants were a continual pain in his ass—just do your job and keep a sock in your pie hole, thank you.

Don didn't bother to react, simply shrugged and gathered his papers, left an hour early to drive home and pack. He tried to summon the conversation with the agents in Spokane; they'd expressed a hell of a lot of interest in the Slango operation, and here he was a few days later, heading there for an in-person visit. The coincidence bothered him.

He stalked into the farmhouse, what he couldn't help but consider Michelle's house, loosening his tie with mounting frustration, spied young master Kurt, home from college classes, flopped on the couch, plugged into a cassette player and reading a *Heavy Metal* magazine with a fancifully-endowed cartoon princess on the cover. Potato chip wrappers and empty pop cans littered his area, crumbs and puddles sprinkled the coffee table. Don guessed he'd actually skipped university for the day and hopped a ride with one of his degenerate upperclassmen friends, of which it seemed he possessed locust hordes. Don didn't bother to upbraid him; he gritted his teeth and went upstairs to undress, shower and gobble aspirin.

Clad in socks and shorts, he sat on the unmade bed, listlessly tracking the slant of heavy red light through the circle window, how it transfigured the knots in the paneling to frozen eyes, the imperfections in plaster to howling mouths, hollowed cheekbones and teeth. His gaze traveled to a framed portrait of a smiling woman in aviator glasses. Dear Mum back when she looked the part of an MGM silent film starlet. An ancient picture, because the boyish iteration of Dad lurked at the edge of the frame—a fuzzy smirk and half-raised hand, bare-chested like a marble cast of Hercules made flesh. A murderous Adonis with Sphinx eyes, on loan to the United States Army Rangers despite his natural proclivity toward the sciences. In those days, Dad had been more interested in meeting new and fascinating people and then killing them. Cheerio, mates. Need someone shot, guvnah? Don beheld a stranger wearing a familiar face. What didn't you tell me, Pop? Why did you have to go mad and get yourself shot to pieces? And Gramps, you grizzled old sonofabitch, how dirty was your laundry anyhow? Nanking, what the hell were you doing in Nanking?

Holly called as he was moping before the mirror, taking gloomy stock of his stretch marks and graying chest hair. He had to run for the phone in the hall. After the operator connected them and ascertained Don would accept the charges, Holly said, "Mom there?" It was a lousy connection. Music honked and bleated in the background. His precious Holly was seldom far from a pub and its gallery of dashing riff-raff, folk-rock singers and beret-wearing activists.

"Hi, honey. How's France treating you?"

"Yeah, hi, Don. It's Glasgow—didn't you get my card? Mom there?" Her accent was decidedly cosmopolitan; she sounded exactly like a BBC broadcast woman who announced special foreign news bulletins.

"She's at work, as I'm sure you're aware, honey."

"Huh. I called the university earlier." Doubtless she had called multiple times—Holly interrupted her mother's work at least thrice weekly to report on current events or petition for more cash. It was endemic of her pathology.

"Ah, I dunno then. Everything okay?"

"What?" Her voice elevated in competition with the riotous music. Highlands metal.

"Anything wrong?"

"No! Everything's great! Tell Mom I'll try again tonight!"

"Love ya." The line had already died. Don threw the phone against the wall; it burst into several satisfyingly jagged pieces that might've been chunks of Big Wayne's skull in a happier world. He pulled on a shirt. He scooped the remains of the phone into the wastebasket and idly pondered the best way to keep this *faux pas* from his hawkish wife. He immediately discarded the notion. She knew all.

Michelle rumbled in, equally pissed at the world. Something about a woman working in a man's field and how academia in general and anthropology in particular could use a nice purgative. Her mood had been savage since they'd returned from the trip to Spokane. She went straight to the liquor cabinet and fixed a drink and sulked at the kitchen table. Don pecked her cheek on his way to making a sandwich and casually mentioned that he'd be flying out of town for the better part of a week. She shrugged and smoked a cigarette, flicking ashes into her empty glass. She only perked up when he mentioned Holly called and immediately wanted to know if he'd gotten a number. He'd failed to do so, as per usual, and her glower became truly and awesomely terrible to behold.

Don fled the kitchen. He retreated to the armchair across from Kurt, who eyed him with the suspicion of a magpie. Don gestured for the boy to kill the tunes which leaked from his earphones at what were likely brain-bleeding decibels and said, "What do you think of the neighbor boy—Bronson Ford? You like him?"

Kurt frowned, an expression that had the unfortunate effect of squeezing his features into those of an anthropomorphized albino rodent. "BF? I don't hang with kids, Pop."

"Really? He lives right next door—"

"Um, he's like, what, twelve or something?" Kurt rolled his eyes.

"I thought maybe you saw him around." Don chafed to ask whether the Rourke boy had access to illicit drugs (obviously he did) and if the little refugee might be moonlighting as a junior dope pusher. *Yo, sonny, you scoring grass from that Ethiopian kid down the road? Oh, and by chance have you seen a pair of goons lurking in the shrubbery? They look like a couple narcs.*

What was it the thugs in the cheap suits at the reception had said? He couldn't pin it down, the conversation was a static-laden mumble. The thought of them frightened him a little. But so did thinking of that Bronson Ford boy. As a matter of fact, thinking of the boy caused his hands to shake. He folded his arms to hide them from an oblivious Kurt and renewed his vow to cut back on the booze forthwith.

"Get real." Kurt jammed in his earphones. After a thoughtful moment, he lifted one muff and said to Don, "Jeezus, Pop. You and Mom are acting weird."

Speaking of weird, that night as Don and Michelle lay in bed after a brief, furious screw, she lighted a cigarette and regarded him as she lolled in her rumpled teddy, one leg still draped over the footboard where Don had flung it. "You're going where?"

"Nowhere. Place in the Olympics."

"Sounds like somewhere."

"Slango Camp. Old site in the mountains. Astra C is running some tests. Wayne asked me to fly in and check on the team. You haven't heard of it, huh?"

She studied him and her eyes were huge and dark as they became after sex, or when she was furious, drunk, or working voodoo on him. "I've heard of Slango."

"Oh. Wayne says."

"I'm tired of Wayne bossing you around."

"Because it interferes with *your* bossing me around."

The room was lighted by a black candle she'd taken from the dresser drawer. Her face reminded him in its wildness of the expression she'd worn that one night at the Wolverton mansion, except less vulnerable. Her snarled hair and cruelly glistening lips, the marble tautness of her neck and bare shoulders, were those of a pagan goddess etched into one of the woodcuts she so diligently collected. A drinker of blood, killer of men, harvester of skulls, and fecund as the dark soil of the ancient forest. She was a savage druid contemplating whether to fuck him or slice his heart out with the wavy obsidian knife she stashed under her pillow. This spooked him, but it also made him hard again.

She said, "I wonder if he knew I was flying to Russia this week."

"He doesn't. And if he did, he wouldn't care. Wayne suffers from an increasingly common malady among management—rectal cranial inversion."

Michelle stubbed her cigarette into a bone ashtray she'd balanced on a cushion. She slithered on hands and knees across the bed and mounted him so he was pressed against the pile of pillows. As his cock went in, her eyes rolled back and she gripped with her knees and leaned down to kiss him softly. She said into his mouth, "Quit."

He grabbed her waist and she slapped his hands away, snatched his wrists and pinned them to the mattress. "Quit? I can't." He spoke with some difficulty.

She bit his lip and moved her hips. "There's a village way out in the taiga, in the mountains. These aren't Inuit folk. Boris Kalamov made contact with them nine months ago, although I have a hunch he's lying on that score. He's a cagey bastard; might've found them years ago. He claims the people have seen outsiders three times in the last decade… trappers who didn't have a blessed clue they'd stumbled across a bloody miracle of modern anthropology. Kalamov is the only scientist on the planet who is aware of their existence. He told me, that's it. Lou was his confidante and now that Lou is gone… I'm going to participate in a ritual with the natives. Maybe. Depends on whether Kalamov can pull the matriarchs over to his side."

"Kalamov…I thought he was ruined. The debacle…"

"The man is tough as a cockroach. Can't kill him. Keeps coming back for more. He got tortured by natives once. Lived to tell."

"Baby, you're killing the mood." Don thrashed a bit; he couldn't break her bruising hold. Age was draining the life from him while she just got stronger.

"My mood is fine." She licked his ear and ground against him. The ceiling over her shoulder blurred into soft focus. "Don, your hair is going white. A whole shock right down the middle. When did that happen? It's sooo sexy."

He was sure he didn't know. Not even a flash of Bronson Ford looming taller than a basketball player, his face that of a shark, could derail the moment.

When they were done, Don's manhood felt as if it had been used for football practice. Wheezing, he said, "What kind of ritual? Better not be a fertility ritual or I'm going to be jealous."

"I don't have their word for it," she said. "It's a croning. After a fashion."

"What's a croning?"

"Don't go to Slango."

He cleared his throat and hummed "Baby Please Don't Go."

After she'd drifted away into dreamland he arose and went to the toilet to urinate. A light flickered on the drive leading to their yard. He squinted, trying to discern a real shape in the black-on-black landscape. The light flared again—the eye of a penlight inside the cab of a car parked down the driveway. Don froze, not certain of what to do next. Moments later the car drifted away without engaging its headlights, reversing down the road and vanishing into the night.

The next morning Michelle headed for Siberia. Everything was different after that.

2.

Don arrived at the Olympia Airfield as night receded into its cave. He experienced several seconds of disorientation when attempting to penetrate the snowy gap between slapping off the alarm on the dresser and climbing metal stairs into the cabin of a company jet.

Standing atop the platform, he glanced over his shoulder at the gravel parking lot which arced before the radio shack and the row of beige hangars gone blue-gray in the filtered light of dawn. He tried to pick his car from the silhouetted lumps of vehicles and failed—wait! Ronnie had driven him; Don abruptly recalled the morning talk show beamed live from Seattle, the dingy and desiccated air freshener bobbing from the rearview mirror, a thermos of coffee and Schnapps in the console between them; a mudslide and flashing red lights and his confusion boiled over again. White-gloved hands floated from the darkness of the cabin and politely ushered him inside the plane, sent his disjointed and inchoate misgivings away in a cloud of smoking dust.

The jet was a four-engine model, manufactured in the '50s judging by its appearance, equipped with a bar and a young attendant named Lisa whose presumably lovely features were squashed under layers of makeup and mascara. Three fellow passengers shared the accommodations.

Don recognized each of them from the list of names Wayne's secretary had printed for his reference, and in turn they'd been briefed regarding his role as the liaison dispatched by HQ to crack the whip and right the ship: A droll elderly lawyer named Geoffrey Pike; Dr. Justin Rush, an urbane gentleman with glistening hair and a Clark Kent smile; and the hotshot Oklahoma archeologist Robert Ring, a rangy, athletic man who claimed one of his ancestors was a famous Chinese noble exiled from the motherland. Perhaps five years younger than Don, Robert Ring dressed like a model in a *Field & Stream* catalogue—plaids and corduroy; his deep dark tan didn't appear to have come from a shake n' bake spa; undoubtedly the byproduct of skiing or bicycling or royal heritage, and his grip was intimidating.

Lisa dispersed coffees and Danishes and the quartet chatted as the crew ran down the last-minute flight check. Each was headed to Slango Camp with particular business on their agendas. Pike was to run interference against BLM officials. Rush had been sent to attend minor ailments afflicting various members of the team. Two surveyors had sickened from bacterial infections and another sprained an ankle navigating a sinkhole; all quite routine, perhaps better than routine—these remote operations were prime for frequent and grievous accidents. Ring was charged with examining several structures for hazards known and otherwise.

Structures? Don perked up. Historical monuments hadn't been mentioned in any of the previous briefings, although such wasn't his particular area. He asked Ring if these buildings were remnants of the logging camp that, though less infamous than the lost colony of Roanoke, was just as vanished in the mists of history.

Frick and Frack had made a cryptic reference to the camp's status as an official mystery and Don did a little digging of his own—two hundred men, women and assorted animals disappeared from the face of the earth in the late fall of 1923. Even the equipment, including boxcars from a train, and the shacks vanished. Unlike mass disappearances such as Roanoke or various wartime events, the Slango situation defied easy explanations such as attacks by angry natives or enemy forces, or high seas. It defied complicated explanations too. Don hadn't given the matter much attention prior to the previous weekend and the unsettling comments of the alleged NSA agents. There wasn't much a man could do with such lore except nod sagely and quote Hamlet. Right then, listening to the big engines rev for takeoff, a mere hour or two from visiting the legendary site, his already vivid imagination began to stir, eager to flex its muscles.

Ring wasn't forthcoming with details. He smiled enigmatically and changed the subject in a manner that achieved obliviousness and insolence in equal measure. He boasted about the red clay tennis court at his summer abode in the South of Italy, an ex-supermodel girlfriend and a brown belt in Jujitsu, his disdain of engineers' and geologists' underwhelming social competence, present company excluded, naturally. Don decided to hate him just a little bit.

Once they lifted off, it was a puddle jump flight to an airport outside of Portland to grab some equipment, then a forty-minute swing back into Washington and the Olympic Peninsula. Don had one bad moment after he buckled in and they gradually rose to cruising elevation. He'd closed his eyes for a few seconds as gravity pulled him into the plush recliner and when he opened them, the cabin windows were going dark. The stain advanced like fast-flowing syrup, a gush of blood spilling through a sluice. As his own window blackened, he detected the crinkle of dry ice, a knifepoint scraping bone, stones cracking under tremendous heat. Motion reflected in the onyx glass: the baggage compartment across the aisle silently swung open; inside, a membrane glistened, a colloidal plexus, the bulk of which nestled in deeper shadow.

The overhead lights flickered rapidly. Bands of utter darkness cycled through the cabin followed by flashes of red emergency light. All the lights shorted as one, snapping with the violence of a string of firecrackers, dry bones under tank treads. Wind shrieked against the fuselage and the plane shuddered, knocked slightly sideways by heavy turbulence. Someone cursed and metal clashed in the galley, pans clattered to the deck. Don dug his fingers into the armrests as the seat threatened to vibrate from its moorings.

Mr. Dart whispered from the adjoining seat, *Nanking, Don. A train loaded with fifteen hundred souls—soldiers, tradesmen and peasants, mothers and kids, chickens and goats—lost. Not wrecked or ransomed. Just lost, like a soap bubble pops and it's gone. Do you suppose they fell into a crack in the earth? You think Martians took them?*

As a boy, Don once asked Luther if he believed in aliens on account of all those secret government projects the documentaries and non-fiction books talked about. The old man had regarded him with eyes brittle and cool as those of a snake. Luther seemed almost prepared to eat his grandchild, such was the manner he hunched forward and widened his mouth. Then he laughed that horrible, phlegmy laugh until tears squirted and his nose went purple. *Idiot flesh of mine, O precocious whelp. Magic 8 Ball says try again later.*

The plane yawed and Don's gorge filled his throat and he almost believed his hands were losing coherence, that he was dissolving in the suffocating blackness—

—the train was so cold his breath steamed despite the stifling mass of humanity pressed from stem to stern. Such a tiny, tiny boy; his name was Xin or Hin and his mother crushed him against her as the windows disappeared, smothered in tar, and the lamps failed and the tube of the hurtling train became a blind canister full of groaning metal, of muffled cries, the sour stink of unwashed bodies, milling animals, of terror. His mother's arm fell away and he floated above his seat as the carriage began to revolve—

Don moaned and clamped a hand over his mouth and bit his palm and fell into himself—

—the capsule revolved and the Earth slewed below the rim of infinite night and someone's water bottle floated toward the nose of the shuttle, someone's belt, an alabaster string of lower intestine, a wristwatch, the crucifix and rosary end over end. The Lieutenant vomited inside his helmet; window plates turned black as empty sockets and bloody light seeped from somewhere deep within the ticking heart of melted circuitry. One of the others babbled through the headset and beneath that a discordant tone, an animal growling, wires sputtering, a train wreck, an avalanche and who was shrieking, who—

Mr. Claxton said from directly behind his right ear, *It didn't hurt much. We liked it. You should try it sometime. You will. You are.* Don was afflicted with a crystalline image of Dart and Claxton, Frick and Frack, pinned in the front seat of a government-issue sedan. Blood poured from faucets in their skulls and covered their faces. They screamed and ejected bubbles of gore, soundless. Bronson Ford ducked his head into the frame. He smiled and waved and the agents flailed like drowning men.

The boy said, *They eat children. The Children prefer children, haha! The brain, while alive, is their favorite. She's with them at last. Your wife finally knows everything. Maybe you will too, before the end.*

Don groaned and covered his face and bit his tongue. This phantasmagoria had to be from exhaustion or heavy drinking or payback for prior indiscretions— a bad hit of purple haze or microdot, he hadn't lived the choirboy ideal in his youth. The imagery assaulted him with the heft and force of a suppressed memory that once unleashed possesses the force and violence of a tidal wave or an avalanche. The icy, diamond-headed conceit that this might be a real memory filled him with despair.

Then the jet punched through the clouds and sunlight blazed into his eyes. The pilot came over the intercom, to apologize for the rough ride and promise smooth sailing the rest of the way. Don glanced around at the other men, noted their discomfort—Pike had dropped his glasses and Rush slumped sideways, green around the gills; meanwhile, Ring glared at the disheveled attendant when she uttered her conciliatory lines. Nonetheless, even as Don observed them, their momentary terror evaporated with awkward chuckles, snorts of relief.

Lisa unbuckled and briskly sealed the softly bumping door of the baggage compartment. She graced Don with a strained professional smile before ducking into the galley. He swallowed and wiped his face with his sleeve. Thunder clouds raced below them; black-crowned and murderous and shot through with white-hot licks of fire.

They landed without incident. Unfortunately, the driver slated to acquire the passengers and their luggage was nowhere in evidence and Ring vociferously questioned his companions and sundry about the logic of packing them into a car instead of a company chopper, but no one could answer that because no one really knew what was going on, least of all Don who felt much like a sacrificial lamb. After nearly two hours of loitering in the mechanic's lounge, they convinced an off-duty pilot to ferry them to a nearby diner for lunch. Don ordered a hamburger and a grape soda, chewed doggedly while the other men conversed in low tones, except for Ring's abrupt barks of sarcastic laughter.

The diner sat within spitting distance of the highway among a drab confederation of minor businesses including a locally operated grocery store and a car dealership flagged by a balloon giant, a Cyclops jabbing its claws at passersby. The whole comprised a strip town, one of the essentially anonymous blights that had eaten into the country and spread like cancer since the beginning of the previous decade. Low mountains rose in the east, bearded and misty. The sun shone small and hard and white through a film of iron overcast. Don noticed he'd been scribing a crimson doodle on the plastic table, tracing irregular lines between discolorations and blemishes with his wet fingertip. He shook his head, concentrated on bits of ice decomposing in his soda, tried to recall how he'd pricked his finger.

The driver finally appeared; a surveyor sent from base camp who rolled up in a muddy Blazer. Elli Mills was a grubby woman with oily, shoulder length hair and a wide, tanned face. She was missing some teeth and Don noted that her knuckles were large and scarred. Ring started haranguing her when they gathered in the parking lot to load the vehicle. Elli shrugged and laconically suggested that pretty boys should watch their mouths and that put a damper on his theatrics. Don was mildly impressed.

The party got rolling as the light softened into violets and oranges. A few minutes north of town, Elli took a narrow spur road that wound through dense forest and rugged hills and meandered toward the mountains. She warned everyone that it was another hour to camp and the ride would become "rough as hell." Long shadows swept over the potholed roadway and the country music radio station descended into static as they entered a gorge of jagged cliffs towering one hundred and fifty to two hundred feet above the surrounding firs and the angry river coiling through their roots. Don sat in the back of the Blazer, wedged between Rush and Pike. His head brushed the cab's roof with every savage jounce and he thought his kidneys might be jellified if Elli persisted in driving at Baja 500 speeds.

Night descended without stars. Don lost his sense of direction or the real shape of the land; he strained to follow the lane beyond the headlights until his eyes hurt. He'd actually nodded off when they left the spur and bashed along a severely rutted dirt track squeezed by boulders and trees. Dust caked the windows, filled his mouth with grit, sifted into his nose, his tear ducts.

Elli clanged gears and made the engine roar as they barreled up a slope, skirting a sheer drop into the invisible trees, the river and the rocks. She explained this had been a logging road and that one or two ridges over a railroad track snaked its way from the mountains toward the lowlands and civilization. The Pickett-Maynard Line historically serviced a string of mining and logging camps that died off shortly after WWII. The line was mostly forgotten; rails overgrown and blocked by slides; trestles rotting; and tunnels carved like arteries through limestone were now empty cylinders except for bat guano, moldering bones of small animals and the faux occult graffiti of bored teenage campers. The state nominally maintained the Pickett Road because of the weather station atop Mystery

Mountain, although it too was practically abandoned eight months out of the year, tenanted by the infrequent hermits, meteorologists or astronomers who'd escaped into the wild. This was a lonely territory.

Camp Slango occupied a shallow basin ringed by shale and granite bluffs on the opposite of Mystery Mountain from the Mystery Mountain National Park. Half a dozen small tents nestled near a central pavilion, a powder-blue dome that glowed like a firefly. Plastic beads of electric light festooned the camp, wrapped the clustered tents in shimmering coral, mingled and counterbalanced the sharp lamplight that streamed from open flaps and through mosquito netting, refracted from the hoods of several parked vehicles.

Don extricated himself from the Blazer and inhaled deeply of the cold, dry air while his companions wrestled with luggage and exchanged greetings with several surveyors who were loitering about. Leroy Smelser, head man prior to that moment, emerged from the confluence of surreal lighting and shadowy confusion to shake his hand and escort him to the "office", which was a partitioned niche inside the central pavilion.

Smelser proved genial; a ruddy, energetic man with a trim white beard and a wry smile, his skin was cracked and hard and there was dirt under his thick nails. Don knew in an instant he was in the presence of a workhorse. Men such as Smelser comprised the backbone of field operations and at the end of their tenure they received the aforementioned Taiwanese watch and a retirement condo in Florida where a fellow could suffer with his rheumatism in peace and quiet. Or they died in their traces. Such a fate might've befallen Don if not for Michelle's pleasant, though relentless prodding that he branch out, explore management and design, indulge his latent artistry.

Who the hell are you kidding, Miller? You're afraid of the dark. You've gone soft. By the way...what was that about two hundred loggers disappearing from this very spot? A fragment of the nightmare he'd suffered on the plane revisited him—Frick and Frack screaming while Bronson Ford laughed—and he set his jaw with grim determination.

Smelser waved Don to a folding chair and fetched a bottle of Dewar's and they had a drink while Don took in the cubby—a small metal desk and half-stack filing cabinet, a computer and numerous electronic components piled willy-nilly, a folding shovel and oodles of rope and a frame pack hanging against the canvas wall. Smelser disappeared for a few minutes and returned with leftovers from mess hall; pork & beans and biscuits.

After Don had eaten, Smelser broke out several geophysical maps and stretched them across the wall with brightly colored pushpins. The two large ones were circa the latter 1970s during the most recent BLM flyovers. Three much smaller maps were the handiwork of Smelser and his able photogrammetrist, Carl Ordbecker, who was currently in the field. Ordbecker was at The Site, as Smelser emphasized in his convivial manner.

"What kind of site?" Don inwardly damned Wayne to hell for making a fool of him.

"Eh?" Smelser's wrinkles deepened and he scratched his chin, obviously calculating the ramifications. "I thought…"

"I mean of course there's a site. They just didn't go into detail. If I'm called in, it's generally a personnel matter."

"A personnel matter. Right."

"I'm generally not greeted with pomp or enthusiasm, Mr. Smelser."

"Oh, I bet. On a Roman galley you'd be the gentleman with the whip. As it happens, we do have a bit of red tape mucking the works, and there are some minor staff difficulties. That's why we asked for the mouthpiece and the sawbones. But that isn't our problem."

"Aha," Don smiled with dread and crossed his arms. "Lay it on me."

"This area was always rich in timber and minerals. Big companies logged here in the 1920s. Then there were some…incidents, I suppose you'd say, and shop got closed for about a decade. Mining companies moved in, bored a few holes, and so on. The mines are dead; nothing suggests anybody would make a profit by reopening them, and so far the chance of dredging up any sizable measure of placer, leastwise what would turn a corporate bean counter's crank, is fairly remote. We've got to stick it out another eight to ten days to fulfill our contract and that's that. Except for Lot Y-22." The older man turned the computer monitor toward Don and conjured a matrix of topical maps and photographs. The photos captured trees, rocks of various shades, the skeletal remains of buildings (perhaps shacks or cabins), and a ragged discoloration akin to a lopsided seam. "Y-22. This was a small village about a jillion years ago, probably abandoned the same decade as Slango Camp, so far as we can determine. No name on record except a notation that B. Kalamov had surveyed the area in 1849, discovered a cave system. Can't vouch for the authenticity of that because I can't find corroboration that such a cave exists."

"B. Kalamov," Don said. "Huh. That's a coincidence."

"What is, sir?"

"Eh, nothing. Please, what else?"

"There really aren't any records except for a reference at the library archives in Port Angeles, and that document came from a decrepit historian who everybody considers a crackpot. A passage in a local history book mentions several ghost towns and this was one. There was an old, old picture of a queer little village with guys in furs and ladies in Puritan bonnets standing around in front of a stone tower like you'd see on a castle in England. A very serious crowd, which was basically the norm in those days, I expect."

"A mining camp."

"Maybe. But it's sixteen miles as the crow flies from the nearest vein—and no roads, no trails, nothing to suggest the homesteaders traveled that way. Carl figures it was an isolated community of hunters and trappers, or something along those lines. Coulda been a religious commune eking out a living in the hills. It's all very interesting, but the site is the peculiar thing. A bunch of ruins, except for that sinkhole you see there." Smelser traced the quadrant of the map with his fingertip.

"Damn. Must be ninety meters horizontally—"

"And about twenty across at the widest point. Yup, it's formidable. You want another drink?"

"Thanks, no." Don's glass was yet untouched; he'd sniffed the whiskey and been transported into the recent unhappy past. "Very impressive. So, what's the problem, exactly?"

Smelser poured another three fingers of pitchy liquor and drank it with a grimace. "It opened six days ago. Carl and our pilot Burton were buzzing the area in the chopper and noticed it probably five or six minutes after the event."

Don stared at the monitor and its stark images. Cheek bones, left orbital, teeth, a black wedge where the throat began. He looked up at the older man and met his shiny eyes. "That's—there must be a mistake."

"Yeah. I thought so, too. The equipment checks out. Carl and Derek know what they're doing. The sink opened when it opened. Best part is, this isn't the first time. Look at the topo from '64 and compare it to the one in '76 and the ones we shot five days ago."

The 1964 photo showed a noticeably smaller version of the sinkhole. It was utterly absent from the 1976 record. Don had the unsettling impression of a vast, earthy maw opening and closing with geological implacability.

"Okay." It wasn't okay by any means. Sinkholes were unstable by definition, but they didn't behave this way. This was something beyond his experience.

"The thing is, we've had people looking into this from the get-go. The brass sent in a couple of specialists. Weird guys—one's a freelance geologist named Spencer Duvall, a hotshot Canuck. He's cooling his heels in the infirmary—sprained an ankle when he was mucking about the site. The other one is a physicist named Ed Noonan. They flew him in from the University of Washington, don't know why. All very hush-hush. Nice enough fella, seemed to know his business. He spent about seventeen hours walking around the sink, taking readings and whatnot. Then he went AWOL. Strangest damned thing I've seen."

"Noonan ran off? Where'd he go?"

"He's holed up at the weather station. It's about two kilometers north of the village. We tried to talk him out of the building, get him back on the job, or at least figure out why he hightailed it in the first place. He won't talk to me and he won't budge. I left some emergency supplies and reported the incident to HQ. They said carry on and that's what we've done. I mean, maybe we should call the forestry department or the troopers."

"No, the company would have our heads if we jumped the gun and created bad press. I'll drop in on him after I survey the site."

"Well, thank God. Mr. Rourke said you'd take care of this—"

"Mr. Rourke? You spoke to him?"

"Uh, yes. And you're one hundred percent right—he absolutely positively wanted this Noonan situation resolved without police involvement. He gave me explicit instructions."

Don nodded calmly while inside his thoughts ricocheted from one another. What was Barry Rourke up to anyway? Frick and Frack, the creepy photos, a sinkhole that apparently defied the laws of physics, and now this, a loony scientist who'd locked himself in a fire watch tower. He was sorely tempted to back away from the whole mess, radio HQ and inform them that this crap was *way* above his pay grade. Something stayed his hand, compelled him to proceed, to follow the breadcrumbs and see where they led. This compulsion was more than duty, more than stubbornness. A slow burning fury had kindled in his heart. He said, "Is that everything?"

"There's some other details. Best they wait until you see for yourself, though. It sounds crazy and I've been onsite." Smelser wiped his mouth and capped the booze and stuffed it in the top drawer of the file cabinet.

"I'll take your word for it."

"Like I said, headquarters gave us our marching orders—hold the fort and wait for further instructions. This is your show from here."

"Appreciate the recap." Don's heart quickened as he contemplated the possibilities of landing in the center of a momentous geological find. "Where I do I bunk?"

3.

Don snapped awake, trapped in the coils of a down mummy bag. Irrevocable darkness filled the tent. "Am I dead?" His chest throbbed. The wind rattled the canvas tent and it was bitter cold. "Am I dead?" Repeated and repeated in breathy whispers until, "No, you're alive." He wondered, as his skin prickled, if that was his own voice returned from the void, if a double of his own face floated pale and unearthly.

Then he was asleep again and dreaming of Michelle. She stood naked and smiling before the entrance of a cave. Strange, bony hands emerged from the shadows and caressed her, drew her into the cave. The moon flared.

The Man in the Moon turned his misshapen head, beamed green cheese eyes upon Don's cocooned form. The Man in the Moon said, *It feels good, my boy*. A black swarm of insects poured from his chasm mouth, took wing and scattered into the icy void of limitless space.

4.

Derek Burton took Don and Ring up in the chopper right after breakfast.

Don tried not to stare. He recognized the pilot from another era of his life, or in the creeping smoke of a dream. *I should know you. We have met.* Ah, the question was where.

Burton moved with a hitching gait reminiscent of Bronson Ford's crow hop. Haggard in the glare of sunrise, his drinker's face sallow and dented and pocked, eyes twinkling, thin mouth pursed in the midst of a tuneless whistle, a culling song. His flesh hung loose as the sloughing wattles of an uncured pelt. His hair was white. He grinned at Don and winked. *Yes, Don, we've met,* that grin said.

Don shook the fellow's hand, suddenly averse to climbing into a cockpit with this unwholesome character. Too late, too late.

Burton chatted with Ring regarding the locations of various structures, the mostly buried remnants of the ruined village. Don eyed the pair, mildly disturbed at Ring's deferential, almost obsequious behavior; a lapdog that had met his new master. When the chopper was aloft, Don awkwardly donned the headset to cut the engine roar and listened as Burton explained the various landmarks. The trees lay green and plastic in the folds and rumples of the land. Here and there small rivers and creeks slashed through valleys. Nothing but miles of crag and trees and low, misty clouds. The shadow of the chopper passed over a trench in the earth. From a height of five hundred feet the gash of yawning rock and dirt and subterranean darkness gave Don a chill. He swore under his breath as the engine stuttered and a series of lights twinkled in the cockpit.

"Hang tight," Burton said, his voice crackling through the headset. "She's old and cantankerous. U.S. Army surplus. Bloody rotor could break off any second now." After a couple of beats the man laughed. Whether in jest or to reinforce his observation, Don couldn't decide.

They landed near a pup tent on a delta in a narrow river valley. An elderly man in a wool jacket and cap fiddled with pieces of video equipment recently unpacked from several large crates. Carl Ordbecker ceased adjusting a tripod-mounted laser camera and cheerfully greeted Don and Ring, clapping both hands to his wool hat until the blades ceased spinning.

"Ah, the blokes I've been waiting for, then. Good show!" He doffed his cap to swipe at a cloud of gnats. "You'll be wanting to see our find. Right around the corner, Mr. Miller, Mr. Ring." Without ceremony he led them through a copse of mixed fir and cedar.

The trio splashed across a shallow expanse of swift-flowing water and through a hundred yards of tall, brown grass, and then they were among the remnants of the nameless village. There was a hollow of weeds and bushes and from the morass jutted the lines of a low, shattered palisade like a piece of art from the set of a Revolutionary War movie, and beyond the palisade a handful of partially burned cottages. The central longhouse was roofless, but its walls stood. The ominous canted tower from the photographs rose at a crooked angle on a plot toward the far edge of the community. Don spotted a few more rotted cottages on a steep, forested hillside.

"Holy shit!" Ring said. "This is..." He closed his mouth and simply stared.

"Ayep, watch your step, boys." Ordbecker gestured to a section of ground where the sinkhole began as a crevice and rapidly widened to a chasm. "Mr. Miller, I don't have to tell you the footing is perilous yonder."

"Any changes since your last report?" Don said. He tapped his watch, a fancy digital model allegedly good for climbing Mt. Kilimanjaro or deep-sea diving. The blocky numerals flickered, faded, came back to life.

"No sir. The sink is stabilized for the moment. Obviously that's not going to last. I got some film on it, taking some readings with sonar. But, well..." The old man took Don's elbow and drew him aside from the vacuously stricken Ring and Burton who hung back near the longhouse, smiling his strange, devious smile and rolling a cigarette. "Sir, I was given to understand this is a feasibility study. We're looking for copper, gold, natural gas."

"That's my understanding as well," Don said.

"Okay, I'm game. No boat rocker. That said, you're a consultant. You aren't AstraCorp to the bone, am I right?"

"Where is this going?"

"I'm saying that if you're playing straight with me, then somebody on high is keeping information from us. I recognize Ring. He's famous. That physicist, Noonan, he ain't a slouch either. Ask yourself why the company needs a physicist on this job."

"Their business is their own. I'm also wondering why it's anything to you."

"It's on my mind because this hole isn't correct. You and I both can see that. The numbers are screwy." Ordbecker turned to regard the chasm. It ran along level ground for roughly seventy-five meters and dug into the flank of the hillside, a low mountain, gradually narrowing to a fissure before it disappeared among the underbrush. "What happened to Noonan is screwy too. Then there's the cave."

"I hadn't heard of a cave."

"See, that's what I mean. We're mushrooms—keep us in the dark and feed us shit. Yep, yep, a cave just yonder in the heavy brush. Whoever built this place excavated the entrance of the cavern. Can't see why—no evidence of mining. There's a honeycomb under this mountain. A whole system, completely undocumented, unrecorded, maybe unexplored. Although, I ain't sure I'd bet the house on that last part."

Ahh, why did he have to say that? Don regarded the great trees and steep foothills. Birds chirped, water chuckled, and that was it. The sun tried to burn through the clouds and created that flat light that always gave him a headache if he didn't wear sunglasses, and of course he'd forgotten to pack them. "With due respect, if there was a system around here it'd be in the books."

Ordbecker gave him a cynical smile, then lowered his voice even further and said, "Look, it's probably nothing. I checked the sink for gas, and it's real baseline methane venting. No radiation. Deep, though. I pinged two hundred meters and didn't hit bottom."

"Equipment malfunction. Gotta be."

"The crevice widens to the point there's...nothing. It's registering as an abyss. I'm hoping it's a glitch." The old man's eyes glittered with what Don finally recognized as fear.

Don said, "Okay. Leave it there for the moment. You check inside any of these structures?"

"Hell no. Mr. Ring can have that pleasure. Bet he doesn't find much. Fire burnt everything to a crisp from what I can tell." Ordbecker spit and stuck his hands into his pockets. "Got the feeling it's for the best, too."

Don thanked the surveyor and approached the near end of the crevasse. He'd disposed with thinking of the phenomenon as anything so mundane as a sinkhole the moment he'd seen it from the chopper. A crevasse, or if Ordbecker's readings were correct, an abyss. He stood at the rim where soil and rock crumbled into a gulf and eyed the striations and demarcations in the exposed substrata. A breath of subterranean air riffled his sleeve. It was dank and strong and cold. Faint metallic groans were carried on the breeze. He retreated several steps and called to Ordbecker. When the surveyor hustled over Don said, "Did you hear anything down there?"

"No sir."

"There's movement below. Major shifting. Stay the hell away from this thing."

"I won't argue with you."

"Pack your gear. We can squeeze you on the chopper."

Ordbecker laughed. "I don't think so."

"Okay, take my seat. I need to hike to the station and try to coax Noonan down from his tree. You know anything about the man? Is he a drinker? Seem like a loon? Beyond the obvious, that is."

"Real pleasant fellow. Eager beaver. He was all over that sink. I had to drag him into camp for supper after it got dark. He stayed up by the fire for hours, going over some papers and a manual by flashlight. Next morning started fine, then around lunchtime he disappeared into the cave I told you about. I followed him for a few yards. Too spooky a situation, what with no supplies and nobody topside to come after us right away, so I retreated. Couldn't raise base camp on the horn due to interference. After maybe five hours I was getting a mite panicky. Noonan sort of stumbled from the cave. He didn't seem right. He turned and wandered up the mountain. Later, I managed to contact Smelser and he came and tracked our boy to the station. Couldn't make any progress, couldn't even get him to talk."

Don noticed that Burton was watching them just out of earshot, grinning broadly now as he braced one boot atop a stump. *What the devil is wrong with his face?* Don had seen a few victims of cave-ins and fires and strokes, and the pilot's soft and drooping visage was similar, yet completely different. The skin fit like a bad mask. *Syphilis? Syphilis could do it. Or St. Vitus's dance... Or leprosy. Does this guy have leprosy? Does leprosy make your face look like it's going to slide off at any second? Maybe he's not grinning and giving me the evil eye. Maybe his face is just screwed beyond repair.*

Bronson Ford whispered, *They took his skin and wore it for a while.*

Don tried to remember when and where Bronson Ford had uttered such a cryptic line, and failed. "I get the picture, Mr. Ordbecker. Go on, then." He whistled to Burton and walked over and explained that the man was to return Ordbecker and Ring to base camp at once.

Ring overheard the conversation from where he'd knelt to take pictures of the charred and fallen center-beam of the longhouse. "Hold on a dang second there, Miller. We just got here."

"I'm aware of how long we've been here. Stuff your camera and get your butt back on the chopper. That's not a request." Don kept his tone bland, but he secretly enjoyed Ring's shocked expression. Guys like Ring only respected brute force; to reason with them was to exhibit weakness. "You've got enough shots to get started. Pick a team, return to the site tomorrow." And as the archeologist took a breath to protest, Don finished with, "This is my call. In matters pertaining to company safety policy, I'm God. Want my head on a stick, file a report."

Ring stood and marched past Don toward the helicopter, jaw hard, brows furrowed. Ordbecker covered his smirk with a cough.

Burton said through his lazy grin, "What about you, *God*? Going up the hill to pay your respects?"

"Give me two hours," Don said. He checked the map he'd borrowed from Smelser, which showed the ranger station—the village had been penciled recently. He tucked in his shirt, nodded curtly to the pilot and the surveyor, and set forth, past the outskirts of the ruins, into the forest, up the flank of sleepy, lovely Mystery Mountain…

5.

The Bobcat Peak Ranger Station loomed atop the crown of a bluff, forebodingly gothic; a medieval watchtower accessible solely by a vertical wooden ladder that ascended to a trapdoor. Its darkened ring of turret-like windows overlooked miles of wilderness. The station was a forest sentinel, weathered and battered by the many storms it had suffered over the decades, mute and grim and implacable.

A house of secrets. Don wiped the sweat from his brow with a bandanna. He cupped his hands to his mouth and called Noonan's name, listened to his voice boom from gullies and boulders until it became that of a stranger's and was lost. A carpet of fir needles lay underfoot, and beneath the tower proper were several dusty crates and a stack of gray and wasted firewood. This outpost obviously didn't see much action. Probably received an annual inspection and was staffed for a couple of weeks if the weather was dry, or was used as a staging platform for search and rescue operations. Otherwise, deserted as a tomb…

In a way he was relieved to receive no answer as his disgruntled determination had withered a bit in the face of the hike, the remoteness, and the gloomy menace of the station itself. Either Noonan had moved on (the guy *had* to return to camp sooner or later, or hike to a trailhead unless he wanted to starve), or he wasn't in the mood for visitors. Don didn't plan on attempting to force his way in either. So, duty dispensed, he tucked the bandanna into his shirt and turned to leave. The trapdoor creaked and dropped open, revealing a black rectangle.

"Hi, Don. Come on up. Tea's on." A man's voice, and familiar, though distorted by the acoustics of the building and the encroaching trees.

Don cursed his luck. He hesitated as the reality of his predicament crashed over him in a sea-cold wave. Was he really planning to blithely traipse his way into the lion's den? The scientist could be a lunatic, given the way he'd abandoned his work. Could be waiting to brain Don as he came through the door. "No thanks, doc. Why don't you come down? Chopper will be swinging back around. Everybody's worried about you."

Silence extended for a long, drawn moment. The hidden man chuckled, and again the familiarity of it chafed and aggravated. "Best scamper up here, old son. If not…"

"Or what?" Don wished he'd brought the revolver he kept stashed in the footlocker in the garage. A brute, heavy weapon that he didn't recall the model or make, a gun he'd fired once at the range in Poger Rock, then replaced in the case and forgotten. It would've felt comforting hanging from his belt right then.

"I've got something very important to tell you. It's about Michelle."

Don's belly tightened. Was that even Noonan? That damnably familiar voice… "Who the hell are you? Show your face!"

The man chuckled again. "Come on. You aren't safe down there. The children keep pets in the trees. The critters come out of the woodwork at night. Gonna be dark soon."

Don glanced around, then at his watch which was still behaving erratically. He estimated it was around 11 A.M., surely no later than 11:30. "Hey, Noonan!" No answer this time, no chuckling, just the door, the black rectangle. He didn't know what to think except that whoever was inside, whether it be Noonan or whomever, knew something about Michelle. Everybody did, it seemed. *Baby, I've had it. We're having a little talk when you get home.* He sighed, felt in his jacket for the folding knife he always carried while hiking. It was proceed or turn tail and wait for Burton in the clearing. Charging headfirst into what was potentially a dangerous situation bothered him less than spending more time with the creepy pilot.

He mounted the ladder and climbed at a measured but swift pace the three stories to the hatch and ducked through. The interior of the station was gloomy. To his immediate left were several more crates similar to those stacked below the platform; in the center of the circular chamber were tables and wooden chairs and a bank of equipment that included a shortwave radio set, reel-to-reel recording machinery, a seismograph, and a telescope mounted on a complicated dolly. The air smelled of must, mothballs, and peppermint. A camp stove hissed upon one of the tables, and a pot of water emitted curls of steam.

The windows were shuttered except for a bank with an eastern exposure whence filtered dull hazy light. A man stood silhouetted against that bank of windows. He said, "Glad you could make it, Don." Barry Rourke's voice, clear now that the men were in proximity.

"Barry. What are you doing here?"

"Waiting for you." Rourke was pale, his eyes sunken. "And you are here because I called you here." He wiped his mouth with the back of his hand and slouched over to the bubbling kettle. His back to Don, he took a pair of mugs from a cabinet and poured from the kettle.

"Did you say there are children here? Pets?"

"Yes, yes—actually *servitor* is closer to the mark than pet. Heh, as guard dog is to poodle, or minnow to shark. The Crawlers, the Limbless Ones; call 'em what you will, you don't want to meet one. Stay near me, you'll do okay."

"I think you'd better start from the beginning," Don said. He'd recovered from the scramble to the ridgeline and the subsequent climbing of the ladder, but now his breath came short and heavy and sweat soaked his shirt. He took a breath and considered his options. Obviously the man had cracked under the pressure. Likely things weren't rosy at the Rourke mansion; maybe he had a gambling debt or was being blackmailed by a lover. The possibilities were endless. Whatever the cause, it didn't require a medical degree to assess Barry Rourke as a mental case.

"Ask me anything," Rourke said. "I'm the answer man, tonight only."

Don said, "Are you in trouble? It occurs to me after the government spooks and all the secrecy surrounding this project that AstraCorp is pulling the wool over someone's eyes. I've seen these kinds of shenanigans. People cutting through the red tape any way possible. Are you trying to screw the BLM? Did you find native burial grounds and can't decide whether to hide the fact? It's only money."

"Ha! And exhibit A Miller remains poor to his dying day while the banker and the merchant die of gout on their yachts. Seriously, though. I'm pondering how to do this delicately. It's easiest to tell you that I belong to an order. A cult. This cult has taken in interest in you and your wife as we have certain members of Mocks and Millers for so many generations it would blow your mind like the heaviest dose of Windowpane you ever did."

Don kept the tension from his voice and smiled glibly. "Okay. The spooks at the reception were keen on grand conspiracies. Tell me about it, this cult of yours."

"It has been around since prehistoric times, when men gibbered in caves and dragged their knuckles. We venerate the Great Dark, the things that dwell there."

"Lovely. Satanism is big with the kids these days, I hear."

"Don't patronize me."

"Wouldn't dream of it. This is a lot to swallow. You don't seem…"

"Don't seem the type? Don't you know anything about the world besides plate tectonics and substrata? The rich are master cultists. We've the means, motive and opportunity to indulge our wildest peccadilloes."

"What I was going to say is that you seem to have such a stick up the ass it kind of surprises me to learn you're a closet hedonist. What do you call yourselves anyway?"

"The cult is nameless. Chief among our deities is one known as Old Leech. Worship of Old Leech is the primary activity of the Terrestrial sect. This worship was transmitted to us by a race that exists on the rim of the universe and spreads like a mold crawling across meat. We call this race the Children of Old Leech. They dwell in the depths and the shadows, they inhabit the crack that runs through everything."

"Aliens with an alien divinity," Don said. "*Chariots of the Gods* is Michelle's favorite book."

"Aliens? Why not? Vampires, demons, devils. Hobgoblins of a thousand cultures."

"I have to admit this is some strange territory," Don said. He hastened to add, "Not saying I don't believe you."

"Look, Don, it's all true. The Rourkes, the Wolvertons, the Mocks, others in this state and across the world, all serve the Great Dark, each in his or her own way; some with enthusiasm, some with reluctance, but completely and without mercy. I can't explain everything. You don't want me to explain everything. Our cult is monolithic with tentacles in every human enterprise throughout history, into *prehistory*."

"Ah, like Amway."

Rourke smiled a real smile and laughed. It was only then that Don noticed the man was dressed in a stylish terrycloth robe and slippers à la Hugh Hefner, precisely as if he'd stepped out of the house to check the mail. His hair was mussed, and up close he appeared unwell—pallid, blotchy, exhausted. A jaundice victim. Tics and twitches raced across his cheeks and jaw. Rourke said, "Even we don't screw with Amway." He sighed and his eyes were oh, so cold. "Man, you don't know when to let sleeping dogs lie. Always meddling. You simply *had* to go hunting for Michelle in Mexico instead of listening to sage advice and spending a couple extra days drunk at the hotel bar. Got crosswise with some real hardcore disciples. Those feds at the reception who were milking you for intel—couldn't just walk away, huh? Exactly the sort of shit that's marked you goddamned Millers since the days of yore."

"I don't like your tone."

"Like it or lump it. We've got important matters to discuss. You are a mosquito trapped in the sap of a sundew. Your existence hangs in the balance."

That definitely sounded like a threat to Don. "Where's Noonan?" The unasked question being: *What have you done to Noonan?*

"I'm fairly sure that Burton ate him. Or the servitors did."

Don couldn't think of a response to such an outlandish statement. He stared at Rourke's back in stunned silence, helplessly awaiting the punch-line.

Rourke said, "In case you hadn't noticed, Burton is...well, he's not really Burton...He's one of *them*, a Dark One, dressed to appear human. Cheap facsimile, though. How the hell you got onto a chopper with him is beyond me. I mean, Jesus, Don. Didn't you see his *face*?" He ran his hands through his hair, and his shoulders trembled. After a few moments he collected himself and brought Don a mug of tea that smelled too strong, too sweet.

Don sniffed his tea. "Good grief, Barry. Fear tactics and propaganda I expect from government attack dogs. *You* really disappoint me. Are you doing your part to fight the Cold War? My wife on a list somewhere because she had drinks with the wrong professor in the 1950s? Or she accepted funds from a flagged trust? Are you bastards after us because my grandfather pissed somebody off during the Boer War? What the hell is it with you people?"

"Dark Ones aren't people."

"Right; they're a bug-eyed alien species who vivisect cattle and abduct people on lonely highways and subject them to anal probes and such."

"Would you care to know what their idea of fun is?"

"The Dark Ones?"

"Right, them."

"Screwing with my life? Administering anal probes?"

"They worship a deity that ate the fucking dinosaurs, several species of advanced hominids and the Mayans. Opened a gate and slurped them through a funnel."

"I'm not going to say that you're crazy, because I don't wish to belabor the obvious. Let's try this: put on a coat and follow me down to the river. We'll chuck some rocks, take in the sights, wait for Burton to fly us home. Whatever booby hatch they stick you in, I promise to visit once a month. We can shoot the breeze and play cribbage. Or backgammon. I got the feeling you're a backgammon man."

Rourke smiled sadly. "Tell me, how bad has it gotten—the memory loss, the blackouts? You convinced it's early dementia? That's not what's happening. I bet you're healthy as an ox with a memory like an elephant. You're a smart fellow, too. No, no, Don. You aren't addled. The masters have this effect on people. They exude an aura that kills little patches of brain. It's like radiation poisoning of the mind. After a few exposures, your memories begin to rot and fall out. You're not really going senile, but isn't that what you've feared?" He sipped his tea, then quickly stepped forward and blew a cloud of steam into Don's eyes.

A gong sounded in the recesses of Don's consciousness and sent bats winging toward the light. He dropped the mug. The scent was that of Bronson Ford's miracle weed, albeit steam rather than smoke. Its effect was much more visceral. Don understood this wasn't marijuana; it was a more ancient, more primitive extract, a hallucinogenic of frightening potency.

A kaleidoscope of images fractured in his mind's eye: Frick and Frack hunting him at the Wolverton Mansion; naked men dressed as horrors from Aztec mythology menacing him with axes and knives; a ruddy young man in a ridiculously tight sweater stepping into a dolmen; Kurt, bronzed and middle-aged running through the woods, screaming, screaming; Bronson Ford, bloated to gigantic dimensions plucking Don from the floor of a dim museum gallery in one huge paw—

He blinked and his hands were leathery and gnarled; the hands of an old man; and his clothes hung on his shriveled and stooped frame. Were there a mirror, Don knew it would reveal a few wisps of white hair on a bald pate and a face carved like a bust from granite. His knees buckled and he collapsed into a wooden chair, still gawping at his withered hands, and as he watched they shifted back to their customary musculature, then shriveled again. The oscillation reminded him of acid tracers. "Please, help me. Tell me what's happening." He could scarcely whisper. The room undulated as though it was a heat mirage.

Barry Rourke said, "I *am* trying to help you. Alas, you married poorly. The Mocks are favorite pets of my masters. Your wife is the last of that line and I know *they* want to keep her happy and compliant. Only reason I can figure that Bronson Ford didn't swallow you whole. Or drag you screaming into the dark. One of your ancestors made the mistake of crossing the

Dark Ones. I get the feeling you're being preserved for something quite hideous. The Children of Old Leech have long, long memories. But *you* aren't important. You're a flea on the belly of a mastodon." He grasped Don's arm and helped him stand, led him to a window.

The sun was an orange streak descending behind the summit of the mountain. As the man had said, night was coming fast. A handful of cumulus clouds scudded past, images in a frame traveling at 4X normal velocity. Don bit hard into the palm of his hand to stifle a giggle. Were he to laugh now there was no telling where it would end.

Rourke said, "Steady, steady. Give it a moment, let the wave roll on by. You've tasted the nectar of the void before, eh? Not to worry—this stuff is more concentrated and it filters through the blood rapidly. It's not my intention to drug you. I only want you to have a moment of clarity before your Swiss cheese brain gets fogged in again. There is something you need to see."

6.

Rourke spoke the truth in regard to the drug—within a few minutes Don's disorientation eased and he came to his senses bit by bit. His resurgent memories lingered, frightful acuity mitigated by their fragmentary nature; a ten-thousand-piece jigsaw puzzle cast into the air.

"We have to move," Rourke said. He snapped on a flashlight and guided Don to the trapdoor and threw it open. Night had descended with unnatural swiftness and Rourke's beam illuminated a narrow shaft, the first half dozen rungs. "I'll go first. Whatever you do, don't look down."

Don was too busy concentrating on maintaining a death grip on the ladder to worry about looking anywhere besides his knotted, arthritic hands. Maneuvering his decrepit self was difficult enough; meanwhile, memories (precognitive visions?) continued to leak through the ruptured membrane: the twins as middle-aged; of Argyle ageless and peering through binoculars; of a beefy young fellow named Hank slipping into the maw of a dolmen—

His treacherous fingers lost hold and he would've fallen, except Rourke caught him under the arms and righted him without much effort. Don was a sack of feathers. *I dried up like a prune in my dotage.*

Rourke set aside the flashlight and ignited a torch—the old-fashioned kind with a big crown oozing pitch that shed a reddish glow and fumed with smoke. The torchlight revealed the shadowy contours of a cliff covered in brush and saplings. A cave waited. The approach was split by the sinkhole/abyss, that narrowed here to a crack six of seven feet across. Mist drifted from the crack and mingled with the torch smoke.

Christ, this has to be a dream. There's a field at the bottom of the tower, a ridgeline. I'm high off my ass. None of this convinced him. The crunch of gravel beneath his shoes, the scents of sap and soil were too pungent. The rock wall and the cave were too solid. Don thought of Milton and Dante and had a keen urge to pee.

Rourke said, "This is the cave in the woods at Y-22. A bit of trivia: Your elder cousin burned the village down in 1923. Admittedly, the burning was a consequence of a gun battle when the villagers ambushed Miller and his fellow loggers with the intention of sacrificing them to Old Leech. What the hell your cousin and his friends were doing this far from Slango is a mystery. Did your father ever mention the incident?"

"No." Don hadn't heard of this particular family legend. He was aware of distant relatives having served as snipers and spies during World War I, and another who'd been a so-called great white hunter during the 1920s and '30s, and another who'd died of a wasting illness after assisting with an excavation of a tomb in Egypt about that same period. Certainly there was Dad and Granddad, villainous heroes in their own right. As for this yeoman logger and his link to the Slango vanishing, nada.

Rourke gestured with the torch and led the way into the earth. As they walked, Don caught hold of Rourke's belt for balance. He recalled a similar cavern system in Mexico and the men who'd beaten him and laid him upon a prehistoric altar to some prehistoric god. He remembered their shrieks as they were snatched away into the shadows. What had occurred thereafter was yet a blank.

The tunnel twisted in steady descent and after a while opened into a grand cavern bristling stalactites. The cave was bone dry and shored by rude timbers. Its walls were scribbled with chalk drawings of stick figures bowing *en masse* before towering worms with humanoid skulls, and stranger things. "I've seen a painting of this." That wasn't quite accurate—*I will see a painting of this. In the attic at the farmhouse. About thirty years from today.* Nearby were several formations, their true parameters distorted by eons of flowstone; and a pit that exuded a foul odor.

Don knew this place. "It's the same gallery as one I saw in Mexico."

"All caves are the same. All of them lead to the Great Dark." Rourke advanced several steps and the fire illuminated a stone structure not unlike a ziggurat, the whole of it rising to thrice the height of a man and encased in flowstone.

The stone was miraculously translucent and studded by myriad knurls and odd disfigurations. Rourke beckoned him and Don reluctantly approached the edifice, immediately noting two details: a perfectly round hole penetrated the ziggurat at eye level; the disfigurations were the intact skeletons of children. Hundreds of them, petrified and preserved as foundational calculus, mortar between bricks.

"The Dark Ones don't procreate as we do," Rourke said. "Their system of reproduction is via assimilation, absorption, transmogrification. Babies and toddlers are a delicacy. Much as I groove on a plate of nice Beluga caviar, they munch on fetuses. Although, toddlers are preferred for peak sampling, that fine line between ripeness and self-awareness. Screaming turns them on. The men and women who dwelt in the hamlet over a hundred years ago worshiped the Children of Old Leech as gods and offered their newborns as sacrifices. The women here were always pregnant. Such was their purpose in life; to breed as animals do, to provide grist for the hungry darkness. Our capacity to breed like rats is a real selling point. That and our quaint fear of the night."

Don was stricken, although he mastered the impulse to flee blindly through the twisting caverns, or fall upon his knees and gibber like an ape. It was a close matter. He wasn't prepared as Michelle would've been—his job didn't ordinarily involve unearthing scenes of primitive bloodshed. He was no anthropologist or archeologist trained and hardened to scenes of ritual atrocity and pagan strangeness.

Even as he observed, the hole in the ziggurat dilated, rapidly expanding to the diameter of a bowling ball, then a hula hoop, and it emitted an icy, metallic keening. His flesh tingled. Blood trickled from his nose and the droplets undulated in a stream of globules that were sucked into the hole. His nipples stiffened, as did his penis, and his body verged upon weightlessness. He said, "Dear God. Dear God. This is unbelievable."

"Behold the portal. To be taken through it is to be carried to the home of The Children of Old Leech, chief among the Dark Ones who serve vast blind things in the lightless wastes where mortal physics collapse into nonsense. Perhaps you'll travel unto Old Leech himself. Were I not such a coward..."

"Cowardice pleases *them* just the same as devotion," Connor Wolverton said. He emerged from the cover of a stalagmite, and bowed slightly. His robes were of a magnificent red silk embroidered with the broken ring in rusty black. He wore many rings set with black gemstones. His eyes were black as the gemstones. "Cowardice tastes like fear, and they enjoy the taste of fear very much. Eh, Barry?"

"Come away from there. The distortions in the time stream are a wee bit dangerous. Hate to see you get fused with your geriatric self, or your infant self. Be awkward to explain the second head at board meetings." Rourke glided across the ground and steered Don away from the yawning black hole that was a deeper, darker mirror of the pit in the floor. He brought Don near the altar slab where Wolverton waited, hands folded in the sleeves of his robes.

Connor Wolverton said, "Miller, excellent to see you again so soon! I feared those vile government chaps would spirit you away from my demesne; a tragic embarrassment. Every so often intrepid do-gooders in the various world intelligence agencies slip their leashes and come sniffing around our business. Seldom does it prove more than an inconvenience. Let not your heart be troubled; those dastards are paying for their temerity as we speak. Their suffering shall last for decades. Those photographic plates you received in the mail? That material is brain-matter rendered pliable by the unspeakable technology of our friends on the other side of the abyssal gulf."

"That's twice," Rourke said to Don. "Twice the Children have interceded on your behalf. You are blessed, or cursed, depending upon your perspective." He laughed, a brittle, humorless laugh, and Don guessed that the man was abjectly terrified of Wolverton.

Probably a grand Pooh-Bah of this cult. I wager he's well aware that man among men Barry Rourke is getting cold feet on this devil worshipping business. Don wasn't sure what to make of this. He filed it away while another part of his brain resisted the siren song of the black portal, the urge to run toward it and hurl himself through. The hole could easily accommodate a man walking upright and it writhed and flickered like black fire.

"Indeed," Wolverton said. "The last time you were here was in the hands of certain loyal and capable servants. I never had the pleasure of meeting Mr. Kinder. A shame. His reputation as acolyte of the dread mysteries was impressive. That worthy bore you here because you were asking questions about your wife, meddling, etcetera, etcetera. Kinder was convinced the Children desired blood sacrifices, that he was bound to be rewarded for slaughtering an interloper. He underestimated our masters, the scope of their imagination, the nadir of their depravity and jealousy in regard to unholy prerogatives. In abducting you he acted impulsively and without sanction. Much like the tragic fate of agents Dart and Claxton, for that transgression, poor Kinder and his merry men suffered a thousand-thousand deaths in a pit that Dante couldn't have imagined in a dozen lifetimes."

Don, mesmerized by the keening of the ziggurat, marshaled the wit to say, "I remember. I remember what they did. Scoundrels were going to split me wide open."

Wolverton and Rourke watched him, obviously waiting for him to connect the dots.

"Barry said I was spared a dreadful fate because of Michelle."

"Yes," Wolverton said.

"Why is she so important? What do you want with her?"

"We want her to do as her ancestors for countless generations have done—to join us, the select few, the elite. To serve the Great Dark."

"To become like Burton, you mean." Don visualized the pilot's grotesque smile, the skins at Wolverton's mansion, and thought of beautiful, vibrant Michelle gone chalky as a corpse, her mouth too wide, her dark eyes glimmering with the evil joy of an alien mind. To break the spell, he slapped himself, hard, grimly satisfied at the jolt of pain and anger. He spat a gob of blood and watched it splatter on the rock floor, then bubble and curve toward the ziggurat, a trail of snail slime minus the snail.

"Still don't recognize him?" Rourke said. "Lupe Ramirez helped bring you to this very cave. Goes by Derek Burton these days when he's in town. *They* put new spawn into fieldwork right away, while their perspective is still fresh. Or maybe the new spawn volunteer."

"Best not to speculate," Wolverton said. "The man known as Burton, or Ramirez, repaid his debt to the great ones after a period of torment. He was absorbed unto the Plenum and reborn. He is at a middle instar of development—more than a man, and thus his need to wear the suit of flesh lest the sun scorch his viscid form— yet neither is he fully of the tribe.

"On the other hand, your wife is not destined to be co-opted as an immortal; not for a while. In the meantime, her talents as an indigenous native are valuable. She will keep her own flesh, as I have mine, most of her brain, as I have mine, and most of her essential humanity. It delights them to invest select humans with subtle enhancements; human identity permits us to maintain our doubts and fears, our qualms. Our terror. She's invited to serve as I serve, and as Barry serves, and untold multitudes of others. We are watchers, liaisons."

"She's an anthropologist!" Rourke said, and chuckled. "Got to love the universe's sense of humor. The irony of it slays me. To have seen the look on her face when Kalamov pulled back the curtain on that 'lost tribe' she's hunted for years... Jane Goodall in Hell."

"The little people," Don said, trying valiantly not to weep. "You must be joking."

"She got the hollow Earth part right—just isn't Terra," Rourke said. "The Children of Old Leech dwell inside the cores of a cluster of dead worlds. These worlds are encased in a blood clot of darkness. Their Diaspora is far from here, beyond an immeasurable gulf between galaxies. A starless abyss. Yet their technology is so advanced it permits small numbers of them to slither across time and space and punch into our lovely little blue sphere, and a thousand others like it. Yonder ziggurat is a portal, an end point of a tunnel. The life-sucking tendril that taps humanity's vein. Its activation occasionally causes quantum fluctuations in our reality. Say, a sinkhole that plunges to Jupiter; time distortions..."

Wolverton smiled with grim kindness. "No need to fret, Miller. By my reckoning the deed is done. Michelle has either fulfilled her destiny and gone to visit the masters, or she's been destroyed. As for you... You're doubtless wondering why we brought you here. Barry, please be so good as to tell the man what's behind door number three."

Rourke nodded. He looked at Don. "The powers on high have invited you on an all-expenses-paid vacation to their domain. They could've sicced the Limbless Ones on you in your home, could've had you bundled to a neat little dolmen not five miles from your backyard. Yep, the Mocks didn't pick that land for the view or the green pastures. No portal in that dolmen, alas. More of a chute for live meat—"

"Barry, let's not traumatize him excessively, shall we? He's been a real sport."

"*Mea culpa*," Rourke said. "As I was saying, this is the kind of invitation very few receive. Make it easy on yourself. The devil only knows what will happen if you decline."

Don considered this for a few moments. Slowly, because of his divided attention, he said, "If these masters of yours are so powerful, why do they need human skin? Rather low-tech solution for infiltrating the ecosystem."

"To monitor an ant colony one inserts a probe," Wolverton said. "It's not a case of simply tearing off a man's skin and wearing it as a cloak. The process is one of grafting, of co-opting aspects of the central nervous system. This process also facilitates communication. I suspect the mechanisms in play are infinitely more sophisticated than our lunar rockets or deep sea vessels, or superconductors."

"Communication is a small piece of the whole deal," Rourke said. "Sol and Luna are too bright, the world too warm. The light isn't their favorite thing—"

"Barry, enough. *They* don't appreciate that kind of talk, do they?"

Rourke licked his lips, glancing around the cavern. He composed himself and continued dryly, "Get down to the nitty gritty, they want to scare the shit out of us. Letting the mask slip and the zipper show in the costume is half the fun! Man, read your old-school fairy tales. Rumpelstiltskin has everything laid out if you squint at it right. That's the Bible on the Dark Ones. What they want, what they're like."

"What about Bronson Ford?" Don said. "Barry, is your kid an ET, or Satan spawn? We had a great conversation at your house last weekend, Connor. Me and the kid yukked it up, big time. I suppose he was trying to clue me in on this whole scene. Too bad for me my memory is a sieve."

"He wasn't cluing you in, he was sucking your fear," Rourke said in a decidedly petulant tone. "He's got it in for you. He likes to watch you dance as the iron shoes heat up."

"It is a rare honor to speak with Him," Wolverton said, ignoring Rourke. "He is powerful among his kind and not given to conversation. It was he who commanded that you be brought here to this sacred nexus and given the opportunity to join our fraternity. Beyond that portal lies a vista of evil splendor. A new life. Go through the membrane and be with your sweet Michelle in the dark. Be changed, and return as part of something much, much larger than one's self."

Without being aware of moving, Don stood fifteen or so feet from the ziggurat, Rourke at his side to steady and direct him. Wolverton remained behind, encircled by a ring of torches that spontaneously burst into flame and revealed more of the cavern—the vault of the ceiling raised still higher than the illumination. Ancient runes and alien carvings decorated the rough walls which were glaciated from eons of water drip and pierced by vermiculate openings. Some of the holes were sufficiently large to admit a small animal, others were fully cave entrances. Don recalled Ordbecker's comment: *There's a honeycomb under this mountain.*

Except, the honeycomb extended farther than under Mystery Mountain, didn't it? This suspicion was confirmed as the blackness of the ziggurat's hole glinted with specks of light, phosphorescent gases and clouds of nebula dust, and his breath billowed forth like frost.

The image rippled and the stars vanished and the veil parted with the soft, wet noise of a live birth. Black yolk sloshed in a minor flood down the foot of the ziggurat where it pooled and stank of offal and innards gone rank in heat. Gazing into the dripping hole was akin to gazing through a reversed telescope. Something large obstructed the throat of the tunnel between stars—a great, squat pillar the dimensions of an apartment building, or an aircraft conning tower, that quaked and quivered as only living flesh may do.

The being uttered a sibilant cry that echoed for miles and scratched at Don's mind, wheedling his name in an alien rebus of maggots and bones and a toothless maw drooling a slow waterfall of gore. The tongue of a colossal, putrefying worm murmured and cajoled and offered to enter his anus and lodge in his cerebral cortex, to inject him with a love greater than the Milky Way. It promised to raise the rotting corpse of Jesus or one of a hundred saints, and make them dance for his pleasure. It sang.

Don's bladder failed. He took a knee upon the hard cold ground while corrupt whispers susserated in his head, and ghostly images of his naked wife, his crying children, a barking dog, lunatics in masks, and rivers of blood whirred past with the gut-churning intensity of a diabolical kaleidoscope. The accompanying sound effects stretched his sanity like a rubber band. Through this cacophony he heard Michelle scream in mortal agony. A shrill, animal cry that terminated within moments.

Rourke leaned over him and took his hand to help him rise. "It's either this or get sliced in a blood ritual, Don old chum. Wish I could do more. Best get moving. They don't tolerate delays."

Don bared his teeth and clouted Rourke with the pointy stone his hand had closed upon as he knelt. Rourke's left eye rolled back in shock. His right eye deformed and collapsed as the edge of the rock squashed it into the socket. The man's blood fanned in a kite pattern toward the hole and the figure that awaited, and suddenly untethered from Euclidean principles, Rourke's feet drifted free of the floor and he rotated end over end and fell with lazy velocity through the opening. He dwindled, dwindled, and the hole irised shut leaving the bare, stony flank of the ziggurat, and the keening ceased upon that instant.

"My stars, Miller. You've got gumption, as the toothless set are wont to say. I like you more and more." Connor Wolverton laughed in genuine wonderment. He turned his head to the left and said, "Well, this has gone slightly pear-shaped, hmm? What shall we do with him?"

Ramirez (self-styled as Burton, apparently) detached from the shadows; a trapdoor spider emerging from its killing blind. His face had slipped nearly sideways and Don only recognized him by his pilot's jumpsuit. He waggled his overlong fingers at Don in greeting. "Oh, I'll think of something fun," he said through a mouth that opened vertically, and advanced, scuttling at terrific speed.

No wonder the man was careful to wear his helmet and walk in the shadows of the trees earlier today—these Dark Ones must fare quite poorly in direct sunlight. Don held on until the last second and then sprang forward and tried to crush his skull with the bloody rock. That didn't work.

Ramirez caught and embraced him. His breath was poisonous. His tongue lolled, fat and toadstool white, and glistening slime. As that horrid tongue wormed its way into Don's mouth and down his throat, Ramirez chortled. "*We knew you'd refuse our offer. One Miller is the same as the next. Your stock never learns, never changes. Take a long look into the Dark, Donnie boy. I'll see you again in thirty years."*

Don was paralyzed as the tongue bore deeper until it tickled his guts. During those moments of agony and fear he longed for death, at least unconsciousness, and was denied both. He felt every moment of exquisitely gruesome violation. The monster's tongue violently retracted with a spray of bile, and Don vomited and shrieked his outrage. Ramirez merely grinned with inhuman malignance and tossed him into the pit in the floor.

Long way down.

CHAPTER NINE

The Croning

(Now)

1.

While Don lay semiconscious in the dark wood after fleeing whatever had emerged slothing and chuckling from the dolmen, he dreamed of choking on Ramirez's tongue; dreamed the brute tossed him into the pit in the cavern floor and Don hurtled formless and weightless, not toward a subterranean abyss or underground lake, but outward into the cosmos. He accelerated through star fields past the reach of the mighty Hubble Telescope. His astral projection zoomed toward a blot of pitch between glinting points of light and as he closed the blot spread in a vast, terrible stain to encompass the width and length of numerous solar systems; a small independent galaxy that seethed and undulated. The moving clot contained many dead, thin-shelled worlds.

Within these hollow planets, far beneath barren surfaces, darkness reigned. Seas of warm blood filled the central caverns. The Children of Old Leech, whose native name was an unintelligible snarl in his mind, lived in the gory seas and writhed upon shores of diamond-hard bone and in millions of tunnels carved and inlaid with more bone harvested from a host of victims from ripe blue and green planets much like Terra.

The Children oozed and squirmed in noisome mounds, and even in the dream Don thanked God he only glimpsed impressions of them. For they were the stuff of nightmares; maggoty abominations possessed of incalculable and vile intellect that donned flesh and spines of men and beasts to shield themselves from the sun and enable themselves to walk upright instead of merely slithering.

Moments prior to waking, Don dreamed of falling back to Earth. He drifted, ghostly and unnoticed, through the living scene of a tale that would one day be scriven in children's books and made legendary.

The Dwarf arrived at court in the dead of night on the dark of the moon. Stunted and misshapen; protuberant of eye, hook-nosed, clothed in the mangy pelt of a wolf from the Black Forest, he hopped and trundled. His legs were deformed and he dragged a clubfoot. He sneered and snickered behind a greasy beard and mocked the soldiers who escorted him, heedless of their swords and ominous demeanor. Every one of them to the last man Jack would've gladly drowned the evil dwarf in a cistern, or cloven his pate with a swipe of a blade.

The Dwarf had come to the capital to claim his blood debt—the firstborn son of the Queen herself. This in return for perpetrating the hoax that the Miller's Daughter could spin gold from flax. Of course, the lady had sought to renege upon the arrangement after she was made queen and became gravid with child. With diabolical perverseness, he agreed to rescind the deal if she could guess his name within three months. Thus, she'd dispatched spies, courtiers, and assassins to the four corners of the kingdom to learn the little brute's name whether it required cajoling, crookery, gold, or a pair of red-hot pokers. As the dark of the moon drew nigh, all reported failure, except for her best man, a wily stable boy and former lover she'd raised to the royal entourage upon her own ascension. He repaid her kindness with good news—he'd spied the little fucker dancing around a bonfire in the mountains, cackling to a covey of witches and demons about how the Queen, dumb sow that she was, would never in million years guess the dwarf's name was Rumpelstiltskin. Etcetera, etcetera.

The royal guards brought R to the Queen's private antechamber. The chamber was dim and the Queen waited alone, garbed in her winter robes. She was pale from fear, her lips pressed into a grim line. They danced the dance that fairytales recounted for centuries afterward, although the coarseness of the Dwarf's language as he mocked the Miller's Daughter pretending to royalty, and the bizarre references he made to diabolic compacts and Dark Ones who dwelt between the stars, were uniformly excised.

When the Queen finally summoned the courage to utter the creature's name, a marvelous, and frightening sequence of events transpired—most of which was also left upon the cutting room floor of children's literature.

First, the dim lamps guttered and nearly failed.

A throng of children entered the room via the main entrance, or crept from behind tapestries and clambered up through grates in the floor. Upon closer inspection these were not children, they shone with a sickly wet pallor of burrowing creatures and moved in a sinister and disjointed fashion. Grubs or worms with vestigial limbs and rudimentary visages. A pair of these abominations fell upon each guard. It was over quickly; cries throttled, the men were ragged from the room and back into the vents.

By the poor light Rumpelstiltskin doubled in size, then doubled again. His dwarfish proportions remained the same, but he towered as a goliath, fully the height of three big men. He laughed that the Queen's spy had indeed witnessed his ritual in the mountains. Rumpelstiltskin wasn't really his name, it was the name of some stupid dwarf he'd molested and skinned ages ago. Nonetheless, a deal was a deal. He grasped the Queen when she tried to flee and lifted her to his mouth. He crunched off her head.

When the Dwarf turned, his face was slick with blood, his expression ecstatic and enraged. The beard had thrown Don until that moment. Across time and space and mutable reality, he recognized, as he always did, Bronson Ford's grin, his inscrutable hatred.

2.

He awoke to weak sunlight streaming through the branches and the bitter taste of pine needles and bile. Thule raised his snout to sniff the air and grumbled. Don spent several minutes working with his cramped and knotted muscles and gathering the intestinal fortitude to make it to his feet. Without his glasses, the world was blurry and strange. He recriminated himself for neglecting to carry the second pair—those were stashed snug in a drawer back at the house. If Michelle had nagged him once, she'd nagged him a thousand times to keep the spares in his pocket. He leaned against the bole of a tree and composed himself, spending a few minutes squinting at the compass. The device seemed to be working again.

Don focused as best he could and took a heading. As he walked, grabbing limbs and shrubs for support, the pink and purple clouds that fogged his mind gradually dissipated and he had an analogue to the reputed out-of-body experience so commonly reported across the world; he shook himself and emerged from the stupor that had cocooned him for years, decades, the waking coma that had divided his personality and diminished him. He thought of that big scientist Cooye who died in a car wreck, the series of plates that allegedly detailed the event, how Ron Houghton had promised to have a buddy give them the once-over for authenticity. What happened to those damned things? What had become of Frick and Frack, the government agents?

After the horrors in the unknown caves of Mystery Mountain, Don had lost his mind completely, had withdrawn into a shell and submerged the atrocities in the primordial muck of his subconscious. Such trivialities as speculation about Frick and Frack, cryptic warnings and photographs no longer concerned him. He became mild and sedate, compelled solely by his research and an ever-strengthening devotion to his wife and children.

Mystery Mountain was a half-glimpsed story on late-night TV.

Yes, the company line went that Wolverton vanished in an unrelated hiking incident, while Dr. Noonan and several others were lost after falling into a sinkhole in the mountains. Don turned up disoriented and amnesiac, for the second time in his life, wandering the river valley near camp. Theory was methane or some other noxious gas damaged his brain. AstraCorp had plenty of money to bankroll any medical or legal cover-up that ensued. Don accepted what conciliatory company reps told him about his missing time; he accepted what Michelle told him as well. He curdled and atrophied and became a mild, toothless old man who feared the night and suffered fugues and delusions for the rest of his life.

Barry Rourke had once told him the degradation of memory was a side-effect of exposure to the Dark. As he weaved through the woods, ragged and traumatized, Don figured the low-grade amnesia was also equal parts self-preservation. His consciousness had evaluated the threat posed by these affronts to sanity and decided to dim the lights and flip the sign to OUT OF SERVICE.

It had been more than the incident at Mystery Mountain. There were also the incidents in Mexico and at the Wolverton Mansion, and Lord knew where else. An entire reservoir of suppressed memories could easily await him, burbling and seething below the surface of his placid consciousness. There was, for one, the matter of Michelle's accident in Siberia; the Jeep rollover that left her hospitalized in critical condition and scarred for life. He'd received the bad news shortly following his rescue from the wilds of the Olympics. They came to him while he was wrapped in an insulated blanket and sitting on the tailgate of a park service emergency vehicle, hands shaking so much he couldn't get the foam cup of cocoa to his lips.

The ranger who delivered the message was an older, laconic gentleman with no bedside manner whatsoever. The man grunted and smoothed the brim of his tall hat and said something along the lines of, *Mr. Miller, your wife was in a car accident. The doctors said it's grim. Here's the number of the Consulate.* Don was sufficiently traumatized from his adventures in the hills that the gravity of the message didn't really dawn on him until he awoke in the night, panicked and crying for Michelle.

It was his turn to fly to her side. Strange, though, that even in the depths of his grief for her condition and numbed by the deluge of malign events, the sight of his wife lying inert at the heart of a shining white bed, her cocooned form tangled in a skein of wires and pulleys awakened in him a momentary callousness, an instant of wary appraisal as of an animal approaching a watering hole on the savanna. For despite Michelle's wounds, her fragile state and its trappings seemed almost contrived; props elaborately staged to create a particular atmosphere and to elicit unquestioning sympathy…to eclipse his rational thought and replace it with instinct. This moment of clarity was a spurt of ice water into his veins, then quickly gone as the clouds rolled in and left scant room for anything other than fear and mourning.

Pausing to catch his breath, Don patted the big dog. "Thule, my faithful friend, what do you suppose is happening in Turkey? What's happening to poor Holly?" He imagined unspeakable atrocities visited upon his daughter. Holly was fifty, the exact age Michelle had been the year she received those permanently disfiguring marks. He had visions of cowled supplicants brandishing knives as they danced around a mighty bonfire while Holly writhed on an altar of obsidian. "There wasn't any damned truck crash in Siberia. My loving wife has lied to me since forever. They carved her with stone knives, flayed her alive."

Later, after returning to the U.S. and healing well enough to totter around on a cane, she refused to speak of anything that transpired during the journey across the taiga and into the mountains. She didn't write a report of any kind that he was aware of. The university must've gotten *some* valuable data as she was feted and promoted, albeit sans fanfare. Possibly this is what Frick and Frack meant when they said she was an "untouchable," a select member of the herd who trafficked with the Dark Ones, protected from interference by government agencies. Or, more likely, abetted by those agencies. The cow handing the butcher his knife and apron, as it were.

These many years after the fact of Michelle's alleged accident, as he trundled half-blind through the brush, he revisited that theatre scene at the hospital, relived his instant of grim clarity that marionette strings extending from his back gleamed in his comatose wife's fist, that every step he'd taken since they met at that fateful art show in 1950 was the jig and jog of a dance she called with small twitches of those wires, that his future promised more of the same. His so-called future, his so-called past, were puppet shows.

Who pulls your *strings, my dear?*

Frick and Frack had tried to tell him. Wolverton and Rourke had also laid it all out, and still Don felt as if he was merely glimpsing the surface of a dense and convoluted pattern. If he stared long enough the fuzzy shapes would resolve into a nightmare image of sufficient potency to smash his mind completely. He suspected that the multitudinous designs, the layers and textures, really were minute oscillations of perfect, illimitable darkness. Neither light nor heat could withstand it; to gaze into that nullity and to comprehend its scope was to have one's humanity snuffed.

Only the inhuman thrived in out there in deep black.

3.

Reality contracted, then dilated, rhythmically as a pulse. Don floated, a helmetless astronaut, across a landscape he no longer comprehended.

An alien sun swung low across the rim of the hills and the shadows glowed purple and red. Stars hung in a belt of crushed glass where the sky darkened from blue-white to seared iron. The house waited, cool and formless in the lee of the twin maples. Kurt and Argyle's vehicles were parked in the driveway. Shiny steel and glass curved backward into invisibility and already seemed well-maintained relics in a museum of humanity, ages after humanity had been blotted from existence. Don was a shambling wreck, but his brain was recording everything and executing a sequence of increasingly dire calculations.

Husks of leaves covered the gravel and muffled the crunch of Don's footsteps as he approached the backdoor. His heart thumped in his ears. This place hadn't felt safe in the past, and now...He went through the door into the unknown, Thule at his heel.

The kitchen was a cave gallery suffused with the dim purple light.

Normal sounds were hushed or suspended entirely—the tip-tap of water dripping somewhere, the creaks and groans of subsidence, the cries of birds in the yard, all muted or absent. The atmosphere was gravid with the electricity of a building storm and he had the impression that the forces of darkness gathered around him.

Through this preternatural hush, a fly batted and whined against the window pane over the sink. The voices of a million doomed souls diminished to a strident drone as they gazed over a city skyline as doom slouched toward them from the depths of space. Their ghostly faces were quite vivid to him until he blinked them away and went to the window and, after a moment's deliberation, crushed the trapped fly and ended a million miseries in one stroke.

"Why you, sweetheart?" he said to the smear on the glass. "Of all the primates on our wobbly ball of dirt, what is it about you Mocks anyway?" He drank water from the tap that went down like acid and looked around the place, ready for the next shoe to drop, the next sign, the arrival of whatever was surely descending upon him. And saw that the cellar door was ajar by three inches. He smiled grimly and walked over and pulled it wide open and stared through the threshold into the musty gloom and its mysteries.

"For the love of Christ, don't do it, Pop," Kurt said. He stood near the kitchen table, hair wild, eyes bulging, clothes in tatters as if he'd tumbled down the side of a mountain. He was covered in blood and dirt. His left arm dangled, broken. "Get the fuck away from that fucking door."

As Don glanced back at his son, he swayed a little, feeling the gravity well of the stairs dragging him toward a swan dive. He caught the frame and steadied himself, and took a breath. "You're alive. Where's Argyle?"

"Alive, yeah. Argyle's...Uncle's gone. The bastards took him." Kurt went toward the pantry. He was missing a shoe and he left a bloody smear like the fly on the window.

Don longed to go to him, extend a comforting hand, but it was all he could do to grip the door frame and hold on for dear life as the proboscis of the cosmos sucked at him. "What happened out there?"

Kurt's shoulders hitched as he laughed silently and took a slug from a bottle of sherry left over from the last dinner party. He gained control of himself with visible effort and said, "They came from inside the trees and took him. Argyle couldn't run, Dad. His hip. He didn't really try. Stood there waving his cane and shouting. I left him. Fuckers didn't follow me. We paid the blood price for trespassing in their territory and that was it. If they were coming here it'd be curtains for us already." There were tears in his eyes and he took another huge gulp from the bottle. "Running won't help, anyway. I don't imagine there's any safety in town, or a bunker. Monsters go wherever monsters wanna go."

They came from inside the trees. Don had no trouble imagining the scene that must've transpired as Kurt and Argyle trudged through the forest, gradually noting the doors carved into the boles of the trees. Then, at a certain moment before sunset, those doors thrown wide and the occupants of the hollows spilling forth. As for monsters roaming willy-nilly, he decided that probably wasn't quite correct. The Dark Ones and their servitors didn't enjoy the light of the sun. Their gods dwelt in pitch darkness. All of them waited for Sol to dim and Terra to cool and glaciate in its twilight. These were not omnipotent entities, simply powerful ones. There was at least a sliver of hope for respite from their menace.

"I take it you didn't find Hank," Kurt said.

"He went into the dolmen. Begged him not to."

"Whatever's creeping around out there probably got him. Thought they were worms, even though that's impossible. Worms don't move so fast. Don't grow so big. Not even in the ocean." Kurt's expression was confused as his gaze focused on a distant vista. "There's doors in the wood. Everywhere."

"I know."

"We should do something."

"Of course."

"Call the cops, the FBI. Somebody."

Don saw a flash of Frick and Frack screaming as blood covered them, drowned them. "I'm certain the government is at least tangentially aware of the situation. This has gone on for a while. My gut says we're on our own."

"Yeah." Kurt nodded. "Mine too. Think Granddad or Luther had any inkling?"

"Doesn't make a difference."

"Makes one to me. I'd like to know which side they were on."

"Again, it doesn't matter. They're dust and we're stuck."

"My world's upside down. Be reassuring to think our kin weren't in on it with the Mocks. Fucking collaborators. Maybe not all of them. Maybe the ones who don't go along with the program get disappeared and that's why we only ever met those biddies Babette and Yvonne. The rest of them…I don't think we'll see Holly again."

"Let's not throw in the towel just yet."

"Get real, Dad. Mom took Holly to a bad scene. An evil ritual, or whatever."

"Safe to say burning bras or celebrating menopause weren't on the agenda. It's no good expecting the worst, though. Could be nothing happened. She loves your sister."

"If you can't indoctrinate the ones you love, who can you indoctrinate? Sis is totally screwed. And if Holly does come back she won't be my sister anymore. Mom hasn't been Mom since I was a kid, has she? She's been a Pod Person since 1980 at least. That's when she found her Hollow Earth people, right? The worms."

"The Limbless Ones," Don said.

"What?"

"That's what somebody called those…creatures in the trees."

"I saw the expressions on their faces. What do *you* know about this shit? Why haven't you told me?"

"I'd forgotten. If I'm lucky I'll forget again. Those aren't what we need to worry about. There are worse things."

"Honestly, it's Mom that scares the shit outta me. She's the ringmaster of this circus. We need to get gone before she comes bopping home from her vacation and sees what we've been up to."

Don glanced at the cellar and smiled sadly. "Too late for that, I'm afraid."

Kurt set aside the bottle. His grubby face was slick with sweat. The broken arm must be hurting, and that pain would intensify with every passing minute as the shock and adrenaline dissipated and cold reality settled in on them. "I feel it. I feel it, all right. Something terrible is down there. You want to go, don't you?"

"Want?" Don shook his head. "Not even remotely. I'm going down there because there's no choice. None at all."

"The hell you are. We're going to hop in my rig and put the pedal to the metal." Kurt snapped free of his daze and grabbed the phone off the wall and dialed awkwardly with his good hand, cradling the receiver with his chin. Dialing Winnie, no doubt, and Don, despite the circumstances, was morbidly curious as to precisely what his son intended to say. *Baby, creatures from Planet X are slithering through a worm hole and we got to make tracks!* There was no answer, though, and Kurt dropped the phone on the tiles in disgust. The younger man's expression was definitely on the crazed end of the spectrum. He wore the hollow expression of someone reacting to a shelled neighborhood or a pile of corpses.

Not for the first time in his eighty-plus years, Don reflected that witnessing a strong man break was among the most terrible sights possible. He said, "Kiddo, you've got the right idea. Climb in your car and go home to your lovely wife. Your baby."

"I can't leave you."

"Your wife and child. Focus, my boy."

"Jesus, I don't even know if *Winnie* is playing for team Earth anymore.

And what are you gonna do?"

"Wait for your mother. We need to talk."

"Dad, that's not a smart move. Mom is…She might walk through the door any second, or it might be days or weeks."

"Oh, my hunch is it won't be so long. Go home, be with your own family. This is between your mother and I."

Kurt stared at him, fish-eyed and blank. Then he whistled a few bars from the *Good, the Bad, and the Ugly*, and grinned with at least a hint of real humor. "All right, Dad. I'm going." He lurched over and gave Don a partial hug.

"Should you see your mother or me again," Don said, "be careful."

"What do you suggest?"

"Check for zippers. That's all I'm saying."

4.

Man and dog were alone in the empty house at the edge of the hills. Don had tried to get Thule to go with Kurt, to no avail. The dog refused to budge from his spot three feet from the cellar door where he growled and grumbled.

The sun disappeared below the horizon and the purple light quickly gave way to darkness. Don snapped on the kitchen lights and a few others on the first floor. This didn't bring much comfort; the illumination was feeble and it flickered ominously and the blackness pressed hard against the windows.

"Oh, Argyle," he said to the empty air. "I already miss you, you old goat." He might've wept then if not for the numbness of body and spirit. He'd looted the bathroom dresser for ancient prescriptions and located a bottle of Demerol. What had he needed it for? Standing in the threshold of the living room, acutely aware of its cramped artificiality, the thinness of the walls, he swallowed half a dozen pills and chased them with a shot of sherry. Exhaustion weighed upon him. His thoughts were jagged, dark bits of glass tumbling through storms of goose down.

He ventured into the cellar and down the rickety steps, his way lighted by a cheap, dirty bulb. The dilapidated stacks of rotten shelving and corroded jars of preserves were as he remembered, and so too the dirt floor and the cobwebs. He was alarmed, but hardly surprised to find the narrow tunnel boring through the south wall where a rack of odds and ends had once dominated. The opening forced him to duck and it smelled damp and ripe.

There was an interruption of time and movement and sound; a cigarette burn in a film followed by a sheared reel. Then power was restored and he stumbled and caught himself at the threshold of the living room. His eardrums popped with a painful pressure change. Though the room seemed stable, his innards sloshed about as if he were falling at terminal velocity.

"Time is a ring," Bronson Ford said. The dwarf was seated in Don's favorite wingback, orientated toward the fireplace so that his face was hidden. Bronson Ford's right hand dangled over the armrest. His gray fingers were so long and sharp they brushed the floorboards. His timbre was rich and modulated. Gone was the broken English, the intimation of mental deficiency. It was a voice rife with the kind of animus and evil that only a deranged genius could emit. Soft as the wind soughing through the canopy and it reminded Don of the men at the tree farm, Mexicans, Hondurans, wherever they hailed from; dark men with wide hats and black-handled machetes, their peculiar fluting cries, the cant of some ancient song that rose and drifted among the green galleries. "We travel the ring, forward and backward, molding it like plastic. Your Michelle can do it too, to a minor degree. She has taken the fumbling infant steps across the lightless expanses as a part of her initiation. Very difficult to maintain any semblance of humanity after one has glimpsed the Great Dark."

Oh, Jesus. He plucked that from my mind. "Frankly, I hadn't thought of you in years." Don grabbed a brass flower vase off the shelf and moved toward Bronson Ford, fully intent upon cracking his nemesis across the back of the skull. Three steps into the room the lights shorted and went dead and an icy breeze ruffled Don's hair.

Bronson Ford chuckled from somewhere in the distance and the sound echoed as if from the depths of a cavern. "It won't last, this clarity of thought. You are suffering from permanent brain damage. This lucidity is a ray of light through the clouds. Soon to be extinguished. Enjoy the interlude."

Don halted, partially crouched, blind, heart thudding, waves of vertigo threatening to topple him. He was overwhelmed by the impression of vast, subterranean space. "Who are you?" The way his words traveled and traveled before rebounding from a wall intensified his queasiness. Faint sparks of starlight refracted from a ceiling that might've been within arm's reach or thousands of feet distant.

"Michelle's fascination with you has eluded me. Then, I gaze into your eyes and note that indeed your double helix spins precisely the same as a certain ancestor. He was a spy. This runs in the family. Your father and grandfather were spies." Bronson Ford's voice drifted, echoing from afar, then crooning near Don's ear. "Should you happen to see young master Kurt again feel free to tell him neither man was particularly brave or wise or noble. Luther knew a couple of things, guessed a few more. We never considered him a threat to our plans. As for your father… A grunt who died for God and Country with the same amount of panache and self-awareness as a driver ant sacrificing itself for the colony."

"I say again, who are you?"

"One who is interested in your species. The bogeymen in your histories and legends. We are far older than you can imagine and have haunted you since you were protoplasmic slime bobbing on the tide line. My kind are epicures. We revel in sensual pleasures, be it as gourmands or sybarites. We sup of blood and fear, we rejoice in flensing away that which occults the truth. Pointless to repeat what you already know. Wolverton and Rourke told you everything. Your recognition of these facts is a chemical bloom that lights your cerebral cortex with fireworks. It is this dawning of horror upon primitive minds that gives me my greatest frisson. I have lived thousands of your own lifecycles and the taste of your revulsion and horror never grows stale."

"Right. We're ants and you're the kid with the magnifying glass. Is that really all there is to this? I'd hoped the universe either had a grand scheme or was at least monumentally indifferent. This Olympus crap is rather disappointing." Don still clutched the vase, hoping for a clean shot. He feared to take another step lest he tumble from a pinnacle of stone into a chasm.

"Despite our superiority to you, we remain but a cog in the gears. We aren't gods, although the distinction is insignificant from your perspective. Whatever our discrepancies as one life form to another, you are certainly handy to keep around. From your babies we draw nourishment—my feast of blood and terror. From your adult population we are provided research and sport. A select few of your kind supply the raw materials to replenish our eternal line. These we decorticate and realign through agony and degradation unto an aesthetic pleasing to our traditions. These lucky few, the prime exemplars of humanity, are made immortal. The offer has been extended *you* in the past. *You* most ungraciously refused. A stubborn breed, the Millers."

Don flung the vase toward Bronson Ford's monologue. He hoped for a cry of outrage, a thud, anything. No response was forthcoming. He waited several seconds and said, "Where are my wife and daughter, you scoundrel? Argyle and Hank?"

"Your associates languish upon a metaphorical anthill. They will endure a right Christian Hell for ages to come. Those fools are beyond help. Your women…That is a more delicate matter."

"If you aren't a god, you're damned well the black Pope. You must want something of me if you're making house calls."

Bronson Ford's answering cackle was thunderous. A section of the darkness rippled with pale fire and multitudes of stars wheeled as if through a pane of warped glass. Alien constellations shimmered and contorted as a black stain spread across them; there was the sun burning low and red, the solar system and its decaying planets, Earth…

Earth was cloaked in a poisonous crimson mist. The oceans were stagnant soup. Festering jungles of maroon and ochre covered one hemisphere; sterile volcanic deserts the other. Most cities were buried under shifting sand or rotting vegetation or had fallen into pits in the earth. Structures that remained intact were webbed in foliage, gummed in amber glaciations, and contorted into spicate towers that bore scant resemblance to their original shapes.

Primates gathered in these marginally habitable regions, but as Bronson Ford's lens swooped to magnify them it became clear these hapless wretches were twisted out of plumb much as the skyscrapers were. The masses shuffled toward a ziggurat the size of the Empire State Building. The mighty ziggurat was constructed of flesh and bone from countless sentient corpses. A dripping black tunnel to Elsewhere opened at its heart. In clots, then droves, the approaching stick figures elevated and were sucked into the shuttering iris. They shrieked as flies shriek.

"Do you understand what awaits in the waning days of your civilization? That viscid hole in the altar doesn't lead to my home. Nay, little man; this is a mouth of our father, Old Leech. That venerable worthy rouses every few epochs and demands provender. Soft, screaming humanity is among the sweetest. What you witness here is only the beginning of the end. The Great Dark will arrive and cocoon your world as it cocoons ours. Terra will be hollowed and refined as we hollow and refine sapient flesh, and the planet shall be added to the Diaspora, dragged from its orbit of Sol, and taken away. This is what always happens." Bronson Ford revealed himself highlighted by a shaft of bloody radiance, a monstrous and bloated giant perched atop a slag heap of bones that floated on the surface of a void. His eyes and mouth were portals that mirrored the iris in the ziggurat, the void itself. He was de Goya's Saturn, Polyphemus, and Satan sans horns. His flesh appeared to be multiple skins stitched together like a quilt. He cracked a smile of benign malevolence.

Don's tongue was dry. He tried to sound brave. "Lucky for me I'll be long dead. Everyone I know will be gone."

"A reasonable observation. Alas, alack for you, one that isn't necessarily correct. The Diaspora won't reach local space for eons. However, it is possible for me to make certain you and those you cherish are preserved to bear witness firsthand of that most dread gloaming. Tell me, little miller, wouldn't you rather be a beneficiary of the inevitable conquest rather than a victim? What of your mate? I am exceedingly curious to discover how much you love her. The females of the Mock line have served us adequately. Yet, I sense her affection for you might prove an impediment to her ultimate absorption unto our ranks. The poor woman is *so* inordinately fond of you, my ancient antagonist. Frankly, I despair that we'll wind up having to devour her alive. Divided loyalties are simply not done in my homeland."

Don had an inkling of what lay in store. Creatures such as Bronson Ford could easily snuff lives or snatch what they desired. That wasn't their preference, however. These devils, like all devils, were manipulators. Time and space stretched before them in an endless wasteland. Ennui was the only enemy immortal monsters possessed. They sought victory through the corruption and damnation of the soft, the innocent, the weak. He considered leaping forward and falling to his doom or precipitating a violent reaction from his demonic adversary, anything to avoid the fate that awaited him as surely as did the grave. Instead, he heard himself say, "Name your bargain."

"It's a small thing." At this, Bronson Ford laughed again, relishing a nasty private joke. "The trade is painless, for you. I'll guarantee the scion of the Mocks maintains her current status as liaison and at the end of your natural life you'll be brought into our fold, forever reunited with her. In return, you'll grant me the precious little gift I traditionally accept as recompense. Refuse and wifey goes on the anthill with Uncle Argyle and hapless Hank, and Frick & Frack, to name a few, while you regress into diapers and perish, drooling and raving, in some dump of a hospice. It has always been about the child. Give me that pound of flesh, so to speak, and we'll be even."

When it hit Don what was being proposed, what child the creature meant, the strength ran from him and he sank to his knees. "But for the love of all that's holy, what you demand isn't even mine to give."

"Oh, don't fret about the details. As you say, we take what we please. I just want to hear you say it."

"I can't." Don raised his hands in supplication and wept. For an instant he beheld a vision of Michelle naked and alight with angelic radiance, hovering in space. This was Michelle as she'd been in the flower of maidenhood. She smiled at him and faded away. The next vision was of a child squalling as claws sharp and steely as darning needles pierced its flesh and blood flowed. "I can't. I can't." Don clouted himself about the forehead and temples. He tore at the remnants of his hair. He prayed for dementia and oblivion, tortured by the knowledge his faculties would deteriorate only after he'd been forced to make his hideous choice.

Bronson Ford merely grinned and waited for the old man to choose.

5.

Someone found him on the dirt floor of the cellar, dehydrated and unconscious. Besides a few contusions and abrasions, Don was physically sound. His mental acuity wasn't so intact.

Time passed. Don lay first in a bed at home, dutifully nursed by

Michelle, then toward the end, his family transferred him to a private room at a hospital in town. He was scarcely aware of the external world, surfacing at odd intervals to note a familiar television jingle, the voice of a loved one, or the tap of rain against the window. He vaguely registered the frequent vigils of his family and almost came fully awake during one visit by a pair of men in dark suits and glasses. The men asked a series of questions and were eventually ushered out by the ladies in white. Occasionally he overheard scraps of conversation between his family and the doctors. A bland fellow in a smock kept referring to *encephalitis* and *vermiculate perforations of the brain,* and *terminal.* There were many tears.

Lucidity smote Don like a lightning bolt one late afternoon, and when it did, he realized he must be dying, although his senses were muffled in gauze and it was difficult to concentrate, much less evaluate his predicament.

The sun was a blood-red band sinking fast. The hospital room lay in darkness except for the beam of light that illuminated his narrow bed. His immediate family stood in the gloom at the foot of the bed—Kurt and Kaiwin and their baby boy; Michelle and Holly to the opposite side. Poor Holly had been in some kind of accident; a wicked scar peeped from the vee of her blouse. The scar was pink and raw.

Don struggled to focus. He was happy that the bed lay in the sunlight because the darkness was so cold. He'd never liked the dark.

Kurt came around and kissed his cheek, followed by Holly and Kaiwin who did the same. They each whispered endearments to him and hugged Michelle on the way out. Michelle stopped Kaiwin and convinced her to leave baby Jonathan with his grandma. "You look so exhausted, honey," she said to Kaiwin.

The door snicked shut and grandparents and grandchild regarded one another in the dying red light. The infant crawled on the bed. The pleasant vacuum of Don's mind began to fill with ice.

"Sweetheart," Michelle said with infinite tenderness. Her red lips gleamed. Her hair was black and lustrous as it had been in youth. She leaned forward and scooped the baby up and pulled him into the shadows. She whispered, "I love you. Thank you."

Don wanted to reply that he loved her, more now than when they first met, wanted to profess that he'd love her forever and a day. Speech was impossible. His breath slowed and he wheezed and choked as his heart labored. The sight of the baby wriggling in Michelle's arms paralyzed him with horror. He couldn't remember why.

ABOUT THE AUTHOR

Laird Barron is the author of two collections: *The Imago Sequence* and *Occultation*. His work has appeared in many magazines and anthologies. An expatriate Alaskan, Barron currently resides in the wilds of Upstate New York.